THE MISINTERPRETATION
OF TARA JUPP

Also by Eva Rice

Who's Who in Enid Blyton
The Lost Art of Keeping Secrets

The Misinterpretation of Tara Jupp

Eva Rice

HERON
BOOKS

First published in Great Britain in 2013 by

Heron Books, an imprint of
Quercus
55 Baker Street
7th Floor, South Block
London W1U 8EW

A CIP catalogue record for this book is available
from the British Library

HB ISBN 978 1 78087 824 9
TPB ISBN 978 1 78087 854 6
EBOOK ISBN 978 1 78087 825 6

This book is a work of fiction. Names, characters, businesses,
organizations, places and events portrayed in it, while at times based on
historical figures and places, are the work of the author's imagination.

10 9 8 7 6 5 4 3 2 1

Printed and bound in Great Britain by Clays Ltd, St Ives plc

Typeset by Ellipsis Digital Limited, Glasgow

In memory of my Aunt, Fiona Armstrong,
whose style lives on.

"Was it proper to sing with such expression, such
originality, so unlike a schoolgirl? Decidedly not.
It was strange, it was unusual."

Charlotte Brontë, *Shirley*

"I must become something."

Nikolaus Pevsner

Part One

The Edge of Land

1

Me and Them

Like I said, everything began with Lucy. And why wouldn't it? Back then Lucy was fourteen and sensational, and quite capable of being the first person on the printed page of any book. She had an appeal that I know I am going to find hard to define, but I suppose I could start by saying that very few have even a little of what she had in spades. She was the Great Looker among us, and the only one of us girls to have inherited Ma's features; in fact, there was so little of Pa in her, it was as though she had been reproduced by binary fission. Photographs of mother and daughter made for curious viewing. Their physical make-up was so similar – the sludge-green eyes, the long, dark hair with its hint of a wave, framing identical, sharp noses and perfect cheekbones – yet it was as if Lucy's picture had been sprinkled with stardust. She was irresistible for the contradictions she inspired; without very much effort she combined a childlike humour with a proper, grown-up allure that made Eve seem merely frivolous.

It was odd; people felt compelled to discuss her the *whole* time. When we were growing up, no one ever stopped saying what a beauty she had become and what a heartbreaker she was going to be, which always struck me as stating the blinking obvious. I mean, from the moment Lucy started to wear a bra, hearts started to break. If anyone, even now, were to ask me what I recall most about my life before the age of ten, it would be the continual presence of boys around my sister. They were all healthily afraid of Pa, particularly as he was the vicar, but not even the threat of his wrath could quell their passion for his eldest daughter. They were always very friendly to *me*, and frequently asked me to relay messages to her: '*Tell your sister I love 'er! Ask yer sister out to the pictures Saturday, will you?*' etc., and I would ask: '*Which sister?*' But I knew perfectly well. She was the only one of us capable of causing havoc simply by walking into a room.

My parents got married and had their first child when they were just nineteen. Ma was forever telling us all that 'in her day people didn't think twice, they just got on and married the first person who asked them' – a statement that never failed to make me queasy with anxiety. She met Pa in Manchester, where he was a cobbler's apprentice and she was spending six months teaching French in a school for the poor, opened by her philanthropic godmother, Lady Elizabeth Wray. Ma, brought up by indulgent, well-heeled parents in the soft-stoned beauty of Bath, was shocked to the very core by northern England – its smoke, fog and industry, its bitter cold, the bleak winter followed by a summer where the sunlight seemed not to sparkle but to spit on the water on the River Tame. Quite apart from learning French and helping Those Less Fortunate Than Ourselves, Ma was a keen amateur dramatist whose greatest pleasure in life was singing – she spent every spare evening listening to records or tramping down to the Theatre Royal to watch some gruesome cabaret or other. The story goes that one evening, after watching an enthusiastic production of *Girl Crazy*, Pa nearly ran Ma over on his bicycle. Off flew her specs (she was almost blind without them), so he picked them up and handed them to her, and promptly asked her if she'd like to go with him to a dance that Friday night. Apparently Ma said yes before she'd even got her glasses back on, which means that either she was scared stiff of Pa's booming voice, or she was so lonely she would have agreed to go out with anyone who showed her the slightest bit of interest.

They went to the dance together, where they drank Guinness and talked about dogs, lemon drizzle cake and a mutual admiration for Arthur Conan Doyle, and that was that; he asked her to be his wife two months later. Pa's height (nearly six foot six) and his girth (gigantic), coupled with a speaking voice of such volume and confidence that in later years his sermons had people practically running out of church and throwing themselves into the nearest river to repent of their sins, made refusal unthinkable. Ma once told me that it had been as though Michelangelo's *David* had proposed to her, he was so strong, so sure, so *overwhelming*. 'Could I have a day or two to think?' would have been out of the question.

It mattered not one jot to Ma that they were from such different backgrounds; if anything Pa's working-class roots were part of the draw. Her own mother – who had despaired of the match until the evening before the wedding, when her spaniel, Warwick, fell into a well, and was rescued by Pa, a thick piece of rope and an excellent pair of boots – often used to say that it was precisely *because* of their differences that the marriage was such a success.

'Sarah Merrywell, you landed on your feet with that man,' my grandmother used to say. 'To think! You almost ended up in the *theatre* – or worse – with an earl! He has saved you from the greatest threat there is.'

'What's that?' Ma would ask, winking at us.

'Oneself, of course.'

He was by any standards a difficult man, was Pa – fixated on tennis, of all things. While most lads around Pa's way and of his age yearned to be like Thomas 'Tommy' Browell, the genius footballer for Manchester City, Pa would rather have been Wimbledon winner Tony Wilding. His enthusiasm for the game had come from his own father who, before the war, had ploughed horses on a big estate north of Yorkshire where a tennis court next to the cowsheds had provided the farmhands with hours of entertainment. To my grandfather's great disappointment, Pa was no good at the sport himself, but what he did have was a great understanding of how to play, and a voice loud enough to bellow instructions from the net.

Very early in their marriage, Pa made two promises to himself. The first was to improve his first service, the second was to *take* his first service. Yes, Pa's second fixation was God, who he claimed he had always known would 'get him in the end'. A year after he married Ma, Pa decided that nothing was going to stop him from joining the Priesthood, and Ma (who, apart from anything else, recognized that Pa was a showman at heart) encouraged him. Their move to Cornwall came back down to the old tennis racket (ha ha). Pa was offered a substantial parish in York, a glorious church with a junior choir twice winners at the Eisteddfod, but he and Ma rejected it in favour of the Rectory, in the village of Trellanack, near Truro, because the house contained within its limited grounds an ancient tennis court. No matter that we would never have the money to restore the court to former glory, no matter that the Rectory – despite being designed by Pugin – had damp patches on the bedroom ceilings from blocked gutters on the leaking roof, an outside lavatory and a reputation for being haunted – Pa had been struck blind by the loveliness it all and the strange notion that he would sire a tennis prodigy through whom he could live – or play – vicariously. He reasoned that if he and Ma had plenty of children, the probability of having at least one with an iota of talent and drive in the sporting arena was fairly high. He was a man of conviction and determination, and with every one of us that appeared, fresh hope for Wimbledon victory emerged.

And plenty of us appeared; my parents had children very easily. The first born was E.J., in 1938 – a year after she and Pa first met. He wasn't called E.J. when he was born, of course, he was merely Jack, but 'Errant' became a prefix when he started skipping school and then much later on decided to become an artist and moved to France. Growing up with Jack at the start of the register was a tough thing: he was that infuriating sort who never remembered birthdays but had that way of making everyone feel so delighted when he appeared that all his sins were instantly forgiven. Eighteen months after him came George, who had poster-boy looks yet wanted to go into the Church like Pa – our mother suggested that it was a sensible choice as it would be the only place he would be able to escape the swooning girls. A year after George came Lucy, about whom you already know plenty. Then came the twins, Florence and Imogen, and fifteen months after, little old me. Bringing up the rear a most unusual eight and a half years later came Roy and Luke, a year and a half apart. Ma felt that she couldn't leave Roy on his own, so far behind the rest of us, which is why she decided to have another baby to keep him company – but I will come to that in a minute.

We lived under Pa's iron thumb, and abided (when he was looking our way) by his twin philosophies: Hard Work Pays Off and Many Hands Make Light Work – a convenient one with a family the size of ours, and one which Lucy was always challenging with her lazy-girl's mantra: 'Too Many Cooks Spoil the Broth.' Yet despite his forcefulness and his desire to have everything in order, Pa, an only child himself, could often be found sitting in his study with a slightly stunned look on his face when we were all at home, almost, Lucy said, as though he'd inadvertently wandered into the wrong house and was trying to work out the quickest way to grab his wife and leave.

Ma gave birth with the same attitude with which she laid a fire or prepared a Sunday roast – with minimum fuss and maximum efficiency. She also claimed that before every one of us was born she knew whether we were girls or boys. She even managed to give birth to Imogen just eight months after Florence, hence them being known as the twins when they weren't really twins at all. What happened was that Ma had popped out Florence, and fallen pregnant a mere six weeks later. Imogen then arrived early (a trait that was to become a habit), and weighed only four and a half pounds, but Ma wrapped her up and put her in the cot with her closest sister for comfort. The doctors warned her that she might always be a little backward, but she wasn't at all, except she stuttered when she was nervous or excited, which unfortunately for Imogen was most of the time.

Imogen was Ma's favourite. She never said so, but I think all of us sensed it. She was a sweet and good and generally helpful girl who aged eighteen became a teacher in the village school, and liked making jam and didn't mind picking up spiders and throwing them out the window. She always said, 'Happy landing, Mr Spidey!' which drove Lucy crackers.

'How do you know it's a mister?' she would ask crossly.

'Because a lady spider would never spend so long in the bath.'

When we were little, Ma's preference for Imo bothered Lucy very much.

'Of all the choice she had, what on earth makes *her* so special?'

'Maybe it was the fact that she was born six weeks early,' George would say.

'I heard E.J. say you should never trust anyone who's ever early for anything.'

'Well, he *would* say that.'

'What do you mean?'

'Beautiful people are never early. They know the rest of the world will wait for them.'

'Oh, shut up.'

Florence didn't mind that Ma preferred Imogen. She just did her own thing and listened – from a very young age – to a great deal of jazz and blues. I was music mad, as anyone with any sense was, and had a thing about a Jewish firecracker called Alma Cogan whom I had spied on the television a couple of times, and who looked like a princess from another land in her outrageous frocks. E.J. bought me one of her records for my ninth birthday, and I played it until it was too scratched and worn to play any longer. There was no one else on the planet I would rather be – I even called *both* my teddy bears Alma, to the irritation of all. But it was Ma who made us play and sing *ourselves*. She would sit at the piano with us every night, singing her heart out as though none of us were there, her eyes half closed, her children worshipping at her feet. She didn't sense us there at all. She was up onstage somewhere, staring out at the lights. She was, while she sang, the girl that she had been before she met Pa. All I ever wanted to do was to learn to play the piano like her, and by my sixth birthday I had taught myself shaky versions of much of the score from *Carousel*. Naturally in love with the instrument, I would sit for hours on end practising until interrupted. It was something that Ma encouraged, just like she pressed upon us that as soon as you could open your mouth to talk – you should sing.

Two of us were better singers than the rest: Lucy and me. The others could hold a tune pleasantly enough – with the exception of George, who had Pa's booming timbre without ever landing on the right note at the right time. I sang because it was something I couldn't *not* do, it consumed me, swallowed me whole. I listened to instruction, I read music, I learned my craft from the masters, and, as a result, I soared ahead even further. Lucy sang for fun, and nearly always with an expression of amused indifference, as if she could take it or leave it, but if she *was* taking it, then she had the clout to keep up with the best of them. Naturally enough, this annoyed me. Why the voice had been given to Lucy, and not to Imogen, who adored opera, made me question the fairness of the Almighty. Ma realized very quickly that she wasn't going to get anywhere by pressing her dreams on to Lucy – so she directed them all at me instead.

As soon as she recognized that I could impersonate Alma, I had Ma's complete attention, the full, chaotic force of her unrealized dreams.

'I wish I could sing like you, Tara,' she would say to me when everyone else had spilled out of the dining room and upstairs to bed.

'You *can*, Ma,' I said, eight years old and puzzled by her, because I believed it to be true.

'If I had had your voice, I would have done something with it.'

10

'Like what?'

Ma would shake her head at the sheer width of possibility.

'I would have used it to become famous. I would have travelled the world, married a film star—'

'But you married Pa!'

'Exactly.' She looked at me, then down at her hands. 'Use what you've got, Tara.'

'How do you mean?'

Ma pulled a thread from the hem of my nightie and snapped it off. She never answered the question.

And it was hard, being part of such a large family; difficult to make voices heard, whether asking for the marmalade across the breakfast table, or for help with homework. Ma was a brilliant yet strangely distant mother, full of contradictions. She was irresistible when something made her laugh, but impenetrable when she disliked someone or something we had said to her. When she was cross, she spoke like a child about wanting to run away from everyone and everything, yet when she was happy it seemed she had the wisdom of all the world within her five-foot-five frame. She couldn't resist giggling when she saw pretty men staring at her, but glared at the boys who whistled at Lucy. She held all of us in the palm of her hand, Pa especially, and she knew it. Her real delight had been with newborn babies; Pa was later to tell me that when each one of us learned to walk and talk, she mourned. Then she would be pregnant again, so the aching ceased. Sometimes she would try to tell us how it felt to carry a baby inside you for nine months. It felt alien, something that I couldn't ever imagine happening to me. She often spoke as though she wouldn't always be with us, something that never struck us as odd at the time.

'You'll always look after the rest of them, won't you?' she'd say to E.J. when he was home.

'Hmm.'

'Just in case.'

'In case of what?'

These short bursts of conversation failed to prepare us for when it happened. Her last baby, our youngest brother, Luke, had been a difficult birth, her worst by some margin. She had gone into labour very suddenly one afternoon, two weeks early; she was at home with only thirteen-year-old Lucy by her side, and Lucy, of all of us, was the most impractical, the one who felt sick at the sight of blood and turned green at the concept of pain.

By the time the midwife arrived, all Lucy had managed to do was surround Ma with glasses of water. A complication with the position of the baby resulted in her losing an awful lot of blood, and the speed at which it happened meant that she gave birth in her bedroom without a midwife. Luke had been the wrong way round, and two weeks later Ma still hadn't properly recovered. She was told that she had a severe infection, and just ten days after this she went to sleep and never woke up. Lucy was wrecked by her death, convinced that it was somehow her fault. It wasn't of course, but Lucy was thirteen and terrified. She once told me that she felt certain that if it had been Imogen with Ma when she was bleeding, she would have known what to do, and Ma would have lived.

'Imo's not a doctor,' I remember Jack saying to her. 'She wouldn't have done any better than you.'

'Too good for us,' whispered George, his new suit falling off his skinny frame at Ma's funeral. 'She was just too good for us.'

The day after Ma's funeral another thing happened that Lucy

and I would never forget. We fell off the bike we were sharing – I was sitting on the handlebars while she pedalled downhill – and both of us ended up in hospital. Lucy was allowed to leave after an hour, but I was sick – so bad was the pain, and the bewildering harshness of knowing that Ma was gone forever. My ankle was bandaged and I went home three days later, and the village felt black then – and every afternoon afterwards and throughout the whole of that bitter winter. Without Ma the world felt horrible. That was the only word I can think of when I look back on that first year without her. *Horrible.* I couldn't seem to lose the limp from that fall – it was a slight, but nonetheless noticeable, thing – a constant reminder of that time, a physical pain stemming from my left foot that symbolized an anguish that we *all* felt.

And after she died, all we Jupp children became more ourselves than ever.

Jack became more Errant than ever before – it was the year after Ma's death that he vanished to France without leaving so much as a note for the rest of us. George became more convinced than ever that he wanted to follow Pa into the Church, and gave up staring at girls on the bus. Imogen became more anxious, her stutter more pronounced. Florence became spikier, harder to read, more fixated with obscure jazz. Lucy was the worst affected of us all, though we didn't find out how until much later. In all, it was as though Ma's complex and contradictory character had been dispersed throughout all of us, with one aspect of her personality assigned to each of her children.

And me? I became more awkward and difficult, and obsessed by horses, who I decided were my only friends in the cruel world, etc., etc. In the years after Ma died, I took to – how shall I put it? – *borrowing* horses whenever the urge to ride became too much to bear. I fancied myself as a gypsy, and would set my alarm and sneak out of the house early in the morning and saunter through the village towards the biggest and grandest place in the district: Trellanack House.

Built in 1764 by the Wells-Devoran family, Trellanack's surrounding park was awash with ponies. The current Lady W-D was a former Olympic three-day-eventer, who – aged sixty-one – collected Shetland ponies like we collected cigarette cards. We only ever saw her in church, where she sat with her daughter Matilda, who went to boarding school and never spoke to any of us, though we were bonded by the unhappy coincidence that her father had died of pneumonia just two months after our mother. Pa had to conduct the funeral service, and famously broke down while quoting from St Mark – something that filled me with shame and love at the same time when I heard about it from Thomas, Pa's indiscreet verger. Pa's tears for our mother were the only ones that fell on the day Sir Lionel Wells-Devoran was buried; the owner of Trellanack House was not a man who appeared to have inspired love in anyone. Certainly his wife seemed curiously unaffected by her husband's departure – she was full of hearty Good Morrows at Easter and Christmas, and seemed to have acquired a spring in her step that none of us had noticed before. She must be as tough as an old bridle, I thought, and Matilda too. I certainly don't think she would have been especially thrilled to know what I was doing on her land, but oh! It was so easy!

I merely had to stand at the bottom of the mile-long drive and hold out half an apple to have whichever animal I liked. Most conveniently for me, there was a dip in the park that meant it was possible for me to scramble under the post-and-rail fence, mount the nearest horse and ride as much as I liked without being seen from the house. I had fabricated a halter from an old girdle belonging to a visiting Roman Catholic priest friend of Pa's, and would slip this formerly holy vestment over the horse's head and ride bareback for a thrill-making twenty minutes or so, before leaping off again and returning home to breakfast as though butter wouldn't melt in my mouth. I can't say that I didn't get nervous – according to Thomas the verger, Sir Lionel was reputed to haunt the house and grounds wearing a life-jacket and shouting for his mother (he had survived the *Titanic*, aged five) but then Thomas liked putting the wind up me and seeing me frightened. My sisters were amused by my equine exploits, and George admired my cunning, yet to me it was nothing to do with providing entertainment, nor being rebel-lious. It was all about wanting to move all the time, to be a part of something bigger than myself.

When I was riding, I could forget that Ma had gone, I could forget that I didn't know where I was going. Singing and riding took me somewhere different, in both the literal and metaphysical senses. And riding at Trellanack was like being transported to a strange, wonderful dreamscape, where I could forget everything in the power of movement. Those early-morning jaunts saved me from the cruel stab of missing Ma and I had no intention of stop-ping – not for anyone.

Above all, when I was on a horse, or part of the choir, I was something more than Lucy Jupp's sister. Back then – it was all that I lived for.

2

The Fairy Wood

In March 1955, just two months after Ma died, Lucy's naughtiness caught up with her. I was just ten years old, but my sister was thirteen going on nineteen, and was caught sneaking out of her bedroom window one night to meet Martin Adams who worked at the garage, which I thought was bonkers on two counts – firstly because Martin Adams was thick as a lump of cheese and not worth the act of such rebellion, and secondly because it was far too cold to *consider* shuffling out of one's bed to meet boys in February – albeit a boy who had – even by Florence's reckoning – Powerful Good Hair. Anyway, sneak she did, and was careless enough to get caught, and after that Pa decided that enough was enough and made the decision to pack Lucy off to stay with our Great Aunt Mary for a week, to think about her behaviour and spend some time on her neglected schoolwork. Mary was Pa's aunt – a thick-set, ample-bosomed housekeeper-turned-cook, whose suspicion of my mother's willingness to marry for love not money had been confirmed at Ma's funeral.

'I thought your mother was a fine woman,' she had said, as though she were bestowing a great honour upon me by saying so. 'Frivolous and flighty in many ways, but good-hearted.'

'Thank you. She was,' I said, not knowing what she meant.

'But I always said there would be trouble when she married my nephew. There's *always* trouble when a lady like her marries beneath herself,' added Aunt Mary. Neat hands folded in front of her, head to toe in black, eyes steel grey, she was one part Mrs Danvers to two parts Mrs Tiggy-Winkle.

'Hard to marry beneath yourself if you're marrying Pa,' I had replied tartly. 'Ma had to stand on tiptoes to kiss him.'

At the last minute, my brother George and I were included on the Aunt Mary visit, mainly because we would otherwise have been cluttering up the Rectory during the school holidays, and without Ma at the helm, Pa was lost in a sea of children whose names he was inclined to forget if we didn't pin them on to the front of our cardigans.

'Aunt Mary scares me,' I bleated as Pa virtually shoved the three of us on to the train.

'That *house* scares me,' added George under his breath.

But the train door slammed shut, and before we could say *knife*, we were rolling east. Aunt Mary lived in Wiltshire, in a pocket-sized cottage next to the post office, but the house where she worked, Milton Magna Hall, was something else. You could have fitted the whole of the Rectory into the Great Hall alone. It was fit for giants.

For the most part, our stay with Aunt Mary was uneventful. We weren't allowed into the Big House except to deliver things to the kitchen — most of the time we were confined to the cottage with stacks of mending and washing, like something out of Dickens. Other times we were sent on tiresome errands around the village, purchasing such fascinating items as corn plasters and turnips, but on the final morning of our stay Aunt Mary decided that she needed one of us to help her prepare vegetables and skivvy around the kitchen of the Big House for the day. Lucy had been locking eyes with some boy who worked behind the counter in the village shop, so was quite happy for it to be me, so that she could saunter through the village on her own all morning. I was to help with the preparation of Sunday lunch for a number of guests. We hadn't even walked through the door before I was sent off into the kitchen garden for some parsley.

I had been instructed to return right away, but like Peter Rabbit I couldn't resist just seeing what was through that gate (a walled garden with an orchard and a dovecote and a statue of a little boy with winged feet, as it happened . . .) and what was over that little stile (a frost-hard field inhabited by an over-weight grey pony who had cast a shoe . . .) and what was around that corner. (Oh! Another gate, and a little path and a half-frozen stream leading up a hill thick with holly trees . . .) Needless to say, before too long I was utterly lost, and thanks to the presence of both my overactive imagination and a wild wind, I was also cold and frightened.

And no, I had not yet entered the phase of my life in which I was to enjoy being on my own in a place unknown, so I sat down on the ground and, to my eternal shame, started to howl. It wasn't just the fact that I was lost, but more that I was living up so completely to Aunt Mary's image of me as hopeless. I needed rescuing, and quick, and for the first time in my life, when I closed my eyes and prayed . . . something actually happened – right away.

When I opened my eyes, there they were, coming towards me with arms linked – two angels in fur and wellington boots. Even from a distance I could see that they were *powerful*, beautiful girls. I recognized one of them as the daughter of the house,

Miss Penelope; Mary had spoken of her often enough, and there was a portrait of her in the dining room of the Big House.

'Little girl, where did *you* come from?' she asked me in surprise.

'Don't cry!' said her friend. She was wearing a black dress under her coat, and her hair was thick and straight. She looked as though she had stepped right out from the middle of a James Dean film. I gulped.

'I'm Penelope, and this is Charlotte. We won't bite.'

'My aunt – I need to find my Aunt Mary,' I sniffed, overcome with shame. 'She told me not to go far, but I got in a muddle through that gate . . .' I trailed off. Livid with myself, I brushed a tear away from my cheek.

'Now come on,' said Miss Penelope. 'Let me see if I can guess your name.'

I blinked. 'How?'

'Well, Mary's *always* talking about her nieces and nephews. You live in Cornwall, don't you?'

I nodded.

'Your eldest brother's called Jack, isn't he?' she said. 'The one who's been away so long that Mary's quite forgotten what he looks like.'

'Quoit forgar-'en!' repeated the tall girl in brilliant imitation. I laughed out loud. There was a mischievousness in their manner that bore no malice towards my aunt – though come to think of it, if she *had* borne malice, I don't think I would have minded. I was just about sick to death with Aunt Mary that week.

'Then there's Lucy,' went on Miss Penelope, taking up the accent with less success. 'Oh, she's a beauty!'

'Oh, she *is*!' said Charlotte.

'But such a *difficult* child! So full of herself, full of fancy ideas over her station.'

'Over her station,' echoed Charlotte, shaking her head.

I giggled. They both had my aunt's expressions so right.

'Ah. But what of yer brother George? Such a loyal, trust-worthy young man! And your twin sisters, Imogen and Florence? How are they getting on?'

'They're all right,' I conceded. 'Imo's a fusser but very nice. Florence doesn't think much of anyone. George is following Pa into the Church, so everyone thinks he's the bee's knees at the moment.'

'And what of the two youngest boys?' asked Miss Penelope, frowning. 'Goodness. I've forgotten their names?'

'The Littles,' I said. 'Roy and Luke.'

'Ah. The baby boys. How old are they now?'

'Um, nearly six months and three months,' I said, frantically calculating.

'They're the ones whom your father wants to see on Centre Court,' said Miss Charlotte.

'Yes,' I said. 'He's bought them rackets already. All they do is bash each other round the head with them at the moment.'

'Extraordinary. A man of the cloth, like your father, with such a passionate interest in such a *selfish* sport. How is it, living with a vicar?'

'Oh, Pa's not just the vicar, he's a tyrant too,' I said, proudly throwing the word out with great confidence. I had heard it used enough times in relation to my father; I assumed it referred to a position of authority.

Both girls laughed very loudly.

'And your mother?' asked Charlotte. Miss Penelope nudged her.

'Oh, she died,' I said.

Charlotte shook her head, and I felt her shame.

'Heavens. I'm so sorry,' she said. 'Curse me, I'm a fool. I knew about your mother, of course. Mary was undone. I'm so very sorry.'

'Aunt Mary thought Ma was a little bit frivo-loose,' I said. Miss Penelope smiled and bit her lip.

'Always a good thing, to be considered frivo-loose by one's aunt,' she said. 'You should know, Charlotte.'

They both laughed again, and I joined in, oblivious as to what was so very amusing. All I knew was that I wanted to stay with these two girls for as long as possible and that Lucy would be beside herself with envy; she longed to meet girls like Charlotte and Penelope, who exuded charm and confidence and possibility.

'Come on!' Charlotte smiled and held out her hand, and I slipped my cold little paw into it.

'Right. Now we can walk and talk at the same time. Penelope and I, we spend all our time talking and walking, you know. Except when we're going uphill. Then it's too much like hard work. Come on; I expect you'd like something to eat. Getting lost makes one terribly hungry.' She dug into her pockets and handed me half a stick of Kit Kat, still in its red paper and silver foil. I hesitated. I was still not used to such luxuries – chocolate was scarce; she might as well have handed me an airline ticket to Paris. Then I took it quickly, before she could change her mind. Imogen had just finished reading me C.S. Lewis; I was Edmund accepting Turkish delight from the Snow Queen. 'Thank you,' I said when I had finished eating.

'Not at all. Stops me stuffing my face – that's the best thing. I have to fit into a dress with the tiniest waist ever invented for Patrick Reece's party next week.'

Party! When someone as glamorous as Charlotte spoke the word, it took on new meaning. I had been to birthday parties, where there was a cake – if you were lucky – and a song and a couple of games, and every August there was a barn dance in the village where, with shins streaked red from running through the stubble fields, my sister Florence and I hid under trestle tables and drank cider until someone was sick. But the way that Charlotte said *party* – well, it sounded like Cinderella time. I envisaged footmen and white horses and princes from every country in the world vying for the next waltz. I wanted to know more, but I said nothing.

It seemed like a fair walk back to where Mary was working in the kitchens. The two girls didn't stop talking, and I stumbled between them, listening in the same way that Imogen listened to the radio soaps in the kitchen at home. They seemed not part of my life at all; they were alien beings, with their height and their age and their laughter. They talked for some time about Johnnie Ray.

'I don't care if he's doing a concert on the moon. We have to be there,' said Charlotte.

'But how?' asked Miss Penelope.

'Don't care how. It has to be done. Chances like this don't happen every day. We have to strike while the iron is hot.'

Miss Penelope looked down at me.

'Do you like music?'

'Um. Yes. But I'm not sure about Johnnie Ray.'

I had seen his face on the covers of the magazines that Lucy read, but being a pop singer, and a *man*, he was, by Pa's way of thinking, in cahoots with the devil.

'I just sing in the church choir,' I went on.

'Oh!' Miss Penelope stopped suddenly and stared at me. 'Of course! You're the wonderful singer! Mary says you're the best in the whole choir!'

22

I blushed as red as the Kit Kat wrapper.

'I'm all right,' I said uncomfortably.

'What do you sing?'

'Oh, songs about God, an' Jesus. You know, church stuff.'

'Mary told us all about how you sang the first verse of "Once in Royal . . ." unaccompanied last Christmas,' went on Miss Penelope.

'Well, someone had to do it. I had a bad cold ac'shally. Don't think I was much good.'

'But you were a *sensation*. Apparently you brought the congregation to its knees,' said Charlotte.

'Already kneeling, most of them.' I shrugged. 'Too scared of Pa not to be. Anyone could've sung it. But people get nervous. So I end up doing stuff just because I don't mind doing it. Don't get worried about singing like others do.'

'You're far too modest,' said Miss Penelope. 'Mary doesn't give praise lightly.'

'I don't know,' I said.

Sensing I felt too illuminated, they changed the subject and started to tell me about Charlotte's cousin Harry, a magician, apparently in love with some American girl called Marina. The whole set-up sounded like something from a novel; I was turning pages as we walked.

Back at the kitchen, Mary scolded me.

'Don't be too harsh on her, Mary,' said one of the girls.

'She's a silly child, Miss Penelope. Always in trouble, this one is.'

'Good,' said the other girl. 'I should hope so too.'

They left the kitchen a minute later, talking about music again.

Mary handed me a sieve full of carrots for washing and slicing.

'You're a saucy thing, Tara Jupp. Fancy being found out in the fairy woods by Miss Penelope and Miss Charlotte. It'll never do.'

Wouldn't it? I thought. I ran the carrots under the tap and let Aunt Mary tie a pinny around my waist.

'Can't have that hair fallin' into the food,' she fussed, rummaging in the dresser for an old napkin and pushing my hair up into it. I winced as she pulled.

You see, I recall all of it so clearly – every word, every step, every sensation of that morning with those two girls – like no other. But here's the reason why. I remember it all because half an hour into the grind of working under my aunt, as if it hadn't been enough to set eyes on Penelope and Charlotte – I met *him*.

3

The Boy from the Big House

'God in heaven, it's cold!'

I heard him before I saw him, and nearly sliced my finger off with the shock of a strange voice in the kitchen. I looked up and saw he had already crossed the room to the fireplace, where he stood, shivering. He was holding a record to his chest, and wearing one of those zoot suits that all the Teds were wearing at the time, but on a boy with such obvious class it gave the impression less of menace, and more of genuine Edwardian royalty.

Mary wiped her hands on her pinny. She gestured over to me.

'S'my niece Tara,' she said. 'This is Master Inigo Wallace,' she said to me, accentuating the *Master*, as if I should even think about him without it. 'She's helpin' me today. An' a good thing too. Fingers are ever so poor of late. Arthur-Ritous somethin' terrible. Pass me the Silvo, Tara.'

Master Inigo Wallace looked at me properly for the first time, and rolled his eyes. I giggled, out of sheer nerves. He was without doubt the most good-looking boy I had ever set eyes on; in fact, being ten years old and only interested in horses, he was the first boy whose looks I had ever noticed at all without Lucy's prompting. Dark hair in a perfect DA quiff, pale blemish-free skin and a tall, skinny frame stood him in sensational contrast to the village boys, with their thick arms and bad teeth. He looked down again. I remember thinking that perhaps he was embarrassed by the length of his eyelashes – they were *absurd*.

'Are you one of the Cornish lot?' he asked.

I nodded, unable to speak.

'Ah.'

'Yer sister and Miss Charlotte found her up in't fairy woods this mornin'!'

'Nice work,' he said. 'No fairies up there any more, sadly. Can't afford the rent.'

'Oh.'

'Can I have a sandwich, Mary darling?' he asked, and I gasped at her being spoken to like this.

'No you can't. I need butter for my parsnips, and the rest of that cheese for my cauliflour. Never known a boy so hungry all the time,' Aunt Mary commented tartly, slapping a vast piece of cheddar down on the chopping board and grating ferociously.

'*Has* rationing ended?' asked Inigo innocently.

'Cheek!' spluttered Mary.

He stole a carrot instead, filled a cup with water from the tap and sat down at the table. He pulled a copy of the *New Musical Express* from a paper bag and sat engrossed, munching loudly and drinking his water without uttering a word. Alma Cogan was on the cover of the magazine; I was entranced. Please, I thought. *Please* can he finish reading, then leave it on the table so that I could stare at her face on the cover. I watched the kitchen clock for fifteen whole magnificent minutes before anyone in the kitchen spoke. I had wanted to ask Aunt Mary where the salt was, to add to the boiling water, but was too afraid to speak. At last he broke the silence.

26

'Have one,' he said, passing me a carrot without looking up from his magazine.

'Just the one. I've yet to prepare lunch,' chuntered Aunt Mary.

I took the carrot; our fingers touched and I jumped as though burned.

Inigo looked at me sharply.

'Are you all right?'

I nodded dumbly.

'Coldest spring I've felt since I were a girl,' said Aunt Mary, apropos of nothing.

'Yes. I've heard that in the Middle Ages the weather was considerably colder than it is now.'

'Gerr'on with you, cheeky scamp!' Aunt Mary swiped at him with her cloth. He grinned and went back to the paper. I could bear it no more.

'I love Alma,' I blurted. 'She's my favourite singer.'

I could sense Aunt Mary's disapproval; I certainly wasn't supposed to be talking to Master Inigo, particularly not about music, and even more shockingly, initiating the conversation myself.

He looked at me for the first time.

'Yeah?' he said.

'Yeah.'

Aunt Mary was shaking her head at me.

'My sister bought me "Dreamboat",' I said. 'Pa doesn't like me playing it, but when he's rehearsing his sermons, we turn it up and all dance round the house,' I said. 'She's so beautiful, Alma is.'

He stared at me, and something clicked.

'Hang on! Aren't you the one who can sing? Isn't she, Mary?'

Aunt Mary looked stranded between pride and disapproval.

'She is,' she said. 'Best in the church choir,' she added stiffly.

'That's nothing,' I said, for the second time that morning.

'Or everything,' observed Inigo. He looked at me. 'Would you sing now? If I play the guitar?'

'No!' I must have laughed with surprise.

'Don't be foolish, Master Inigo,' said Aunt Mary sharply.

'Oh, go *on!*' he said. He almost sounded irritated.

'I don't know what you mean,' I said. 'I can't jus' sing here. What? In this kitchen? In front of Aunt Mary an' you?'

'Why ever not? That's the wondrous thing about singing, isn't it? You can do it any time, anywhere.'

'I'll do it if you let me read about Alma,' I said.

Inigo picked up the magazine.

'If you're good enough, you can *have* it,' he said, pointing it at me.

I shrugged. 'All right.'

'I don't think it's right—' began Aunt Mary.

'Course it is,' said Inigo. 'Go on. Sing.'

I sang "Dreamboat", there and then, in the kitchen, accompanied by the rolling boil of the potatoes on the stove and Inigo on the guitar. The acoustics were favourable; the ceiling was high and gave a resonance, a sustain, to every note. But I couldn't sing like Alma without moving. At first rooted to the spot, I stood up for the second verse and chorus, throwing my hands out to my imaginary crowd, imitating everything I had read about Alma's performance. Inigo laughed and carried on playing, and his hair fell forward over his eyes. At one point he dropped his pick, so he carried on without it, strumming hard, banging his booted foot on to cold slabs of the kitchen floor. When the song finished, he and I just laughed and laughed. We couldn't not.

Aunt Mary, face still resisting the pull of a smile, nodded at Inigo.

28

'Told yer she could sing,' she said in a tight voice.

'Here.' He handed me the magazine. 'You've got some voice, kid. You should do something with it.'

I laughed out loud at the put-on American expression in his voice. Nobody I knew talked like that!

'She's only ten,' boasted Aunt Mary.

Shut up! I thought. In my head I was nineteen, dressed in pink tulle with red lipstick and an engagement ring on my finger, preferably from Inigo Wallace.

'You sing me something,' I begged of him. 'Please.'

He hesitated for a second. 'All right,' he said. 'I'll sing you an Elvis Presley song.'

'Who?' I asked anxiously.

'He's a new rock-and-roll singer from America. My uncle knows him.'

Funny, that my first impression of Elvis was through a fifteen-year-old English boy, singing in a house like a medieval galleon, in the middle of Wiltshire. I never heard Elvis after that without recalling Inigo. It was as though he and the King were one and the same person to me – if anything, I preferred Inigo's imitation of him to the real thing.

Just as he finished the song, a woman's voice called his name.

'Shit, I've got to go,' he said. 'My mother's taking me to get shoes.'

My dismay at his departure was softened by delight at his swearing. He grabbed his guitar and vanished.

I bent down and took his pick between my fingers.

The rest of the day passed in a daze. Twice Aunt Mary lost her temper with me due to my lack of concentration. Yet who could blame me! I dreaded leaving Wiltshire now – Lucy, George and I were due to return to Cornwall the next day, on a slow train. I might never see him again. Then – just before we left the house for the evening – and as if I hadn't caused enough controversy that day by getting lost and singing and burning the bread sauce – I did something that was to haunt me for years to come.

Aunt Mary asked me to return some tea plates from the library to the kitchen. I hadn't a souvenir, I thought, and we were going home the next day. Lucy liked daring me to take a little something from everywhere I visited – and at that age, I'm afraid to say, I liked taking things almost as much as I liked making my sister think I was brave and clever. If I took something from Milton Magna Hall, I could put it in a drawer along with the magazine – and dream about Inigo Wallace whenever I wanted to; it would bring it all back to me in clearer colour. I padded into the dining room and looked around. Hidden behind an old birthday card there was a tiny china ornament of a circus elephant. No bigger than my hand, it was standing on its back legs, dressed in pink and green, obeying some invisible ringmaster. No one would miss it in a house this size, I thought. Swiftly I whipped it up my sleeve.

I was careless in those days, and because Aunt Mary's hearing was poor I gave her no credit at all for her excellent eyesight. We were in her cottage that evening, and packing to leave, when she entered the bedroom and spotted the elephant waiting to be put inside one of my socks to travel home with me. Lucy hadn't been especially impressed – she had imagined that in a house the size of Milton Magna Hall, I could at least have managed to swipe a small painting from some long-forgotten back bedroom, but Aunt Mary saw it, and instantly realized what it was. Crossing the bedroom, she picked it up and stared from it to me, and back to the elephant again.

'I've been looking for this all afternoon,' she said. 'We turned half the house upside down. What in the name of Saint Peter is it doing here?'

'I don't know,' I began.

Lucy, surprise, surprise, made a swift exit.

But denial was pointless. It was quite plain what had happened, and Aunt Mary was not going to let it lie.

'You can put it back, Aunt Mary,' I said.

'Oh no, my girl. You shall put it back. And you shall explain to Mrs Wallace precisely what has happened here.'

'But why?' I wailed, breaking into a sweat with nerves at the prospect. 'Please, Aunt Mary, it was a dreadful mistake. I don't know what came over me—'

'The one thing I cannot tolerate is dishonesty,' said Aunt Mary. 'You took it, so you shall return it.'

'But, please – *please!*'

But she wasn't listening any longer.

The next morning at nine o'clock I stood in the library, awaiting an audience with Mrs Wallace. I held the elephant in my hands, terrified. But it was not Mrs Wallace who walked into the room. It was her son. Inigo.

'Hello again,' he said in surprise. 'What are you doing here?'

I bit my lip. Here was the one person I wanted to impress, more than anyone else in the world, and I had to tell him that I had been stealing from his mother.

'Tell Master Inigo,' ordered Aunt Mary.

'I – I took this.' I held out the elephant in my upturned palm. 'I shouldn't have done it. I just wanted something to remember this . . . this . . . beautiful house by. I'm giving it back. I'm very sorry.'

I placed the elephant back on the table with a shaking hand

and, hating myself for it, started to cry. I didn't care much about the elephant, nor even about Mrs Wallace noticing its absence, but standing like a fool in front of him was a terrible thing. I couldn't contain myself.

'Leave us for a moment, won't you?' Inigo said, nodding at Aunt Mary.

'She was meant to tell yer mother—'

'Mother's having one of her Bad Heads,' said Inigo. 'I'll deal with this.'

Hearing him speak with authority, the pedestal I had balanced him on shot even higher into the sky – he was up with the gods now. Aunt Mary shuffled out of the room, shooting me a magnificent glare – a slit-eyed masterpiece layered with disappointment, anger and a healthy dose of old-fashioned *ye-who-have-brought-shame-upon-this-family* despair. Once she was out, Inigo handed me a crumpled blue and white handkerchief.

'Don't cry,' he said. 'It's pointless.'

'I just feel so sorry,' I said. 'After you were so kind, listening to me singin' an' all.'

'Nothing kind about that,' he said. 'I liked it.'

He picked up the elephant.

'My father gave this to me,' he said simply. 'That's why my mother would have gone so spare over its disappearance. He brought it back from a trip to India when I was a baby.'

'Your father?' I breathed. 'But he's dead, isn't he?'

Inigo nodded his head with so slight a movement that I wondered later that night if he had answered me at all. For a moment his eyes clouded over. 'It's all right. I'm just glad it's back, that's all.'

I felt so appalled by myself that at that moment I doubted

that I would ever laugh again. I certainly knew that I wouldn't steal again in a hurry.

'I . . . I . . . never thought—'

'You weren't to know. I used to nick stuff from the village shop when I was little. Mainly liquorice, but once I got away with a copy of the *Westbury Gazette*.'

'Wh-why did you take that?'

'I wanted to see the photograph of Phyllis Burns's prize-winning marrows. My sister told me they were too big to lift.'

There was a pause. 'Thank you for being so understandin',' I said in a small voice.

'Not at all.' He grinned at me. 'I shan't tell my mother,' he said. 'And I shall tell Mary not to chain you up for too long, or at least to let you read a book in prison.'

I smiled and sniffed.

'When are you going home?' he asked me.

'After lunch.' I took a breath. 'I've got the magazine you gave me,' I said, terrified that the conversation was drawing to a close. Now that I had him on my side, I never wanted him to walk out of the library door *ever* again.

'The magazine?' he said vaguely. 'Oh yes. Good.'

He looked out of the window and frowned.

'I should get going,' he said. 'I've got to go back to school tonight.'

Lucky, lucky school, I thought miserably. 'I'm jus' so sorry to have caused you any . . . any—'

'Don't give it another thought,' he said.

'Fat chance!' I said ruefully, dizzy with the length of the conversation and the odd turn of events.

'Only, if I were you, I wouldn't steal anything else. My mother has an incredible radar for things moving an inch out of line.

33

Especially people,' he added under his breath, turning towards the door.

I didn't look at the *New Musical Express* again until I was back at the Rectory. When I fished for it in my coat pocket, a part of me thought it wouldn't be there, that it had been a dream. But there was Alma on the cover, and the pages all creased where he had been reading about Ramsey Lewis. I breathed in the pages, all ink and carrot, and as I read I had a sensation of something having changed forever, something being denatured, irreversibly altered. I just didn't know what it was.

4

A Photographic Memory for Houses

What happened next only made my little incident with Inigo seem more steeped in fantasy than ever. Only two months later, the Big House burned down. Aunt Mary, who had seen the place going up in flames, wrote her first letter in twenty years, to tell all the details.

No one was hurt, the Lord be praised, she wrote, before going on, in some detail, to recount the way one of the firemen had rescued the best knives and the portrait of the dog from the kitchen before the roof collapsed around him. Pa, who had always harboured admiration for his aunt's 'way with fruit', invited her to stay over the rhubarb season, to recuperate and recover from the shock of everything. On the first morning of her visit, Lucy and I made toast, and dithered around the kitchen table listening to her talking.

'Mrs Wallace has taken up with a man called Rocky Dakota,' she concluded, an hour and a half and five cups of tea later.

'Rocky Dakota!' Even Lucy was startled. 'But he's . . . he's *famous!*'

'Used to come and stay at the house, so 'e did. Works at the pictures, so 'e does.'

I pictured the legendary film producer selling popcorn at the Odeon cinema in Redruth.

'My workin' days are over, I tell yer,' said Mary, picking up another piece of Imogen's ginger cake.

'And not a moment too soon,' soothed Imogen.

'He always wanted to go to America,' I said, without meaning to at all.

'Who?' asked Pa.

'No one.' I frowned at myself.

Mary nodded briskly at my father.

'She means Master Inigo,' she said. 'Very taken with him, was Tara.'

'Their eyes met over a sieve of carrots,' said Lucy slyly. I elbowed her in the ribs.

'It was raining,' I said quickly, as though that explained everything.

'Liked her singin', Master Inigo did,' went on Aunt Mary. 'Not to mention 'ow 'e let 'er off the hook regardin' that elephant.'

'Elephant?' asked Pa sharply.

'It was nothing,' I said quickly.

'You *sang* to him?' demanded Lucy, pretending that she didn't already know.

'He had a guitar,' I said, all defence. 'He sang to me too. Elvis Presley songs.'

'Who's Elvis Presley?' asked Lucy suspiciously.

'Course, they've been good to me.' Mary clearly felt the conversation was straying off track, i.e. moving away from her as the key subject. 'Mr Dakota's taken care of me. One thing I'll say for the Americans, they know what side their bread's buttered.'

'On neither side!' I said cheekily, remembering Aunt Mary refusing Inigo his cheese sandwich.

'Tara!' said Pa, shocked at my outspokenness.

'I'll miss 'em,' announced Mary. ''Specially Master Inigo. Said he'd send me a postcard. Said he'd miss my cooking.'

'Really?' said Lucy doubtfully.

'I worry about him,' sighed Mary. 'I mean, he won't get spotted dick over there, I don't suppose.'

'One hopes not,' said Lucy.

He, in fact, never left my mind. He was always present, always there, that little episode with him bringing me secret delight and awful dread in equal measure. I turned over every line of conversation that we had had together – even the bits in the library when I had made such an idiot of myself. Things that he had mentioned took on heightened significance – elephants, liquorice, marrows. And Lucy, despite her own heart's flightiness, liked to keep my romantic vision of Inigo Wallace alive.

One afternoon, I remember staring at my sister as she sat at her dressing table applying thick layers of mascara in preparation for a cinema trip with Stephen Holmes, who rode a motorbike and looked like Adam Faith.

'Can I give you a piece of advice, Tara?' she said, watching me watching her.

'What?'

She turned around and looked me in the eye. 'Always dress like you're going to bump into James Dean.'

'Fat chance.'

'All right then,' conceded Lucy. 'Always dress like you're going to bump into Inigo Wallace.'

'Even less likely,' I muttered.

'You know how you told me about the way that it felt to sing for him?' she said.

'Yes.'

'Well, don't imagine that you were the only person to feel it.'

'What do you mean?'

'It takes two to tango,' she said.

'I still don't understand.'

'It takes two to feel That Thing,' she said.

'What thing?'

'I don't know,' said Lucy. 'I can't define it. But whatever you felt – he felt it too.'

'Please,' I begged her, 'don't ever tell anyone about Inigo Wallace. Don't even *talk* about him again. Not to anyone.'

Lucy looked surprised.

'All right,' she said. 'He's our secret.' She smiled at me. 'I'll never tell anyone else that you love him.'

'I *don't* love him!'

'Methinks the lady doth protest too much,' said Lucy blithely.

That night I thought about what she had said, and stared at myself in the mirror. My hair was the same colour as Lucy's, so why wasn't it *good* like hers? It hadn't her wave; it was poker straight, and thinner. Were my blue eyes too close together to be beautiful, my mouth too big for my face? I had a smattering of spots that Imogen insisted were the result of too many straw-berries, and I certainly was far shorter than Lucy had been at my age.

'You'll grow,' promised George, but I wasn't sure I believed him. I thought about Aunt Mary, and shivered that I might end up as stout and plain as she, counting my days in sticks of rhubarb.

Plain and stout appeared to be no obstacles to gainful employ-ment; Aunt Mary was in popular demand after Milton Magna burned down. Despite declaring that she was too old to grate cheese, her suspect cooking skills and 'way with fruit' were sought by the occupants of several estates in the years that followed. Although we were pretty incredulous about this, Imogen concluded that aristocratic society didn't like change, and if their own cooks dropped down dead, they'd probably rather have Mary replacing them than some jazzy new French girl who wouldn't know the meaning of a jacket potato. Also, pointed out Florence, she was so deaf now, they could gossip all they liked without worrying that she would repeat what she had heard being discussed at dinner. I had a different view, suspecting that Inigo's mother, for all that she was reputedly a difficult woman, probably wanted to make sure that Mary was all right and had persuaded her friends to use her; it seemed impossible to me that anyone could willingly delight in her culinary creations, but I kept quiet about it. Aunt Mary had been part of my time with Inigo Wallace, and had become, unwittingly, almost as sacred as he as a result.

Over the next two years, Lucy, behaving worse and worse, was often sent to help Mary wherever she was working. Alas, Pa – cleverly recognizing that as long as two or more of us Jupp children were together it was no punishment – insisted that she went alone. At first she resisted, but then a strange thing happened. Lucy started to look forward to going away on her own – and not just for the possibility of firing loaded eyes at young dukes and married art dealers as she helped them to new season's asparagus and Jersey Royals. Almost against her will, and very much to my astonishment, she came back talking about the *houses*, not the people inside them – she found herself falling in love with the buildings themselves. It was, from the start, a very tricky affair for Lucy to conduct – many of these places were falling apart. Some of them had had their path to ruin accelerated by the army's acquiring them for use during the war and subsequently treating them with the careless abandon characteristic of those whose chief preoccupation was to stay alive for one more week rather than preserve the Ruskin watercolours in the hall. Others were too big to keep standing. Many houses were owned by families who had quite simply run out of money, and Lucy's helplessness in the face of their plight seemed to pain her very much. She was reduced to tears on more than one occasion by the doomed romance of these houses; the sense of the inevitability of their descent into rack and ruin. In some ways, she saw them as people.

'The ceilings,' she whispered of Winbourne Park in Hampshire, shaking her head with despair. 'You should have seen them, Tara.'

'Wish I could have,' I said with feeling. Lucy had a way of talking about these places that made them come alive in blazing colour.

'That place won't be standing in two years' time,' she predicted. 'And we just sit back and watch it all disappear. All that work! All that time spent building something that should last forever.'

I thought she was going to cry.

Later that afternoon, Pa listened to her talking to me about the damaged ballroom she and Aunt Mary had cleared for a bazaar at Broad Lynch – a gigantic pile with a moat in Dorset that was plainly on its last legs. 'Lady Reesdale thinks she can make money doing that sort of thing,' said Lucy, 'but it won't bring in enough dosh to replace the kitchen door handle.' She shrugged at me grimly. 'The drawing room was lovely though, despite the fact that some soldier had drawn something unforgivable on the Stubbs above the fireplace. Gosh, *men*!' she added in disgust. I giggled.

Pa looked up at us, and particularly at his eldest daughter, with her beautiful, pale face and wary green eyes. *How often must he see Ma in her,* I thought with a wrench of heartache for him.

'Mary wants you with her at Enys House next weekend,' he said.

Lucy's eyes brightened considerably. 'Enys!' she said. 'I've always wanted a nose around there.'

'I thought you were going to the cinema with Stephen Holmes,' I said.

'He'll have to wait,' said Lucy and Pa at the same time. Lucy grinned.

'Nice to stay in Cornwall with the aunt,' she said. 'The train to Yorkshire last month was no joke.'

'Take Pevsner with you,' said Pa suddenly. 'You might as well learn something about these places from an expert.'

The world stopped for a moment.

'Take it with me?' said Lucy in confusion. 'Oh, Pa, I *couldn't*! It's your copy. Your own *signed* copy!'

Nikolaus Pevsner's books were revered in our house almost as much as the King James Bible. Pa never tired of recounting the story of how the German-born scholar had appeared at the Rectory one afternoon in 1949, to take notes on its origins and noteworthy features. It was a warm afternoon, and the story went that he and his wife Lola had stayed for lemonade, and two of Ma's blackcurrant iced lollies before walking with Pa to the church. When his findings on the county were published two years later, Pevsner – recognizing a minor error in his description of the stained glass in our village church – had written to Pa enclosing a signed copy of his *Guide to Cornwall*. '*Thank you especially for the iced lollies,*' he had written. '*I cannot think of a time I was better refreshed.*'

Now Pa was prepared to give Lucy – the most chaotic of us

all – the very book that he and Ma had loved so much. This was, I can say with confidence – A Moment. Pa picked the book off the shelf and handed it to Lucy, nodding in recognition of the hugeness of the gesture. I hardly dared to breathe. I could almost hear Lucy's heartbeat speed up, like someone had switched the speed of the record from 33 rpm to 45 – much later on, she said that Pa paying you attention had the effect of cocaine on the soul.

'If I take Pevsner with me, I'm going to be forced to learn,' she protested weakly. 'I can't make up my own stories any more.'

'You should be thankful to be forced,' said Pa. 'If Jesus hadn't forced ignorant fishermen to open their minds, Christianity would have petered out around midnight in the Garden of Gethsemane.'

'Saint Peter-ed out,' said Lucy lightly. She grinned at Pa. 'Thank you,' she said. 'I promise I'll look after it.'

So Lucy's education in Great Houses began, and it was quite plain from the offset that this was her calling. House after house she visited, and as soon as she set foot back through the door of the Rectory, Imogen would pour her a strong cup of grainy coffee and Pa would quiz her.

'*When was the south façade re-ordered?*'

'*What famously disappeared from the West Wing in 1896?*'

'*Who laid out the pleasure gardens in 1760?*'

'*Which room was said to be a favourite of Tennyson?*'

And Lucy would answer every question without hesitation – sometimes even closing her eyes and talking us through every room on every floor in minute detail. I was amazed by her recollections.

'I think you've got a photographic memory,' I said to her when she finished describing the complex passages of the upper rooms at Hodsock, a vast priory in Nottinghamshire where Aunt Mary had been asked to cater over the Whitsun bank holiday.

'I've read about such things. You only have to look at something once, and it goes into your head forever.'

'For great houses perhaps,' said Lucy, considering what I was suggesting. 'Not for Pythagoras or square roots, worst luck.'

She underplayed her talent, but once Lucy had an interest in something, she absorbed information like a Weetabix soaking up milk. Her historical aptitude was astonishing – and the more she learned, the more she developed her own strong opinions on what was good and what was bad architecture, good and bad art. Unlike most of us, who were more fascinated by things that had happened in the dark ages of long ago, Lucy's real obsession was with the Victorians.

'But they've only just *been*!' I used to say to her. 'Grandpa Jupp remembered Queen Victoria dying!'

'But think about how bonkers Imogen goes when she misses *Housewives' Choice* by an hour or two. Stuff that's only *just* out of our grasp is by far the most alluring,' said Lucy.

'Who on earth wants *anything* to do with the stuffy old Victorians?' scoffed Florence, Queen of Modern Thinking. 'Most Victorian women were *utter* wet dishcloths. All they did was sit around holding tea parties and following their husbands up the garden path.'

'Sounds all right to me,' sighed Imogen.

Florence looked at her in disgust.

'You're so backward that you're almost a radical,' she said.

'Tell me again about the dining room at Ashton Court,' I begged Lucy.

But the visits didn't last long. Aunt Mary died in 1958, after a bad fall. She was carrying a plate of ham and parsley sauce at the time; her last words were apparently a plea to return the ham to the larder so it wouldn't spoil. I was upset – despite everything,

I had been quietly in awe of Aunt Mary, and of course, she had been my great link to Inigo Wallace, and there was no chance of hearing any more news of him without her around to impart it. But Lucy, of all of us, was the most distressed by the news. Not just because she had spent so much time on her own with our cantankerous old aunt – but also because she wouldn't get to exercise her Photographic Memory for Great Houses any longer.

She looked at me with tears pouring down her face. 'When I turned up with her, I had access to *everywhere*. There was no velvet rope sectioning off the best bits! She was the *key*! Oh, *why* did she have to snuff it before I'd seen Castle Howard?'

I had thought that Inigo might be at the funeral (and got myself into a state accordingly), but when we arrived at the church in Derbyshire where Aunt Mary's spinster sister Jessie had been buried ten years before, the Wallace family was repre-sented only by Inigo's mother, Talitha. Pa took the service – a surprisingly humorous address peppered with stories about Aunt Mary's long life in service gathered from those she had cooked for. Afterwards, Talitha Wallace drank one cup of milky tea, very quickly, before vanishing into a waiting car. I caught her eye once and she smiled at me. I was dumbfounded by how young she looked still. It was as if *he* had smiled at me, they were so alike. I felt the heat rising in my cheeks. All I could think about was that elephant, and how awful it would be if Inigo had told her the truth about it. Was that to haunt me forever?

After the funeral, we took the train back to Cornwall. Lucy read extracts from Pevsner's *Guide to Derbyshire* to an increas-ingly soporific audience, and I fell asleep with my head lolling on George's shoulder. I had strange half-dreams about Milton Magna Hall, Aunt Mary and her carrots, and Inigo Wallace, until we arrived home.

5

Trellanack

Two weeks after Aunt Mary's funeral, I planned one of my secret riding excursions. I had finished my history homework without a fuss, and had helped Imogen to make bread already that morning, so felt particularly deserving of a treat. Up until that point in the year it had been too dark to go to Trellanack House – but now it was early March, and the skies were suddenly spring-light. As I ran through the village, daffodils jogged about by the green and I felt my heart lift.

I stopped at the bottom of the drive and tasted the salty morning. Much as I liked being on my own, I rather wished that Lucy were there with me to crack a couple of jokes and share the cheese roll I had made for myself the night before. As a result of her newly found interest in Great Houses, Lucy had developed a bit of a Thing about Trellanack (described by Pevsner as having 'the most trustworthy chimneys in the county'), but for Lucy the thrill of the place stopped short of the ponies that occupied its park – she wanted to get inside the house, not on to one of the horses, for goodness sake. Pa had been inside just once, after Sir Lionel's funeral, and had been too weighed down with woe for our lost mother to note anything other than the odd smell of tinned pineapples coming from the kitchen. Lucy had to make do with second- and third-hand accounts of the original Tudor tapestries in the dining room, and the garden laid out by Capability Brown, that she obtained from those in the village who had seen inside the place. She would have done anything to get herself into the rooms for an hour or two, but was far too proud to go and ask Lady W-D if she could have a snoop. Trellanack House tantalized her with its closeness and its impossibility.

I finished my roll and surveyed my prey. There were the usual shoal of Shetland ponies scattered about the park – they were always fun for a charge-about if you could stop them from putting their heads down and eating for five seconds – but standing under a chestnut tree, and far superior to any of the little tykes around her, was a grey pony of about fourteen hands that I hadn't seen before. *Sod it, my mother's dead*, tended to be my mantra in those days. Two minutes later I was up on the pony's back, and five minutes after that we were cantering around the 'dip' in the park, to *my* mind entirely privately.

The Shetlands were so close to the ground that one could roll – commando style – from their backs if they didn't want to stop, but this pony – several hands bigger, and full of the joys of a fast-erupting spring – decided to take events into her own hoofs. Thundering up the dip, and straight across the field, she took me – grasping on to handfuls of mane like a child on a seaside donkey – back to the gate that overlooked the house.

It was there that Lady W-D saw us. She was standing between the fence and the front door, holding scissors in one hand and a basket of daffodils in the other. I decided that turning around would be pointless. The pony whinnied loudly – the great sneak – and Lady W-D turned and fixed me with a frown. It seemed like an eternity before she got to where the pony had parked me. I pushed my hair off my face and wondered what on earth I was going to say.

'Off you get then,' she said, not unkindly. I slid off, hoping to bolt back home. Lady W-D had never spoken to me as an individual before, only as part of a crowd, when I was out and about with various of my family. She was wearing a pair of beige trousers and a brown cashmere jersey, with two strings of pearls knotted around her neck. Everything about her seemed a little bigger than other women, from the size of her ankles to the white expanse of forehead, yet she avoided seeming plump because she was so tall. She had wide, watery blue eyes, a straight, elegant nose and a wide, generous mouth. She was unknown to me. I couldn't believe how silly I had been to take a chance on a new pony.

'Never, ever dismount like that again,' she said in a very loud voice. 'Sloppy, *sloppy* riding.'

'I didn't know you were going to be judging me,' I said sulkily. Nerves, as usual, made me answer back in a way that I would never have done under normal circumstances.

Lady W-D ran her hand down the pony's leg, no doubt to check for injuries incurred while being galloped about by me.

'She's fine,' I said.

'So it appears.' She looked at me. 'Well?' she said.

'I'm sorry,' I managed. 'I – I – my father won't let me have a pony.' I didn't know whether this simple truth would hold any sway with her, but it certainly did *something*.

'For goodness sake,' she sighed. 'You may as well come in for a cup of tea. I've just asked Mrs Wilson to bring me breakfast.'

I was shaking as I followed her. It felt wrong somehow that it was I and not Lucy at that point – as though I were performing in a play and someone had underlined the wrong part in my script. The inside of Trellanack was a revelation. Everywhere there were photographs of Lady W-D being presented with silver cups and jumping spectacular horses over vast fences, and on every available surface there seemed to be bits of a bridle or a copy of *Horse & Hound*. For the sake of my sister, I took in the rest of the place too, which looked like a palace to me, though I could see great holes in the curtains and dog hairs coating most of the armchairs. She led me into the morning room, from which there was a wonderful view of the drive and, I noticed with horror, a very clear view of the dip where I took my occasional fix on her ponies.

'You're a decent enough rider,' conceded Lady W-D, following my gaze. 'Nice seat. Appalling clothes though, and your hair could do with being tied back. And yes, I am aware that you've been bolting my ponies all over the park at some ungodly hour whenever it takes your fancy. I was aware of your presence all throughout last summer. Didn't think you'd have the nerve to strike up again this year. It seems I was wrong on that count.'

'I love riding,' I said stupidly.

'Well, you needn't worry,' said Lady W-D. 'I shan't tell your father. Did a similar thing myself when I was young. Not that I want you to continue your free-for-all. It won't do, you understand? Not one little bit.'

'All right. Sorry.'

I felt my heart sinking. I couldn't risk being caught again, or she probably would tell Pa. I was so busy pondering where else I could borrow ponies within a two-mile radius of the Rectory that I missed the start of what she said next.

'. . . to help me. I could do with someone young and impressionable around the place.'

'Huh? I mean, I beg your pardon?'

Lady W-D sighed. 'I *said* I'd like to offer you a job, of sorts. Come up here whenever you can and take the Shetlands out, then help with mucking out, cleaning tack, bedding down, that sort of thing. Victoria, my groom, is getting married,' she said in disgust. 'She's leaving us in two weeks' time, and to be perfectly honest I've had enough of her moods. I pity the poor man who's taking her on. But you,' she continued, nodding her head approvingly. 'You're probably too young for feeling blue, I was at your age. All I could think about was sitting astride my father's hunter and galloping hell for leather over as much of India as I could manage in one afternoon.'

'India?' It was the only word I could manage. It was too much information all at once.

'Yes,' said Lady W-D cheerfully. 'I grew up there. Lived there until I was thirteen, when I was packed off here to Cheltenham Ladies' with nothing more than a tuck box full of cashew nuts and a metal nit comb for company.'

Now she was talking in riddles. I sieved through what she had said to locate the bits that I understood.

'You'd like me to come here? To Trellanack? To help you with the horses?'

'I'll pay you in riding lessons,' she said breezily. 'We'll sort out your seat, and your appalling habit of looking back over your shoulder at the canter.'

I grinned at her like the Cheshire Cat.

'Oh my goodness,' I said.

'I'll take that as a "yes" then?'

'Yes, please. Thank you very much.'

'Good,' said Lady W-D, who seemed awkward in the presence of gratitude. 'Then that's settled.'

49

It felt like a scene from *Jill's Gymkhana*. Even more so when Lady W-D rang a bell and the aforementioned Mrs Wilson appeared with a teapot and looking about a hundred and three. She started in surprise at the sight of me.

'Two scrambled eggs, please,' boomed Lady W-D. 'And another teacup. Oh, and some of that new gooseberry jam with our toast, if Gordon hasn't finished it all, gannet that he is.'

'Yes, ma'am.'

Mrs Wilson hobbled off.

'Gordon minds the garden,' said Lady W-D.

'Oh,' I said.

'I call him Incapability Brown. My husband had a strange devotion to him that I fail to partake of myself.'

'Oh,' I said again. Everything was happening rather too fast – I still hadn't quite taken on board the joyous fact that I would be able to ride whenever I liked, and that Pa would be pleased with me for getting down to some Honest Toil in the process. Lady W-D took a gulp of tea.

'Now, in return for employing you up here and giving you access to my horses, I'd like you to do something for me, if you will.'

Oh no, I thought. *Here comes the catch.* She shuffled in her chair for a moment, then fixed me with a salty look.

'It's Matilda,' she said. 'My daughter.'

I was touched by her need to explain who Matilda was, as if it were remotely possible that anyone in the village wouldn't know of her – even if they only ever saw her standing in the back of the church next to her mother. Matilda Wells-Devoran was the only girl as staggering as Lucy, but unlike my sister, whose presence in the village was so strong it sometimes felt as though there were three of her about the place, Matilda was

50

ethereal, sighted only very occasionally, like a kingfisher, and even then she never actually *said* anything to any of us. She was a boarding school girl, so quite out of our league.

'I think she needs friends,' said Lady W-D, frowning at me.

'What do you mean?'

'She's away so much at school. But when she comes home she needs people her own age to be with. She gets bored, dripping around the place on her own.'

'How could she be bored here?' I said in amazement.

Lady W-D didn't appear to be listening.

'As a child she was just the same. I should have had another, but of course Lionel had trouble in that particular department.'

I didn't know what she meant, nor did I *want* to.

'I'd have sent her to school in the village, were it not for her father,' she went on.

I went very still, which is what I always do when I'm receiving information I'm not sure I should be hearing. Lady W-D stopped herself from going any further.

'In any event, he's not here any more to issue orders, and I think your sister, the eldest of you Jupp girls – what's her name? – Linda?'

'Lucy.'

'That's the one. I think she'd get on wonderfully well with Matilda. They're about the same age, aren't they?'

'Lucy's fifteen. She acts much older,' I said, without thinking.

'And Matilda's seventeen, but acts much younger,' shrugged Lady W-D. 'Where is your sister at school?'

'She's just left,' I said. 'She works at Miss Fitts' in Truro.'

'Miss Fitts?' asked Lady W-D incredulously. 'Who or what on earth is Miss Fitts?'

I giggled. 'It's a hairdresser's. It was started by Yvonne Fitts, you know? Her son just married Ruth Lipson with the funny eye?' Lady W-D looked blank, as well she might. 'Well, anyway, she runs the hairdresser's. You should try it out,' I went on. 'She'll get you a discount.' I looked at Lady W-D, realizing what I was implying. 'I mean, not that you *need* your hair done. Your hair's nice. And of course you don't need a discount,' I added helplessly.

Lady W-D ignored me.

'She's terribly accident-prone, my daughter – she can't walk from one side of a room to another without tripping over herself or spilling something. It used to drive my husband to *ebb-solute* distraction. Now, couldn't you bring your sister up here for luncheon one day? It's half-term next week.'

'Up *here*?' I imagined Lucy's face when I told her. 'Oh, she'd love to. She's always had a thing about this house. She thinks it's the prettiest house in Cornwall.'

'Easy to say when you're not having to put up with it all the time,' said Lady W-D grimly. 'It costs a fortune, and it's far too big for the two of us. It was Lionel's house,' she went on. '*His* family built it, *his* family loved it. Personally I'd rather go East.'

I had the feeling she meant Bombay, rather than Bodmin. I murmured in agreement.

The clock on the mantelpiece chimed nine o'clock and Lady W-D clapped her hands together – signalling that this was as much chat on this topic as I was likely to get.

'Well, that's settled then,' she said. 'Your sister, I mean.'

'Oh yes. She'll be delighted.'

'Good, good.'

Lady W-D looked absurdly pleased, for someone who had just arranged to have someone as cavalier as Lucy taking on her only daughter. As the eggs and toast appeared, she talked more about Matilda. I did little more than stuff my face and offer the odd grunt in response. With Matilda away at school, she was probably lonely.

'Matilda's no horsewoman,' she boomed. 'They make her sneeze. But she's a great beauty, which I imagine will get her further than being able to execute a perfect figure of eight in the show ring.'

'I don't think that's true,' I said unthinkingly. I spent most of my time day-dreaming of being presented with cups for dressage. If I could have executed the perfect figure of eight in the show ring, I think I would have died happy.

'Seventeen's such a difficult age nowadays. Of course, before the war things were so much simpler.'

I groaned inwardly. Sentences like this were usually a prelude to a great long monologue about how the world had changed and hark at the youth of today and what on earth did we need sweets/music/clothing for when there were perfectly good stones and bits of wood to play with/gnaw on, etc. But Lady W-D had already moved on.

''Strordinary how unalike all you Jupps are,' she said.

'People do say we have very individual looks,' I said, quoting the Bishop of Salisbury, who had made this very observation the previous weekend over lunch at the Rectory.

'Hmm.' Unlike the bishop, Lady W-D seemed unwilling to commit as to whether this was a good or bad thing. 'What I would have done for Matilda to have an interest in horses,' said Lady W-D. 'Simply none. She has no natural *balance*, no apparent sense of *space*. It doesn't make for a rider.' For an extraordinary, almost comical moment, I thought she might cry.

I went home and rushed straight to tell Lucy about what had happened – about seeing inside Trellanack for the first time, and tea and toast and gooseberry jam, and Mrs Wilson and everything. Lucy – taking in all I was saying yet refusing to react until I had finished – had been crawling around in the pantry looking for the mousetrap, and when she stood up her cheeks were flushed and there were scuffs on her knees which made her look about twelve. I sensed her irritation that it had been I, and not she, who had managed to wangle the chance to look inside the place – the fact that I was to be a regular within the grounds must have sent her spinning with jealousy. I couldn't help feeling a touch of pleasure in knowing this. Lucy was always in the right place at the right time for all the action. For once it was I who had hit the jackpot.

'Lady W-D wants you to go for luncheon with Matilda,' I concluded.

'Go for *luncheon*? Who does she think I am? Nancy Mitford?'

'Well – probably, yes. She thinks Matilda doesn't have enough friends, and for some odd reason she thinks you'd be the perfect companion.'

'Why would I want to spend any time at all listening to that stuck-up little madam wittering on about school and bloody lacrosse matches and putting itching powder down the history mistress's stockings?'

(Lucy, like the rest of us who had never set foot inside a boarding school, accepted Enid Blyton's accounts without question.)

'Oh, please, Luce. Please and *please* again.'

'*You* can go out for luncheon with her,' she said, and stalked off.

'I *can't*. Lady W-D might not let me ride unless you do this!' I shouted after her. 'I promised her—'

'Well, un-promise her then. It's appalling, trying to force friends upon people.'

'You'll get to see *inside* Trellanack!' I shouted, playing the one ace I had left.

Lucy stopped walking. Slowly she turned around.

'She wants me to go to *Trellanack* to meet her?'

'Of course,' I said.

'*Well!*' said Lucy, 'I had assumed we were to be taken out every week to some awful hotel in town. Tea at Trellanack! That *does* put a different light on things.'

'It was like nothing else,' I said, delighted that she had changed her mind. 'Gooseberry jam and everything.'

But Lucy was thinking about the prospect of the late-Georgian cornicing around the dining-room ceilings, the bathroom allegedly used by Queen Victoria, the maze, uncluttered by the rest of the village. All of this information was mere hearsay. Here was the chance to see it with her very own eyes.

'As a matter of fact I'm rather thrilled that Lady W-D's chosen me to corrupt her daughter,' she said. 'Tell her we'll come over for luncheon on Friday. We'll come up around midday.'

And really, she wasn't joking. Even with Lady W-D and a house like Trellanack, Lucy set the rules.

6

Lucy and Matilda

I'd like to be able to recall that first meeting with Matilda with razor-sharp clarity, but I can't because I was not even fourteen years old, and all I could think about was riding and the horses and how long we'd have to sit at the table before Lady W-D led me out to the stables. I do remember Matilda was wearing a very beautifully made, very clean grey skirt and an ironed white blouse and school shoes, and her hair was tied back in a long plait. Up close, her face was pale and rosebud pretty, like the ladies on the front of a bar of soap. She looked extra-ordinarily innocent, and unopened, quite the opposite of Lucy, with her kohl-blackened smudgy eyes, ringed with purple from reading Agatha Christie into the early hours. But Matilda's immaculate complexion was short-lived. I do remember that she fell over her shoelaces on entering the room, which endeared her to me instantly, and made Lucy grin. I recalled what her mother had said about her clumsiness, and my heart went out to the older girl.

'Lovely weather,' I said firmly.

Lady W-D had the nous to realize that by hanging around she wasn't going to help her daughter to make friends, so she left us to lunch without her, telling me to join her in the stables when I had finished my fish pie.

'I'm sorry about all of this,' said Matilda when she had closed the door behind her. 'I had no idea that Mother considered me such a tragic figure. You must have been dreading today.'

She had the soft, dreamy voice of the only child, a voice not at all battered about by shrieking at any brothers or sisters to hurry up in the bath or help look for missing socks before school. Lucy – a girl who would have made a wonderful only child herself – was impressed.

'I don't dread anything,' she said. She sounded ridiculous, I thought, like Peter Pan. 'How could anyone dread coming to a house like this?' she went on.

Matilda looked surprised, as though the stupendousness of the place she called home had never occurred to her.

There was a pause and we slurped at our soup. I willed myself to think of something to say.

'I've heard you sing,' said Matilda, turning to me. 'In the choir. You did the solo didn't you, last Easter? In the church?'

'Um, yes.'

'It was good. You were good.'

'Thank you. Um . . .' I grappled around for something to say – anything – to make the whole ordeal less painful. Matilda, despite what one would have thought, had terrific clout in the making-one-want-to-impress-her department.

'You're at boarding school, are you?' I asked her finally.

'Yes.'

'Is it fun?' demanded Lucy, spiking a runner bean with her fork.

'It's all right. Better than sitting around here all day.'

'Are there boys?' demanded Lucy.

'Where? At school? Oh no. Gosh no. In fact, what *are* boys? I've been meaning to ask someone for years.'

She smoothed her skirt and laughed, a short little cough-like laugh. It was in that split second that Lucy decided to be nice to her. Don't ask me why. At any rate, I was relieved because it meant I could race off to the stables without feeling awkward.

'You should come out with me on Saturday,' said Lucy.

Lucy did a lot of talking about how Matilda was 'misunderstood' and how all she needed was to be 'brought out of her shell'. By the end of her first evening out with Lucy there were bits of broken shell all over the place, and no sign that Matilda was ever planning to piece it back together. Lucy only took her out to the pub, but she had never been before. (Fancy! In the very village that she had grown up in!) Instead of being jealous of the attention that Matilda received from various of my sister's former, current and future conquests, Lucy revelled in being the one bringing the unknown beauty to the masses, basking in the reflected admiration. Lucy bought Matilda her first drink from the bar (even though Matilda refused it and asked for a lemonade instead) and encouraged her to talk to the boys about her life at boarding school rather as though she had descended from another planet.

'They all think you're beautiful,' she said to Matilda matter-of-factly as we sat around the kitchen table at home the next day.

'Oh, don't be silly,' said Matilda, beaming.

'They're hopeless, most of them,' said Lucy. 'I mean, they'd fancy anyone new in the village, but you're the ungettable girl par excellence. I heard Ricky Wallop saying he thinks you've got the best legs he's ever seen, and he's seen a few pairs, I can tell you – mine included, now you mention it. But I'm not a legs girl; obviously you very much are. Johnnie Alan—'

'Which one was he?'

'The one with the chin – tall, looks a bit like a mountain goat – works up the garage on the weekends?'

'Oh yes, I know.'

'He said that you looked like a *fashion model*.'

'Oh ha ha ha ha! I saw him looking at *you* all night!'

'Oh, he's looked at me quite enough already. Ever since we – no, that's another story.'

'Oh, go on, what happened?'

'Well, it was my birthday two years ago . . .'

And so it went on. Matilda was utterly in Lucy's thrall because Lucy had done things that Matilda hadn't so much as read about, and Lucy didn't care one jot what anyone else thought. Lucy would wear anything, talk to anyone, stay up late drinking, skip school when she felt like it, and she never tripped up – Lucy could juggle with five apples from the orchard, and had been able to drive since she was eleven. The contrast between them was what Lucy found fascinating. Matilda was nearly six foot tall, never swore, and stayed skinny no matter how many Aero bars she ate. She wouldn't smoke – no matter how many times Lucy rolled cigarettes for her.

'I'm sure it would make me dizzy,' she would say.

'How would you know if you've never tried?'

'Prof Harris says it's bad for your health.'

'Who the hell's he?'

'Our science teacher,' said Matilda. 'He thinks smoking can kill you.'

'They all say that,' scoffed Lucy. 'I bet he smokes himself.'

'Like a chimney,' admitted Matilda. 'In fact, he gives smokes to the sixth-formers when they hand in good essays. He's terribly handsome – rumour has it that he kissed Bridget Simpkins behind the Lime Kiln on Founder's Day last year.'

'Sounds like he's wasted on a load of posh girls with high morals,' said Lucy. 'I think *I* should be at boarding school. Free cigarettes and good-looking men with brains. You don't know you're *born*, Miss Wells-Devoran.'

Matilda, like Lucy and I, was obsessed with the cinema, and musicals in particular. We went to see *Gigi* three times in the cinema in Redruth. Afterwards, with Lucy at the wheel, we sang all the way back to Trellanack.

'You should do something with your voice,' said Matilda, nudging me in the ribs.

I thought of Inigo Wallace, as I always did when anyone mentioned my singing.

'Easier said than done,' I said.

'Wouldn't it be wonderful to make a record?' said Matilda dreamily.

'Oh! Look over there!' shouted Lucy suddenly, pointing up to the sky.

We craned our necks out of the car.

'What is it?' I demanded, noticing nothing out of the ordinary about the Cornish horizon.

'A flying pig,' said Lucy. She grinned at me in the rear-view mirror. 'Make a record, indeed!'

'Our mother always wanted to be a singer,' I said. I felt a strong need to talk to Matilda about Ma; it came over me almost every time we were with her. I don't know why it was that I felt anxious for her to know that once we had had a mother in our lives – was it because Pa was so strong a presence now, or because I wanted something in Matilda to realize the extent of Lucy's loss? I never got far with the conversation, because

Lucy would change it, swiftly, in that amazing way that only she could. Usually when Lucy didn't want to talk about something she drifted into farce. Once she made us play that silly game – What would you be if you were a breed of dog/a household appliance/a cake? – and in the latter category Lucy was a dark-chocolate gateau (messy but irresistible, I suppose) and Matilda was a vanilla fairy cake with hundreds and thousands sprinkled on top. And not the dry cakes that you used to get on the stall at the village fête – she was the sort that you got at a smart tea with a rich aunt, the sort you dream about for weeks afterwards. Needless to say, I was a Battenberg, because, as Lucy said, 'Your life is divided into four sections – horses, singing, eavesdropping and eating. And you're very square,' she concluded.

'And not many people like me,' I added sardonically.

For the year that followed that first meeting, Lucy and Matilda were virtually inseparable. Matilda was still away at school while Lucy cut, primped and permed at Miss Fitts', but even then they kept in touch by post and occasionally by telephone. Matilda wrote to Lucy of foreign things like house-points and mufti, and Lucy wrote pages and pages of comedy back to her – stories of old ladies and blue rinses, or Martin Adams's sister's disastrous wedding hairdo. Sometimes she talked about her latest conquests and how they bored her. She always signed off the same way: *Love and other indoor sports, Lucy.*

And those eighteen months were almost continual bliss for me – riding under Lady W-D's expert instruction, working with horses, and begging honey sandwiches and damp, sweet pineapple cake from Mrs Wilson while I cleaned tack on a Sunday evening. Lady W-D employed another groom, called Pamela – who was plump, blue-eyed, spotty and always laughing. She didn't seem to mind that I was only thirteen – and looked even younger. We talked about horses and music and what we would do if we had a thousand pounds. Both of us cried when the robins' nest in the ivy above the tack-room door was invaded by magpies.

When Matilda left school at eighteen, she was ensconced at Trellanack with a tutor in Italian (from Falmouth of all places) for much of the day. Lady W-D didn't like her going out during the week, but on the weekends Lucy worked very hard at maintaining their mystique as a pair, while Matilda remained resolutely innocent. It simply was not in her make-up to throw caution to the wind as Lucy did. She would sit among the village boys and listen to their awful jokes, and would somehow separate herself from it, while being part of it all the time. She was not to be touched, just looked at, and everyone knew that. I suppose that, honestly speaking, nothing that happened to Matilda would have happened without Lucy. Later on she said that she invented Matilda. She was only half joking.

And Lucy, who had always loved Trellanack from a distance, was now deep in its thrall, as much a part of the place as the seventeenth-century urns in the hall. Having seen so many Great Houses with Aunt Mary, she now had one permanently at her disposal. It was true to say that she fell harder for that house than she had ever done for a boy.

It wasn't surprising. Despite its size – the south front, Mrs Wilson never tired of telling visitors, was two hundred feet long and was punctuated with vast windows 'you could drive an omnibus through!' – there was a softness, a *kindness* about Trellanack that made it more than just a house to us. The granite walls – faded over years of Cornish summers and sea air to a rose-pink flecked with silver, seemed to melt into the dapple-grey slate roof, which in turn supported what Professor Pevsner had called its 'trustworthy chimneys'. It combined greatness with sweetness, beauty with humility. It had seen so much over the years – the addition of the east and west wings in 1799, a Gothic chapel in 1820 which went again in the Victorian alterations – yet I could never shake the feeling that it had surely only started to live when *we* arrived there. It felt as though Trellanack had known all along that we were coming, and had been merely biding its time with its past residents, waiting.

'Every time you think you know everything about it, something else comes along and makes you realize that you hardly know a thing,' said Lucy one afternoon.

'Have I ever shown you the Red Bathroom?' Matilda asked her suddenly.

'No. Where is it?'

'It's locked up, but we should really take a look. I think it was last used by Lord Byron's valet.'

'You've known me all this time, and you've never breathed a word to me about Lord Byron's valet!'

'I forgot.' Matilda grinned at her.

'Well, what are we waiting for?'

Their friendship wasn't restricted to Trellanack either – Matilda angled for invitations to the Rectory whenever she could. She was transported by the size of our family, by the unprecedented sensation of being part of a tribe – and after a wary intro-duction, my brothers and sisters decided that she was perfectly entitled to show up whenever she pleased. We spent hours on end sitting around the kitchen table eating cake and playing charades. Matilda, for all her apparent dizziness, was sharp as a razor when it came to games of any kind – and beat us all at

Scrabble every time. She would be reluctant to go back to Trellanack after these evenings.

'You're so lucky,' she would say, 'having each other.'

'Well, you can pretend that you're our sister,' said Imogen, who was in awe of Matilda's face and the way that she appeared to get some sort of odd pleasure from helping with the washing-up.

'Come over again tomorrow night,' suggested George. 'Florence got Cluedo for her birthday last week.'

Pa liked Matilda because she had lovely manners, and even forgave her when she dropped a plate from a set of six that had been given to him and Ma as a wedding present from the Dean of Salisbury.

'These things happen,' he said blandly, as Matilda, horrified, stooped to pick up the pieces.

If it had been one of us, he would have hit the roof.

7

Raoul

One weekend in mid-August 1959, Matilda was swept off to the south of France, to a huge party, held by her Uncle Richard and his wife – a Parisian beauty called Marie-Leon. Such names, such places and such possibilities of sensational food and drink were utterly alien to Lucy and me, to whom the village barn dance was as close as we had ever got to glamour. Longing to be invited too, we had to make do with waiting for Matilda's return and talking about what she would be eating and what people would be wearing. Matilda was gone for just three nights, but Lucy was restless, as though she sensed that there was change in the air. As it turned out, she was right. Matilda returned with stars in her eyes for a boy she had met. She couldn't wait to discuss him.

'What's his name?' I asked her. She, Lucy and I were eating apples in the orchard at Trellanack.

'Raoul.'

'*Raoul?*' repeated Lucy and I in unison.

'He's Spanish,' said Matilda. 'He's a brilliant writer, but can't decide whether to specialize as an architect or landscape gardener.'

'*Landscape gardener?*' I echoed, and at the same time Lucy said, '*Spanish?*'

'Well, half Spanish,' conceded Matilda. 'His father's as English as they come – he was a don at Oxford and taught my uncle Greek before he went to Spain and met Raoul's mother. She was working selling ice creams at a café in Salamanca and he just looked at her and fell in love.'

'Always a mistake,' said Lucy.

'Anyway, Raoul's the most amazing man I've ever met,' said Matilda calmly. 'He grew up in Granada, like Lorca.'

'And we're from Cornwall, like D.H. Lawrence,' said Lucy tartly. 'What of it?'

Matilda didn't register Lucy's snap.

'He speaks wonderful English. Oh, and he's also the most beautiful man you've ever seen.' Matilda blushed becomingly. 'He's coming here next week.'

'To see *you*?' demanded Lucy.

'Well, not exactly,' admitted Matilda. 'He's doing a degree at Bristol. He's obviously terribly clever.'

'Hmm,' said Lucy.

'He's writing a thesis about Capability Brown,' said Matilda. 'When he told me I said, "Well, he had a go at our place, why not come and see it?"' She nodded at Lucy. 'You two will be up until three in the morning, talking about things like how the kitchen was used in the days of yore and all that.'

'You've invited him to stay?' I asked, amazed.

'He's never been to Cornwall. He's going to come here for a month,' said Matilda.

'A *month*!' spluttered Lucy. 'How on earth did you square that with your mother?'

'Oh, she thinks he's *marvellous*,' said Matilda. 'She wants him to write the definitive history of Trellanack. He's always wanted to write fiction, but he feels there's more money in the truth.'

That shut Lucy up. She stared at Matilda.

'Don't joke.'

'I'm not!' squealed Matilda.

She actually danced a little jig with excitement.

'Since when has your mother given a monkey's about the history of the house?' asked Lucy. 'She never stops telling us how she couldn't care less about who lived here or how the West Wing came to be built, and by whom.' She was stung, I could tell. If anyone was to compile a history of Trellanack, it should be her!

'I know,' agreed Matilda. 'I thought it was odd too. Then I realized that she has something else in mind.'

'What's that?' I asked.

'I think she rather likes the idea of Raoul and I spending time together – you know.'

She raised her eyebrows at us. '*You* know,' she repeated meaningfully.

'Are you trying to tell us that she's setting him aside as a possible husband for you?' asked Lucy with a bark of laughter.

'Mother likes him,' explained Matilda patiently. 'His family are all riders. He's clever and handsome, and he's sure to succeed – you never saw anyone so determined to work. Anyway, Mother never saw me marrying an Englishman. I don't think she wants me to suffer like she did.'

'Not all Englishmen are like your father. And you're only eighteen, for goodness sake!'

'My cousin Tatiana was married at seventeen.'

'And divorced by twenty-two,' pointed out Lucy.

'Her husband had an affair with the nanny,' snapped Matilda. 'They started out with every good intention.'

'Well,' I said, shaken by Matilda's unusual defiance, 'he certainly sounds lovely.'

'Coming from someone of your great age and experience, that's very encouraging,' said Lucy.

'We sat and talked for hours,' said Matilda. 'And it was like nothing else. It was as if nobody else in the world existed.'

'Oh Christ,' said Lucy wearily.

'It was eleven o'clock at night, but so *warm*,' said Matilda dreamily. 'We sat on the stone steps away from the rest of the party and ate greengages straight from the bushes.'

'I'm no expert, but I imagine, *anyone* can fall in love on a summer's evening surrounded by greengages,' I said doubtfully.

'Of course,' said Lucy. 'It may not be quite the same back here in Blighty.'

'Why don't you *want* this for me?' asked Matilda with sudden violence. 'What's *wrong* with me falling in love?'

'Falling in love!' Lucy gave the phrase the full weight of the absurd.

'Wait till you meet him,' said Matilda. 'Then you'll see what I mean.'

We none of us said anything for a moment, just let what Matilda had said sink in. Then Lucy spoke up.

'I just don't want you to get hurt,' she said. For an odd moment I saw something resembling anxiety in her face; there was a sudden, sharp jolt of the premonition that old Lorca was so famous for. *It was as if she already knew.*

He turned up at Trellanack a week later, right at the end of the month. Summer hadn't made much of an impression that year – it had been cold, and hadn't stopped raining for three days. Matilda had fussed about the weather continually in the lead-up to his arrival.

'I prayed for sun, to no avail,' she said, agitated.

'I'll ask Pa to put in a good word for you,' yawned Lucy.

The afternoon that Raoul arrived, Matilda and her mother met him at the station. As soon as he had set down his bags, Matilda bought him into the tack room to meet Lucy and me. Lucy was helping me clean a mountain of filthy saddles – something that she never normally did, but I think she wanted to be on the scene when he turned up. I was dismantling a bridle when they walked in; my fingers were black with dirt and I had tied my hair back into spiky bunches with several of the little rubber bands we used for plaiting manes. I didn't look my best. Lucy, huge, moon-pale breasts falling out of an old white vest stained with blackcurrants from the fruit cages, tiny shorts and a smudge of grease across her left cheek, looked ready to be photographed for *Playboy*.

'Tara,' said Matilda, 'Lucy, this is Raoul.'

Her face was glowing with delight.

'Hello,' he said.

'Hello there,' I managed.

He was traffic stopping enough. I don't think that I had entirely believed the bit about him being Spanish until I saw him in the flesh, but there he was; even in the gloaming of the tack room at Trellanack, there could be no mistaking his exotic credentials. He was wearing a white shirt and a thin blue tie; in his hands was a pale blue jacket. His thick black hair was swept up into a duck's ass quiff, Teddy boy-style, just as Inigo Wallace had worn his back in the day – but he wasn't English enough to look like a Ted – his dark skin was far too good for that. When he smiled, I felt Lucy breathe in.

'How do you do?' he said.

He stretched out his hand, and I stepped forward to shake it, and spilt a can of hoof oil over the floor.

'Shit!' he said, stepping back. 'My father will *kill* me if I ruin

69

his shoes. I borrow them so I can look like I know what I'm talking about when I arrive here.'

Like I said before, I loved hearing boys swear. Hearing boys swear with a heavy Spanish accent was just about heaven on a plate.

Raoul smiled, and picked up the can. 'I miss riding,' he said. (His accent was something else. 'I *meees* riding!')

'I'll get a cloth,' I said.

I wiped the floor with the underside of an old numnah. Raoul picked up the can, sniffed the contents with his eyes closed and placed it on the side of the table. Then, apropos of nothing, he reached into the pockets of his blue jacket and took out four pieces of what looked like exotic fruits. He stood for a moment holding two in each of his dark hands as though he were about to juggle.

'What are they?' I asked.

'Avocado pears,' said Raoul. 'I bring them from home for you to try.'

He handed me one and I felt its softness under the smooth green skin.

'We should eat today,' he said. 'Or they will be over.'

I don't know why that stayed in my head for so long. *Eat today or they will be over.* But it did.

We all walked back to the house, Lucy and I hanging back a little so that Matilda could lead the way, but Raoul kept stopping and asking questions about the garden, and much to Matilda's distress, she was unable to answer even one of them with any confidence at all. We walked through the orchard, through the little gate in the dry-stone wall. Raoul was unable to tear himself away from it.

'This remarkable wall,' he said – and he actually stretched out his hand and stroked it, as though he were touching an endangered animal. 'Matilda, when was the orchard laid out? It has to be the seventeenth century, no?'

'Oh heavens!' said Matilda, laughing. 'I should have known you'd be full of impossible questions. All I know is that I used to hide behind the wall eating apples when Father was in one of his rages. Apples or tins of pineapple,' she added.

She was actually giving him far more information than she had ever imparted to Lucy or me – I would have liked very much for her to go on – but Raoul wanted dates, facts, not the emotional stuff.

Lucy, unable to contain herself any longer, blurted, 'The Domesday Book records this as being "one of the fairest orchards in the country".'

Raoul turned and stared at her, as if seeing her for the first time. She looked down at her feet, almost embarrassed.

'You get sick of apples, after a while,' said Matilda, like the Lady of Shalott and her shadows. She tried to laugh but there was a great sadness in her voice. 'I much prefer greengages myself,' she added archly.

This last remark was no doubt meant to be A Moment, something that reminded Raoul of the night they spent together in greengage heaven at the party, but he didn't seem to register that at all. But then any need to react to what she had said was obliterated by Matilda sneezing suddenly in any case, three times in rapid succession. Her eyes watered. I felt desperately sorry for her, falling at the first hurdle like this.

'Bless you,' I said, feeling like an oaf for saying it. Matilda had barely time to recover before she was off again. Another three violent sneezes. Lucy and I – used to it – stood back and waited for her to recover.

'Are you all right?' asked Raoul, all concern.

'Oh yes. Don't worry.' Matilda gasped and pulled out a hand-kerchief. 'It's nothing.'

'*El fiebre del heno*,' said Raoul. 'My brother suffers the same fate every year. For him, it's lime trees. Put him anywhere near one, and the game's over. It's a bugger.'

I snorted with laughter at the unexpectedness of the expression. Raoul grinned.

Lucy raised her eyes almost imperceptibly to heaven. Like most robustly healthy people, she had little sympathy with Matilda's hay fever and its accompanying disruptions.

We walked around to the other side of the house.

'Such a place!' said Raoul, taking in the back of Trellanack, in all its time traveller's chaos.

'It doesn't look as wonderful from this side,' said Matilda. 'All those bits stuck on by people in different eras. Mother says if aliens were to land at Trellanack, no one would know what century they were in.'

'If I were an alien, I'd take my chances and settle in for the next millennium,' said Lucy.

'That'd suit me,' said Matilda lightly. 'I'd jump into my space-ship and zoom off to Mars. Or London at the very least,' she conceded. 'Anything for a change of scene,' she added, looking up at Raoul from under her eyelashes. I suppose she thought that presenting herself as the dancing spirit, as the flicker of light that didn't want to be trapped in a village in Cornwall forever, would appeal to him. In actual fact, it was quite clear to me that Raoul had never been as transfixed by anywhere as he was by Trellanack. Mars, London, Granada – none were as intoxi-cating as this little corner of south-west England.

Once in the drawing room, I started to mess around on the

72

piano as I always did after a ride. Raoul walked slowly round the room, taking in every detail of the panelling around the Georgian bookcase, the fireplace, the paintings. Lucy sat down and picked up *The Field*, appearing to read an article about the perils of colic in Connemara ponies, but all the time watching him.

Eventually he came and sat down next to me and joined in "The Entertainer", and I could see that although he was letting me play most of it, he was a very good pianist.

'Won't you play something else?' I begged him.

He shook his head.

'No, thanks. I'm horrible in front of an audience.'

'Unlike Tara,' said Lucy. 'Once she gets going, you can't stop her.'

'You play in concerts?' he asked, looking at me with the good grace not to sound astonished.

'Oh no. Not play. I mean, I sing. It's nothing. Just a church choir . . .' I glared at Lucy.

'Still,' said Raoul. 'Church choir. Everyone has to start somewhere, do they not?'

'I suppose so.'

'Church choir one night, then Glyndebourne before you know it,' he said. He gave a shout of laughter, as though the concept were hilarious.

I laughed too – it *was* hilarious. 'I prefer pop music actually,' I said.

'Of course,' he said. 'Me too.'

'Really?' I looked at him with suspicion. 'Who do you like?'

'Roy Orbison,' said Raoul promptly.

I laughed.

'"*Only the lonely* . . ."' he sang, in surprisingly fine imitation, without a shred of embarrassment.

We all gasped at him, then laughed.

Raoul's dark eyes fell on the backgammon board in the corner of the room.

'Matilda's the reigning champion,' I said, following his gaze.

'When it's too cold for picnics in the summer, we play backgammon as though our lives depend on it,' explained Matilda.

I looked out at the pewter sky. 'So you can imagine how good we are,' I said.

'In Spain, I play my brother when it's too *hot* to set foot outside,' said Raoul.

He sat down and straightened the red discs on the board.

'Well, what are we waiting for?' he demanded.

Matilda laughed and sat down opposite him.

'I'll adjudicate,' I said.

'Lucy, you come help me,' said Raoul. 'You know how she works.'

'Ah, now that's where you're wrong,' said Lucy, pushing the blue armchair up close to watch the game.

Raoul's hands opposite Matilda's looked so strange – I had never seen someone so dark before. I was shocked to find myself picturing him without his clothes on. Shaking the thought out of my head, I heard Lucy asking: 'How do you find Bristol?' I don't think she was as at all sure how to act around him; he had confounded all of us by surpassing his blurb.

'I've been there two weeks. It's August, and it has rained every day. I love it.'

'I'm not sure you'll feel quite so well disposed towards the weather here by the end of the year,' said Matilda.

'I have a feeling he will,' said Lucy.

An hour later, and Matilda and Raoul had won two games each. Mrs Wilson came in with jam and toast, and it looked strange to me – Raoul, all dark-eyed and mysterious, yet completely at home sitting on the dog-haired, faded tartan armchair that Lady W-D favoured for her elevenses. He looked out into the bleak afternoon.

'Only in England,' he said slowly, and we followed his gaze out into the garden. The sky was wet seal grey, the Shetlands stood huddled together in the dip where I used to ride in secret.

'Only in England, what?' I asked.

'I don't know. I just always wanted to say something like that, looking out of a window like this.'

I had never seen anyone so pleased to be anywhere.

And so his stay at Trellanack began. Lady W-D – who welcomed him in a way that left Lucy and I in no doubt that Matilda's reading of the situation was correct – gave him the whole of the top floor of the house, his own bedroom, bathroom and dressing room that looked out over Capability Brown's years of hard work in the garden below. She put shortbread biscuits beside his bed, and Matilda filled a vase with roses from the garden for his dressing table.

'He's landed on his feet,' muttered Lucy, running her finger along the bedpost and encountering no dust. 'She's never bothered getting out the Pledge for me.'

'That's because you're a girl,' I said. 'I think she's imagining that he's going to be the one who saves her. Anyway, I wouldn't like to stay up here. It's weird.'

It was the part of the house that Matilda never took us to; the nanny had lived up there when Matilda was a little girl and it was full of reminders of that time, but without the presence of children, the top floor of Trellanack certainly had a haunted atmosphere. The bathroom was decorated with painted nursery-rhyme scenes featuring all one's childhood nightmares – a sinister-looking Humpty Dumpty, a reproachful Jack and Jill with bandaged heads, a scarred-for-life Miss Muffet, stuck forever on the same tile as her very own Mr Spidey with fangs, three squint-eyed mice fleeing tail-less from the knife-wielding farmer's wife. The bedroom Raoul was sleeping in had wooden floorboards and a sparse feeling. There were shutters behind the curtains that entirely blocked the light, and therefore any sense of when the morning had come. Raoul frequently overslept, and if I was in the house Matilda would send me upstairs to wake him up.

'Matilda used to sleep up here when she was little,' I said to Raoul on one such morning. I felt that talking about her might inspire him to reveal a little of how he felt about her; there had been scant evidence so far to suggest that he was ready to propose.

'Why would she want to be at the top of the house on her own?' he asked me, knotting his tie.

'She wanted to be away from her father, I suppose,' I said.

'Was she afraid of her father?' Raoul asked me.

'He wasn't very nice to her,' I replied. I didn't know if I should be saying this, but I felt that perhaps it was good for him to know how hard her childhood had been. I would evoke sympathy, and love, from a man who would want to protect her. 'He had a difficult life. He was on the *Titanic* as a little boy.'

'I know,' said Raoul simply. 'Lucky him.'

'*Lucky?*'

'If you survived that, you have something to talk about for the rest of your life.'

'I'd never thought of it in such terms,' I confessed.

'What doesn't kill you makes you stronger.'

'Or in his case, makes you into a mean old man who bullied his only daughter.'

'Poor Matilda,' said Raoul.

Later that day, he asked her – straight out – about him, and Matilda described how her father had punished her for not liking cabbage, and for not being able to recite her thirteen times table at breakfast – but most of all for her perpetual clumsiness, her lack of coordination for the simplest of tasks. Matilda confessed that he had made her wear her left shoe on her right foot and her right on her left for a week, so infuriated was he by her permanent lack of ability to get from one side of the room to another without falling.

'I had blisters for three weeks,' said Matilda. 'Mother was in India at the time, and Nanny was too afraid of Father to go against his wishes. It was awful. But then Father suffered a great deal,' she said. She was incapable of talking about him without automatically adding this caveat. 'He had poor health all his life after what happened on the Ship.' (Neither Matilda nor her mother ever used the name.) 'He had no hearing in his right ear, and arthritis from the age of twenty-one. Some days he could hardly move. There were always doctors in this house, in and out, all hours of the day and night.'

'I wasn't sad,' whispered Matilda. 'I know I should have been, but I didn't like him.' She started to peel an orange. 'Isn't that awful? My own father, and I didn't like him.'

It was curious that Lucy and I learned all of this through her conversation with a boy she hadn't known a few months before. I felt proud of Matilda for it. Lucy, though she touched her friend's arm in sympathy, seemed fractionally annoyed that she had opened up to Raoul and never to her.

'I expect your father wanted you to be a boy,' said Raoul. 'My father always wanted a daughter, but never got one.'

Then Matilda replied with something that stuck in my head and wouldn't leave from that moment forth.

'Oh no,' she said lightly. 'He didn't want me to be anything at all.'

'I'm sure that's not true,' said Raoul gallantly.

'Oh, but it is. It's all right. Mother always said that I was born into the wrong nest,' said Matilda. 'She always wanted me to ride, but of course I was afraid, and horses have always set off my hay fever.'

She spoke without any self-pity, but I wanted to kick her under the table and tell her to stop. I wasn't sure that all this talk was going to help her campaign to win Raoul's heart – certainly if I was a boy listening to this it would have put me right off. On cue, her mother called from the hall.

'Tara!'

'Yes?' I scrambled to my feet.

'I need you out here right now. Hester appears to have cast a shoe.'

'You see,' said Matilda as I pulled on my boots. 'She'd have been much better off with Tara. I don't know the first thing about casting shoes.'

'Some might say that looking the way you do will get you further in life than anything else,' observed Raoul.

It was the first time he had spoken about Matilda's appearance. She tried – and failed – to hide her delight.

'I don't know,' she said skittishly.

But I did know. I knew that it was nothing more than a well-brought-up man responding to a woman who needed a compliment. Because it was perfectly obvious to me, as it should have been to everyone, that there was no chance that Matilda was ever going to get any further in her mission to win Raoul's heart.

He was completely in love with Lucy.

8

Chaos in the Detail

As soon as I had worked it out, I chose to hide the fact that I knew how Raoul felt about Lucy – I wonder whether we all did. At any rate, I didn't want anything to change. Having Raoul in the village seemed to spill sunlight into the most overcast of days – he was one of those rare people one was *always* pleased to see. My sisters loved him – even Florence who, as a rule, held everyone she knew, including her family, in great suspicion. When Raoul came up to the Rectory, he liked to play around in the kitchen; his cooking was unbelievable. Effortless, delicious food just materialized as if by magic – and even with our limited ingredients he succeeded in bringing a bit of Spain to west Cornwall. Imogen stood in awe while he made *churros*, soft sugar-coated doughnuts, and advised us that the only way to eat them was dipped in melted chocolate. In turn, he admired Imogen for her superior pastry and her imaginative use of rosemary in cakes and tarts.

I talked to him about Roy Orbison and Frankie Howerd, about his work on Trellanack's history, his childhood in Spain with an English father, and our shared love of rhubarb. I was at school again during the week, but on most afternoons I would go directly to Trellanack to help with the horses, and then have tea with whoever was around. Quite often Lucy was still working until after five; she wouldn't appear until later in the day, when I was due to head back to the Rectory. But Matilda was always there. Writing essays in Italian in the afternoon, she would sail into the drawing room for cake and Darjeeling at five o'clock, with roses in her hair and eyes for nobody but Raoul. I couldn't blame her. What was there not to love about Raoul? The mere fact that he was Spanish combined with his ability to swear in English so deliciously was quite enough for me to consider him an excellent person – but something happened towards the end of the third week of his visit that set my admiration for him in stone.

The Saturday afternoon in September was as a child's drawing – an azure sky punctuated by jaunty little clouds – and for the first time in weeks there was a strong breeze – the sort that gets under the tails of horses and sends them spinning when they should be walking. On this occasion Lady W-D had asked me to exercise Cathedral Boy – a chestnut hunter of nearly seventeen hands, whom she had on loan from a friend in Ireland. Cathedral Boy was about the only horse I had ever met of whom I was a little bit afraid – he had a suspicious, wide face, and he had bitten me twice when I was picking stones out of his hoofs the afternoon that he had arrived.

'Just take him out for twenty minutes,' said Lady W-D, flinging the saddle on to his back. 'He needs the exercise.'

'He doesn't look like he's in the mood,' I said, dodging as Cathedral Boy nipped me again.

'When I was your age I was hunting every weekend on a horse that my father couldn't hold. How many times have I told you? Good horsemanship – like everything else in life – is entirely about belief in your own ability, and nothing more.' She laughed, which was rare for her.

I could go on about how from the moment that I clattered off down the drive I sensed that there was going to be trouble. I could remark upon Cathedral Boy's abject refusal to do anything that I wanted him to do, or I could tell you about the way that he shied at the rabbits on the verges, and stopped stock-still when he heard the woodpecker on the roof of the stables before we rounded the corner on to the bridle path. All of this was mere prelude to what happened once we turned on to Mrs Otley's path. Jet-charged, stuffed full of oats and in cahoots with the increasingly sharp wind, Cathedral Boy decided that enough was enough and gave one of those bucks that you see in cowboy films, sending me flying through the air and landing painfully on my ankle, which crumpled beneath me. Shocked by the fact that I had fallen, I made the terrible mistake of letting go of the reins, so that the next thing I saw was the wretched horse breaking into one of those horrible fast trots and vanishing into the woods beyond.

I sat up, practically seeing stars. Staggering to my feet, I knew that I had to find Cathedral Boy before any further damage was done. I don't think that I had ever read a pony story in which a loose horse didn't veer on to a road only to be hit by the only car for miles around, but when I tried to walk my ankle gave way, and I fell back on to the ground with a cry of pain. I took off my boot and my ankle swelled up like a Swiss roll, so that I couldn't even get the boot back on again. Worse still – the sun had been taken hostage by a host of indigo clouds. It started to rain again.

'Please God,' I muttered. 'Get me help.'

My head was still spinning ten minutes later, when I saw him coming towards me from the wood, wearing a thin red shirt, new jeans and old boots, his black hair swept back off his face, smile wide like Ritchie Valens. He was leading Cathedral Boy, who walked alongside him, rolling his eyes and snorting, but very much aware of the fact that the Game Was Up. Raoul had him.

'He threw me!' I shouted, the wind eating up my words.

'Are you all right?' Raoul shouted back.

'Don't know,' I confessed. 'My ankle's gone.'

'Is it your bad ankle?' he asked me. Raoul had never mentioned before that he had noticed my limp. I felt myself going red.

'N-no,' I said. 'It's the other one.'

Raoul sat down and picked up my foot, letting Cathedral Boy snatch up great mouthfuls of dandelions and daisies beside us.

'Can you walk on it?'

'Not really.'

Raoul pulled a hip flask from his back pocket, unscrewed the lid and handed it to me.

'What is it?' I asked weakly.

'Don't ask, just get it down you.'

I took one gulp and nearly threw up.

'Ugh! It's *revolting*!'

'Cooking sherry,' confessed Raoul, grinning. 'I was too afraid to take anything more important from Matilda's mother. My father didn't believe in going anywhere without a shot of something in his back pocket. Go on, have some more. Once you get past the first mouthful, it's really quite satisfactory.'

I gazed at him gratefully.

'What were you doing in the woods?' I asked.

'I wasn't in the woods. I had been posting a letter home and was walking back through the village. *El Chico de la Catedral* came out the other side of the bridle path and was heading towards the village green.'

'How did you catch him?'

'He knew he'd met his match when I appeared. Oh, and I had half a bar of Crunchie in my pocket.'

Cathedral Boy snorted his approval. I laughed. Raoul had a great weakness for English confectionary, as we all did, having been so starved of it during the war.

'Beautiful horse,' said Raoul. He looked at me. 'But too strong for you, Tara. Is she trying to kill you?'

'She says that in her day she was galloping horses bigger than him all over India.'

'Everyone behaves like a cowboy in India,' said Raoul dismissively. 'In England, it's a different story.'

The wind had picked up again, and I shivered. Without saying a word, Raoul unbuttoned his shirt and handed it to me. I did a double take. Under the shirt he was wearing nothing at all. Raoul had proper *hair* on his chest, like the illustrated heroes of fiction in the magazines that Lucy read. I supposed I had known it was there from when he wore the top two buttons of his shirts open when he was working – but seeing it in all its glory, reaching right down to the top of his denims, was another thing altogether.

'What are you *doing*?' I asked, embarrassed and thrilled in equal measure. 'You'll catch cold.'

'You very well know that I *like* the cold,' he said. 'Now. I'm going to ride both of us home. You sit behind me.'

'Oh no, I don't think that's a good—'

'We have no choice,' said Raoul. 'You can't walk, but I can ride, and this animal's built like – how do you say it? – a *breek preevee*. He can take us both.'

I laughed, delighted. 'A brick privy! Raoul, *where* did you hear that?'

'Your sister,' said Raoul, heaving me up on to Cathedral Boy. 'She uses the most uncouth expressions. Before I met her, I thought all English girls wouldn't say boo to a duck. How wrong was I?'

'Boo to a *goose*,' I corrected him.

'That too,' he said.

I watched him as he sprang into the saddle in front of me. My sister, it seemed, appeared never to be far from Raoul's thoughts.

We set off back down the track to Trellanack together, and Cathedral Boy didn't put a hoof out of line. Raoul rode with the confidence of a matador – and with a style that was quite at odds with how I had been taught. He held his hands high, and appeared to do all his steering with his legs..

'I learned to ride *Doma Vaquera* style,' said Raoul. 'I was taught by my mother's brother, Ricardo. You and the horse have to become part of each other in order to assert complete control, and therefore experience absolute freedom and unity together.'

'Would you teach me?' I asked him.

'My hostess would not approve,' said Raoul. 'Matilda's mother is not someone who appreciates the Spanish style.'

My head was hurting, and my ankle was hurting, and I was exhausted by the complex exercise of keeping my arms wrapped around Raoul's waist without touching too much of the smooth skin on his back. I was fourteen, and I had never felt *any* man's bare body before. To do so for the first time on horseback was almost too much; I didn't know how to place myself at all. He looked around at me and grinned. 'Do you want me to take you all the way home?'

'Yes, please,' I muttered.

It was in that moment that I realized who Raoul reminded me of most strongly. He was like Errant Jack, only he was actually *here*, not prancing about on the continent like my adored eldest brother. As Cathedral Boy carried us homewards, I didn't ever want him to go back to Spain. He could have led me into the Rivers of Babylon and I wouldn't have minded. I had never felt so safe as I did on the back of that horse with the Spanish Boy. It seemed inconceivable that we had known him such a short time. He was already so much part of all of us.

When we arrived at the Rectory, Lucy, Florence and Imogen were pegging out washing on the line. They looked up as we rode towards them, and Lucy straightened her back and pushed out her chest. Imogen blushed and widened her eyes at the sight of Raoul's lack of clothing, and Florence tried to look as though she had seen it all before – even though I was quite certain she hadn't.

'What's going on?' Lucy asked, as Raoul pulled Cathedral Boy to a halt. 'Trick jumping? You've missed the circus. They were here at Easter.'

Raoul dismounted. Carefully he lifted me down. 'Tara had a fall and she's hurt her ankle,' he said.

'Your bad foot?' asked Imogen quickly.

'No,' I said, irrationally irritated.

'I'm delivering her back to you for ice and rest. Lavender, arnica, witch hazel,' he said, ticking them off on his fingers. 'All good for sprains.'

'How do you know?' asked Florence suspiciously.

'My great-aunt is a witch,' said Raoul simply. He looked at the expressions on our faces. 'A good one,' he said quickly. 'Not the broomstick kind. She has powers,' he added with a shrug. I

86

giggled. 'But in the absence of Aunt Sophia, I suppose you should get Tara's foot looked at. One of your brothers is a doctor, no?' asked Raoul.

'No,' we all said together.

'None of the boys has ever bothered to learn anything that will be of any use in the real world,' said Lucy.

'But if it's tennis, God, or Parisian houses of ill fame you're after, look no further,' added Florence drily.

Leaning against Cathedral Boy, I pulled off Raoul's shirt and gave it back to him.

'You know, you really should watch out,' said Lucy. 'Showing up half naked on the back of a horse like this. We're not accustomed to such beauty.'

Raoul laughed, but there was weight in what Lucy was saying. It was the first time she had thrown him one of her compliments, and she knew it.

'My grandmother used to say that Spanish men have a habit of turning up in the wrong place at the right time,' he said.

'Indeed,' said Lucy. 'Look – you're doing it up wrong.'

She stepped forward and pulled his hands away from his shirt. With steady fingers she undid what he had done, and did it back up again correctly. Raoul glanced down at her and her chest, opened his mouth to say something, but looked away instead. Imogen stood beside them, frowning slightly.

'Thank you,' I said to Raoul. 'I don't know what I would have done if you hadn't found us.'

'You would have been fine,' said Raoul.

'It's not me I was worried about. That horse is almost worth more than Trellanack,' I said. 'Anything could have happened.'

'But it didn't,' said Raoul. He looked right at Lucy as he spoke. 'Disaster was averted.'

'Yes,' said Lucy. 'Disaster was averted.'

Holy Smoke – once the fire had been lit, I felt its heat everywhere. That last week that he was at Trellanack, everything seemed to crank up a gear. They knew they were on borrowed time. The odd thing was how little Matilda seemed to sense it, although the fascinating thing about Raoul's adoration for my sister was that it was based almost entirely on conversation and common interest rather than his desire for her body. I'm not saying that he hadn't noticed her looks, but they were secondary to what really mattered to him. He never appeared to care what she was wearing, or if her hair had been washed that morning or how much make-up she had on – he focused entirely on what she had to say, with particular reference to her Photographic Memory for Houses (Trademark). He was transported by her description of Mosse Hall in Hampshire, a recently demolished house that she and Aunt Mary had worked in over a fishing week; he made her repeat her stories about the chapel at Awns Court in Northumberland over and over again. They discussed endlessly the scores of houses that had gone, lamenting them like old friends. Lucy had never spoken to a boy like this, without the need to flirt, or reapply her lipstick.

When they weren't talking about houses, they were laughing, incessantly, over nothing at all. Raoul seemed to feel everything that Lucy felt – his delight at everything good that happened to her was palpable. I hovered in the background, worried. I think I knew that we were really in trouble when I heard Lucy telling him, in faltering tones, about Ma's death. Lucy never talked about Ma, and still less about her own place in the story, about how she blamed herself. She and Raoul were sitting in the dining room, alone. It was a warm afternoon, but it was always cold in that room. They didn't hear me padding into the kitchen.

'I couldn't save her,' Lucy was saying. Her voice was high, bright, as though she had temporarily forgotten where she was and to whom she was talking.

I heard Raoul reply, 'But how could a little girl of thirteen know what to do in such a situation? It is impossible.'

'She never recovered,' said Lucy. 'She never recovered. I didn't know how to help. I just didn't *know*. I was scared.'

It was the first time I had ever heard Lucy confessing fear. I felt sick. Frozen. I waited to hear what Raoul would say.

'You cannot go on for the rest of your days blaming yourself for this, Lucy. It's not right.'

'What else can I do?'

'It is the easy option, to do as you are doing,' said Raoul.

'What?' I mouthed the word as Lucy spoke it out loud.

'It is the easy option,' repeated Raoul. 'You can wring out your hands and wail at the moon for as long as you want, but it won't do any good.'

'Well, what would *you* do then? What would *you* do if you had this hanging over you every day of your life?' Lucy must have banged her hand on the table; I heard a thud and the rattle of the candlesticks.

'I would turn it all around,' he said. 'Shake it up.'

'Shake it up?'

'Yes. I don't know how to say in Eenglish, Lucy. *Como se dice?* You think that you did wrong? The only thing you can do is to *learn* from that. Don't waste your time over things that you can't change.'

Lucy must have stood up because he said: 'No, don't go—'

'Why not? All this is so easy for you to say.'

Perhaps – I thought – perhaps he had pushed her too far.

The morning before he was due to go back to Bristol, Lucy

spoke to me about Raoul for the first time.

'What should I do?' She was staring out of her bedroom window and picking at her fingernails.

'What shall you do about what?' I asked her. I was full of dread – right up to the brim with it.

'Raoul,' she said. 'Matilda wants me to ask him how he feels about her. She thinks he's just shy; that's why he hasn't kissed her. Oh God.'

She looked at me, and her eyes were full of pain.

'She loves him,' she said. 'She *really* loves him.' She looked at me. 'Do you think he loves her, Tara? *Do* you?'

'How on earth should I know?' I said. There was a pause. 'No,' I confessed.

I felt slightly sick, as though I had boarded a train travelling very fast in the wrong direction. Lucy shook her head, gritted her teeth and slammed her hand down on the windowsill. 'He should never have come. He's going to ruin *everything*.'

'Lucy? You're not *crying*?'

'No, I am *not* crying,' she said, swiping the tears away angrily. 'It's just a mess, all right? Not that you would understand.'

But I absolutely did. When Lucy spoke again, her voice was so soft I had to strain to hear what she was saying.

'Sparks between us,' she said dully. 'Bloody disastrous sparks. From the moment he first arrived. I willed them to vanish. But they didn't. They're all over the place. But I can't do it to Matilda. She'd never forgive me. Oh, I think I should go.'

She walked out of her room, and minutes later I heard her telling Pa and George that she wanted to go with them to Southwold for two nights, to keep them company.

'Who are you avoiding?' demanded Pa.

'Matilda,' confessed Lucy.

'Spanish chap in love with you, not her, is he?' said George, with shocking perception for someone who was meant to be renouncing all that sort of thing.

'Something like that.'

George shook his head.

'No good running away. He'll only come and find you.'

Later that afternoon Raoul showed up at the Rectory, and said it. George was right, as he nearly always was. Running away was pointless.

I saw him through the kitchen window.

'Raoul!' I shouted. 'Aren't you supposed to be packing?'

He seemed to hesitate when he saw me, and then beckoned me outside. I dropped the dishcloth into the sink and went out to meet him. We stood under the copper-beech tree and he pushed his hands through his black hair. Even so early in the day I felt the sun pricking my skin, and shaded my eyes with my hand. But where it handicapped pale English girls like me, it seemed to give Raoul more power, more glamour. He drank in the sunlight, seemed to photosynthesize.

'Listen,' he said. 'I've gone and fallen in love with your sister.'

'Which one?' I asked automatically.

He looked at me blankly, as though he hadn't realized that there were two others to choose from. 'Lucy, of course.'

I'd heard it enough times from other boys, but this was the first time it really hit me that this sentence was going to change everything.

'Oh.'

'I don't know what I should do. I mean, there's no chance I'm going to get over it, so I may as well tell her how I feel.'

'I thought you might think like that.'

He looked at me. 'You think I should?'

91

'Oh, Raoul,' I said. 'What about Matilda?'

Raoul frowned. 'Matilda?'

'She's – she's – she likes you a great deal.'

Why was I talking like this?

'Oh,' said Raoul. He looked thoroughly taken aback. 'Ah. How very tricky. Are you sure? It hadn't occur to me that she—'

'Oh, come *on*, Raoul! She lights up every time you walk into the room, she hangs on your every word. You can't tell me you hadn't noticed.'

He sighed. 'I think perhaps it is a little – how do you say it? A little *crush*? I don't think it is anything more. She cannot love me,' he said dismissively. 'We are not alike. I would drive her to distraction.'

He frowned and shook his head. I opened my mouth to say, Look, Lucy falls in love like Roy and Luke fall off their bikes, but then I shut it again because I knew she was really mad about him and if he left without telling her it would hang over me forever.

'Well, if you really feel you can't go without telling her, then you should say something,' I said finally. 'Tell Lucy how you feel. I think she . . . I think she should know.'

He looked at me intently. 'You think so?' he asked. 'You really think so? You think I should say something?'

'I do. Otherwise, well, it's a waste, isn't it?'

Raoul looked at me.

'Tell me, have you ever felt like this? You know, the thing where you cannot sleep, where everything is . . . all over the place, you can't concentrate.' He looked confused. 'I don't understand it. I thought I had loved before, but that was just nothing.' He looked at me. 'That was just nothing,' he repeated. He sighed. 'You are too young to know,' he said.

'Once I thought I loved a boy who played the guitar and sang like Elvis,' I blurted.

Raoul didn't look surprised.

'Of course,' he said. 'If anyone play guitar like Elvis, you will think you're in love.'

'Maybe.' I gave a brief smile.

'Where is she?' he asked me. 'I should find her now.'

'She's at work,' I said. 'She'll be back in half an hour.'

'Could you ask her to come to the green?' he said. 'I'll wait for her by the bus stop.'

I nodded. 'All right.'

There would have been no point in refusing him. He was going to find her somehow, whether or not I passed on his messages.

At supper that night Lucy had grass seeds in her hair and she didn't mind when Pa told her off for forgetting to tell Mr Bell that choir practice was cancelled. I knew that Raoul had told her, and I knew that she had told him right back.

Everything that had been so tight, so close, so protected for the two and a half years that she and Matilda had been friends – had been shattered. I stood back, shielding my face with my hands, and waited to see what would happen next.

9

Black Ink

Raoul went back to Bristol as he said he would, but the great romance swelled to crescendo after crescendo with every postal delivery to the Rectory, with every ring of the telephone bell. He and Lucy saw each other only once between the end of the summer and October, when Raoul came back to Trellanack for a weekend. Matilda was blind to everything.

'I think he may have been missing me,' she said to Lucy after supper. 'He said that I looked well.'

And Lucy had turned away, horrified, but so very protected by love. She knew he had come to see her. It was she who had changed his life forever.

At the end of this second stay, Lucy dropped the bombshell. Standing in my bedroom, she told me that Raoul had asked her to marry him, and that she had said yes.

'*Married!*' I very nearly fainted. Staggering towards the nearest chair, I stared at my sister in disbelief. Nothing – no amount of clocking her love for Raoul – had taken my imagination as far as a wedding, at least not *yet*. It seemed impossible. I was partly terrified for her, partly bursting with the sudden, tremendous thrill of knowing that this would make Raoul the brother I believed him always to have been.

'*Married!*' I repeated. 'Oh, Lucy, it can't be true!'

'Why would we wait?' Lucy said. She offered me her left hand, and I stared at the simple gold band on her fourth finger.

'Shivers!' I whispered. Then I shouted with amazed laughter, and stared at her as a sudden thought struck me. 'Oh my gosh – you're not . . . ? Oh, Lucy, you're not going to *have a baby*, are you? Is that why you're doing all this so fast?'

'Don't be idiotic,' said Lucy, snatching her hand away.

I looked at her and still I couldn't take it in.

'But what about your hopes for the future?' I said shakily.

'*Hopes for the future!* Why are you talking like Mrs Bennet?' laughed Lucy – but she knew exactly what I meant. Since my sister had first opened Pevsner, she had spoken about her longing for work in the field that had drawn her in so thoroughly. She was an architectural historian in the body of a French actress, George was fond of saying, and marriage, I suspected, would end her hopes for a career, as it tended to end *every* girl's hopes for a career. Having a husband, even if he was as different and wonderful as Raoul, would mean cooking, cleaning and running a home, and – one day – producing children.

'Raoul believes I can still do everything I want to do,' she said. 'Only it will be easier, because he'll be by my side.'

I looked at her slowly. I was only fourteen, but I knew in a flash that it wouldn't be easier. I couldn't see how it could be.

'It just seems very sudden,' I managed. 'I think Pa will say that. He'll say it's too sudden. Too *soon.*'

'Raoul's been to ask Pa,' said Lucy. 'He asked him for my hand all good and properly. And Pa said yes. He gave us his blessing.' She looked at me, unable to stop grinning; then she took my hands in hers. 'He gave us his blessing,' she repeated, sounding as amazed as I was.

'*When?*' I asked, incredulous.

'Yesterday evening.'

'He gave you his *blessing*? Is that all he said?'

Lucy looked out of the window and laughed.

'Well, you know Pa. He likes to play things his way. As soon as Raoul told him that he'd come to ask for my hand in marriage, he went and asked him what colour eyes I had.'

'Huh?'

'He asked Raoul what colour eyes I have.'

'He did *what?*'

'Raoul said he didn't know but he thought they were brown.'

'But they're green!' I gasped.

'I know. Pa said that not knowing the answer to this question settled it all. He said that if he had answered correctly right away, it would have meant that we had spent too much time gazing at each other and not talking. Talking, he said, was what started a marriage in the proper fashion, not swooning.'

I could scarcely believe it – and yet of course I could. It was *terribly* Pa to behave in this *answer-me-this-riddle-young-man-and-ye-will-pass-the-swamp-of-fear* way.

'So in answering *wrongly*, Raoul proved that he loved you for something more than your face? Everything's all right because of *that*?' I asked, shaking my head.

'No,' said Lucy. 'Everything's all right because it was only *ever* going to be all right. It's all right because we were *meant* to be together.'

'But Matilda,' I said, almost unthinkingly. 'How are you going to tell her?'

'That was the other condition that Pa had,' said Lucy. 'He

wants nothing hidden. He insists upon my telling her tomorrow.'

'*Tomorrow?*'

Lucy gulped and looked at me.

'Please be there,' she begged. 'I'm not sure I can do it without you.'

'I can't be there!' I said in horror.

'If not for me, then for her,' said Lucy. 'I don't know why, but I think it would be easier for her if you were with me. Sometimes when it's just the two of us, it's too . . .' She paused. 'Too much,' she concluded confusingly.

I could see no way of refusing. She was still my older sister, and I would have moved mountains for her if I could – and I think there was a part of me that must have wanted to see Matilda's reaction first-hand. I felt rather as one would have felt in the days watching death at the gallows – compelled to be there, despite the horror of it all. And so the next day we went together to Trellanack, together to tilt Matilda's world at a different angle. Raoul was back in Bristol. Without him to confirm it all, I still felt as though everything that was happening was dream-like, untrue. But I only had to look at my sister's face to believe it.

'You're getting *married*!' said Matilda. Her sweet, soft voice was unsteady – it cracked in the middle like crème brûlée. 'You and Raoul! You're getting *married*!'

She stared straight ahead, as if waiting for the information to sink into every part of her brain. It was a warm morning. Lady W-D had gone hunting.

Matilda crossed the morning room to embrace Lucy, catching her foot on the rug and propelling herself into Lucy's arms with considerable force. I looked down at my feet because it was plain that despite her fixed smile of delight and her outward show of affection, Matilda was devastated. Under her smile and her warm words there was *fear*, something that I hadn't banked on at all. Anger, yes. Tears and despair perhaps. Not fear. Lucy saw it too, and realized at once that this was going to change everything more than she had ever thought it would. Matilda was not over Raoul. She was as crazy about him as Lucy was – only she couldn't have him. I tried to make myself as small as possible behind my lemonade and wished I had asked for something stronger.

'We never meant for this to happen,' said Lucy. 'It wasn't on the cards. I know how you felt about him. It's made it hard.' she bit her lip and tried again. 'It's made it hard to tell you. I – I've been worried that you might disappear and never speak to me again.'

'Nonsense!' jabbered Matilda. 'How could I? Goodness, won't Mother be surprised? She'll have to go and find me someone else now – she was so very keen on Raoul taking me off her hands. Although deep down I don't know that she ever trusted the Spanish. Not since the Crimean War.'

There was a short silence.

'But the Spanish weren't involved in the Crimean War,' said Lucy, who could never resist picking up on historical inaccuracies.

'*Weren't* they? Mother thinks they were.'

Matilda laughed and pushed her hands over her head, dislodging several hair-slides. Now her blonde hair was sticking up at odd angles.

'I should have known he'd fall for you, anyway,' she said. 'They always do, don't they? Tara – *you* told me that.'

'They like the same things,' I said stupidly.

Lucy looked down at her hands around her glass of water.

'Of course,' said Matilda. 'I mean, what would *I* have to talk to him about? We'd run out of conversation pretty quickly.'

But it was suddenly too much for her. Sitting down heavily on a green and yellow footstool in the middle of the room, Matilda crumpled in front of us. Her head in her hands, she started to cry. For a minute, neither Lucy nor I moved, both of us hesitating about how to react.

'I'm sorry,' said Matilda, looking up again. 'I just didn't expect it. I don't seem to have any suspicion in me. It's a terrible disadvantage.'

Lucy stood up; she didn't know where to put herself.

'I never wanted to upset you,' she said, standing over Matilda, addressing the top of her head. 'Please don't cry. I hate it.'

Matilda pulled a handkerchief out of her sleeve and blew her nose.

'At least I'm going to India with Mother next month,' she said. 'A change of scene will do me good.' She blew again. 'I expect you thought of that.'

Lucy said nothing: she had thought of nothing else.

'And you and your new job,' said Matilda. 'It's all worked out very well, hasn't it?'

'That's not for me to say,' said Lucy. 'Oh, please don't cry,' she said again.

'It's just the shock — that's all,' said Matilda.

Just the shock. I don't know whether that explains or justifies what Matilda did next. Sometimes, you know, I actually I think it does.

We left Trellanack a short while afterwards. Matilda claimed that she had to write some letters, and Lucy had to get up for work in the morning, but we all knew that in the old days both girls would have skipped anything to be together — even if all they were going to do was lie about the house talking about their fingernails. When we got back, Lucy seemed lighter, less anxious now that she had revealed her hand – however Matilda had reacted. I went up to my room and wondered if Matilda would ever get over it.

I knew the answer the next morning, when she pushed a note, addressed to me, through the front door of the Rectory. I was at choir practice, so didn't get it until just before lunch.

Dearest Tara,

By the time you read this, I will be on my way to London to stay with friends of Mother's in Kensington. I couldn't face going to India. London has to be better than wilting around here like a fool with a broken heart. I can't see Lucy any more, You understand that, don't you? It would be too painful. With things as they are, everything feels pointless. This house came to life while Lucy was my friend, but now it's back to how it always was. Empty.

Don't stop dreaming.

Love, Matilda.

She was full of phrases like 'don't stop dreaming', which tend to sound ridiculous when spoken, but bring a lump to the throat when read in black ink on Basildon Bond.

I pushed the letter into my pocket with shaking hands, and walked to Trellanack. I knew I wouldn't be in time to see Matilda again, but at least I could see Lady W-D and the horses. I had to be sure that I could still ride there – or I would have been punished for Lucy and Raoul as much as Matilda felt she had been. Being caught in the middle was the tragic fate of a younger sister, I thought. I didn't care, as long as I wasn't going to lose my time at Trellanack, but I had an awful feeling that it wasn't going to work out like I wanted at all.

10

Beautiful Debris

Lady W-D was going through papers in her library when I arrived; I sensed that it wasn't the best time to show up.

'Hello,' she said. 'Pass me that waste-paper basket, will you?'

Into the bin went several old copies of *The Field*.

'Gordon is going to have a bonfire,' she said.

'Is there anything I can do to help?' I asked. 'Should I move Hester to the top paddock? She and Cathedral Boy are getting on very well now—'

'No,' said Lady W-D sharply. 'I'm sorry. I mean, no, thank you, Tara.'

She pushed her glasses on to her nose and looked at me.

'It's a good thing you're here,' she said. 'I need to talk to you.'

'About Matilda?'

'In a manner of speaking.'

'And Lucy and Raoul?'

'Yes.' Lady W-D frowned at an old letter and sighed. 'You see, Tara, I had high hopes for Matilda and that man.'

'I know.'

'Thought he would have made a good husband for Matilda. He's a one-orf, you know.'

'Yes,' I said. 'I know.'

'I can't blame him entirely for falling for your sister's charms,' said Lady W-D. 'She's one of those girls who men seem to . . . like.'

'Yes,' I agreed.

'But she shouldn't have led him on. It wasn't right. Matilda trusted her, and she hasn't trusted anyone. Lionel never took to her, you know. Lucy was the first person she ever really loved.'

I was torn between a desire to cry and beat my head against the wall, berating my sister for being who she was, and another contrary urge to shout that these things just damn well happen, and wasn't it time that everyone realized it? Lady W-D hadn't finished.

'I liked your sister, I really did.' Lady W-D pulled open a drawer in her desk, revealing an old apple core, a cracked thermometer and a syringe for administering medicine to horses, and closed it again. 'Yes, she's different to Matilda, yes, she's a little wayward and she talks too much, but I liked her. I thought she was good for Matilda.'

'She is,' I said boldly.

'But I've never seen Matilda like this. It will never do.'

'Perhaps when she comes back from London—'

'You know, it sounds peculiar, but I never imagined that I'd feel her pain like this, but I do, and that's all there is to it. More than that, I feel she and I have been made to look jolly silly indeed.'

'Oh no—' I began.

Lady W-D held up a hand to stop my protestations.

'I'm sorry, but that's how it is.' She looked me right in the eye. 'I'm afraid that you're not to come up here any more. Pamela will manage the horses without your help in future.'

It was what I had feared.

'But what about Hester? None of this is anything to do with me!' I bleated.

'It's unfortunate' agreed Lady W-D. 'But I've made the decision. Matilda is my only concern.' She blinked, as if she were surprising herself with such statements of staunch loyalty to a daughter she had always considered a very queer fish.

'But Matilda won't even *be* here!' I squeaked.

'It's the principle of the matter,' said Lady W-D. 'I'm doing what I believe to be right.'

I was going to cry, I knew it. I looked down at my shoes, my eyes blurring.

'You're a good rider, and you've tried hard. You happen to be caught in the crossfire, and for that I'm sorry. But we must have a clean break if Matilda is to make progress.'

Now she was making her sound as though Matilda had lost the use of her legs.

'No one will ever love your daughter, or this house, more than Lucy and I,' I said shakily.

Lady W-D walked to the door, implying that I should follow.

So I lost the horses, and the house, and felt for weeks as though I had nothing. Racketing around the Rectory in a bad temper, I came to blows with Pa on more than one occasion.

'*Work hard and become a leader! Be lazy and never succeed!*' proclaimed Pa, quoting from Proverbs when I said that I didn't want a Saturday job at the garden centre.

'*Where is the one who is wise? Where is the scribe? Where is the debater of this age?*' I demanded, almost in tears, throwing Paul's first letter to the Corinthians back at him in despair.

In the end, Pa came good and found me a job at some stables

five miles away, run by an old boot called Marcia Thorne whom nobody liked. She had horses, I supposed. But not perilous, beautiful hunters like Cathedral Boy, or sweet-natured, delicate mares like Hester. Even her Shetlands seemed devoid of the humour and spirit of those at Trellanack. I wanted to blame Lucy somehow, but I couldn't. Raoul loved her, and as a result we all had him, and for me, that alone made everything all right.

Lucy and Raoul were married, in our church and with a small ceremony and Pa giving the address. Raoul's mother and father attended the service – his pink-skinned, cheerful-eyed father delighted with the match, but his mother – whom he resembled acutely – remained deeply uncommunicative from start to finish, making her disappointment in Lucy perfectly apparent.

'Silly cow,' said Imogen, shocking me with her choice of words. 'Who does she think she is? Anyone should be so damn lucky as to have Lucy as a daughter-in-law.'

I wasn't sure. Raoul's father – bowled over by Lucy's fairy-tale looks – couldn't see beyond his son's honeymoon. But there was something in his mother's eyes that suggested doubt. Lucy was only eighteen. She had a long way to go before she proved she was worthy of her beloved boy.

We Jupps sang our hearts out, and threw confetti into the air and over their heads like stardust. No one said it, but Raoul's mother's disapproval was not the only thing that jarred the day. For all of us, Matilda's absence was felt. I don't think that she even knew that Lucy and Raoul had gone ahead and done it. She hadn't written to me, or to anyone else. All that we knew was that she was in London, from where Trellanack, it seemed, had ceased to exist.

After their honeymoon in Dorset, Raoul and Lucy moved

into Rose Cottage – whose name spoke for itself. Just the other side of Truro, it was still close enough to the Rectory for Lucy to be back within smelling distance of Imogen's shortbread whenever she wanted. Raoul began writing his book about Capability Brown, working three days a week teaching history in the grammar school in town, and Lucy still cut hair at Miss Fitts' – distracted regularly by Victorian crime novels and stained glass, in which she had developed a great interest, thanks to Professor Pevsner's writings on the subject. To me – deprived since Ma's death of living proof of a perfect marriage – they had to do. I invested *everything* in them. Cramped into the cottage with little space for his legions of books, I wondered sometimes if Raoul regretted coming to England and falling in love with someone as untidy and domestically incapable as Lucy. But if he did, he certainly never said so.

They had just celebrated their first anniversary when Raoul asked me to come to Rose Cottage with a pile of books he had left in Lucy's bedroom in the Rectory. George – home after a mission in Syria, and always good for a favour – had offered to drive me there, and Lucy had promised me Sunday lunch – I suspected it would be Raoul doing the cooking. I struggled from the study to the car – swamped by ancient hardbacks with Raoul's indecipherable comments covering every margin – but as I opened the boot I dropped several books on to the ground, still wet from a February downpour.

'Bugger it,' I muttered under my breath. The heaviest tome of the lot – *An Illustrated Guide to Important Houses of Ireland* – had fallen into a puddle – open at a picture of an ugly neo-Gothic stately home in Belfast. Marking the page was a white card with Raoul's name underlined at the top and a few sentences below. There was something familiar yet unexpected about seeing *that* handwriting and the indigo ink. Picking it up, I noticed that it was written on the back of an old postcard of Trellanack – confirming my suspicion that it was her writing. *Matilda.* It was dated October 1959. Just before she had gone to London, I thought.

Raoul, it said. *I don't feel right telling you this, but under the circumstances* (spelled wrong) *I feel you ought to know that Lucy will never be able to give you children. Sadly, she is BARREN. I think that this will matter a great deal to you, and I am telling you this because I don't want you to be broken by this news in years to come. She won't tell you, but it is true. Do with this information what you will, and please don't think the worst of me, the messenger. Matilda.*

I read it again, and again.

George came out of the front door, holding a brolly and an apple strudel.

'Imo says can you take this over. I think she's hoping for one of Raoul's chocolate mousses in return,' he said, opening the driver's door and getting in. Seeing me still staring at the card and not moving, he beeped the horn and wound down the window.

'Will you get moving?' he said calmly. 'I've got to be at the bring-and-buy in the town hall in forty minutes, which is not something I'm relishing, I can tell you. I said I'd help Peggy Payne erect the tables. Her breath could strip paint.'

Shoving the card into my jeans, my heart thumping, I sat down in the passenger seat.

'Hold tight,' said George. 'I haven't driven since I got back from Syria. You'd better put your belt on.'

Queasy with the discomfort of George's driving and the horribleness of the card burning a hole in my pocket, I walked up to the front door of my sister's house. I knocked once, and then let myself in. I could hear feet creaking about through the ceiling. The uneven beams and low windows gave rise to a feeling of seasickness and claustrophobia. I would say nothing, I decided. It was too difficult – too awkward. Lucy and Raoul came out of the kitchen. Raoul was holding a plate of his home-made cheese straws. I took one.

'They are a *leetle* overcooked,' he said. 'I tried putting cumin seeds in them. What do you think?'

But it was no use. I was a terrible actress, and pretending that nothing was wrong was never going to work. I couldn't help myself. Lucy came into the room and I blurted out:

'This fell out of one of Raoul's books in your room at home. What does it mean?'

I handed Raoul the note. Lucy – seeing it, actually pulled her hand up to her chest in an instinctive gesture of horrified recognition.

'What's she doing with that?' she whispered, looking at Raoul. 'How did she *find* – *where* did she find it?'

'Raoul asked me to bring some books over,' I said. 'This was inside one of them. I didn't mean to read it, but I could hardly help it.' The look on their faces unnerved me even more than I already was. 'Please,' I said, 'just tell me it's a joke.'

Lucy looked at Raoul, her face white.

'Some joke,' she said softly. Then she looked at Raoul. Her face was sharp – pinched in a way that I had never seen it before. She stared at him, half bewildered. 'Why did you keep it?' she asked. 'Why didn't you throw it away?'

He crossed the room and took her hands in his.

'Please, Christ in heaven – I thought I had. I thought I had!' he repeated. 'I would never have asked Tara to go through my things if I thought she would find—'

'Bloody stupid,' said Lucy under her breath, still staring at him. He took the note from me, and ripped it up into little pieces.

'Only a year late,' said Lucy. 'Why couldn't you have done that at the time?'

He threw the pieces into the fire. They curled up and died.

'I don't understand,' I said.

'I'd have thought Matilda's done all the explaining you could ever wish for,' said Lucy. 'What more do you need to know?' She looked at Raoul. 'Would you leave the room?' she asked him. 'Please?'

Raoul reached out a hand and touched his wife's arm; Lucy pulled it away.

'Maybe it's best that Tara knows,' he suggested softly.

'Maybe it's best that you leave us alone,' said Lucy even more quietly.

He walked out. I looked at my sister, and then back into the fire.

'It's not true,' I asked her, and my voice didn't sound like me at all. 'Is it?'

Lucy threw another log on top of the burning embers.

'Yes,' she said. 'As a matter of fact, it *is* true.'

I stepped forward one pace, like in Grandmother's Footsteps.

'I can't have children,' she said.

'No,' I said firmly. 'No, that's wrong.'

Dazed, I walked to the edge of the sofa and steadied myself on the arm. 'It's not true,' I said again. And then I said what I really wanted to say, because I couldn't keep it inside any longer. 'And even it *were* true – why did Matilda know and not me?'

Lucy hit her fist on to the side of the sofa, and swore again under her breath, then pushed her hair behind her shoulders.

She was wearing a pair of Raoul's pyjamas and a thick, red, knitted cardigan that had belonged to our mother. She should have looked awful, but as usual, her inherent beauty made that an impossibility. On the table in front of us was a pile of mending. Had I not been so shocked by what was happening, I would almost certainly have commented on the oddness of Lucy actually darning a pair of tights.

'Since you know now, you may as well know it all.'

'Tell me. Please, Lucy. Tell me.'

She looked down, as if composing herself, then up and into my eyes. When she spoke, it was as though she were reading something she had rehearsed a million times but had never actually spoken out loud.

'I always knew there was something not quite right,' she said.

'What do you mean?'

'Just let me speak, Tara. All right? God, you never give anyone a chance to finish a sentence!'

I nodded, and gulped.

'I'd known since the accident,' she said. 'Since we fell off the bike on the day of the funeral.'

'*My* accident,' I said. '*You* were all right. I was the one with the bad ankle. My limp! I've still—'

'I know,' said Lucy. 'But for three weeks after that day, I didn't stop bleeding. From *there*, you know,' she said, pressing her hand on her lower abdomen. 'From here,' she said, as if I could be any doubt about it.

'I – I know,' I said, my mind scrambling around to locate the truth of that awful time just after Ma had died. 'You told me,' I said. 'You said that you'd got the curse, and that when I started I should come to you if I wanted help, because Ma had been pregnant so much that Pa thought that monthly bleeding was a myth.'

Lucy gave a sad little laugh. 'Gosh,' she said. 'You remember that?'

'Of course,' I said.

'Well, as it turned out, that was the only time I had it.'

'What do you mean?'

'Do I have to spell it out to you, Tara? I never got it again. That was it, that one time. A couple of ruined sheets and several hours of scrubbing my knickers with cold water and Pears soap after lights-out, and then –' she raised her shoulders and widened her eyes – 'nothing.'

'Not the next month?'

'Nor the month after. Nor the year after.'

'But you were seventeen when *I* started,' I said. 'I sat on your bed and you talked to me about it for hours.'

'Yes. That was tricky.'

'Tricky? I don't understand! You made me feel as though everything was going to be all right, because it had always been all right for *you*!'

Lucy shrugged. 'Big sister's job, isn't it? Even if I did have to rely on eavesdropping on Marie Hudson and Sandra East in the salon on Saturday mornings, comparing length of cycle and whether or not tampons made you "walk funny".' Lucy grinned at me sadly. 'What a pair of bananas,' she said.

'You *pretended*?' I whispered. 'Just for *me*?'

'I thought that if you knew that I was all right, then you'd be fine too.' She shrugged. 'It seemed like the right thing to do, at the time. Ma wasn't around. Someone had to tell you *something.*'

I thought back to the occasions too numerous to count, when I had sat on Lucy's bed asking her if it was normal for it to hurt so much, and why did it seem to last so long? And would everyone know? And could I still ride? And was it all to do with the moon or was that just gypsy talk? Lucy had reassured me with her usual, casual confidence.

'Put up with it, like the rest of the women in this world,' she had said. *The rest except for her,* I thought.

'Why didn't you go and see Dr Hawley?' I asked, knowing the answer.

'Ugh! That old letch? Would *you* have?'

'No,' I admitted.

'I didn't tell anyone until I was eighteen!' She looked at me in astonishment, as though she were only just computing the facts for the first time.

'Eighteen! But then you told *her,* but not us? *Why?*'

'Come on, Tara. What on earth could you have done about it? Matilda's old man had spent half his life seeing doctors for one thing or another after the bloody *Titanic* failed to finish him off. Matilda spent her whole childhood seeing men with brown leather bags dispensing advice into her father's dressing room.'

'Yes, but—'

'Matilda's godfather was a doctor. She simply telephoned him one afternoon and asked him if he could recommend a specialist for a friend who needed advice.'

'A specialist? What kind of specialist?'

'Oh, antiques and eighth-century rugs, of course.'

I looked blank.

'A gynaecologist,' she explained patiently. 'The next thing I know, Matilda and I are off to see a Mr Hooper at Treliske hospital. Such a lovely, *lovely* man.' Lucy's voice caught, but when I moved towards her she held her hand up. She wanted to finish talking. 'Matilda came with me, you see. She paid for my appointment with a fat cheque her uncle sent her for her birthday. She made us flapjacks to eat on the way there and bought peppermint creams on the way back. No one else ever knew.'

I pictured the two of them arriving at the hospital, Matilda's face creased with worry as she waited for Lucy to emerge from the doctor's room – both girls causing a domino effect of second glances by virtue of their appearance.

'What did . . . ?' I stopped and tried again. 'What did . . . ?' But I couldn't finish.

'He had a good rummage around up there,' she said. 'Then he did some tests and asked lots of questions and suggested that I came back again the following week. When I did, he said he was "terribly sad to tell me that I wouldn't be able to conceive".'

'But how did he *know*?' I whispered. 'He can't just say that to you! You're too young to hear that!'

'I know,' said Lucy. 'But he said he'd seen cases like mine before. He said that even without the accident, the lack of a menstrual cycle was a concern. He said my womb was under – under . . .'

Siege? I thought wildly. *Arrest?*

'Underdeveloped,' said Lucy, wincing as though the phrase tasted of lemons. 'He said it was the uterus of a thirteen-year-old, which wasn't right for a woman of eighteen.'

She looked at me and sighed wearily.

'Ma,' I said in a whisper. 'You were thirteen when Ma . . .' I stood up.

'He said that a trauma just before the onset of puberty can halt the growth of the womb completely. I said to him, "Well, my mother died in childbirth when I was thirteen, and I couldn't save her, if that's traumatic enough for you." Poor man. He was quite shocked. There was a woman in the waiting room about to give birth. He must have welcomed her into his room with open arms. Delivering babies must be easy compared to telling people that they can never hold their own child.' She spoke so quietly now, it was hard to hear her. 'I'm – I'm sorry, Tara,' she said. 'I wanted to keep this from you, more than anyone. I know how much you wanted it for us – for you.'

'For *you*,' I said. 'For you and Raoul.'

'I was never going to tell,' she said. 'I would rather have pretended that I didn't want babies than have people bearing down on me with sympathy because I wanted them so much but couldn't do it.'

I sat down again and stared out of the window where a robin was picking crumbs from the bird table.

'I can't believe it,' I said. 'I *won't* believe it.'

I was horrified by an irrational swell of anger towards my sister, and kicked it down as quickly as I could.

'You *have* to believe it,' said Lucy.

'And the note?' I said at last.

'Isn't it obvious?' said Lucy. 'Matilda told Raoul. It was just before she left for London. A last-ditch attempt to make him forget about me, I suppose. *Barren!*' she said with a hollow laugh. 'Makes me sound like some crone out of St Luke. Only Matilda would use such a word.'

'What did Raoul say when he read it?' It was the question I most needed answering.

'He asked me if it was true, and I said yes. Then he asked me if I was planning to tell him, and I said I didn't know. Then I said that he could go.'

'You told him to *leave*?'

'I opened the door for him, and said that he didn't need to stay with me,' said Lucy. 'We weren't yet married, there was no reason for him to stick with a girl who wouldn't be able to provide him with children. And he walked out.'

'He walked out?'

'Yes. But then he walked back in the next night. He said he didn't care if we never had children, and I chose to believe him. And the rest is history.' She sat on her hands. 'Good story, isn't it? I always said that one day someone should write it down. This sort of thing shouldn't happen in real life, should it?'

'Matilda failed then,' I said. 'She tried to ruin it, but she failed.'

'Then she went to London and left us to get on with it,' said Lucy sardonically. 'Leaving barren little me behind forever.'

She said nothing more, but I knew, and it made sense to me now. Her refusal to talk about Matilda, the odd remark since Matilda had left that it was Matilda who needed to be forgiven, not the other way around, was suddenly understood.

Two minutes later, Raoul came back into the room, carrying a tin of ginger biscuits and a cup of tea. Putting them down, he sat down and took Lucy's hands in his. Lucy pulled her hands away again.

'I wish she hadn't found it,' she said to him. She was still looking at him as though she had partly turned to ice.

'I'm very glad I found it,' I said. I was knocked back by a wave of horror at the prospect of going through life not knowing this about Lucy, then knocked back again by the even greater horror that was the truth. *She was never going to be able to have children.* Lucy blew her nose, pulled up her hair and stood up.

'I don't think I want to talk about it any more,' she said. 'I'm feeling a bit sick.'

'Sit down,' urged Raoul. 'Let me get you water.'

'No, no. I want to go out. Let's go out.'

She walked to the door and pulled on her shoes.

'The truth of it is that it's boring,' she said, and she sounded thirteen again as she spoke. 'It's *always* been boring. Not being able to do things is boring. Everyone else can have children, and that's exciting. I can't, and it's boring. Talking about it is even worse.'

'We don't need to say any more,' I heard myself saying.

'Thank you,' said Lucy. 'Because the thing is – there's really nothing to say.' She picked up a lipstick and smelled it. 'It was just that she promised not to tell anyone,' she said suddenly. 'She promised, because she was my best friend. It was my secret. It was *our* secret. She broke it. She must have hated me for what I did. She must have hated me *so* much.' She walked quickly to the door.

'Or perhaps she loved you, and relied on you too much,' said Raoul.

There, I thought. He had said what I hadn't been able to articulate. That was the truth. Lucy had been everything to Matilda, and losing her was way more terrifying for her than losing Raoul – yet even she couldn't see it. That was why she had attacked her in the way that she had.

'Enough,' said Lucy, her hand on the door. She glared at Raoul, and for the first time I had a sinking suspicion that he didn't always understand her like I thought he did. 'It's sad, all this stuff. Just so *sad*. That's why I don't want anyone else to know – not Pa, or the girls, or George, E.J. and the Littles. Everyone's had enough sad, haven't they?' She laughed, lightly. Yet she, Lucy, had had the biggest dose of all, I thought. Just as she had been given extra points for beauty, she had had to lose out elsewhere.

We went out for lunch in the end, and talked about Florence's crush on Halo Jackson, and whether the boys' backhands had improved, and nothing was different at all, except that I felt a distance between my sister and Raoul that I pushed aside and ignored and pretended wasn't there at all.

11

Fruitcake

I would love to write that by the start of 1962 I had all shaken off my childhood and was in the midst of conquering the world with my talent, wit and beauty, but it would all be fabrication. In fact, all that is notable is how little seemed to have altered since Lucy had married. All of us – bar Errant Jack and Lucy – lived at home still – drifting through days punctuated by the thwack of tennis balls across the court in all weathers, and the sound of Florence's new jazz records floating through the house from Pa's gramophone. Imogen, meanwhile, had developed a liking for a round-faced Welshman called Matthew Bell who had arrived in the church to invigorate the flagging choir that Pa had insisted I joined.

'But the practices are all at the wrong times! I'll have to give up some of my rides.'

'There will be no argument. You can sing, and it is your duty to the Lord and those around you to do so.'

'But I can ride too!'

'Anyone with half a brain and no mind for their own physical well-being can sit on a horse and gallivant around the countryside after foxes,' said Pa, who for some reason only gave credence to riding if it was practised on the hunting field – something that I had never been given the chance to try, worst luck. 'Your mother would have insisted upon your using your voice for something other than bellowing instructions at a pony. And pull your hair back,' he went on in irritation. 'Contrary to what you believe, you've a pleasant enough face, quite hidden under that mane.'

I ran to my room and burst into tears. Was I pretty yet? If so, I didn't know it. I was sixteen now, but for all the promises that I would grow, and one day would be as tall as Lucy, I remained about five foot one, skinny and flat-chested. I would be too small for the new choir robes, I thought. I would look *ridiculous*. What's more, I knew that the choir contained a bossy madam called Antonia Jones, who thought herself important because she could hit top E with her eyes shut, and several other dolts who had been in the class below me at school and couldn't sing to save their lives. The last thing I wanted to do was associate myself with such people – yet Pa was far too scary to refuse. But there's a lesson here, and no mistake. You see, if I hadn't joined the choir, then none of what was going to happen would have happened. Only I didn't know that yet.

A month later, and the morning after my first rehearsal with Mr Bell and the choir, Florence barged into my room and woke me up. Coming into my bedroom in her wellingtons, treading mud into the rug beside my bed, she was pink in the face with excitement.

'Meet me downstairs in the orchard in five minutes. You won't *believe* what I've got here.'

'What is it?' I demanded, pulling on my socks. But Florence had already rushed off again. Excitement rather suited Florence, I thought. On the rare occasions that she displayed it, her suspicious, denim-blue eyes became sapphires – she lit up and was almost beautiful.

By the time I reached the orchard and everyone else, I could see Florence waving *Good Housekeeping*, which struck me as very odd as Florence had never shown any interest in housekeeping, far less housekeeping of the good variety, and she never wasted her money on the kind of periodicals that the rest of us pored over.

'Look!' she said. 'Matilda!' She thrust the magazine into my hands, dramatically. And there she was. Staring out from the cover, eyes sparkling, very white hands in a clear bowl of sinister things that in my view always ruin puddings and cakes – like sultanas and glacé cherries. Irrationally, all I could think was how if it had really been Matilda cooking, then the bowl would certainly have ended up on the floor at some stage.

'No!' cried Imogen. 'Oh my word! It *is* her, isn't it, Ta?'

I studied the picture. 'It's her all right,' I said. I looked at Florence suspiciously. 'Is this an April Fool?'

'Certainly not,' replied my sister. 'It's real all right. She's a model. A *fashion* model,' she added darkly.

'Lemme see,' demanded Luke, now six, snatching it out of my hands.

'She's the one who went spare when Lucy married Raoul?' asked Roy in wonder. The Littles had been too young to appreciate the saga at the time, but had heard enough stories of Matilda to show considerable interest in her picture.

'She's the one,' I said grimly.

'She's pretty,' said Roy, with the authority of an eight-year-old Warren Beatty.

'She's changed her name – that's interesting. It says here "our m-model, Matilda *Bright*",' said Imogen, scanning the page.

'That was Lady W-D's maiden name!' I squeaked.

'She must be twenty-one now,' I went on. 'She's a year older than Lucy.'

'And the photograph was taken by *Digby O'Rourke*!' gasped Imogen.

'Who's he?'

'Oh, he photographs *everyone*. Supposed to be jumping in and out of bed with more women than Marlon Brando.' She blushed at her own words.

'Very good-looking though. I bet Matilda's at it with him,' said Florence.

'They're *full* of it all at the shop,' went on Imogen. 'They're thinking of framing the picture and hanging it up for all to see, apparently. Local girl makes good in London and all that.'

'None of them *knew* her,' I said, staring at the picture again. 'At least – not like we did.'

Yet there she was, the girl who had vanished from our lives for so long. I had the strangest feeling that the triumphant smile looking up at us from the crumpled magazine cover was directed at my sister – the one who had stolen her one true love. Revenge was sweet, and tasted of fruitcake.

Of course Lucy found out. She couldn't *not*. In no time at all, Matilda Bright was everywhere – the opening night of this, the cover star of that. She divided the village into two camps. Those over forty said things like, 'See what a sight she's become! What *would* her father have thought had he been alive today?' to which the unsaid answer was: not a lot, probably. Not talking about her was impossible – but we restricted our conversations to times when Lucy was not with us. Three years on, I still avoided all references to the girl we had once known. Occasionally Trellanack came into the conversation – on a crunchy bed of eggshells – for I feared where talking about it would lead. Raoul was sometimes unable to resist talking about the place – I don't exaggerate when I say that it haunted him.

'How can it sit there, empty?' he asked after lunch at the Rectory one day. 'Such waste!'

'Oh, Miss Bright will be back now,' said Florence. 'Perhaps at Christmas. She'll waltz into the church as though she's never been away, and everyone will stare and she'll sign autographs on the way out like Bette Davis.'

'I expect that once Matilda gets her hands on Trellanack again, she'll sell it,' said Imogen.

'Well, wouldn't *you*? What fun is Cornwall when one could be in Monaco with Grace Kelly?' demanded Florence, slicing a scone in half.

Raoul said nothing, but I knew that, despite everything, this sort of chat would be a body blow to him. If it was sold, who could tell what would happen to it? It was still the house of dreams for him and Lucy – the place where everything had started. And three years into their marriage, they seemed to rely more and more on memories of how it had all been back then – when they had nothing but the inextinguishable crush of newness to support them through more or less everything. When they had first announced their engagement, it had never occurred to me that anything would go wrong between my sister and the Spanish boy. Yet every time I saw them after that fateful Sunday I felt the distance getting greater, and I knew more than anyone that Matilda's arrival in the popular press was hardly going to help.

Fame and fortune had happened to someone Lucy used to spend hours with – and someone who had then threatened to destroy her and Raoul – and that was never going to be an easy

122

pill to take, however many nips of gin you took to help it down. But I worried about something else too – something that could cause more trouble than everything else put together. Lucy never spoke about what had happened that afternoon in Dr Hooper's rooms ever again. She buried it somewhere inaccessible and shut it down completely. This was probably what I would have done too, to be perfectly truthful – were it not for the fact that the result of all this squashing down of emotion meant that it had to burst forth from somewhere else. In Lucy's case, it seemed that she acquired a restlessness, a light, barely visible lack of still-ness in her marriage to Raoul. She started doing dangerous things, like looking over horizons and wondering if this was it – and her dissatisfaction with her life was thrown into even sharper focus when Matilda was so inescapable. Raoul, believing that the only way to make her happy again was to get his book published and become the man he felt she wanted him to be, buried himself in his work. It seemed to me – who paid far too much attention to everything that he and Lucy said to each other – that they were two people pulling very gently, but relent-lessly, in opposite directions. If they had no children, then how could it ever hold together?

'I've had a letter,' said Pa, a week after we had talked about Trellanack. 'It's from Matilda Wells-Devoran.'

I stopped trying to fix the handle back on to the milk pan and stared at him.

'Matilda *Bright*,' corrected Imogen. 'Oh, come on, Pa, what on earth does it *say*?'

Pa read it through to the end.

'She's getting married to someone called Mr Billy Laurier.'

'Getting *married*!'

'Oh my *goodness*!'

123

'Who *is* he?'

'Bet he's rich!'

'Of course he is!' It was I, delivering this statement. 'He's one of the most successful men in the music business. He's a manager, of sorts. He's *American*. He started Bilco Records.'

Even Pa must have heard of the label, I thought. Along with Mercury, Capitol and RCA, it churned out hit artists by the baker's dozen. The trademark 'B' was the label's logo, stamped red in the middle of each single and as identifiable to me as the signature of Mr Kellogg on the back of a cereal packet.

'He started Bilco Records?' asked Roy, who through no fault of his own had absorbed my love of the music industry. 'Is that really *true*?'

'I read *Melody Maker*,' I said promptly.

'Matilda's not *really* marrying him, is she, Pa? What does he look like, Tara?' asked Imogen.

'Don't know,' I admitted.

'Well, he's not Spanish, that's for sure,' said Florence.

'She'd like me to marry them,' said Pa, cutting into our conversation and folding up the letter. He was hiding a delighted smile. Pa loved a wedding.

'Oooh!' wailed Imogen. 'Let me read the letter, Pa, do,' she begged.

To our astonishment, he relented.

'"Dear Jonathan,"' she read. 'Gosh that's rather forward, isn't it? It was Reverend Jupp in the old days . . .'

'I hope you don't mind my writing to you to let you know some exciting news. I am engaged to be married to a wonderful man called Billy Laurier, and I can think of no other person I would like to perform the service but yourself. My great dream

is to be married on Saturday 9th June in the village, so long as the dates are appropriate with the church. It is rather short notice, but we are keen to start married life right away, and to have a summer wedding, when the sweet peas are out.

We hope to hold a big party at Trellanack afterwards, and invite the whole village. I do hope that all the family can come. I have missed your daughters greatly during my time away. I look forward to seeing Lucy, in particular.

With much love
Matilda W-D.'

A great, rare whoosh of emotion came over me; I actually felt myself shaking.

'But, Pa,' I said, 'Matilda made everything very difficult for Lucy.' I stalled at telling him about the note to Raoul. 'You can't agree to marry her—'

'It is perfectly plain from this letter that Matilda Wells–Devoran wants to make right whatever was wrong,' said Pa. 'The girl was born in the village, and her father's family has been at Trellanack for years. If she wants to get married here, I'm the only person who can perform the service.' He picked up the envelope to replace the letter, and frowned.

'There's a note in here for you,' he said, handing me a piece of paper.

'For me? For *me*?'

'Yes, you. You're Tara Jupp, aren't you?'

He handed it to me.

Dearest Tara (it said)
I hope you don't mind my writing to you, especially as it's been so long. I have a favour to ask you, and I'd rather put it

down on paper for you to think about than risk your refusing me straight away over the telephone.

I would simply adore for you to sing for us, while we are signing the register. Do you remember how much we loved Gigi? Well, it would make my day if you could sing 'Say a Prayer for Me Tonight', just like you used to. I've told Billy what a wonderful singer you are, so he's longing to hear you too.

Oh, please say yes! I shan't put it in the Order of Service, so you don't have to decide until the last minute. But I would love it.

I suppose you think what's happened to me is very odd. I do too! London has been such an adventure, but I want to come back to the village to get married. I don't know why, except that I can't not.

I do hope to see you at the wedding. Please think about singing for us.

With love and fond memories,
Matilda.

I handed the letter to Lucy that day. She had come home to do some washing, in the hope that Imogen might iron it afterwards. When she had finished reading, she handed Matilda's request back to me, and picked up a bar of carbolic soap.

'I don't think I should do it,' I said.

'Why?'

'Well, because of you. It wouldn't feel right.'

'Oh, come on, Tara. You won't get an audience this big at bloody Harvest Festival. You'd be a prize idiot not to do it.' She dried her hands on a clerical shirt awaiting the wash, and looked at me.

'I thought you wouldn't want me to do it,' I said.

She sighed. Pushing back her hair, she reached out and took my hand. Such a gesture was a rare thing; I nearly jumped backwards with the shock.

'Just because Matilda and I made a complete mess of everything, it doesn't mean that *you* shouldn't take this chance.' She took her hand away again and pulled a packet of cigarettes from the front pocket of her pinny. 'All of London will be there. All the beautiful people and beyond.' She turned her back to me and pretended to be looking for her matches, but I could hear her voice shaking. 'Ma would . . .' She gulped and cleared her throat and started again. 'Ma would expect you to do it. She'd have gone out of her mind to hear you doing such a thing. Do it for her, won't you?'

There was a silence.

'But *you* won't be there,' I said.

'That doesn't matter.'

'Isn't there a part of you that wishes you could bring yourself to go?'

'There will be,' said Lucy. 'You.'

And with that I had to be content. Mr Bell started rehearsing me the next day, much to Antonia Jones's fury. She was coming back – the girl who had hurt Lucy so much. And I was to be the one singing her through her marriage. It felt wrong, yet somewhere in me there was the stirring of something. A feeling that if I got it right, perhaps I might just manage to heal them both after all.

Pa may have been thinking the same thing. He was all over the place in the lead-up before the wedding. He tried to act as though this occasion was no different to any other, but I had caught him twice – twice! – standing in front of the long looking

127

glass in Imogen's dressing room, proclaiming verses from Daniel and flashing his eyes around at her collection of stuffed toys.

'Gosh, Pa, you're not going to go *too* Old Testament on them, are you?' asked Imogen in alarm.

'You, of all people, should know that there's no such thing as too Old Testament,' said Pa.

Everyone in the village kept saying things like, 'Well, we always knew she'd come back to get married!' and talking as though they knew her, although none of them really did of course. Pauline, an old biddy with bat ears who used to clean at Trellanack, discussed her endlessly with anyone she bumped into in the village.

'Never thought I'd live to see the day!' she said to me in the village shop. 'Prettiest girl I've ever known. Always so considerate of others! And treated so ill by that boy of yer sister's. Left her at the altar, so 'e did.'

'Hardly,' I snapped.

'Oh, she were distraught! But in't it lovely she's found such a wealthy man? And done so well fer 'erself? Must be makin' a pretty penny wearing them fancy clothes all over the place.'

And so it went on. The closer the village got to the wedding day, the more feverish the gossip became.

'They say they met in Paris,' said Imogen one afternoon, buying stamps in the post office.

'It were Californica,' corrected Pauline.

'Sounds more like it,' muttered Florence.

In the end, Lucy didn't need to fabricate an excuse not to attend. Something happened five days before the wedding that made it quite acceptable for her not to be there. Raoul fell off a stepladder in Truro library and broke his leg very badly. He was to stay in hospital for at least six weeks, with his leg in the

128

air, which gave Lucy the perfect excuse.

'I need to stay behind and look after my husband,' sighed Lucy. 'The Lord works in mysterious ways indeed.'

Imogen and I went to visit Raoul in hospital, bearing old copies of *Country Life* and the biscuits he loved. I was shocked by the sight of my brother-in-law lying on his back, his leg suspended in plaster. Imogen, naturally enough, started to cry.

'I'm not dying,' he said. 'Shut up, Imogen, and pass me my hip flask.'

He picked up the Spanish book I had selected for him from the foreign-literature section of the library.

'*El Coronel No Tiene Quien Le Escriba*,' he said in disgust. 'Bloody hell, Tara.'

'What? I thought it looked nice.'

'Depressing,' he said, staring at the ceiling. 'Marquez leaves me cold.'

'In that case, take a look at these,' said Imogen. She placed three of her Georgette Heyer books on to the bed beside him with all the flourish of one presenting the king with bullions of gold. He looked at them without interest.

'Novels for bored women,' he said. 'But thank you anyway.'

'They're unputdownable,' said Imogen.

'*I* am unputdownable,' said Raoul in despair. 'I shall be lying up here for weeks on end. How will I get through it? By the time I'm out of here, Matilda and her wedding party will be back in London, and the chance to see Trellanack again will have vanished,' he said.

'Now that Matilda's welcoming us all back, you could ask Lady W-D if she would let you have a look around next month?' Even as I said it, I knew it would never happen. Raoul looked boot-faced.

'Even if she agreed to that – which she would not – she would be there all the time, waiting for me to put a foot out of line. I wouldn't relax. That's why the wedding would have been the most perfect occasion to be everywhere, with no need for excuses. She would be too *bee-see* with the other snoopers to notice me. It was the one chance, the *one* chance to go back. Now that chance is destroyed, and all because I fell off a ladder like some idiotic Spanish 'Arold Lloyd.'

Imogen giggled.

A young nurse appeared, brandishing one of those suspect mechanisms that measures blood pressure. If I had been Lucy, I would have noted and raised my eyebrows at her prettiness; Raoul didn't appear to notice, nor care.

'Bad time to take it,' grumbled Raoul. 'As if it's ever going to go down while I'm trapped in this *casa de locos*.'

'Visiting hours are over,' said the nurse, nodding at me and strapping the monitor to Raoul's arm. She pumped the rubber bit briskly.

I stood up and took a biscuit from the tray beside Raoul's bed.

'Don't worry,' I said to him. 'I shall report back to you.'

I pulled on my cardigan.

'Gawd,' muttered the nurse. 'This thing can't be working right. No one's blood pressure's that high.'

She pulled a pencil out and started to scribble something on Raoul's notes. Raoul rolled his eyes.

'Hey,' he said, as I prepared to leave. He touched my arm. 'You have a good time, won't you? Look over Trellanack for me?'

'Of course I will.' I could have cried.

'Who knows?' said Raoul. 'You might even fall in love with one of the guests.'

'Not likely.'

But later that night as I ironed my choir robes in the kitchen I thought about what he had said. I didn't want to fall in love. I put it off, like a visit to the dentist. It sounded too painful for words.

12

Wedding at Trellanack

The day they got married was curiously still. The whole world felt flat calm. A blanket of white cloud sat static over the village until midday, when the sun broke through, milky white and hazy at first, then by the time the church started to fill, strong and yellow-bright, like the sun in a child's drawing. It filled the top of the church with slanting, biblical rays. The fifteenth-century stained-glass window in the chancel, much loved by Lucy, of John baptizing Christ in the Jordan, gave sufficient clout to the occasion. If there was a God, He was watching all of us that afternoon, with our quickened heartbeats and polished shoes. He was watching all those who waited, at the end of the land, for Matilda Wells-Devoran's return.

Even inside, the afternoon air hung warm and sticky, at blood temperature. I used my Order of Service as a fan and Antonia Jones, head soprano, glared at me. Pa was muttering to himself behind the pulpit, his hair standing on end, which made him look chaotic but determined. He glanced over at Mr Bell and gave me a brief raise of the eyebrow. I felt off balance, unnerved by the distinct possibility that for the first time in my life I might actually perform to more than ten people.

And lo, 'twas was just as Lucy had predicted. The church was heaving with beautiful people. It felt hilarious to me, heady, naughty, as though the contents of some London restaurant had been tipped in here for a joke by a bored magician. Two girls with eyes like sugared almonds stopped Pa on his way to the vestry and asked him something and I saw him gesticulating at the altar and had to sit on my hands to stop myself from laughing, suddenly fiercely protective and hideously embarrassed at the same time. My fingernails were in shreds, so I closed my eyes and thought deep, relaxing thoughts as recommended by Imogen, and was just starting to feel my nerves subsiding a little when Sarah Cartwright nudged me fiercely in the ribs.

'Ow!'

'There's the groom,' she hissed. 'Isn't he beautiful?'

I followed her gaze. It was the first time Sarah Cartwright had ever been right about anything. He *was* sensationally good-looking. He stood on his own facing the altar, swaying slightly to Mr Long the organist's confident but hopelessly inaccurate rendition of 'Nimrod'. He stared up at the roof of the church, then down at the floor, then intently at his hymn sheet. His hands, I noticed, were absolutely steady, his dark red hair swept back, advertisement-ready – his eyes were as blue as the ink Pa used to write his sermons.

I had read in the papers that he was six foot five, but seeing him up close, he looked taller still. Unlike Pa, who often seemed oblivious to the effect his stature had on those around him, Billy Laurier seemed very aware of the power of his own height. He straightened his back and smiled at the front row of the church with beautiful, even teeth. How *white* he seemed compared to Raoul. How straight, somehow. I glanced round at the rest of the choir; every jaw was open in ill-disguised amazement. He was having the effect of a film star, and I rather think he knew it.

Then 'The Arrival of the Queen of Sheba' struck up and a hush filled the aisles of the church at last.

'Apparently she's even more beautiful than she used to be,' hissed Sarah as the bridal party began their ascent.

'Shut up,' I murmured.

She was even skinnier than I remembered, and although she was wearing a dress so demure it would have gone down well in a nunnery, there was something *unexpected* about her that I couldn't quite place. Her hair had been drawn up into a chignon and a veil of slightly yellowing antique lace spilled down her slender back and into the chubby hands of her five bridesmaids and two pageboys (I didn't recognize any of them; they must have been connections on the groom's side) – but the expression on her face was the strangest thing. She stared at her husband-to-be as though she couldn't quite get over the fact that he was there at all. Perhaps all brides looked like her, I thought. And I would be grateful too, to be marrying a man like him. I welled up, of course. I mean, who *doesn't* at weddings?

Then I saw Lady W-D and was ready to start bawling. Seeing her in a dress was almost as difficult to digest as it would have been if my own father had turned up in a tutu. Her handsome face was bronzed and lined by the Indian sun, her round body was entirely covered in a vast linen tent of pale blue and white flowers, which – combined with a boxy hat of the same pattern, and a *this-must-I-do-or-die* facial expression of grim determination – gave her the unfortunate appearance of a giant teapot poised to pour. Once she arrived at the altar, she almost seemed to fling Matilda at Billy and Pa; if she could have dusted down her hands and said, 'Right. That's that, then!' she probably would have. She was horribly uncomfortable with it all. I suspected that after years of trying to palm her off, she was now finding giving her away more painful than she had imagined she would.

I had half worshipped her. Was she delighted that Matilda was marrying into money? I doubted it. Money had never been of much value to Lady W-D, in the way that it often isn't to those who never have to worry about it. No, all she had ever wanted was a daughter who could ride, who could hunt, who could kill foxes and whip up a hearty meal for six from a badger carcass and water from the nearest puddle boiled over a fire sparked by rubbing sticks together. Yet as she looked at Matilda now, it was as though she was seeing her for the first time. She pulled out a handkerchief and blew.

Pa began his welcoming address, and I had to look down at my hands for fear of catching Matilda's eye and it throwing me off balance completely. We sang 'Tell Out My Soul' and said a few prayers, and Pa introduced the choir, and the groom smiled at us, and like the Garden of Eden in reverse, all I could think about was how shameful it was that such an immaculately attired man should see me clothed in my sack-like choir robes. Not that I had anything in my wardrobe that would have suited such an occasion. New clothes for me were about as likely as a telephone call from the Everly Brothers.

'We are gathered here today to witness the joining in matrimony of William and Matilda,' began Pa – and I'm certain Matilda was holding her breath. I opened my Order of Service. Pa sauntered through his introduction to the marriage service, throwing in a few jokes at the expense of several of the apostles. (Pa realized long ago that the way to hold an audience was to dance on the edge of controversy as precariously as possible without actually overstepping the mark.) Billy looked properly impressed throughout, agreeing to honour and love his bride, and speaking his vows with what I decided was nonchalant intensity, if such a thing were possible. His voice was low and soft. And American.

Matilda galloped through her side of the bargain, which I supposed was the logical thing to do, and just after he had pronounced them 'man and wife', Pa made a crippling announcement.

'And now, my daughter Tara will sing "Say a Prayer for Me Tonight" from the popular motion picture *Gigi* –' Pa's northern tones fell comically hard on the G's – 'as the bride and groom sign the register.'

I could hear everyone who knew my father gasping in unified amazement – it was so unlike him to introduce me, even more so as I was singing something from a *musical*, for crying out loud, that I almost forgot to stand up and sing at all. I understood why he did it though. He was afraid that if he didn't announce it, I would back out. At any rate, there was a murmur of interest as people craned their necks to see who I was, and Mr Bell signalled for me to move forward.

'Good luck!' hissed Sarah.

'Here goes nothing,' I muttered.

The organ stuttered into action for the start of my solo, and I felt that wave of excitement mixed with nausea that I always experience in the split second that exists before I open my mouth to sing in front of a crowd. Mr Bell's arm came down to start me off. *Don't worry*, I wanted to reassure the congregation. *I'm not going to mess this up.*

When I finished there was a slight pause, while the rest of the choir looked right at Mr Bell, awaiting his signal to stand for the next piece we were singing together. It was at that moment that an astonishing thing happened: someone at the back of the church started to clap. There were a few frowns and horrified, purse-lipped glances from the sort of people who know that clapping in church isn't just not done, it's *never* done, but there must have been enough sunny-side-up, didn't-she-do-well? folk out there to squash this lot entirely. Within seconds, the whole building had joined in.

It wasn't a polite smattering of appreciation that someone might receive after a solo in a concert in the town hall, it was proper, full-bodied applause, and it echoed around the church very loudly. In a daze I listened to the word 'Bravo!' coming from a man's voice around the nave. I stared straight ahead, face blazing, hardly daring to imagine that this cacophony was for me; I could almost see a raised eyebrow from the carving of St Peter on the stalls opposite where I was sitting. But I was thrilled. Thrilled beyond belief. Mr Bell looked confused and delighted at the same time, hovering uncertainly at the front of the choir stalls, considering taking a bow, then deciding against it. Everyone in the choir stared at me with expressions of outright amazement – I don't think that any of them had ever considered me particularly clap-worthy, particularly not after singing something as blousy as a song from a musical. The noise didn't die down until Matilda, who had been clapping hard with the rest of them, had one of her old sneezing fits – six huge ones in a row – and Pa had to lean over and ask whether she was quite all right to carry on. I saw her nodding frantically and blotting her eyes with a tissue.

When at last we had changed out of our robes and had left the church, the choir pressed around me.

'I've never heard anyone clap during a service before. Not even when Antonia hit that unexpected high C at the end of

"Seek Ye First" at Harvest Festival,' said Sarah.

'No one should clap in church,' said Antonia Jones, puffing to keep up with us. 'It's not right. Not respectful.'

'To whom, exactly?' demanded Sarah.

'God,' said Antonia instantly. 'And Jesus and the Holy Ghost and all.'

'I'll Holy Ghost you,' muttered Sarah. 'I'm sure if everyone inside the church enjoyed Tara's singing, then God would have too.'

We darted back home to change. I pulled off my choir robes and zipped myself into a yellow and cream dress, mended too many times to count. It had a Peter Pan collar that Lucy said was fashionable, but I thought made me look about twelve.

'You can take Mrs Otley's path to Trellanack,' Lucy had suggested on her way out of the door to visit Raoul in hospital. 'That way you can walk barefoot through the fields and carry your shoes until you get there.'

She was very practical when it came to this kind of thing, was Lucy. Years of experience of sneaking home late and covering up blistered feet from dancing till dawn. It only occurred to me later that day that most of Lucy's dancing had been done with Matilda. As I pushed on my shoes I decided that not to be at the wedding of the person you've danced the most with was something close to tragedy.

13

Billy

Florence, Imogen, Roy, Luke and I all piled out of the house again, and into the still afternoon. Every house we passed was empty. Everyone had gone to the wedding; the whole *world* had gone to the wedding, it seemed to me. And why wouldn't they? The village shop was shut, the post office closed. I could feel the pull of the party from before we even reached Trellanack. My shoes were too tight, and my dress but I didn't care. There didn't seem to be enough of the village to contain the summer; it seemed to be spilling everywhere, the verges were dotty with wild flowers, the air heavy with butterflies, hay seeds and powdery little thunder-flies. Why marry in June when you suffer from hay fever? Didn't Matilda *mind* that her new husband was seeing her so undone?

We arrived at the bottom of the drive in time to see Lady W-D's old Shetlands having a field day, and behaving as badly as Shetlands always do – rubbing their impish rumps against the fence and shoving wet, grass-stained noses into the pockets of anyone silly enough to say hello to them. A woman in front of us shrieked as a large begonia was taken out of the hat she was unwisely holding over the rails.

'I'm worried we're missing lunch,' panted Imogen. 'The invitation said one o'clock sharp.'

'Don't be so silly,' said Florence scornfully. 'Weddings like this *always* run at least an hour late. No one will have taken into account how long it takes to walk from the church to Trellanack in high heels.'

I hadn't been up the drive for three years, and in that moment all I could feel was relief at the sight of its beauty. *It's just a house*, Matilda used to say. But she could say that because she was born with it; it had become unremarkable. To Lucy and me, it remained astonishing. It never lost the power of that first hit.

I felt sick with nerves and excitement and the fear of not knowing how my head and heart would react to being there again; yet it was just as it is when you go back to a place from childhood – both exactly the same and quite different. If the gardens had been in terrible disrepair, as Raoul had suspected, you would not have known it. Florence managed to discover that a collective of ten gardeners had been in to pull, prune and repair before the place was on show once again, though all their work could not disguise the underlying lack of care the place had experienced since Matilda had left. Yet where it had been left to fend for itself, the garden was at its most spectacular. The nineteenth-century Egyptian obelisk, given to the house by Lady Joanna Robinson – a favoured guest of Sir Lionel's great-grandfather and rumoured to have arrived at the house every time with a different female lover – was almost knee deep in foxgloves. There was a wildness to the garden now, which combined with the precision of Capability Brown's designs made for dizzying, if confusing, viewing.

It made my heart jump, seeing the place swarming with people again; it was like watching someone stirring from a deep sleep. Half the West Lawn was covered by a marquee the colour of icing sugar. We all stood and stared and dithered in our smart shoes until a man in a white apron handed us all glasses of what was probably the most spectacular champagne.

'Tastes funny,' said Imogen, who had never tried champagne before. She screwed up her face.

I refilled my glass and threw myself headlong into the crowd, because, knowing Trellanack as I did, it was easier being on my own. I knew exactly how to work through across the lawn, and how to sneak around the back of the fruit cages for the best view of the newly arrived guests. All around me, people were talking about the place – 'What a terrific house! Have you seen a garden like it?' etc. – and I felt pride and irritation in equal measure. It felt far more mine than anyone else's. I saw Lady W-D and walked the other way. I didn't want to hear her talking about selling the place to someone who wanted to turn it into a hotel. Not today. Today I could pretend that it was just as I had left it, and always would be.

My attention was taken to a string quartet, which had started to play to a small crowd under the cherry tree. The first violin was excellent, but the cellist, who was blonde and beautiful, kept giggling and making mistakes.

'Whaddaya think?' asked a man's voice behind me, and I knew from the church that it was him. I turned around halfway, not wanting to face him. He felt too close; it was as if I was afraid I should be knocked down, simply by looking him in the eye. He felt that powerful.

'The cellist can't play,' I said bluntly. 'She's ruining it for the others.'

As always when confronted by someone with good style, I felt out of my depth and volatile. I stared at him defiantly. I wanted, very badly, for him to disappoint me. I was fighting, fighting all the time.

'She looks great, though, doesn't she?' said Billy. 'So what she's playing doesn't really matter.'

I frowned, confused by his response.

'Can you play the cello?' he asked me, smiling.

'Probably. Never tried, but it can't be that hard.' I flexed my fingers over an imaginary bow.

He had a straight, elegant nose, smattered with freckles, like nutmeg over ice cream.

'It's a perfect afternoon for a wedding,' I said.

He smiled at me; there was no doubt that he was enjoying my discomfort. He was aware of his power, and how couldn't he be?

Imogen marched up to us, her disgust at my smoking obliterating her nerves. Florence was following her; I noticed her glass was empty.

'For goodness sake, Tara, put out that thing,' hissed Imogen. 'And I've been watching you. You've drunk too much.'

'*You* haven't drunk enough,' said Billy, handing her his glass of champagne.

'These are my sisters,' I said to Billy.

'Which ones?' asked Billy quickly.

So he knows about Lucy, I thought. Matilda had told him about all of us.

'Florence,' I said, 'and Imogen.'

'Beautiful names,' said Billy.

'Are they? I rather thought Ma and Pa had run out of steam by the time they got to me,' said Imogen.

142

'Tell me, you two,' said Billy. 'What are the chances of your father letting me take your sister with me to London, to make a record?'

Imogen and Florence looked at each other and laughed immoderately, as if it was a huge joke. I joined in weakly. The champagne was sending my head spinning.

'Oh, he'd jump at the chance to get shot of her,' said Florence.

'Pa says London is full of fools,' said Imogen pertly.

'So it is,' agreed Billy. 'But you can sing,' he said to me. 'Shame not to try to do something with a voice like yours. We'd put it out on Bilco. The label was *made* for singers like you.'

For a moment, he gave me the full blast of his light, his eyes torch-bright into mine. I felt hypnotized by him, half afraid, half delighted. He was repeating the same words that Inigo Wallace had said to me. *You've got some voice, kid. You should do something with it.*

'Pa believes in hard work. I wonder sometimes if I only believe in fun,' I said lightly.

Oh, I thought myself terribly cool for this remark! I may have been a spinning top inside, but I wasn't going to let him know that no one had ever said anything as exciting to me, ever, in my whole life. I thought about what Lucy would say. Preserve some kind of mystery.

'Where I come from, work is more fun than fun,' said Billy.

And before I could think of a suitable response, Billy Laurier had been stolen away from me by some man and his wife who were shrieking at top volume about a hotel they recommended he try in Austria.

'We go every year at the end of the season, darling, when most people are heading back, yet it *always* seems to snow for us,' said the woman. 'We enter the lobby, and they fire up the cable cars. Of course, Karl is the most superb instructor.'

I slunk off, unable to stop myself from grinning like a fool. Florence followed me.

'Go to London,' she scoffed. 'With whose bloody money? We wouldn't get further than the station. Come on,' she added. 'You know this place better than I do. Where can we hide and watch people?'

I'd love to report that Florence and I drank just enough to glitter and swing with every alluring boy in the room before retiring to bed as the sun rose, but of course it never works out like that. I was no stranger to alcohol – we frequently snuck half-bottles of sloe-gin into choir practice – but it was the combination of alcohol and adrenalin from the church and from talking to Billy Laurier that got me so very high and far too quickly. Imogen was very cross.

'Why do you have to be so silly?' she demanded. 'I'd say you were just showing off. You're overexcited, the pair of you.'

Mortifyingly, the new Mrs Laurier happened to be coming off the dance floor at that moment.

'Overexcited,' she said with a smile. 'I should certainly hope so. Hello, Tara, you've completely floored my new husband with your voice.'

The first thing that I noticed about her was how she spoke. There was a husky edge to her voice that had never been there in the past. I was further confounded by the fact that she had a cigarette in her left hand.

'You're *smoking*!' I gasped, unable to keep my astonishment a secret.

Matilda looked surprised at the observation.

'Tara darling, *no one* can drink champagne without a Lucky Strike.'

144

'You *drink* too?'

Matilda threw back her head and laughed.

'I had my first real drink the night I arrived in London. I'm sure you can imagine that I needed it.'

'Well, you look beautiful,' I said truthfully.

Matilda rested her hands on my shoulder and looked into my eyes.

'Thank you,' she murmured. 'You look beautiful too, Tara Jupp.'

Lucy had always seemed much older than Matilda, yet now that wasn't the case. It wasn't how she looked, but how she spoke, her *fame*, I suppose. It wrapped around her like a shawl. Now she stood back and smiled at me.

'The first thing my new husband said to me when we left the church was, "You were right about the singer."'

'I don't know,' I said, not very modestly.

So, where's Lucy?' asked Matilda, looking around.

'Oh. She's so very sorry, but she couldn't come in the end. Didn't you get the message?'

'She's not *here*?' Matilda wailed.

'Raoul broke his leg. He was up a stepladder trying to reach a book about the Golden Gate Bridge—' began Imogen.

'Too much information,' I hissed at my sister.

'Lucy could have come without him then,' said Matilda swiftly. 'Where is she? I *wanted* to see her. I wanted her to meet Billy.'

'She didn't feel she could leave Raoul on his own. He's going to be in plaster for six weeks.'

'Six weeks? But he's a grown man, isn't he? If he's in the hospital, there's nothing more she can do, is there?'

So she really was over Raoul, I thought – but not over Lucy

at all. Matilda wobbled for a second in her heels. She stretched out her hand and steadied herself on my arm.

'She was the person I was most looking forward to seeing,' she said. Matilda's honesty always put one on a back foot. For a second she looked cross, like a little girl denied a packet of sweets – but she was the bride, and the great gift to the bride on wedding day is that she should be interrupted whenever she wishes. Within seconds, her wrists were in the tight grasp of a woman in a green silk suit with the biggest row of pearls I had ever seen wrapped double around her neck. Florence and I stood by for a moment, and then melted off, leaving Imogen to deal with an increasingly silly Roy and Luke. In any case, none of us Philistines could add anything to a conversation in rapid Italian.

We ran up the stone steps to the greenhouse, where we picked handfuls of ripe tomatoes, still warm from the evening sun. We ate them lounging on the patch of lawn beside the herb garden, the hum of the party seeming to glitter below us. Above us hung a pink moon, almost full; the night air smelled of mint and warm earth and roses. Occasionally a couple of guests walked past, mostly very drunk. Some of the women had taken off their shoes. I don't know how long we stayed there; I think I might even have fallen asleep for a while. My head was full of nothing but Billy Laurier and his new wife, and how strange she still was, yet how the same. At one point I think they walked past us, arm in arm.

'Thank you,' I heard her saying to him.

'For what, baby?'

'Thank you for rescuing me.'

At least I *thought* I heard this. But then that could have been a dream too.

★

It was just after two in the morning when we walked home – my sisters, the Littles and me.

'I could have stayed longer,' complained Luke, who had spent two hours asleep under the bar.

'Me too,' agreed Roy.

'Matilda certainly shone, didn't she?' sighed Imogen.

'She's strangely attractive,' agreed Luke.

'Luke!' cried Imogen. 'Where did you get that expression from?'

'You. Talking to Gwen Parsons about Mr Bell on the telephone last night.'

When we got home, I smoked a cigarette and collapsed on top of my bed. I closed my eyes and slept, squashy and queasy with the combination of gin, overheard conversations and over-ripe tomatoes.

14

After Midnight

Lunch had almost finished when I staggered downstairs the next day. For a second I looked in at the dining room, where we always sat on Sundays, with the eyes of an outsider at the scene gathered around the table: the old blue willow china spilling over with Imogen's gravy, the mouths all moving at once, pushing, pulling, demanding, passing, laughing, scowling. As I walked through the door, Roy threw a bread roll across the table at Luke.

'Being late for lunch is not something I'm prepared to tolerate,' said Pa in my direction. 'Next time I'll feed your beef to the swine.'

'We don't have any swine,' muttered Florence.

'Really? You could have fooled me. Judging by the state of your bedroom, I'd say we were overrun with people living like pigs.'

'Sorry, Pa,' I said.

He turned to address us all.

'After yesterday's excitement, I expect all of you in bed by nine o'clock. Florence, tomorrow morning I would like you to deal with the flowers left in church after the service.'

'What am I to do with them all?'

'Sell them to the rich, give them to the poor, press them between books or wear them in your hair. Use your imagination, for once,' said Pa briskly. 'Roy, Luke – I'd like you to come to my study to go over your homework.'

The Littles, grumbling, followed Pa out of the room, and half a minute later Lucy left the table to telephone Raoul. I think she knew that we wanted to talk about the wedding, and I don't think that she felt safe listening to the conversation at all. George turned another page of *Truro Today* and frowned at a picture of a dog on a surfboard. 'I'm sure that's Janet Dicer's collie. I was with her for tea last week.'

'My God,' said Florence. 'You should get out more. Janet Dicer must be coming up to a hundred and three, isn't she?'

'She's ninety-one,' said George with dignity.

'What are you looking for in a wife anyway?' asked Florence idly.

George shrugged and turned another page.

'Just a sweet girl with a nice smile who wouldn't mind my being the vicar,' he said. 'That really is all I ask.'

'Sweet girl, nice smile, good cook, big boobs,' said Florence, picking up a pen and pretending to make a list.

'Oh, shut up.' George grinned. 'Come on. Won't you tell me all about the party?' He plopped a piece of apple pie into a bowl. 'Didn't dare to ask about it until Pa pushed off. Damn those irritating people, holding me up all day in Yorkshire. I've never had my spirit of tolerance pushed to such limits. I don't know how on earth Jesus put up with half the riff-raff that hung around him wanting a piece of the action.'

'You're not sounding very vicarish,' I said, piling potatoes on to my plate.

149

'Hard to be vicarish when you're missing the party of the century,' said George miserably. 'Was it *very* ridiculous? How was Pa?'

'Oh, on fire,' I said. 'Hard as nails. Lots of guff from Daniel and Samuel.'

'*Quelle surprise,*' said George.

Imogen was looking at me intently. After a minute or two she couldn't bear it any longer.

'Tell George what Billy Laurier said. About your voice.'

'Let me guess,' said George. 'He wants to take you up to London to make a record?'

I stared at him.

'How did you know?'

'Stands to reason,' said my brother. 'He makes his money when people sing – you can sing, he makes money.' He put a large mouthful of pudding into his mouth and shrugged.

'Really, you're wasted on the Church,' said Florence.

'He'll want to steal you away from Cornwall, Ta. He'll take you up to London and turn you into Helen Shapiro,' said Imogen.

'Hardly,' I said, rattled.

'Ooh! It's like "The Little Mermaid". Once you've given up your voice, you won't get it back!' she went on, spreading butter on a crust of bread.

'Don't be so silly. I'm not going to London. Not ever.'

'I don't understand you,' said Florence. 'Isn't it the sort of chance that Ma would have taken?'

'I'm sure he was only joking,' I said. 'He doesn't really want to make a record with me. Can't you lot just forget about it? He was probably just joking around.'

'I've heard that Americans don't joke about anything,' said Florence.

'I'm going to bed,' I said. 'I feel I could sleep for a thousand years.'

'You'll be lucky, around here,' said George.

It was two thirty in the morning when I heard the noise. A heavy sleeper with a tendency towards complex dreams involving the Littles playing at Wimbledon, I didn't stir at first. Then I heard it again; a sound that I recognized from the days when Lucy used to sneak out at night to meet Adam Young, who had three nipples and claimed to be descended from vampires. Stones were being thrown at my window.

I sat up, my heart thudding in my throat, and padded out of bed to the window. There was someone there. Lucy, who had been staying with us since Raoul's injury as she didn't like to be alone at Rose Cottage, looked out of her window at the same time. We stared at each other.

'Did you hear that?' she asked me in a shaky whisper.

'Yes.'

'Who's there?' I asked, voice quivering, deafening in the still-ness of the garden.

There was no answer, but the sound of muffled sobbing.

'Who's there?' repeated Lucy.

I strained my eyes at the shape below. Whoever it was, was crouched low in front of the rose bush. There had been a robbery from George Welch's farm last year. But why would someone throw stones up at the window of a house they were stealing from? And what on earth would anyone want from within the Rectory? Imogen's rock cakes?

Someone stepped out of the shadows, and for a second I felt fear sticking in my throat. Then I saw who it was. Standing just in front of the roses, wearing a nightdress and wellington boots, stood Matilda. Her face was as white as death.

'Christ!' said Lucy, appalled. She ducked her head back into the bedroom in haste. I was left staring out alone.

'It's me,' hissed Matilda. 'I had to come and see you.'

'It's the middle of the night!'

Matilda looked baffled – as though that were the least of her considerations.

'Couldn't you have knocked at the door?' I asked.

'I didn't want to wake your father.'

She had a point.

'I'll come down and let you in,' I said.

'I have to talk to you.'

She stepped forward and caught her foot on the rose bush. She fell forward with a howl of pain.

'Oh, my nightdress! My hands! Oh my goodness! The thorns!'

'God in heaven,' muttered Lucy, who had returned to the window to view the scene unfolding. 'Go and let her in, Tara, before Pa wakes up. She must be out of her mind.'

She shot her head back into her room and seconds later was in mine.

'What kind of woman behaves like this?' I whispered to Lucy.

'The drunk sort,' said Lucy instantly. 'I imagine the rumours about her are true.'

'Won't you come and say hello—'

'No,' said Lucy. 'You want to let her in, you can deal with this one, sister.'

There was no use arguing. I was going to have to face Matilda on my own.

A minute later I led Matilda up the back stairs and into my bedroom.

152

'Where should I sit?' she asked.

I indicated towards my bed, pulling the covers up. I perched on the wooden rocking chair in the corner of the room. It creaked heavily as I sat down.

I lit a candle, so that we could use it to fuel the inevitable cigarettes. Matilda, now that I could see her properly, was wearing a nightdress that had surely belonged to her mother, buttoned up to the neck, the ripped hem trailing on the floor. Her hair, so perfect at the wedding, fell over her face in blonde disarray. She had chosen to apply red lipstick before leaving Trellanack to find us, but it had smudged out of place, and combined with running eyeliner gave her a ghoulish look. The force of her fame – the familiarity of her bone structure to the world – afforded her a certain punch, a strange authority. Outside an owl hooted from the big oak at the end of the lawn. I offered Matilda my hip flask.

She looked around at us – the relief at being inside, with a cigarette and a whisky, was all over her face. Still, it startled me afresh to see her smoking and drinking.

'I'm so sorry,' she said. 'I didn't mean to frighten anyone.'

She looked at me properly for the first time. Then, without warning, she started to sob. Burying her face in her hands, she sat there, my bed gently wobbling with her.

I stared at her in alarm. Whatever happened, Pa must *not* wake up now. Hysterical women in the middle of the night were not on his list of favourite things.

'Don't cry,' I said. I heard the sound of creaking coming down the corridor. 'Don't cry,' I repeated more desperately.

'I can't stop!' She sat up, gasped, then back down again, head back into her hands.

I patted her gingerly on the back. She was so thin that I could feel her spine through the thin cotton of the nightdress.

153

'Come on,' I said. 'You're going to be fine. I'm here. I'm here.'

I kept repeating this, over and over again, and the more I said it, the stronger my patting became, until I was holding Matilda to my chest.

I'm here, I'm here.

I didn't even know whether I even was. I felt as though I were on another planet.

Eventually Matilda's sobs shuddered to a halt. She looked up, and ignoring my hand proffering my best handkerchief, embroidered with my initials and given to me by Imogen for Christmas, she picked up my dressing gown from beside her on my bed, and blew her nose into it.

'I never meant this to happen,' she said.

'I know,' I said.

That dressing gown was a twelfth-birthday present from Pa! I wanted to shout.

Matilda's lip started wobbling again.

'I can't do anything on my own,' she said. 'Billy thinks I'm stronger than I am. He thinks I can look after myself, now that I'm home. He thinks it's easier for me to be here than London. But it's not.'

'How long are you going to stay at Trellanack for?'

'A week,' sniffed Matilda. 'But it feels like a century alone.'

She had always been a mistress of exaggeration.

'Why?'

'Too much space,' she said. 'All I was thinking about when I knew I was coming back was that I wanted to make everything all right again. I was a fool. I wanted to say I was sorry. I should never have got so tied up over Lucy and Raoul. I'm so sorry about it all. I'm so very sorry.'

There was a long pause.

Sorry. There it was, the whole world made good in those two syllables. All the village thinking Lucy a harlot, that terrible little note to Raoul, breaking the secret they had shared . . .

'You should be saying sorry to Lucy, not to me,' I said.

'I know.' She sniffed. 'It's obvious she doesn't want to see me.'

'I'll try and get her to see you,' I said. It was more to get her out of my room before Pa appeared, than anything else, but Matilda couldn't hide her appreciation for this remark. Throwing her arms around me, she unbalanced me completely, and I staggered back, steadying my hand on my ancient wardrobe, and sending a framed photograph of Ma and Pa on their wedding day crashing to the ground. I could hear footsteps now, and they meant business.

'Pa!' I gasped. 'Hide!'

Matilda displayed admirable presence of mind for someone who had finished the contents of my hip flask just seconds before, and shot under my bed. Pa was in the room within seconds.

I stood rooted to the spot, holding the photograph in its smashed frame.

'What on earth is going on?' Pa tried to whisper, but he couldn't – his whisper would have woken the dead. 'I'm due in Bristol at ten o'clock tomorrow for a three-day meeting with the bishop. I'd like to get some sleep, young lady.'

'I got up to get a drink of water and knocked this over.'

'A likely tale,' said Pa. 'Since when was there running water in your wardrobe?'

'I woke up all confused,' I said desperately. I could see Matilda's nightdress sticking out from the end of the bed.

'Confused? What the dickens were you confused about?'

'Had a Wimbledon dream. Roy and Luke were playing doubles

155

against Pat Hughes and Fred Perry. When I woke up I was disorientated. I thought I'd get some water, but I crashed into the wardrobe. That's all.'

I rubbed my arm.

'No one under the age of sixty-five needs to get up at night for water. It shows weakness of character. Jesus fasted for thirty days and thirty nights! And what do you think they did in the trenches?'

'I don't know what you mean, Pa.'

'No. That's exactly the problem. Get back into bed, and go to sleep.'

I flung the covers over me, barely breathing.

Pa stomped to the door. He was pathological in his loathing of slippers; none of us was ever allowed to wear them in his presence, but the floorboards groaned under his bare great canoes.

'Tara?' he said, just as he was about to step back in the corridor.

'Yes, Pa?'

'Who won?'

'Who won what?'

'The doubles, of course! Roy and Luke, against Hughes and Perry! Who won the match?'

'Oh, I don't know. The game was interrupted because one of the ballboys turned into a dragon and started breathing fire over the court. It was a messy business, Pa.'

'Very convenient,' said Pa tartly. 'They'd have thrashed them otherwise.'

He left my bedroom, closing the door behind him.

Matilda emerged seconds later.

'He's still as frightening as ever,' said Matilda. 'Thank good-ness he didn't see me. What would he have said?'

It was a question that I thought didn't bear answering.

'I think you should go,' I said in a low voice.

'*No!*' Matilda shouted the word out in a loud whisper.

'But Pa will—'

'I can't go now,' said Matilda. 'Not until I've said what I came here to say.'

She looked at me and took a deep breath.

'There's another reason why I came here, now, in the middle of the night. I had to tell you. I'm – I'm – I'm going to have a baby.'

She sat down on the bed, staring down at her own stomach with wide-eyed incredulity, as if she expected a child to emerge fully formed from under her nightdress, there and then.

'Congrats,' I said, finding my voice. 'Quick work.'

'I'm already nearly six months gone,' said Matilda. She looked up at us, her eyes watery.

'I beg your pardon?' I said in confusion. I opened and shut my mouth, staring at her again, trying to see how such a thing was humanly possible. 'You can't be! And anyway – you were only married last week.'

Matilda stood up and pulled her nightdress tight around her. There was a slight swelling in her stomach, which simply served to make her look more like a normal woman.

'When you see it like this, it's huge!' said Matilda, running her hand over the bump. She looked at me anxiously.

'It's flatter than Lucy's stomach after a three-week diet,' I said, with perfect truth. 'You can't be six months gone,' I said again.

'I am. That's why the wedding had to be planned so quickly. I was worried enough as it was that everyone would notice. I get this awful morning sickness, all day long,' she went on. 'Night's the only time that I'm free from it.' She hung her head. 'And all day, the only sound that I can hear is the door slamming shut.'

'What does that mean?'

'I don't know,' she said. 'I don't *know*. I just hear it, and I see it, and I know it's happening.'

I was almost too shocked to speak. 'Are you happy?' I asked her cautiously. 'Are you happy to be having a baby?'

'I suppose I shall just have to make the best of it,' said Matilda. Her lip wobbled, her lipstick smudged again. She was crying, her hands covering her face – her whole body rocked with it all.

'You'll be a good mother,' I said desperately. 'You were always the one wanting to look after the kittens at Trellanack. You've got a very good instinct.'

'Have I? Gosh, I don't think so, Tara.' She blew her nose again. 'I just had to come and tell you. I don't know why. It just seemed that if I didn't tell you, I might burst.'

She seemed to gather herself together a little.

'Perhaps you should get back to Trellanack,' I suggested. 'It's nearly light. You could sneak down to the kitchen now with me and out the back door.'

'Yes, all right.' Matilda stood up. 'Or I could just climb out the window, like you and Lucy used to—'

'I wouldn't,' I said quickly. 'Not with the baby and everything.'

Matilda grabbed me by the hand.

'Coming back here,' she said, 'all I wanted to do was make it right between us again. All that stuff about Raoul – I'm just so *sorry*. Please – come to Trellanack,' she said. 'Tomorrow night, for dinner. Just you and Lucy. I don't know how much longer we're going to have the house. I couldn't bear for it to go without you seeing it again.'

'Go?' I asked sharply. 'What do you mean, go?'

'Mother's had a decent offer. Some hotel group or other.'

'Hotel!' I said. 'They'll turn the park into a golf course, knock down half the house and start again. You shouldn't let it happen,' I said with some urgency. 'You should talk to your mother.'

But even as I said these words, I recalled my first conversation with Lady W-D, where she had expressed so little emotion towards the house. Talking to her would do nothing.

'I can't do anything about it,' said Matilda. She gave a defiant shake of her head. 'The house never meant to me what it did to Lucy and Raoul.'

She sniffed again.

'I shouldn't drink,' she said. 'At least, I don't *think* I should. But really, it has this awful way of making one feel so much *better* somehow.'

She walked to the little cracked mirror in the corner of the room. 'I look awful,' she said. Then she seemed to gather herself up again, to realize that she needed to pull herself out of wherever she had been. 'Billy won't stop going on about your voice.'

'Oh,' I said. I didn't know what else to say.

'I've told him all about you and Lucy,' said Matilda. 'All about her Photographic Memory for Houses, and everything.'

'I'm sure he's fascinated,' I said.

'Well, he *is* actually' said Matilda. I felt the flurry of a trump card appearing. 'He's got a proposition for you.'

'What do you mean?'

'He's got an idea for both of you — something that he wants to talk to you both about. You have to come over tomorrow. Please.'

At that moment, I didn't know whether anything that Matilda was saying had any truth in it at all, but I knew that if I didn't go, I'd only sit around wishing that I had.

'All right,' I said. 'We'll be there.'

'Both of you,' said Matilda again. 'It must be *both* of you.'

'I'll ask Lucy,' I said.

'And tell her . . . tell her my news,' she said. 'It's difficult, knowing she . . .' She stopped talking, clearly wondering if I knew the truth about my sister and babies.

'I know,' I said. Then, because I couldn't stop myself, I said, 'I was clearing some books for Raoul, and I found your note inside one of them.'

As soon as I had told her, I regretted it. Her face fell again; she stared at me in horror.

'That note! I am haunted by it! How could I have done that?' she wailed. 'I – I didn't think. I never think. I was just so sad! I'd lost them both—'

'It's all over now,' I said. I didn't know what I meant by this. Matilda took a breath and looked at me. There was determination in her face.

'I shall make it better,' she said. 'It's what I came back here to do. Please,' she said, taking my hands in hers again. 'Please bring her to me.'

'I'll ask her,' I said.

That must have been enough for her.

'And I warn you that Billy won't drop this idea of your coming to London to make a record. And when he asks you, you really should say yes. You really should do it.'

That was how she said it, as though it were little more than a trip to the dentist. *You really should do it.*

Then she was gone. I watched her patter off down the drive, stumbling occasionally, under the light of the swollen moon. Being on the cover of *Vogue* hadn't stopped her from being the type of person who fell over her own feet.

Moments later, the door opened.

'She wants to be friends again,' I said to Lucy. 'She's deranged from wanting to make it all right. She wants us to go to Trellanack tomorrow night. Billy Laurier wants to take us to London.' I looked at my sister. 'Please come,' I said. 'Even if only to see Trellanack again. She talked of it being sold.'

There was a pause. I could hear George snoring across the corridor in the room he shared with the Littles.

'All right,' said Lucy. 'I'll come.'

'And she's having a baby,' I said. 'She's six months pregnant already.'

Lucy went white. 'Don't be ridiculous,' she whispered.

'She seems unprepared,' I said. 'I think it must have come as a shock.'

'She can't be having a baby,' said Lucy. 'It can't be true.'

But it was true, and even though there was no evidence of it, as yet, I knew that Matilda hadn't been lying.

'How can she have all that she has?' asked Lucy. 'And have a baby too?'

I don't think that she meant to say this out loud, but she did.

'I don't think she's very happy about it,' I said.

Lucy looked away. There were no tears in her eyes. No sadness, I thought. She was just angry.

I fell into a strange half-sleep. No dreams of Wimbledon, or even Matilda Bright in my bedroom. I dreamed of Trellanack melting into the sea, disappearing forever, before Raoul had had a chance to take a look at the Yellow Room and its dry rot ever again.

15

Of London and Pineapples

I hurried downstairs for breakfast four hours later. In the kitchen, Imogen was standing by the window reading a postcard.

'I just got this,' she said. 'From Matthew. He was in the Isle of Wight the week before the wedding.'

I looked at Imogen's flushed face. She handed me the card.

Dear Imogen, weather is fine, and the sailing has been grand.
Had lunch in a wonderful little café in St Ives. Caught crabs
all afternoon. Wish you were here! Matthew.

'What do you make of it?' she asked doubtfully. She held it up to the light, as though some secret message would be revealed beneath.

'Interesting handwriting,' I observed in surprise. 'And take heart from the "wish you were here".'

'But *everyone* writes that,' wailed Imogen. 'That's just standard postcard-writing practice. I don't think it means anything at all.'

'He's obviously not used to putting pen to paper in this way,' I said. 'His S's look like treble clefs.'

★

I didn't track Lucy down until the evening – an hour before we were due to leave the Rectory for Trellanack.

'What are you going to wear tonight?' I asked her.

'My emerald and cerise Christian Dior ball gown, of course,' she said ironically.

In the end, Lucy wore a dress Pa would never have let her step out of the house in, had he been present that night. It was long to the ground and red, and dangerously low in front, so she had pulled on an old grey cardigan over the top. Lucy often did this – shoving some manky bit of material on top of something sensational; it was as though she suffered from last-minute embarrassment for the havoc she knew she was capable of causing. I had red eyes from trying out black eyeliner that I had bought off Sarah Cartwright for a bob, and not liking it. By the time I had finished scrubbing it off, I looked as though I had been in a fight. I cursed Lucy for stealing all of Ma's genes. It wasn't fair. If I looked like her, I thought savagely, I wouldn't care about anything else in the world.

They had torches burning outside Trellanack, like they had on the night of the wedding. It was the first really warm evening since then; the windows on the ground floor had been flung open, so that it would have been possible to enter the house through any one of the downstairs rooms. Seeing Trellanack so open was the first shock to Lucy's system.

'It's alive,' she breathed.

I was saved from responding by Matilda appearing at the front door. She was wearing black, down to the ground in thin satin – it was a beautiful dress, but for the fact that, being Matilda, she had trodden on, and ripped, the hem. I looked down at her stomach with a certain amount of incredulity. How could she be having a baby? Pale and stick thin as ever – she looked about as far from carrying a child as it was possible to look, without being a man. The only evidence of the previous evening's events was the presence of a scratch on her left arm where she had catapulted into the roses. She was holding a glass of something dangerous; the ice clattered like dice in a shaker as she waved hello to us. Being Matilda, as she waved, she looked about six again. She was as capable of an outward show of serenity and perfection as she had always been. But under it all she was as accident-prone as ever; it was something that she simply didn't appear to be able to shift with the passing of time, and the arrival of fortune.

'Lucy,' she said when she saw her. She almost whispered her name – there was incredulity on her face, as if she had never imagined that I would actually stick to my promise and get her there.

'Hello,' said Lucy.

Matilda stepped forward as if to embrace her, then seemed to sense Lucy's distance.

'How – how did you get here?' she asked.

'Remarkable, really,' said Lucy smoothly. 'We put one foot in front of the other and somehow ended up right outside the door.'

'Stop it,' I muttered under my breath.

'I can't tell you what it means to see you again,' said Matilda.

'It's all right,' said Lucy, shrugging. 'You don't have to tell me anything.'

A cloud scudded over the sun, the back door banged shut and Matilda jumped. Lucy, secure as a fell pony in her four-inch heels, stood her ground.

'Should have worn my plimsolls,' I said, wobbling in the heels Imogen had worn for her confirmation.

'Take them off,' said Matilda, nodding at my shoes. 'I always think of you barefoot.' She grinned at us. 'Come on. Billy's dismissed the idea of anyone else cooking, and he's putting together a spectacular feast all by himself. Lucy, you must come and see the garden. I can't believe it's been so long.'

I don't think that Lucy wanted to follow Matilda, but the urge to see Trellanack again was too strong.

'I'll just put my shoes inside,' I said, by way of an excuse. I wanted Matilda to have some time with Lucy on her own, even if it was just half a minute. I wanted, very badly, for everything to be all right between them – suddenly it seemed like the answer to everything. I knew there was a long way to go. Lucy might be here, but there was nothing resembling the old friend-ship that she and Matilda had forged all those years ago. It was achingly apparent by its absence. As we made for the gate that led into the garden, I slipped through the back door and into the cool of the cloakroom.

Once inside, I stood still and took deep breaths, such was the overwhelming oddness of being back inside the house again. It was the *smell* of the place that transported me so thoroughly back in time to when Lucy and Matilda had first become friends – that mixture of sweet peas and slightly damp dog, of silver polish, wisteria and warm horse. It was still there. My feet were cold and silent on the red flagstones. I moved out into the hall.

I hadn't expected Billy to be at the top of the stairs, and he clearly hadn't expected me. We both jumped, and then laughed. He was dressed in a pale grey suit, his dark red hair swept back off his face. Behind him, the Irish mirror that Matilda had checked her face in a thousand times during Raoul's first stay was filthy. Someone had drawn a heart shape in the dust with a finger.

'Nice shoes,' said Billy, winking at me.

165

'Thank you,' I said. I looked down at my bare feet. 'They're all the rage. Cheap as chips too.'

'Come with me to the kitchen,' he said. 'I was going to make us some drinks.'

He reached the bottom of the stairs and opened the door in front of him with such confidence that I followed him, assuming that there had been some sort of rearrangement of the rooms. For a moment we stood in the cool quiet of the pantry, staring at tens of tins of pineapple and baked beans. I snorted with nervous laughter.

'There were always tins of pineapple at Trellanack,' I said. 'Lady W-D said they reminded her of India.'

I thought of Mrs Wilson's famous cake and felt a sudden wave of melancholy.

Billy closed the door again and grinned at me.

'I suppose you know your way round here like the back of your hand. I've been here nearly five days and I'm still getting lost.'

'The kitchen's through here,' I said, opening the next door along.

There in the kitchen, everything was the same; it was as though the room had been wrapped in cheesecloth, tinned and preserved – like the pineapples – for Matilda's return. I could even see the same packets of tea on the shelves, the same post-cards pinned up on the wall above the dresser.

I was certain that Billy still didn't know about Matilda's escapade the night before. I felt odd, uncomfortable, knowing something about his new wife that he didn't. He started to chop up a cucumber.

'Thank you for getting your sister to come tonight.'

He was giving me credit for something that still meant nothing.

'It's nothing,' I said uncomfortably. 'Should we go and find them?'

They had taken down the marquee, and without the bunting and the fanfare of the wedding, the garden looked naked somehow. The lawn opened up, and contrary to the popular belief that childhood places become smaller when one sees them as an adult, the garden seemed to stretch on further than ever before. I joined Lucy and Matilda, who were standing a little apart, talking about the lightest of things: the weather. Lucy's face was suspicious, her outward show was one of confidence and nonchalance, but I could see how unnerved she was by the flick of danger in her eyes. Things were not as they had been, and it was jarring to hear Matilda pretending that they were.

'I expect Raoul would think I'm the most awful girl for letting the garden get so out of control,' said Matilda. Hearing her say his name to Lucy like that gave me a jolt. Lucy felt it too. I could see her eyes darting over the beds, the mulberry tree where she and Matilda used to go to talk about what had happened in the pub the night before. I hadn't seen Lucy look as shocked since Errant Jack had come back from France for the first time with a beard and moustache. She wasn't going to be drawn in at all.

Billy came and sat next to me and handed me a glass of champagne. I accepted it as though it was quite normal for me to be handed such thing – *Thanks, darling! Don't mind if I do!* One sip of the stuff, and I felt myself most violently, brilliantly alive. The garden itself felt suddenly keyed-up, the very branches of the old cherry tree we sat beneath felt like an embrace. We ate around the rusting white iron table, with the lion's feet on each corner, and I kicked off the high shoes again, feeling the grass still warm through my toes, the flickering of the candles Matilda had put in the middle of the table throwing out soft, impish half-light and casting unfamiliar shadows on our faces.

'I was serious when I talked to you about making a record,' said Billy.

'Were you?' I asked, hearing my voice high and anxious and excited all at once. Out of the corner of my eye, I saw a barn owl fly ghost-pale out of the copper beech on the far side of the lawn.

'Entirely.'

'Go on,' urged Matilda. 'Tell them your idea.'

'What idea?' asked Lucy sharply.

'Well, here's the thing,' said Billy. 'How would it be if you *both* came up to London for a while?'

I stared at Lucy, and she frowned. She cleared her throat.

'*Both* of us?' she said. 'What do you mean?'

'I'd like you to come and sing for me, and I'd like *you* to work for a great friend of mine,' he said, nodding at Lucy.

'She's called Clover Napier,' said Matilda, unable to contain herself. 'She lives in the most beautiful house in Chelsea, but it's going to be pulled down to make the road wider. She's trying to save it. Billy's already spoken to her, and she's *desperate* for help. Lucy – you would be researching the history of the house, and sorting through all the stuff there. You should *see* what's in this place. It's a perfectly preserved piece of Victorian delight. Oh, and she says she'll pay you to do it. Oh! *And* she's the best cook in London.'

So this was what she had been bursting to say before she left the night before. She looked at Lucy, her eyes round with the thrill of imparting such information.

'Why would she want me to come and stay with her when she's never met me?' said Lucy.

'Clover runs Napier House as a sort of exclusive hotel,' explained Billy. 'Whenever I have anyone over from the States, they stay with her. I pay her to look after my guests, as she's the best hostess in London.'

'Says who?' asked Lucy rudely.

'Johnnie Ray, Natalie Wood, Marina Hamilton,' said Billy, ticking the names off on his fingers. 'Oh, and I think she had Spike Milligan there last week. She said he kept writing poems all over the bathroom walls.'

'All right,' said Lucy, hiding a grin. 'I get the picture.'

'I want you to come to London because I think *you're* good.' He pointed at me, and however hard I tried not to, I felt myself blushing. 'And *you're* her sister,' he added, gesturing towards Lucy. 'From what I know of girls, they're always at their best in the company of their sisters. When Matilda told me that you're an expert on the era that Clover needs help with, it seemed too good to be true,' he said. 'Although what a clearly very intelligent woman like you sees in the darned Victorians, I do not know. I'm with the best of them. Get rid of the lot of it, and don't look back, I'd say. Awful, claustrophobic rubbish, most of what they put up.' He looked at Matilda and winked. Lucy flushed.

'I could give you plenty of evidence for why what you've just said is unjustified.'

'I don't know much about how it was in London at that time but what I do know ain't pretty,' said Billy. 'Dickens, factories, slums, soot and workhouses, the Thames stinking all through the summer, the fog terrorizing you all through the winter,' he shuddered.

'Brunel, Bazalgette, Stevenson, W.G. Grace, Ford Madox Brown and Florence Nightingale,' retorted Lucy sharply, counting them off on her long fingers. 'Look them up,' she snapped.

Billy hid a smile.

'Napier House is the worst of the lot,' he went on unrepentantly. 'Rooms full of junk, pre-Raphaelites hanging mournfully from every picture rail, old Chinese porcelain cluttering up the landings and old wallpapers covered in fruit everywhere. *Ugh!*'

I could see that Billy was goading her. Whether or not he believed what he was saying was debatable, but Lucy took the bait.

'The wallpaper covered in fruit was probably designed by William Morris. He was a visionary.'

'If you say so,' said Billy. He swept his hands through his hair and looked at us both. 'Now, you can turn me down, and we'll go our own ways, and no more will be said about it,' he said. 'Or you can get out of here and try something new, because, God damn it, girls, you're only young once.'

I was nearly blinded with the thrill of hearing words like this. I was a terrible sucker for the American accent, and the lure of what it promised.

'This is the only chance you're ever going to get. Not because you're not good, because you are. But because you're down here, way out in the middle of nowhere. You don't question these things, baby. You just do it.'

'I don't question it,' I said, and I heard my voice shaking.

'It's all right,' said Lucy. She looked at Billy coolly. 'I can't leave my husband.'

'How long would we be away for?' I asked.

'Hard to say,' said Billy. 'Why not just call it a few weeks? You can pop back for weekends here and there of course.'

'A few weeks?' I asked blankly. How long was that? The rest of July? Half of August? All of September too?

He looked at Lucy. 'I took the liberty of telephoning the hospital and talking to your husband to explain the situation.'

'You did *what*?' said Lucy and I together.

'I wanted to make sure that when I came to you with the plan, he was already on board.'

'On board?' demanded Lucy. 'What does that mean? You telephoned him without asking me? That's very strange.'

If I had the measure of her correctly, she was half furious, half thrilled. I admired her for speaking out.

'What did Raoul say?' I asked, struggling to imagine him and Billy in conversation.

'Well, he agreed that it would be a good chance for you to pursue your interest in houses of this period. You'll be making a bit of money, which he says will come in useful. As soon as he's able to write again, he wants to continue with his book, even if it's from the confines of his hospital bed. I reassured him that you'll be back to visit him regularly of course.' He looked at Lucy, pre-empting her expression. 'Of course you'll miss each other, but this could be something that may very well change the rest of your lives for the better.'

'I'm not being rude, but how do you *know*?' asked Lucy, sounding confused.

'I just do.'

I could picture the relief in Raoul's face as Billy had suggested all this to him. All he ever wanted was for Lucy to have a chance to do something with the knowledge that she had assimilated from Professor Pevsner and beyond. He would have embraced any chance for her to get out of Cornwall, because he knew it

171

was right for *her*. He, of all people, believed in setting people free to do what they needed to do.

'Well, Pa *certainly* won't let Tara go to London,' said Lucy, trying a different tack.

'Oh, *that's* all taken care of,' said Billy with a wave of his hand. 'I ran into him and your *adorable* sister Florence outside the church this afternoon. He's quite satisfied with the prospect of you getting on and doing something with your lives. He's not a problem.'

Lucy's eyes widened in shock, as did mine. Florence had never been called adorable in her life.

'*Not a problem*,' I said in wonder. 'I've never heard Pa use that phrase.'

He laughed. 'He's a great man, your father. He says that your mother was a singer.'

Lucy looked at him helplessly – she was cornered by the confusion of hearing Ma mentioned.

'Yes.' I choked on the word. 'She always said to me that I should use my voice if I could.'

'Well, here's your chance. Do you think she'd want you to take it?'

'I think we should,' I said slowly. I looked at Lucy, unable to stop the grin from spreading across my face.

'Thank you,' said Lucy, briefly meeting Billy's eye. 'It seems that you've covered everything, and there's no point in refusing you. If there's any chance that I can help with Napier House, I should certainly take it, especially as Raoul agrees.' She looked at me. 'I wouldn't like Tara to be out of Cornwall without me,' she said. 'She's really too young to be on her own.'

'I'm seventeen,' I bleated. 'When do we leave?'

'Thursday,' said Billy. 'So you've plenty of time to pack and get ready. Matilda, darling – pass the champagne, won't you?'

Now that he had us, the tension had evaporated. He was calm, replete, a panther after feeding. I came back to the table and sat down.

'You all right?' Lucy asked me.

'I think so.'

And then, as if what had just happened wasn't enough, *he* appeared.

16

Him

I heard him laugh loudly before I saw him; I nearly jumped out of my skin. We all swivelled round to the secret gate, where he stood in its entrance. Matilda stood up, knocking her glass of wine across the table.

'He's here, Billy!' she cried. 'He's actually made it!'

'Who?' asked Lucy, retrieving the glass.

Billy stood up. A huge grin spread across his face and it struck me that it was the first time I had properly seen him smile.

We all watched as Matilda loped across the lawn to greet the stranger.

'He's from America,' Billy said, as though that explained it all away. 'He's one of my best songwriters. Wrote three number-one hits in a row for Jules Harrison. He's a genius,' he added lightly, as though the world was full of them.

The stranger and Matilda walked towards us, still laughing, casting black dragonish shadows across the lawn. In his left hand, he carried a guitar case.

'Dear boy, you told us you would be back in London by now,' shouted Billy as they approached.

'Ah well,' he called back. 'I decided that the chance to come and snoop around this place was too much to resist. I've got to leave for the Big Smoke by six thirty in the morning, so I'm debating whether it's worth going to sleep at all.' He grinned at us. 'Hello,' he said, nodding at Lucy and me.

I gave a gasp, then nearly blacked out. It was, of all people, Inigo Wallace.

'Inigo!' Billy shook his hand delightedly.

Lucy widened her eyes and stared at me, and then at him. I kicked her under the table. Thank heavens she and I had communicated with sign language – raised eyebrows, subtle flicks of the fingers – so many times in Pa's presence that she twigged not to say anything else that might give the game away. Instead she took a great gulp of champagne and started to cough as her eyes watered.

Looking at me properly, Inigo frowned.

'I've seen you before,' he said.

The world stood still. He remembered me. He actually remembered us in the kitchen at Milton Magna, when I was ten years old. He hadn't forgotten it. And if he hadn't forgotten that, then he wouldn't have forgotten the elephant. I felt faint with horror – I wanted to disappear under the table. A look of realization hit him and he sighed with relief.

'Oh, I know. You're the girl who made them clap in church. I told my sister about you – she was quite shocked.'

'You – you were at the wedding?' I asked him faintly.

'I left straight after the main picture,' said Inigo.

'Inigo had to finish a recording in London the next day,' explained Matilda. 'He missed the party.'

For just a moment I nearly said to him that we had met before, nearly gave away the fact that I knew exactly who he was from our encounter seven years ago, but I stopped myself. All I could feel was that terrible, terrible wave of shame that had swamped me when I had confessed to him, in the library at Milton Magna Hall, that I had stolen the elephant. Nothing in my life had been as embarrassing, as awful, as time-stood-still-while-I-died as that moment. I couldn't laugh about it now; it had haunted me for too long. And even worse, I thought, with an inward gasp of horror: what if he *didn't* remember it? How could something as significant to one person mean so little to another? I could remind him who I was, and he could have forgotten about it entirely. It was an awful prospect.

'This is Tara's sister, Lucy,' said Matilda. Oh dear God, I thought. He would fall for her. He was a man, after all. He was human.

But Inigo shook her hand and nodded. If he thought she was as beautiful as everyone else did, he had chosen not to show it at that point, for which I was very grateful. I had known boys to fall over at the sight of my sister. Matilda also looked at him for his reaction. Force of habit, I thought. It was as though they had never been apart.

Lucy wrapped her cardigan around herself, attempting to dilute her beauty, to uglify herself somehow. She sat next to me, very still, as though if she moved the world might explode or something. Usually easily bored and distracted, she seemed uncertain how to act under tonight's circumstances.

Inigo started to pile up his plate with food, talking all the time to Matilda — had she seen Jean and Chrissie lately? Had she heard Brian Jones's new rhythm and blues group? All the time that he talked, I noticed that his accent, that public-school drawl that had so captivated me, had half drowned somewhere in the middle of the Atlantic. I couldn't tell if he was putting it on or not. All I knew was that he didn't recognize me – at least not from the time that we had actually met before. And why should he? I had been a kid of ten, the great-niece of a woman who had cooked for him, who had tidied away the plates after he had eaten, who had been to all intents and purposes a slave of sorts.

I picked at the candle in front of me and studied his face.

For someone who I couldn't imagine had experienced much post-war austerity with Rocky Dakota as a stepfather, his face still had the elegantly undernourished look of the perpetually hungry schoolboy – in fact, he hardly seemed to have aged at all. I wouldn't have known Savile Row from Woolworths at that stage – but his clothes looked good, as though someone had taken some time to make sure that they fitted him perfectly. His dark hair was shorter – the DA replaced by the sort of cut that all the boys in the village attempted and never quite pulled off, and his blue eyes were ringed with indigo shadows. He looked successful, I realized. Not through his clothes, or his hair, or his skin – but because of how he was behaving. He talked to all of us as though we already knew who he was.

'You want a smoke?' he asked me.

'I promised Imogen I wouldn't,' I said. 'She thinks it looks awful on girls.'

'Who's Imogen?'

'Another sister,' I said.

'The sensible one,' added Lucy.

With every clue that I gave him, I imagined he would suddenly twig and say '*Oh! It's you! The little tyke who stole the only present my father gave me!*' but he didn't. Instead he pulled a cigarette out of a silver case and lit it off the candle in the middle of the table, his hand shaking slightly. He took one puff, then offered it to me. Last time it was a carrot, I thought wryly. I bit my bottom lip. I wanted to sit there and listen and watch; it was a pity I couldn't make myself invisible.

I wondered how he was seeing me – a surreptitious glance in my hand mirror before we had sat down had confirmed that my hair looked terrible, and my skirt and blouse so old-fashioned, that they wouldn't have looked out of place at Imogen's 'Wear What You Wore in the War' birthday party last year. I didn't expect he was very impressed. I cursed myself for finally proving Lucy right. I should *always* have dressed as though I were about to bump into him.

'Where do you live?' Lucy asked him. I could see her thinking that she needed to speak for me, to Gather Information, yet she was still loath to give too much to Matilda.

'I've lived in New York since I was fifteen,' he said.

'What's it like?'

'Just how you imagine,' he said.

'*Guys and Dolls*,' said Lucy promptly. 'And don't tell me I'm wrong. I couldn't bear it.'

Inigo grinned at her. 'There's a Nathan Detroit on every street corner,' he said.

'Do you miss England?' asked Matilda. 'Where exactly did you live when you were growing up?'

I had to sit on my hands to stop them from shaking.

'Westbury,' said Inigo. 'East of Salisbury.' I sensed reluctance from him. He didn't want to talk about it, but Matilda had never had a radar for this sort of thing.

'What happened to it? Did your mother sell it?' she asked.

'It burned down,' said Inigo.

Hearing Inigo tell us that it had burned down shocked me as much as it did the others, even though I already knew it to

178

be true. I had spent so many nights thinking about Milton Magna, so many evenings asking Lucy with her Photographic Memory for Houses (Trademark) to take me through every room in that place, that I had placed the fact of its destruction into myth, legend, rather than reality. Now here he was, saying that it happened. It was true.

'Was anyone hurt?' asked Billy, the ultimate People Person.

'Astonishingly they weren't. But the house was wrecked.'

'How dreadful,' shivered Matilda. She pressed her hand to her tummy.

'Well, it was – and it wasn't. We couldn't afford to stay there. Mama had met Rocky – she wanted to get away from the place, out of England. At least it put an end to the worry.'

'But it must have been the most awful shock,' said Matilda.

'All I thought about back then was this,' said Inigo. He banged his foot against his guitar case. 'I was going to be England's answer to Elvis.'

'What happened?' I asked. I couldn't help it; I needed to know.

'Cliff Richard,' said Inigo.

'Who have you written songs for?' I asked. I wanted to hear it from him. I wanted every detail from him that I could possibly get; nothing felt true unless he had spoken it.

'Nina Sharp, the Georgettes, Helmut Stevenson,' said Matilda, counting them off on her fingers.

'*Really?* You wrote "Hold Me"? And "Georgina"?'

'Well, I think so,' he said. 'I can't remember writing half of them, but I see my name's on the record sleeve so I suppose I must have.'

Billy looked at him with something I was at a loss to inter-pret – sympathy, gratitude? I didn't know. Whatever it was, it was just there for a second, for a flicker of time before Billy said, 'I want to make a record with Tara. She and Lucy are going to come back to town with us next week.'

Hearing him say it made my legs tremble. Inigo forked up a stack of new potatoes and said nothing.

'A record in the style of whom?' he asked eventually.

'In the style of herself,' said Lucy, unable not to remark. I kicked her.

'She can do whoever you like,' said Matilda eagerly. 'Alma, Ella, Helen . . . Tara, sing for us now,' she begged.

'Yes, go on, Ta,' said Lucy. She nodded frantically.

I wanted to refuse, but some part of me wanted to sing too.

Inigo looked at me. 'What do you want to sing?'

'Oh, I don't know,' I said. *Something as far from Alma Cogan as possible*, I thought. I couldn't *bear* for him to know me now. 'How about Etta James – "Stormy Weather".'

'On the stillest night of the year?' said Inigo, taking his guitar out of its case. 'Is that a bad omen?'

'No,' I said. 'It's just a damn good song.'

Holy mother of God, the wine had given me confidence I would never have had in any normal circumstances. I could impersonate Etta and sound nothing like Alma, I thought. I was safe. Inigo tuned his guitar while I sat still as a cat.

'Ready?' he asked me.

I nodded.

I heard myself sing, felt myself looking in on us all, listening, tapping my foot on the sidelines. I made plenty of mistakes with the words, but it didn't matter; everyone but Inigo Wallace was too drunk to notice. By the time we finished the song, Matilda had all joined in, shouting out the words, right up into the starry sky, as if the universe depended on it. He would know me now, I thought. How could he not?

'Wonderful,' said Billy when I had finished. He looked delighted, as though I were his own daughter. 'You had her voice perfectly.'

'Thanks.' I smirked with relief and took a puff of my cigarette.

'But not her soul,' he went on. 'You can't imitate that. You can't fake suffering and heartache. You can't fake being a coloured girl in a white world.'

I stared at him. 'Wh-what?'

He laughed. 'For what it was, it was cute. I liked it. But it's not *you*.'

'What does he mean?' I looked at Inigo dumbly.

'Billy likes girls like you to sing sweet songs about marrying the boy next door,' translated Inigo. 'That's what sells records.'

Billy laughed, but there was nothing funny about it.

'So I can't ever sing Etta James because I'm *white*?' I felt my lip trembling.

There was a pause. Inigo lit a cigarette and raised his eyes at Billy.

'No one's gonna believe you, baby. You have to make people believe what you're singing,' he said.

'Just because I'm white doesn't mean I haven't suffered. I get my blues from something else.'

'What, exactly?' asked Inigo. He looked amused.

'My mother died,' I said.

'That's not blue,' said Matilda. 'That's black.'

'Too right,' I muttered.

'I was thinking she could record that wonderful song you wrote for Susan Vaughan,' said Billy. I don't think he was even listening to me.

'"May to September"?' said Inigo. 'Well, she *could* do it. It was never released.'

'Why not?' asked Matilda.

'Susan discovered she was five months pregnant, and decided to get married.'

I glanced quickly at Matilda.

'The point is – it's a great song that's never seen the light of day.' Billy buttered a water biscuit and crunched. 'Susan did the most *wunnerful* job . . .' (He said 'jaıb'.) 'All Tara would have to do is copy the way that she sang it. She could do that standing on her head. We'd have a smash-hit record on our hands.'

'She's certainly got the necessary skills to make a record like *that*. We could do it in a couple of hours,' said Inigo, stifling a yawn. 'Three songs. A-side, B-side and a spare. In and out of the studio in no time. Then the rest is up to you,' he said, gesturing to Billy.

'You know, that song's been in my head ever since you wrote it. I was just waiting for the right person to come and do it.'

'Oh, Tara,' said Matilda. 'When he says this sort of thing, it happens! It *always* happens!' She spoke as though he were a magician, casting an unbreakable, irreversible spell. For a moment, I shivered.

'If anyone can do it, Tara can. She's been singing for as long as she could talk.'

'What about you?' Inigo asked Lucy, turning away from me. 'Do you sing, too?'

'No,' said Lucy hurriedly.

'But she's coming to town with her sister,' said Billy quickly. 'She's gonna help Clover save Napier House. She knows *everything* there is to know about the Victorians.'

'You're married?' asked Inigo, looking at her left hand.

'Yes. My husband's broken his leg.'

'Sometimes time apart can be a good thing,' said Inigo. 'Makes you see things more clearly, you know?'

Lucy looked as if she wanted to say something, but Inigo gave her no chance.

'So you married her for the house,' he said to Billy.

It was as though he had decided to change the record, or at the very least flip it over to the B-side.

Matilda raised her eyebrows at him.

'Not at all,' she said. 'My mother wants to sell it.'

She looked at Lucy as she said this.

'Why?' asked Inigo.

'It was my father's place. Her only real contribution was to shove a couple of horses in the fields. She's always wanted to travel. Since he died, she's spent most of her time abroad.'

'These houses are all splendour and heart-shaped topiary to the outside world, all crumbling ceilings and ruined dreams for those inside,' said Inigo. 'My sister says that she only started to live when Magna burned down.'

'Inigo's sister is married to Harry Delancey,' said Matilda.

'The great magician,' said Inigo archly.

'I know . . .' I began again, then checked myself. 'I know he's supposed to be on the Royal Variety Show next week, isn't he?'

'Probably. He's in the Palladium so often I'm surprised they don't just let him move in and redecorate the place. He's far too pleased with himself.'

'Cliff and the Shadows were on the show last time,' I said. I couldn't resist the dig; I felt as though with every word that was coming out his mouth, Inigo Wallace was letting me down more and more.

'I suppose you love Cliff,' he said.

'Imogen thinks he's dreamy,' I said. 'Our sister Florence isn't interested – she's only into jazz – but our little brothers, Roy and Luke love the Shadows.'

'Jeez. How many of you are there?' asked Inigo, frowning.

'Too many,' said Lucy with feeling.

'Well, prepare for chaos ahead, because if Brian Jones's new group comes to anything, you'll be wishing Cliff back again. They're kind of wild,' said Inigo. 'Cliff can only appeal to kids of a certain age. Once they move on, he'll be out.'

'What if you're wrong?' I said. 'Maybe they'll move on with him? Maybe Roy and Luke will be singing along to "The Young Ones" when they're sixty?'

I didn't really believe what I was saying, but I was irritated enough with Inigo to say anything that opposed his views.

He laughed. 'I doubt it,' he said in a voice that I can only describe as deeply patronizing.

'Sixty,' said Matilda. 'Seems a lifetime away.'

Matilda stood up, or rather, she staggered to her feet.

'You don't have to go anywhere, but I'm going to bed,' she said.

'You've drunk too much,' said Billy. I don't think he meant to say this out loud.

Inigo drained his glass, then shivered violently.

'Cold?' asked Billy.

'No,' he said. 'Just being back in England,' he said. 'Brings back memories,' he added, more to himself than to any of us.

But not the memory of little ten-year-old me, I thought. And that was the thing. I would have known him from the sound of his voice. I would have known him from the way that he played. I would have known him from the mere shape of his shadow. But he didn't know me. He didn't *know* me.

17

The Yellow Room

An hour later and it was plainly time to go. Lucy and I set off down the drive – she holding my hand to stop me from falling. I had drunk far too much; nothing seemed grounded in reality any longer.

'Wait!' I said suddenly, stopping in my tracks.

'What is it?'

'Raoul wanted me to see if the dry rot in the yellow room was any worse.'

Lucy rolled her eyes. At least I assume she did; it was too dark to see for sure.

'I'm going back.'

'What possible excuse do you have for walking back into the house ten minutes after we've left?'

I looked down at my feet. 'I forgot my shoes.'

I padded back through the front door, which had been left slightly open. Matilda had always been berated for leaving doors open. Now she could do what she liked. I walked towards the morning room as I had done that first afternoon with Lady W-D, hoping that no one would see me and wonder why I was back again. All I wanted, I thought, was a quick glance in the corner of the room where the damp had been. That was all.

But just outside the door, I heard voices and stopped. Billy and Inigo were in there. I was just about to go in there and pull out the shoe story, when I heard Billy talking.

'What did you think of my little singer, then?'

I froze, terrified, unable to move forward or backwards.

'Typically English,' said Inigo. 'Odd-looking scrap of a thing, isn't she?'

'I think she's rather beautiful,' said Billy.

It was the first time I had heard such a word used in connection with me. I should have taken that as my little going-home present and padded away immediately. But who hears that sort of thing and doesn't stick around to hear what follows?

'*Do* you?' Inigo sounded amazed. 'Listen, I don't rate conventional beauty, but I don't know about *that*. She's got those huge blue eyes like saucers, with not much pay-off in front. She's too thin, and tiny. She could pass for thirteen, no problem.'

'Clover can sort that out.'

I heard the sound of ice clanking in Billy's glass.

'What's her name again?'

'Tara. Tara Jupp.'

'Tara Jupp,' repeated Inigo. 'No. It's an awful name for the front of a record. You'll have to do something about that. Rename her. Try the old first-pet's-name-followed-by-mother's-maiden-name method. It worked for Bluebelle Gillespie.'

'You know, when I try that trick, my pseudonym is Harper Stevens,' mused Billy.

'Perfect,' said Inigo. 'When you release your first country-music record, we'll know what to call you.'

Billy laughed. There was a pause.

'Was Harper a dog?' Inigo asked politely.

'A canary,' admitted Billy. 'My mother was allergic to fur.'

I leaned forward slightly to hear, my heart thudding about in my chest.

'So you're not entirely convinced by Miss Jupp,' said Billy, returning the subject to me.

'Ah. Is it that obvious?'

'It is. What don't you like? You *can't* be unsure of the voice?'

'Oh, the *voice* is all right. I have no doubt at all that she can deliver a perfect Susan Vaughan. No, it's not the voice I'm worrying about.'

'What is it then?'

'*Everything* else. She doesn't *look* like she can sing even if she can; she's clearly got a mind of her own, which is always a bore, yet she's so fresh out of the box that I'm not sure she'd even know how to sell anything with any degree of sophistication. She needs to sing like she means it, but I'm not sure she'd know what to do if any man wanted to do so much as take her out for tea.' He sighed so loudly that I could hear him from outside the door.

'Well, the singing with conviction is *your* field,' said Billy. 'The rest of it is up to Clover and me. We've got a month. I went for the whole summer but that didn't cut the mustard with the vicar.'

'What was he like?' asked Inigo.

I drew in my breath, rooted to the spot.

'Like an Old Testament prophet, only fractionally more terrifying.'

Well, that was just about as good a description as any. The whirlpool of awe around Billy Laurier increased its suction. So what if he had slammed the Victorians? He had called me beautiful!

'What's the limp all about?' Inigo asked. 'Polio?'

'Never noticed it myself,' said Billy, the great liar! 'I'll get her in with Madame every morning. She sorted out Laura Mollier's feet in two weeks flat. Or two weeks arched, as they were by the end,' he conceded.

'Ha!' said Inigo. 'You know, the sister looks like she would have been a better bet.' He yawned. 'She's very pretty.'

'She's married.'

'Don't get me wrong, she's not my type. But I gather that voluptuous, innocent-yet-knowing thing pushes buttons for the rest of the nation.'

'Difficult, according to all sources. And she can't sing like Tara.'

'Who's her husband?'

'A Spanish architect and writer of sorts called Raoul Fernandez. Matilda was crazy about him years ago, but Lucy Jupp got in there first.'

'Luckily for you,' said Inigo.

'Luckily for me,' agreed Billy.

'Still,' said Inigo, 'I stand by my point. The little sister's going to be hard to sell to anyone.'

'Once Clover's taken over, you won't know her. She can turn a sow's ear into a silk purse overnight.'

'I'm not sure this one *wants* to be a silk purse,' said Inigo. 'London will eat her alive.'

An hour later I was lying awake in bed running through that terrible conversation in my head. He had no faith in me, whereas it had been his words at Milton Magna that had given me faith in just about everything for the past six years. I would go to London, I thought savagely, if only to prove him entirely and completely and *utterly* wrong.

The next morning, hands trembling, I spoke to Pa.

'Is it true, Pa, that Billy Laurier spoke to you about my going to London?' I asked him.

Pa looked up from the paper.

'It's perfectly true. He says you'll be properly fed and watered. I can't see what use there would be in trying to keep you here.'

'Are you sure you think it's the right thing to do?'

'That's what I said, isn't it? You need to climb down off your high horse and realize there are people out there who would give anything for what you have, Tara Anne Georgina Jupp.'

'I'm Tara Anne *Cynthia* Jupp.'

'Are you?' Pa looked astonished. 'Which one of you has a Georgina?'

'Florence,' I said. 'Florence Catherine Georgina Jupp.'

'Florence Catherine Georgina,' mused Pa as though hearing the name for the first time. 'Well, I stand by what I say, whatever your wretched middle names are. You shouldn't waste what God gave you.'

'And what did he give me, Pa?' I asked despairingly.

'A voice, you silly girl,' said Pa. 'Take it, and use it, and do what you will.'

'You really think so?'

Pa stood up to his full height, his hair on end, his blue eyes flashing. He pointed his specs at me, more Gandalf than Moses. 'The only thing that matters, Tara Janet Margaret Jupp,' he said, 'is that *you* believe in what you're doing. No one else can believe for you, you see.'

It was extraordinary how he could deliver such a pretty line with such vigour.

'All right, Pa,' I said. I thought I was going to cry.

He put on his glasses again. I walked towards the door.

'Don't know where you get it from,' he said.

'What?'

'Your voice.'

'Ma was always singing,' I said.

'She was always singing,' agreed Pa. 'Only never in tune.'

'I remember her voice perfectly. She was very musical.'

'When we were first married, she used to have to stand right at the back of church because her inability to hit the right notes was a distraction to the choir.'

I laughed at the absurdity of what he was saying.

'But that *can't* be true! She taught us every song in the book!'

'Of course,' said Pa. 'You were all children; you didn't know any better. But the wonderful thing about her was that she didn't care. She knew she couldn't sing for toffee, but she did it anyway, because she liked to.'

'Lucy said Ma had a better voice than I do,' I said.

'And she believes it,' said Pa. 'I wouldn't tell her otherwise.'

'Perhaps my voice comes from you, then, Pa,' I suggested tentatively.

Pa boomed with laughter, an infectious roar that was as rare as hen's teeth back then, so always set me off with the sheer surprise of hearing it.

'Volume,' he said, 'does not a great voice make.'

'I know Aunt Mary was in the church choir back in the Middle Ages—' I began.

Pa held up his hand to stop me.

'Mary made your mother sound like Vera Lynn,' he said. 'No, Tara. It comes from *you*. That's all there is to it. Just you.'

I turned my head away from him. One blink of the eyes, and there they were – tears splashing on to my bare feet.

'So you think I should go?' I said in one of those high, odd voices that pretending you're not crying gives to you.

'As long as you're doing something that makes sense to you,' he said.

I nodded, back still turned.

'I'd like to see you read Paul's letter to the Romans. He has a great deal to say about keeping oneself free from vanity. Focus on the important things.'

'Like tennis, I suppose,' I said, with a hollow laugh.

'Tennis is a discipline,' sighed Pa. 'The more disciplined we are, the better we are. Jesus would have played tennis, had the game existed in the ancient Graeco-Roman world.'

'Whom would he have played? John the Baptist? He'd have been a great player, wouldn't he, Pa?'

'John would have been too wild, too unorthodox. I suspect his backhand would have let him down. He'd have amazed you occasionally though. He'd suddenly do something unexpected and brilliant. He'd have shocked the crowds.'

'Peter?'

'Not confident enough. He'd lose his nerve under pressure.'

'Paul?'

'He'd challenge the linesman continually. He'd want to analyse every shot. He'd refuse to admit defeat.'

'So Jesus would have won then, against all of them?'

Pa shook his head.

'Not at all,' he said. 'He'd let the others win. Every time.'

'So his weakness was making people believe they were great when they were quite ordinary?'

'No, no, no,' said Pa. 'That was his great *strength*.'

We were interrupted by the Littles.

'Roy's put his foot in his shoe, and there was a wasp! And it's stung him!' panted Luke.

'Pity the wasp,' said Pa. 'Is it all right?'

I found Imogen upstairs in my bedroom, crying.

'It's not that I don't want you to go,' she said. 'It's just that I – I – I don't want you to go.'

'It's not for long,' I said. I desperately wanted her to stop crying. I felt as though I was stepping off the very edges of the earth without the slightest clue where I was going to land.

'I just don't want you to stay away forever – like Matilda did.'

'You're making this much harder than it needs to be,' I said. 'Please don't.'

With that, I ran upstairs and started flinging things into the old suitcase that I had inherited from Aunt Mary. Then, worrying that Inigo Wallace might somehow see the case and know it to have belonged to the woman who had worked for his family, I took everything out again. Lucy walked into my bedroom.

'How was Raoul?' I asked her.

She shook her head. 'Don't ask me, Tara.'

'What do you mean?'

Lucy started piling my clothes back into Aunt Mary's case. 'I mean, don't ask me,' she said. 'Sometimes it's better not to know stuff.'

'You will be . . . you will be all right, won't you?'

'I don't know,' said Lucy.

'What do you mean, you don't know?'

'What do *you* mean, by what do you mean you don't know?'

She sighed and rolled up a pair of my stockings.

'We can never have children, Tara. Sometimes it's a hard thing to keep up with.'

I stopped and looked at her. It was the first time she had mentioned this since the morning I had found Matilda's note to Raoul.

'I – I know that,' I said. 'But Raoul doesn't mind. You said he doesn't mind.'

Lucy lifted her shoulders a little. Her eyes were swampy – impossible to read.

'Last night I read a letter he'd written to his brother before he broke his leg. Turns out that he minds a great deal.'

'You read a *letter?*'

'He left it on his desk.'

'But you don't understand Spanish!'

'No, but I cracked most of what he was saying with the aid of the dictionary. *Please tell Mama that she is wrong if she thinks I do not care that I will never be a father. It is a constant sadness to me. But she must learn to accept it, as I have.*'

'You shouldn't go around reading other people's letters! And maybe you translated it wrongly anyway.'

'No,' said Lucy quietly. 'I don't think so.'

She turned on the tap of the basin in the corner of my room and splashed her face with cold water.

'Today when I visited him I asked him straight out if he ever thought about it.'

'What did he say?'

'He said no,' said Lucy.

'Well, what are you worrying for?'

'I know he was lying,' said Lucy simply.

She dried her face, briefly pausing with the towel over her head as though she wanted to stay like that forever. Then, when she looked at me again, her face was quite changed.

'Enough,' she said. 'We're going to London. Everything else is unimportant now.'

I didn't know whether she was referring to Raoul's sadness, my crippling anxiety or her marriage, but whatever she meant,

I knew that by the time we got to the capital city Lucy would be a different girl again. She was more capable than anyone else I had ever known of casting off the past and running as fast as she could towards something new and sparkling. Only this time, I was coming with her.

Part Two

The Golden Haze

18

Arrival of Cherry Merrywell

Lucy and I travelled by train, arriving like a couple of refugees at Paddington, where on Billy's instruction we found a taxi. Lucy – whose experience of London was limited to Raoul's descriptions of the protests over the demolition of the Euston Arch the year before – took control.

'Beaufort Street, please,' she said, as the porter flung our bags into the back of the cab. She took out her purse and tipped him, and I noted that Lucy's charms were obviously translating with just as much power in the city as they did everywhere else.

'Is your ankle all right?' she asked me. She knew how my limp became more pronounced with tiredness.

'Of course it's all right,' I said. My leg was hurting, certainly, but what of it? I was in London now.

That first journey – from the station to Chelsea – was one of the most thrilling twenty minutes of my life. Here were all the places that I had been told existed, but had never actually believed in until I was gawping at them from inside a black taxi. vast Hyde Park, the Royal Albert Hall, then up to Knightsbridge where we could see Harrods spewing shoppers into the evening sun. We saw buildings still black with smoke and pollution that seemed to coat them in the authenticity of years past – I had never seen such dirt, nor such glamour, such height, beauty, chaos and order all thrown in together. We passed streets still injured by bombing, and streets where new buildings were rising from old. Drills sounded ominously, then bells from a huge neo-Gothic church.

Lucy stared out of one side, and I the other, yelping at each other as each new wonder was witnessed. I didn't want to get to Billy's house. There could be nothing more perfect than riding around London like this, with the un-buyable joy that seeing somewhere for the first time can give you. I had worried it wouldn't live up to what we imagined, yet I hadn't even known *what* to imagine. I was already another person, I thought. Surely I was.

The taxi turned into Beaufort Street and it felt as though someone had turned down the volume. When the driver pulled up outside Billy's door, Lucy rummaged in her purse for money. It would be enough for me to go straight back home now, I thought. Suddenly I was aware of my own innocence, and the high probability that if I wanted it to, London would very probably steal it away forever. Then there was Matilda, on the doorstep, waving.

'Come in!' she shouted. 'I've been *so* looking forward to you getting here!'

Lucy stiffened, and we followed her into the house. And what a house – I had never seen anything like it.

I had no eye for art back then, nor any concept of the obsessive need to collect beautiful objects that grips certain people, but even I could tell that whatever the stuff was, it was *good* stuff. A statue of a cowboy astride a rearing horse stood on a wooden table, thick with dust and flanked by four black glass figures of leopards in various poses that I would later recognize as Lalique. In the four corners of the room there were lamps with enormous gold shades shining 40 watts of unapologetic light on to tables crammed with photographs – Billy with the Shadows, Billy and Alma Cogan, for God's sake – and I jolted even more at a colour picture of Inigo squinting and playing guitar next to Billy Fury. The walls were so white that Billy should have handed out sunglasses to everyone who stepped through the door, and on each side of the room was hung one vast, impossibly difficult piece of art – works so modern that I felt the paint wasn't even dry on their surfaces. Beneath our feet was an enormous cream rug patterned with black trees against a huge orange blob of a sun. Our dusty feet in our sandals looked ridiculous standing on it.

'It's Danish,' said Matilda, as though that meant anything to me at all.

'Oh, a Steinway!' I exclaimed, noting the piano with relief. I played a run of notes. As usual I felt that pang when I saw a piano, that emptiness without Ma. I squashed it hard out of my head – I couldn't get sentimental now. I distracted myself with the rest of the place – the cream curtains, the Wurlitzer Jukebox stocked with American records I had never heard but desperately wanted to, lines of hardbacks in height order on built-in, red and white shelves and Billy's desk, standing in the corner of the room – immaculate – black and polished, and clear of everything but a large pot of blue ink, a pen and a telephone.

Against one wall a stack of boxes, bags and packages had been piled, mostly wrapped in fiendishly expensive-looking paper and ribbon. Matilda kicked off her shoes.

'Wedding presents!' she said with glee. She picked up a bag from Tiffany and Co.

'Ooh!' she said, peering into it. 'Two boxes inside.'

Holding it under Lucy's nose she said, 'Go on. It's like Roy's birthday all over again. Lucky dip.'

Lucy raised her eyebrows. I think she wanted to refuse, but she couldn't help herself. She extracted a pale blue box and pulled the white ribbon from around it. It contained army-style identification tags in silver with two hearts engraved on them.

'Nice,' said Matilda. She looked at Lucy. 'Keep them,' she said suddenly. 'Go on. Keep them. From me.'

'If it's not a packet of liquorice allsorts or a bar of saddle soap, I'm not interested,' Lucy lied, giving it back to Matilda.

'Poor you – all those thank-you letters,' I said.

'Billy will deal with it,' she said. 'He sends flowers to say thank you. It's ridiculous really – then they have to thank us again. He says the safest place to keep most people is in one's debt.'

'What a charming way of looking at things,' said Lucy.

'We didn't give you anything,' I said.

'You did,' said Matilda quickly. 'You gave me your voice and your friendship again. That means more to me than any of this crap.'

Lucy, to her credit, looked uncomfortable. There were miles between them.

Matilda gasped as she opened another present – a little statue of a clown holding a cockerel.

'Who's that from?' I asked.

'Andy Warhol,' said Matilda. She had the good grace to blush. 'He has such wonderful taste in beautiful –' she paused, looking at the statue – '*pointless* things. Oh, come on, Billy – get some champagne or something, won't you?'

A minute later Billy came back into the room, champagne under one arm, glasses under the other.

'Shall we do the post?' asked Matilda.

'Now?' Billy frowned. 'You hate doing the mail.'

But Matilda had already pulled a huge pile of letters off the table in the hall and on to the sofa beside her. It was all a big show, I thought, and all for the benefit of Lucy. When Billy had poured us all champagne, he sat next to his wife on the sofa and opened invitation after invitation, casting those whose dates had passed into a waste-paper basket.

'Opening of a new gallery on Dorset Street next Thursday,' said Billy.

'Not likely,' said Matilda.

'Champagne cocktails and Salvador Dali's meant to be turning up.'

'Oh, all right, then.'

'On Friday there's two. Drinks at Bazaar, then an early view of *The Man Who Shot Liberty Valance*.'

'Yes to Mary, no to the movie.'

'Supposed to be very good,' said Billy.

'So's liver, but I still don't like it. I don't want to go.'

I laughed. Matilda looked at me, delighted.

'How about this? A wedding invitation, for next month. The pleasure of your company, bla bla bla, at the marriage of Anton Bower and Mara Southgate.'

'Who the hell—?'

'Some couple I met in Nashville, last year,' said Billy. 'They came to our wedding.'

'So you've seen them recently enough. We don't have to go.'

It was an act, and one that she thought was impressing Lucy. If only Matilda could realize that Lucy was never going to be drawn in by this new version of herself that she was parading in front of us. It was the old Matilda that had left us. It was the old Matilda who was going to have to win Lucy back.

Just then the telephone rang and Billy went off to answer it. Through the gap in the door I watched him talking, his back to us, padding around the room as far as the telephone wire would allow, the fingers of his right hand running over and over again through his fox-red hair, then picking things up, examining them, putting them down, all the time talking, listening, laughing. Lucy sat down on the floor, stretching her long legs out over the rug, and lit a cigarette.

'That was Clover,' said Billy, coming back into the room. 'You're to meet her tomorrow at midday, Tara. She's going to take you shopping for something to wear to Digby's party on Saturday. Thereafter, you'll be staying with her. You'll be in good company. Inigo always stays there when he's in town. He has his own room in Napier House.'

'Why can't we stay with *you*?' I bleated, horrified. *And was this Digby O'Rourke they were talking about?*

'I'd *adore* you to stay with us, but Billy won't have it,' said Matilda sulkily.

'You haven't been to London until you've stayed with Clover,' said Billy. 'She's the glue that keeps everyone in Chelsea together. I've known her since she was twelve,' he went on. 'Her mother and mine were best friends.' It was the first time he had mentioned his parents; the idea that Billy had once been a little boy with muddy boots and crumbs all over his face was preposterous. He had been born how he was now, hadn't he?

'Clover's *forty-three*,' said Matilda, as though the achievement of being so old warranted some sort of National Award. 'You would never believe it. She could pass for twenty-five, couldn't she, Billy?'

'I wouldn't go that far,' said Billy.

'Why do I need her to go shopping with me? I'd rather go on my own.'

Nerves were making me say things I certainly didn't believe.

'Shopping with Clover is as close to childhood delight as anything else I've ever known in life,' said Matilda.

Recalling Matilda's childhood, I couldn't very well think of a single moment that anyone would have classified as remotely delightful until the arrival of my sister, but I realized I was beaten so I just said, 'Well, if you put it that way.'

'She will love you both,' sighed Matilda. 'As will all of London, if you give the place a chance.'

'There's another thing we need to talk about,' said Billy. His voice had thickened. 'Your name.'

'What about it?' I asked, all innocence.

'Tara Jupp is a sweet name, but it's not really . . . *enough* for someone making records.'

'Not enough?' said Lucy, frowning. 'What do you suggest she does about it?'

'Well, we come up with something else.'

Lucy looked at me, astonished.

I nodded. I had known this was coming; I had had time to prepare. 'All right,' I said. 'I'll be whoever you want me to be.'

It was the first time I had said anything like that to Billy. He looked relieved and surprised.

'There's a way of getting a name that we've tried with singers before. It can work quite well.' He looked from me to Lucy. 'What was your mother's maiden name?'

'Merrywell,' we said together.

'Merrywell,' said Billy thoughtfully. 'That's good.'

'I don't know,' I began. 'It seems a bit odd – taking Ma's name.'

'But wasn't she the one who always wanted to be a singer?'

'Yes, but—'

'Just try this for me, won't you?' asked Billy. He was on a roll now, enjoying himself. 'Indulge me, girls. What was the name of your first pet.'

'Pet? *Pet?*'

'Yes, you know. Cat, dog, rabbit . . .'

'Splish,' said Lucy.

'Splish?' repeated Billy, confused.

'He was a goldfish. We had two. One was Jack's, the other was mine. Splish and Splosh.'

'Dear God!' said Billy, alarmed. 'Anything else?'

'What about that guinea pig? I think he was George's. We called it Cherry,' said Lucy, who appeared to be rather enjoying herself.

'Cherry Merrywell! That's even *more* ridiculous!' I said. But it was as though a light had gone on in Billy's eyes.

'Cherry Merrywell.' He said it again. 'Miss Cherry Merrywell. Cherry Merrywell.' He nodded and looked at me. 'What do you think?'

He had that awful hypnotic thing going on with those yellow-green eyes again. He had a way of looking at you as though the next words that you uttered were to be the most important of his life.

'Do you think it's the right thing to do?' I asked him.

'I think that people won't forget that name,' he said.

'Hang about!' said Matilda. 'What was it again?'

That night Lucy and I slept together in Billy and Matilda's spare room – a vast space, empty but for the bed and a table beside it stacked with Ian Fleming novels. I stayed awake, flicking through *Live and Let Die* unwilling to close my eyes. Beside me, Lucy fell asleep the moment her head touched the pillow.

I lay awake listening to London. A street lamp shone orange light through a chink in the curtains, the sinister orange of a candle in a hollowed-out pumpkin. I was amazed at the great claw of homesickness – despite having Lucy close to me – and it came upon me so suddenly I was powerless to fight it, ill-prepared. One minute I was laughing with Lucy in the bathroom, the next I was virtually unable to move for fear of its power taking me completely, rendering me useless. It wasn't just Imogen, Florence, Pa and the Littles I missed, it was the whole shooting match – the smell of my bedroom, the thud and squawk of the boys on the tennis court, the gentle cooing of the wood pigeons that had nested in the roof, the hope of Shreddies, then a boiled egg with plenty of salt in the morning . . .

My heart sped up with fear for how far away we were; I spent an hour planning my escape. Tomorrow this whole crazy thing would start in earnest, with Clover Napier, who was older than my mother had been when she died, but apparently looked younger than all of us, and Digby O'Rourke, who appeared to be having a party and couldn't walk past a woman without commenting on the shape of her legs and photographing her in as few clothes as possible. Lucy was all right with sex, I thought, looking at her unrepentant little face beside me in the bed, her leg hooked over the sheet, showing her wretched, sinful black lace knickers. She understood boys; she knew her own body, had never feared what it could do, she had embraced it from an early age. I was afraid. If this were to be my great awakening, I feared I would run from it.

I closed my eyes, and prayed.

Our father, who art in heaven . . .

I started again.

Our father, who art in the Rectory . . .

That first night in London, the fourteen days and nights ahead could have been fourteen years. I cried myself to sleep.

19

Clover

Lucy and I awoke at the same time, sat up in bed and looked at each other. That monster Homesickness had vanished with the night; I felt none of it with the dawn. Matilda knocked on the door.

'Clover's meeting you in an hour,' she said. 'I'd get your skates on if I were you.'

Then we heard her running to the bathroom. Minutes later she was outside our door again.

'Sorry,' she gasped. 'Morning sickness.'

'Hangover, more like,' muttered Lucy.

'I can't get used to Matilda drinking so much,' I said.

'Evidently neither can she,' observed Lucy.

Lucy was quite prepared to tone down her excitement when Matilda was present, put up that unbreakable barrier she had constructed, but with me, safe in the knowledge that today she had the whole of Historical London at her feet, she was a child, thrilled.

Now she was flipping through her book, breaking back the spine like Pa told us never to do, like a child, thrilled. '*The interior of Leighton House invokes a compelling vision of the Orient,*' she read. 'I'll be the judge of that.'

Lucy was notoriously harsh on those who wrote information for guidebooks.

'You must take notes for Raoul,' I said.

Lucy looked momentarily confused, as though she had clean forgotten that she had a husband at all.

Napier House stood apart from the other houses in its row by virtue of its size, and also because it was set back from them and was reached by opening a small gate and walking down a short path to the front door. Mid-Victorian, I thought – with Regency frills. I wasn't Lucy's sister for nothing. *Please Ring* said the sign hanging on the railings. A short flight of wrought-iron steps led to a basement door that would have been used by the servants. There had to be some mistake, I thought. They can't tear this place down. *A stealthy plague of people with no vision*, Raoul had called those who wanted to kill these buildings. And they were coming to get this one too.

Then on the first floor, a window was flung open. I looked up, shielding my eyes to block out the sun. Clover stuck her head out of the window and looked for me.

'You! Are you Tara?' she called.

'Yes, I am.'

'Here. Catch!' And out of the window came a pale blue velvet jacket. I watched it fall.

'I said catch, didn't I?'

'Sorry.' I picked it up and a shoal of coins, several playing cards and a confetti of ripped cinema tickets spilled out of the pockets.

'I'll be down in five minutes. Here, read this. It'll give you something to think about.'

Out shot a copy of *The Feminine Mystique*.

At last the front door opened and Clover emerged into the light. Despite heels and a huge floppy hat the colour of the aubergines Imogen used to make moussaka, Clover was tiny – even shorter than me. Her skin was vampire-white, enhanced by a slash of dark red lipstick. She was wearing huge red-rimmed sunglasses; her hair fell perfectly straight, the black of George's polished boots. She looked like one of the pixie drawings from an Enid Blyton story. I wouldn't have been surprised to see a wand extending from her tiny hands, and Matilda was quite right – if I hadn't been told that she was forty-three, I would have said she was fifteen years younger. She looked at the book in my hands.

'Well,' she demanded, 'what do you think?'

'My sister Florence has read it,' I said.

'What did she think?'

'It started fires in our house,' I admitted.

'*It is easier to live through someone else than to become complete yourself,*' said Clover. 'I have a terrible suspicion she's right.'

She looked at my suitcase.

'Leave that in the hall,' she said. 'We're going out.'

I caught a brief glimpse of Napier House as she shoved my bag through the front door, and craned my neck to see and opened my mouth to ask the first of a line of questions about the place, but Clover anticipated my interest and put up her hand to stop me.

'Time for all that later,' she said quickly. 'If I start talking about the house we won't ever get down to the more immediate problems, such as your clothes.'

'I like your hat,' I said. *If you can't think of the right thing to say, throw a compliment* was one of George's adages. Clover laughed, removed the hat and put it on my head.

'Better already,' she sighed.

She looked at me properly, really up and down, sizing up the linen smock, the sandals, Imogen's boating shorts.

'Crumbs,' she said with feeling. 'You're not from round here, are you? Still, where there's life . . .'

She bent down and picked up my foot, just as though I were a horse she was inspecting at a show. I was too surprised to speak.

'How many times have these been resoled?'

'Oh, I don't know. Not that many. Five at the most.'

'They're terrible, truly terrible. Now, beautiful shoes can hurt and it doesn't matter – you just push on and know that however much agony you're in, it's all right because half the world thinks you don't cook your own breakfast. But those!' she shook her head. 'No words can describe the terribleness of those. Come. We must walk and talk.'

'They're not terrible!' I protested weakly, breaking into a trot beside her. 'They belonged to my mother.'

'Ah. Now I hear you. *Belonged*. Did she die?'

'Yes.'

'You poor girl. I lost my mother to the south of France two years ago.' Clover bit her lip.

'Oh.'

'These things happen.'

'Is she very like you?' I asked, not really knowing what to say.

'She's a difficult, capricious hypochondriac, so yes. She lives with her second husband, whom I refuse to call my stepfather. I suppose you were mad about your mother, weren't you?'

'Yes,' I said, struggling to keep up. 'Everyone was. She was a wonderful person.'

'*Cela va sans dire*,' said Clover. 'And your father?'

'He's a vicar.'

'Good Lord. Terrifies you, I expect.'

'Yes.'

'Didn't want you to come up to London?'

'Actually, he encouraged me. He thinks you may as well follow your dreams if you can.'

'Sounds my sort of man. Has he married again?'

'No!' I laughed, briefly arrested by the thought of Pa and Clover together. 'No woman would want to have him now. He's actually a full-time tyrant.'

'Perfect. I suppose he's soft as butter underneath it all?'

I considered for a moment.

'No.'

'Good. I can't stand those irritating types who come over all tough, then fall apart listening to *Play for Today*.'

She was bustling me over the road now. A cab driver hooted his horn at us, or rather at *her*. Her fairy's legs, despite the heat, were encased in brown tights. She wore sharp heels that clicked along, giving her an atmosphere of great efficiency. She never stopped talking.

'So, Billy tells me you've a wonderful voice,' she said briskly.

'He seems to think so. Oh, sorry,' I said, bumping into Clover as she stopped short to look in the window of a shop selling tweed jackets.

'Hideous,' she muttered under her breath. Turning back to me she said, 'Apparently you can sound like anyone. Billie Holiday, Etta James, dear old Alma Cogan?'

'I suppose so.'

'He must think you're special if he's got Inigo Wallace involved.'

I didn't say anything.

'Have you met him yet?' asked Clover.

'Yes,' I said. I nearly opened my mouth to tell her the whole story – Clover had the effect of making you want to tell secrets – but closed it again. Clover looked at me.

'Difficult,' she said. 'You shouldn't worry if he seems a bit odd; it's what makes him brilliant. You know they call him Father Hit-mas in New York.'

'That's a stupid name,' I said, with more venom that I intended.

'Makes the point accurately enough though,' said Clover. 'He's always so terminally unavailable. I was rather obsessed by him for a while.' I gaped at her frankness. 'As it turned out, I had confused love with deep admiration for the way he styled his hair. It just took me a couple of weeks to realize it.'

I laughed.

'Still,' said Clover, 'he stays with me every time he comes to town and appears to write his most successful songs in my great-grandfather's study. It contains a grand piano and a large amount of Victorian pornography, which could be the reason he so loves coming back to Napier time and time again.' She gave me a serious look. 'No one else is allowed to enter that room,' she said. 'Just Father Hit-mas and his *genius* –' she splayed out her fingers into the air as she delivered this word, injecting it with more than a touch of irony. 'It's his sacred ground,' she added.

'Do *you* think he's a genius?'

Clover looked surprised at the question.

'It's hard to say. I suppose it's a tricky thing, writing songs that millions of people can relate to. I couldn't begin. I don't have any clue how the rest of society operates. He seems to have a knack for getting into the minds of the great unwashed, which is strange considering he went to boarding school and grew up in a house that – I *promise* you – would have dwarfed

Kensington Palace. I used to know his mother a bit, actually, when she was a widow in Wiltshire, before she married Rocky Dakota and vamoosed off to New York.'

As usual, mention of Magna set my nerves on edge. Perhaps Clover might have heard about the stolen elephant?

'Still,' Clover went on, oblivious to the hammering of my heart. '*Somebody* loves the boy. He's had two half-hour telephone calls from New York since he's arrived here, which is extravagant spending by anyone's standards.'

'A girl?' I asked, amazed.

'A girl,' confirmed Clover. 'When I asked him about her, he sort of clammed up and went red which is most unlike him. I heard him saying "*I hope everything's all right with you, baby.*" She put on a disconcertingly accurate, posh-boy drawl as she spoke these words, and I laughed uneasily. Clover smiled knowingly.

'No doubt that she's the muse behind all those relentlessly up-tempo pop songs he churns out every ten minutes.'

'Well, good luck to her,' I said tartly. Whoever she was, she could keep him. He was no longer the boy I had kept wrapped in the magic of my own imagining.

'So,' said Clover, sweeping any further chat about Inigo aside, 'we're to find you something to wear to Digby O'Rourke's party.'

'If that's what Billy wants,' I said. 'I've never been invited to a party by someone I don't know before,' I added, fishing around for some encouragement.

'No, I don't suppose you have,' said Clover pityingly, looking down at my shoes again. 'Keep close to me when we cross the road, darling. We're not in Yorkshire now.'

'Cornwall.'

'That's what I *said*. Now, apparently you've got a sister who looks like Julie Christie. What a *bore* for you.'

'Doesn't bother me,' I lied.

'Nonsense, you only *think* it doesn't because you're so used to it. And I imagine she's jealous of the attention you get when you sing?'

'I don't think so. She can sing too. She just never bothered to practise.'

'The very good-looking never need to bother with much at all. They can afford not to. The rest of us have to work hard at being liked, unjust though it seems. Right, we'll take a look in here first. How much has he given you?'

I turned the notes out of my pockets and handed them in a crumpled pile to Clover. She whisked them through her fingers, muttering under her breath.

'Hmm. He's not taking any chances, is he?'

She halted to light a cigarette and handed the money back to me.

'I have a whole life on credit. It's the only way to exist. The only person worth paying in cash is one's cleaner. Round here, they get more loot than anyone else.'

'Why?'

'Everyone's too afraid they'll start talking, of course. Digby O'Rourke's cleaner, now *she's* seen a few things in her day. They say she's the best in London, but she keeps threatening him that she's going to sell her story to the papers.'

'I can imagine.'

'Can you?' Clover looked at me and laughed. 'I'm not sure that you can. Not yet, anyway.'

She hurried me across another street.

'You know, I loathe smoking,' she said. 'I only did it in the first place to give myself something to do when I was bored at parties, and now I find I can't live without it. Like sex really,' she added as an afterthought.

I gulped. 'My sister Imogen believes I should stop if I want to see old age.'

'What, smoking or sex?'

'Smoking of course!' I wished I didn't sound so shocked.

Clover laughed loudly. 'Of course,' she said. 'And anyway – who the hell's going to be around to see old age? Everyone knows the world's going to end in 1984.'

Now she had stopped outside a shop with a window display like the cover of Pa's battered old Hans Christian Andersen. Fairies with gauze wings, dolls in white lace and frogs with gold paper crowns on their heads stared out at us from a tea table spread with spotted plates and a red velvet cloth.

'Cee-Cee's,' explained Clover, teacher to imbecile. 'Elizabeth Taylor, of all people, was in here last week, so all of a sudden everyone wants to be seen here too. I know the girl who started it. I've asked her to shut the place for the morning so we can concentrate. Hold your head high, breathe in and don't knock anything, rip anything or even *think* about buying anything until I tell you we can.'

She put her hands on my shoulders and looked into my eyes. 'One day, far into the mists of time, you'll tell your grandchildren that you shopped here.'

She was hard to read; I was unable at this stage to tell whether she was joking or not.

'If the world's going to end in 1984, I may have no need to,' I said lightly.

Clover laughed and, peering into the letterbox, shouted: 'Police! You're under arrest!'

20

Cee-Cee's for Beginners

A minute later, the door was opened by a girl of about Lucy's age, with thick blonde hair tied back in a red handkerchief. She beckoned to us both and fled back down the steps, as though the sunlight might steal away her cosmic powers or something. Clover pushed me ahead of her.

'Go on,' she said.

We clattered down into the basement. It wasn't until my eyes had adjusted to the gloom of the shop that I saw Clover's friend properly. She didn't recognize me, of course. But then, why should she? I had only been ten years old when we had met for the first time, back in 1956 – I doubted whether she even recalled the event at all. Yet her face and clothes had stayed with me as clearly as if I had seen her yesterday – in the way that all details leading up to an hour of great significance do. She had been one of the two who had found lost little me that day at Milton Magna when I had met Inigo Wallace. She had given me the stick of Kit Kat. It was Miss Penelope's friend, Charlotte Ferris. My mind raced. I said nothing.

'This is Cherry Merrywell, one of Billy's creations,' said Clover, nodding at me.

'You're staying at Napier House?'

'She could be one of my last guests,' said Clover.

'Delighted to meet you,' said Charlotte, putting down a ham sandwich and offering me her hand. 'And you could have blown me down with a bicycle pump,' she said to Clover. 'I thought you were joking when you said you were coming in this morning. What went wrong with Henry?' she demanded gleefully.

Clover looked at me.

'What do you think?' she said. 'Ran off with someone else.'

'How could he! Oh well, I always said he was unreliable.'

'Oh, not him, *me*. Met a French guy in some bar. You can guess the rest.'

'Who?'

'You wouldn't know him.'

'Want to bet?'

Clover covered her face with her hands.

'Michel Grangier? Friend of Bailey's?'

The girl whistled. 'Micky G? Always had him down as one of *those*, darling.'

'Oh, I think he is. And one of the others too. Still, Henry went out of his *mind*. Spent all of last night trying to convince me to join him in India next week. I told him he had more chance of getting me on a shuttle to the moon.' Clover turned to me to explain. 'Henry's a psychoanalyst,' she said. 'Terribly interested in telling people the precise moment in their child-hood that everything went wrong. He makes a criminal amount of money for it. Poor Hope Allen – do you know Hopey? No, silly me, of course you don't – well, anyway, she sees him three times a week. Not that it's done *her* any good.'

'Oh, but it *has*,' said Charlotte. 'Telling people that she goes to Dr Henry Wright to discuss her state of mind is the best medicine in the world.'

'My father thinks that there's nothing anyone can teach you about yourself that you can't learn from the story of Joseph and his brothers,' I said. 'Genesis,' I added hastily.

'Joseph? The one with the coat?' asked Charlotte.

'That's the one.'

'I always rather liked the idea of him.'

'What do you *mean*?' demanded Clover. 'He was another one who never stopped telling people how to live their lives – interpreting dreams and seeing into the future . . .'

'So what you're saying is that if he'd been around now, he would have cleaned up,' said Charlotte.

I blinked at them both; it was impossible to tell if they were serious.

'He *did* clean up,' I said. 'Became ruler of Egypt based on correctly predicting the weather forecast over a fourteen-year period.'

'Well, *I* say that's just showing off,' said Clover.

I laughed, delighted with her exegesis.

'Come on, then. You'd better come in,' said Charlotte.

'Is Henry your – your . . . ?' I didn't know what word to use. Charlotte stepped in for her.

'Not any more,' she said. 'How *can* he be?' She looked at Clover. 'When your heart's not in it? When your heart's *never* been in it?'

Clover took off her dark glasses for the first time and looked at us.

'How *can* he be?' she repeated softly.

I was astonished to see the expression in her eyes overcrowded by pain.

'Are you all right?' I asked her. It was an instinctive question – so sharp had been her transition from complete control to sudden vulnerability. She snapped back with equal speed.

'Perfectly, thank you,' she said.

Charlotte swung a bottle-green cloak around her shoulders, which seemed to signify that all lines of this particular conversation were now officially over.

'Christopher found this in Morocco last month. Isn't it wonderful?'

'Where the hell is Christopher? I never see him any more.'

'He's not here much,' said Charlotte. 'I've started calling him the "Lost Cee". He doesn't find it very funny.'

Clover stubbed out her cigarette on a blue glass ashtray, shaped like a naked girl sprawled across a sofa with her hands outstretched. Actually, I don't know that it was an ashtray, but it didn't seem to matter much either way.

'So, you're a singer, are you?' Charlotte asked me.

'Well – I sing.'

'Billy says she's *sensational*,' said Clover, impersonating his accent.

'If he says so, she must be,' said Charlotte promptly. Then she glanced down at my feet and her expression changed. 'Look at her shoes,' she said, barely concealing her horror. 'Surely you should start there?'

Clover raised an eyebrow.

'Poor thing. Shall we get going? Let's have a pot of tea. Cherry, darling, take a look around and point to anything you like the look of.'

I pointed to a full riding habit, hung on the wall, probably simply as decoration.

'That belonged to my Aunt Clare when she was a girl,' said

Charlotte. 'She only used to go hunting because the MFH gave her a toot of cocaine before they set off.'

'*Cocaine?*' I hadn't come across *that* in the Pullein-Thompson novels.

'It was legal in those days,' said Charlotte airily.

'I'd love to try it on,' I said, touching the stiff black material with my left hand. Charlotte and Clover exchanged looks.

'Sit down,' advised Clover. 'Read this.' She tossed *Harper's Bazaar* at me.

Charlotte took an amber rock from a collection in a clear jar.

'It's not drugs, darling,' she said, seeing my face.

'Yet,' added Clover under her breath.

'I don't go anywhere without frankincense and myrrh,' explained Charlotte.

'Like the three wise men,' I said.

'Only thing I'm lacking is gold,' said Charlotte.

And that was funny really, because all I could see when I was with those two was glitter.

They wanted to talk about Billy and Matilda's wedding. Charlotte had been away in Africa and unable to get back in time for it. I supposed refusing the invitation was the last word in cool.

'How did she look?' she asked us.

'Beautiful,' I said, perfectly truthfully.

'A Pre-Raphaelite dream,' said Clover. 'Typical of her, of course. I'm surprised Billy allowed it.'

Then followed a long discussion about who had been at the party and when they had last seen them and what everyone was wearing. Clover and Charlotte together were like no two people I had ever met, talking over each other, handing one another pieces of fabric, smoking, pouring oil from tiny bottles and smelling each other's perfume-covered wrists – to me they were half-children, half-witches.

'I sang the solo when they signed the register,' I piped up when they got to that bit in their reminiscing. Clover actually stopped rifling through the rails and stared at me.

'Was that *you*?' she asked accusingly. 'Singing from *Gigi* and getting applauded at the end as though we were in the Royal Festival Hall? I couldn't see a thing – we were right at the back. I overslept. Opium,' she added to Charlotte, by way of an explanation.

'Yes. That was me,' I said.

'*Well!* Henry and I had a *terrible* row over you!'

'How's that?'

'It was all that rousing praise you generated after you sang. He said it was wonderful that people felt they were able to clap in church and why on earth did they have to be so reserved about everything all the time and church should be a place where breaking into applause should be – well – *applauded*, so to speak, and I said I didn't agree one bit, and clapping in church was just not on, however stupendous the voice.'

I couldn't tell whether this was a compliment to me or not, so I said, 'Ahhh.'

'Then he said that was rich coming from me as he'd never known me to go to church, and I had no right to get sanctimonious over such things – silly man. It's only because I won't marry him and he can't conceive of how refusing him could be possible for any woman – anyway, he went on and on and on, and I got so bored by it that I hopped into a Bentley with Kate Wentworth and we shot off back to her hotel, which was about a thousand miles away in some town called Falmouth.'

'So she was good?' Charlotte asked.

'Astonishing. So unbelievably un-English, you'd never guess it came from her. From *you*!' she added, remembering I was in the room. 'Such a voice! I imagined some six-foot, dark-skinned beauty had been flown in from Jamaica for the afternoon. And it was *you*! Well! You could knock me down with a feather.'

They both looked at me with new respect. I squirmed.

'I only did it because it was Matilda's wedding,' I said. 'Wouldn't have sung that for anyone else.'

'Where *was* Matilda before she was everywhere?' asked Charlotte.

'Cornwall, with us,' I said. 'She was my sister's best friend.'

'She's come a long way,' said Charlotte. 'I heard she was the most photographed woman in the country last year. *Vogue* called her the "definitive female beauty".'

'My sister's far prettier,' I heard myself saying. 'She just never went to London and pushed herself around like Matilda.'

For some reason, Clover and Charlotte found this extremely funny.

'Charlotte,' called Clover across the shop floor, 'tea, please. Now, get your clothes off and we'll have a look at what we're dealing with here.'

She went up to the door of the shop and flipped the sign over so that it said 'Closed' to the rest of the world.

'What do you mean, get my clothes off?' I stammered.

'Darling, we all went to boarding school. We've seen it all before. Why on earth aren't you wearing a bra?'

'Never thought I needed one.'

'Everyone needs one. Here.'

She whipped her hands under her blouse and in about three movements pulled off her own.

'How did you do that?'

'Years of practice.' Clover was deadpan. She tossed her brassiere over to me. It was black and tiny and padded and warm from her skin.

'I don't think it will fit me. I don't like bras.'

'Are you out of your mind?' Clover looked at me in amazement. 'Are they all like you in Derbyshire?'

'Cornwall,' I corrected her again.

'Potato, potahto, darling.' She handed me her rolled-up cigarette. 'Have a smoke. We're going to be here for some time so you may as well relax.'

I took several pulls on the cigarette. It tasted strange. Probably drugs, I remember thinking, then, oh well, when in London. But after another puff I felt the world spinning. I pulled off my top and squeezed into Clover's bra. She was right, of course, it changed me straight away. Suddenly I had more of what I had always envied in Lucy.

'You see,' said Clover.

'Yeah,' I breathed, grinning stupidly at my reflection.

Charlotte went over to the gramophone and put on *South Pacific*, of all things. Clover rattled through the rails of clothing, squint-eyed from cigarette smoke, muttering under her breath. '*Too long, too much detail, wouldn't work with her colouring, yes I'll try that, oh, Jean borrowed that last week for the book launch, didn't she, yes but without the belt, no but possibly if we could find the right shoes . . .*' and so on. I stood staring into the long cracked mirror, bare feet paddling in a sea of crushed velvet, listening to Mitzi Gaynor waxing lyrical about her wonderful guy, my ancient grey and white school knickers an absurd accompaniment to the black push-up bra. I didn't mind one bit, because of course by then I was entirely stoned. Charlotte's terrier – who had been introduced to me as Dobbin – lay on my shed clothes behind the screen. Clover and Charlotte talked on and on, occasionally throwing the odd question my way – '*Are you all right, darling? Could you lift up your arms for a second?*' – and I did everything they asked, as if in a trance.

'Hmm,' said Clover said. 'How about this?'

'Not for sale,' said Charlotte firmly. 'It's an antique piece of Victorian lace, inherited from Aunt Clare.'

'At least let her try,' said Clover, and before Charlotte could object, she took it from her.

Clover wrapped the black material around my legs, so that it fell right to the floor. Standing behind me, she stuck pins into the back so that it flowed into a long skirt.

'I'm too short to wear this sort of thing,' I said regretfully.

'Beautiful stuff,' muttered Clover. 'It's a sin not to use it.'

'Far more of a sin to send her to Digby's wearing it, where the drunkest people in London can spill their revolting cocktails all over it,' said Charlotte.

'Just walk over to the stairs and back, darling,' said Clover.

I can't say what it was that caught my foot under the shoes and the makeshift skirt, it could have been anything – the corner of a Persian rug, a dog-eared hardback of *Peter Pan and Wendy*, Charlotte's feather boa – but down I went, falling forward on to the floor, accompanied by a horrifying ripping noise. I was too surprised to say anything; I ended up sitting on my bottom, legs stuck out in front of me, Clover's hat entirely covering my eyes. I felt more winded by that fall than any amount of tumbling from the backs of ponies, but then that may have been the lack of air in the room. I tried to stand up, and failed, falling down again, ripping the fabric further.

'Shit.'

Clover started to laugh.

'Holy smoke, darling, are you all right? Still breathing?'

'Never mind whether she's still alive! What about the lace?' wailed Charlotte.

'I'm so sorry!' I gasped.

Charlotte took hold of a piece of the material and pulled at it, but the whole thing had torn in strips, giving the impression of someone removing the bandages from an Egyptian mummy, so that the remaining material hugged my thighs and stopped at least eight inches above my solid white knees. With nothing but the hat and the push-up bra on top, I looked like the victim of a gruesome attack.

'It's ruined,' I said, panic gripping me. Suddenly I felt the overwhelming need to get out of Charlotte's shop, I felt like the magician's assistant, smoke and material closing in on me before I was sawn in two.

At that moment that the doorbell rang. From where I was lying on the floor, I could see through a crack in the curtains and into the street above us.

'Holy mother of God,' I said, scrambling out of the way. 'It's Inigo.'

'Father Hit-mas himself,' said Charlotte sardonically. 'Billy's probably sent him to check on us,' she added, stubbing out her cigarette.

'Shall we just ignore him?'

Inigo rang the bell again.

'You'll have to let him in,' said Clover. 'If you don't, he'll only come down the chimney.'

Charlotte left Clover unravelling pieces of me so she could open the door. Clover and I listened to their exchange.

'Hello, darling. We're just dressing your little singer.'

'Can I take a look at what you've been doing? Billy wants me to—'

'No, no. Off you go and play, there's a good boy. We haven't got anything together yet.'

'Have you been smoking?'

'Well, we might have been. *I* might have been. *She* hasn't.'

'For Christ's sake, Charlotte, the girl's seventeen years old!'

'Inigo. I don't want to remind you what *I* was doing aged seventeen. She's not a baby!'

'She's a backward child compared to you!'

'Oh, and *you're* such a model of good behaviour—'

'We're not talking about *me.*'

I opened my mouth. Clover closed her hand over my indignant gape.

'You're a dreadful bore, you know, Inigo,' went on Charlotte. 'Still, nothing changes. You've been a pain in the neck since you were fifteen years old.'

Clover put her hand up to her forehead in despair.

In seconds, and before I had a chance to rearrange myself, he was downstairs.

The basement of the shop was so small that Inigo stopped on the bottom step.

'Well, she can't go out like *that*,' he said instantly.

'I know,' I said between clenched teeth.

'Although we'd probably sell a lot of records if you did,' he added. He turned to Clover, speaking with some irritation. 'For crying out loud, get some clothes for the poor girl. She hasn't been in London for twenty-four hours, and you've already got her stoned and half naked in the most —' he threw his hands in the air, looking for the word – '*louche* basement in the whole city.'

'I don't know what *louche* means, but I'm presuming wonderful—'

'She's trying things on for the party,' said Clover. She looked at me, barely able to move and standing there shrouded in black lace. 'Get behind that screen and put your clothes back on, darling,' she said.

Behind the screen I stood, face burning hot. I pulled my linen smock up to my face and smelled it. *Imogen*. I fought a powerful urge to weep. Clover was talking in tones of great irritation.

'Every time Billy asks me to dress a girl, the *same* thing happens.'

'What? Priceless pieces of fabric from a bygone age end up ripped to shreds?'

'No. Someone *always* has to interfere.'

'Just doing what I was asked to do,' he said. 'All Billy said to me was that if the clothes weren't right, then nothing else comes right either. He's just seen some pictures of Susan Vaughan and he wants Cherry in pink and white.'

'Well, he can't have her in pink and white,' said Clover. 'It won't work with her colouring.'

Inigo pulled a magazine out of his back pocket. I don't think he was enjoying being Billy's messenger boy.

'Here,' he said, pointing to it. 'This is what he wants you to work from.'

Clover pulled the magazine up close and frowned.

'She's too young to be dolled up like she's off to some fundraiser in Manhattan. For God's sake, Inigo – surely *you* can see that?'

'It may have escaped your notice, but I am merely the song-writer.'

'What are you doing here then?'

'I'm asking myself precisely the same question.'

At exactly that moment, the bell rang again.

'Who is it *now*?' asked Clover.

Charlotte walked to the window and peered up.

'Just some model,' she said. 'I'm casting here this afternoon; she must have got the time wrong.'

I followed her gaze.

'That's not a model!' I squeaked. 'It's my sister! She's cut her hair. Pa will *kill* her!' I said this last bit out loud without meaning to, but the shock of what Lucy had done was too explosive to be kept to myself.

I waved frantically; I don't think I had ever been so thrilled to see Lucy in my life.

'Your *sister*?' asked Clover in amazement. 'Snakes alive! I didn't think she'd be *that* beautiful.'

'No one ever does,' I said.

'I'll go and let her in,' said Charlotte, escaping with relief.

Clover had taken control again and was pulling a pink sundress off the rails.

'Actually, this will be lovely on you,' she said firmly.

Lucy clattered down into the basement. Standing on the bottom step, she grinned at us. Inigo shook his head, in a gesture of wonder or despair – it was hard to tell which.

'Leighton House was unbelievable,' she said. 'I could have stayed there at least another hour.'

'Never mind that – what's Pa going to say when he sees what you've done to your hair?'

Lucy shook her head defiantly.

'Who cares?' she said. 'I walked all the way here from Kensington. I went past a hairdresser's with a picture in the window of a girl with the shortest hair I've ever seen. I walked in and asked for the same thing. What do you think?'

'Miss Fitt will explode,' I said.

Lucy had become Jean Seberg in *Breathless*, the shortness of the cut making her eyes even bigger, her cheekbones even more geometrically astonishing.

Charlotte spoke. 'Wish I had the nerve to cut mine off,' she said. 'Apart from anything else, you'll certainly save on shampoo.'

'What will Raoul think?' I said, not meaning to speak out loud.

'He probably won't even notice,' said Lucy.

'Who he?' asked Clover.

'Husband,' said Lucy and I at the same time.

'*Where* is he?' asked Charlotte, turning as though she expected him to be standing behind her and holding out his hand in greeting.

'Cornwall,' said Lucy.

'Might as well be on the moon,' said Charlotte beadily. 'Poor man.'

She picked up the remains of the skirt.

'Are you going to Digby's party?' she asked Lucy.

'Yes,' said Lucy, Inigo and I all at the same time.

'All right,' sighed Clover. 'What Billy wants, Billy gets. Let's try you in that pink tunic over there. No, don't take off the bra.'

I picked up the tunic and stared at it in dismay.

'You,' said Clover, pointing at Lucy. 'Come over here. I've got an idea. A way to mend what your sister's just destroyed.' She winked at me, and I knew she was on my side, but I felt hot tears pricking my eyelids. I didn't want Clover's ideas to be for Lucy – she was meant to be here for me!

Lucy, who usually hated being bossed around, shuffled obediently to where Clover was standing. Clover picked up the remains of the skirt and wrapped a piece around the top of Lucy's legs.

'Take off your trousers,' she said. 'I need to see if this is going to work.'

Inigo raised his eyes to heaven.

'I'm off,' he said.

'You can report to Billy that both girls will be arriving at the party at nine thirty,' said Clover.

'It starts at eight,' said Lucy.

'Darling, dressed like *you're* going to be dressed, you can't possibly arrive on time.'

Inigo went back up the stairs two at a time. I watched him leave the shop and lope off down the street, one hand in his pocket, the other holding a cigarette.

Charlotte looked at what Clover was doing, head tilted sideways.

'A bit short, isn't it?'

Clover looked at her, her mouth studded with pins, and frowned. Lucy and I stared at her reflection as Clover worked. I stood slightly behind my sister in the pink tunic, my short, skinny little body looking absurd next to hers – like the reflection from the Hall of Mirrors at the fairground. Feeling my discomfort, Lucy looked at me. She tried to raise her eyebrows to show how absurd she was thinking everything was, but she just couldn't manage it. She had to bite her bottom lip to stop herself from grinning.

The phone rang, and Charlotte melted off to answer it. We heard her shrieking with delight and then talking in rapid French.

'Hold still!' ordered Clover.

When Charlotte came back into the room, Clover was pinning Lucy into the little skirt.

'Charlotte, get this girl some water, get me some thread, the scissors, and take the bloody telephone off the hook.'

'Yes, sir,' said Charlotte.

She worked for half an hour on the skirt, almost in silence. Neither Lucy nor I spoke to each other, for fear of breaking the spell. When she had finished, she stood up, arching her hands behind her back.

'Well?' she said. 'What do you think?'

The skirt was now tiny, no more than a fraction of what it had been before. It clung to Lucy's thighs, at least eight inches above her knees, its brevity drawing the eye inevitably to the length of the legs below.

Feeling Pa over my shoulder, I spoke before anyone else.

'She can't walk into a party like that! She looks half naked!' I bleated.

Clover shrugged. 'The material's beautiful, and so is she.' She spoke the facts without any sentiment.

'But won't everyone stare?' asked Lucy.

'I most certainly hope so,' said Clover.

'Billy'll think it too much,' said Lucy regretfully.

Charlotte laughed.

'You don't know Billy very well, do you?'

'How much do I owe you?' asked Clover.

'Twenty,' said Charlotte firmly.

'But there's nothing of it!' protested Clover.

'Sentimental value,' said Charlotte airily. 'It belonged to my beloved Aunt Clare. I can't possibly put a price on that.'

'And yet you just have.'

'Twenty,' said Charlotte. 'Clover, darling, I've got to make a living somehow.'

'Fifteen!' said Clover. 'You're hardly scraping by. This is the most talked-about shop in west London, and if this goes down well tonight, you're going to have all of Digby's little slaves in here

231

wanting a piece of the action. This isn't any old skirt,' she went on, warming to her theme. 'This is a Skirt with a capital S.'

Once again, the doorbell rang. 'You see, it's started already,' she added. 'The Skirt is born.'

Charlotte glanced out of the window.

'It's André. We must get him down here to look.'

Years later, I read that Charlotte's friend André had invented the miniskirt. Well, it was either he or Mary Quant. But I rather think that we all did, that afternoon in Charlotte's shop on the King's Road. We *all* invented it. Charlotte's Aunt Clare, with her penchant for Victorian lace, me with my clumsy great feet that ripped the material, Charlotte and Clover with their witches' brew of incense and jasmine tea, and Lucy with her effortless ability to wear anything and make it look like a piece of art. Later that night she would get to wear it, of course. I couldn't do that – and no one even suggested that I should. I had to stick to my little dress and to Billy's rules; it was what I had come to London to do. If he wanted to dress me like an ice-cream sundae, then he was allowed to. It didn't stop me from feeling like crying though.

Afterwards, Clover took us for a late lunch on the Fulham Road. Lucy and I wolfed down milkshakes and hamburgers, unable to hide our delight. Clover drank black coffee and ate a croissant.

'I'd like to go to Buckingham Palace now,' said Lucy. 'I think it's a sin to come to London and not look at the most famous house here.' She opened her bag and took out her guidebook. Two girls at the next table gave Lucy and her short haircut interested glances, to which Lucy appeared oblivious. 'Would you take me?'

Clover was so astonished, she actually said yes.

21

Napier House

'Holy Moses!'

Coming in from the squint-making sunlight of the July afternoon, having witnessed the red and gold ceremony of the Changing of the Guard an hour before, our eyes took several moments to adjust to the hall of Napier House. Its immediate atmosphere was one of precision and order, despite the huge number of objects on display. It was stifling hot.

'I can open the windows,' said Clover. 'But you never get cool in this place. I've been known to cook in nothing but my knickers. Highly recommended,' she said. 'Though I'm not sure that was how they went about things in my grandmother's day.'

I looked up, rather with the same instinctive action that I did in church, to find a ceiling covered in tulips.

'William Morris,' said Clover, though she needn't have told us. Lucy would have upholstered her entire life in his wallpaper if she'd had the chance.

'He's all over the shop in this house,' went on Clover. 'They went off him for a while, but came back to him in the end. Like all the best love affairs,' she added.

Lucy peered at the gold mirror hung close to a mantelpiece

covered in faded orange velvet, and saw not herself, but everyone who had walked past it one hundred years earlier.

'This is exactly how I imagined the Darlings' house in *Peter Pan*,' I said out loud, not meaning to – through Lucy I knew enough about Victorian furnishings to offer something a bit more substantial than this, but it was all I could think at that moment.

'J.M. Barrie was a friend of my great-grandmother's,' said Clover. She put her bag down over the banister. '*When Margaret grows up she will have a daughter, who is to be Peter's mother in turn; and thus it will go on, so long as children are gay and innocent and heartless.*' Clover shrugged at Lucy and me. 'Come on,' she added briskly.

For the second time in as many days, my dirty sandals looked ridiculous – this time not for the contrast of their shabby child-ishness against the restrained, clean, grown-up modernity of the Danish rug in Billy's flat, but for the exact opposite. We were back in time now – these stairs needed leather and polish, and laced boots. At once I understood Clover's choice of shoes, even on so hot an afternoon. It would be impossible to live here and not adhere to the past. As Clover swept up the stairs – past a vast display of seashells and ferns on the landing that stood in front of a selection of ostrich feathers in flirtatious vases, Lucy and I hung back a bit to observe, so as not to miss anything. As we reached the top of the landing, I tripped, almost knocking over a pair of matching statues – bejewelled African men standing on wooden bases decorated with fruit and gold leaf, smiling and holding trays.

'Help,' I muttered, holding them steady.

'Help indeed,' whispered Lucy. She stopped and peered into the faces of the men with their ivory teeth and beautiful glass eyes. 'These are Blackamoors,' she said. 'Venetian. Early nineteen-hundreds. Worth a fortune.'

'Do you think Billy would buy such things?' I asked.

'Not a chance,' said Lucy. 'They're far too exotic for him.'

Billy seemed allergic to intricate patterns – allergic to anything small. He wanted a big, white space with large, singular pieces of art that required a comment from whoever stepped into the room. Here at Napier House, all life appeared to be in the detail, the tassels, the richness of fabrics. And yet those who had created this house had wanted just what Billy wanted now: acceptance from those around them – and just a little bit of envy – they had been as modern as he in their time. The density of paintings and photographs – hung so closely that in some cases their frames touched, was almost unnerving.

'My great-grandparents could have found something to buy in the middle of a desert,' said Clover, reading my mind.

As if on cue, from inside the drawing room a grandfather clock struck five.

'How long have you . . . ?' Lucy trailed off, too busy staring to complete the sentence.

'My father ran off with an Italian countess two years after I was born, so my mother moved back here with me and my brother, James. It was where she grew up,' said Clover.

'Poor her,' I said.

'Not really. She loved my father, but really there wasn't an awful lot of space for him in her life. She had me before she was twenty. Her parents were the most important people in her world, and subsequently, in mine, too.'

Lucy touched the top of a marble bust of a woman with a bridal lace around her head, as though she expected it to come to life. Clover smiled.

'I loved my grandmother more than anyone,' she said simply.

235

'My mother's mother – Colette Napier. Once you knew her, no one else measured up. She simply stole the top place and everyone else had to fall in after her. Simple, really.'

She jerked her head towards a small pencil drawing in a black frame just above the hall table.

'There she blows,' said Clover. 'Good nose, don't you think?'

'*Your* nose,' said Lucy, peering in for a closer look. '*And* your eyes. What a beautiful woman.'

It wasn't really like Lucy to comment on female beauty of any sort – not so much because she didn't rate it, but because any mention of another girl's prettiness only ever seemed to emphasize her own.

'I'm nothing like as havoc-causing as she,' said Clover. 'But thank you very much, I appreciate the comparison. She never lost her looks with age. I have the photographs to prove it.'

'Colette Napier,' I said. 'Was she the first of your family to live here?'

'She was the second generation. But she's the reason that the house is how it is. No one could bear to change it. Most people call it sentiment, but I call it keeping history alive for the dolts in the future. And it's not easy, I can tell you. You both know that this house is existing on borrowed time. That's why you're here. They're widening the road,' she went on. 'And this row of houses stands, very inconveniently, right in their way. They want to send the bulldozers round and pay me off.'

'But they can't!' I said, appalled.

'Want to bet?' said Clover. 'They can't stop themselves. It's like an addiction for these people. Once they've started pulling stuff down, they can't stop. Everyone hates the Victorians. They're so *unfashionable*,' she added in a mocking voice. 'Such hideous taste! Such awful, cluttered rooms with terrible oppressive gloomy colours everywhere!

'Idiots,' said Lucy, glaring at Clover as though these were *her* words.

'You,' said Clover, pointing at Lucy with equal accusation in her tone, 'are a rare thing indeed, because you can see past the end of your nose. You can see past tomorrow, and past yesterday, and you know that one day someone's going to step inside this house and thank God it stayed how it was.' She waved her hand up the staircase. 'I only hope we make it through to the end of the summer. I hear the Coal Exchange won't.'

'Don't,' said Lucy. 'Just don't say it.'

'Come on,' said Clover, grinning suddenly. 'There's no time like the present. Let me show you around.'

She kicked off her heels, and in diminishing her height even further became more, rather than less, powerful. Outside I could hear the roar of another drill, but inside, at least for the moment – we were safe.

'This was my great-grandmother's study,' said Clover, pushing open a door. 'When she died, it became Colette's. I use it now. I thought for a while that perhaps I shouldn't – scared of damaging it, I suppose. But I can work here. It was designed as a room to get things done in. So I do.'

Lucy actually laughed with joy. It was her dream room. From the red and gold leaf fabric on the walls – faded over time like many of Napier House's once-bright interiors to a deep russet and bronze as though a perpetual autumn were reigning throughout the house – to the dark green doors decorated with painted foxgloves. It was perfect; a little box of Victorian Turkish delight, the like of which neither of us had ever seen. It wasn't that we hadn't been in rooms untouched for forty years – far from it. It was just that we hadn't ever seen a room and its interiors so revered. So absolutely *loved*. On the wireless the month before, I had heard talk of man flying to the moon before the decade was out – people could run a mile in four minutes and telephone America afterwards to tell their friends – and yet this room was unchanged through all of this, and in its defiance it felt strong. As our pupils dilated wildly, it felt as though Napier House was not so much a feast for the eyes, as a singular, delicious bite from something long out of reach. At the back of the room, behind the desk, was a little stained-glass window of a woman holding a violin to her chin, eyes closed in rapture. Lucy shot across to look at it.

'Let me guess,' she said. 'Francis Owen Salisbury? It's St Cecilia, of course. Patron Saint of Music.'

'Well done,' said Clover, laughing in surprise. 'Inigo says a prayer to her every time he stays here.'

Lucy looked at me. Every time his name was said, she looked at me. It was still as inconceivable to her as it was to me that he was to be staying here too.

On every surface, all over the house, were extraordinary photographs – a man in a suit holding an iguana, the wedding of a couple taking place next to an elephant, a small boy dressed in his Sunday best and standing among a crowd of hens, eating what looked like a radish – and most stare-worthy of all, a portrait of Clover, slit-eyed and grinning, crouching beside a fire wearing nothing at all but a trilby hat.

'Gosh,' I managed. 'Is that you?'

'About ten years ago,' she said. 'Don't I look evil?'

I laughed. 'You do a bit.'

'I was about to steal someone's husband,' she said. 'Look at my eyes! Not a shred of remorse there. I did that sort of thing back then,' she said. 'Morocco,' she added, as though that explained it all. She was looking out of the window now; she seemed distracted.

'There they are again,' she muttered.

'Who?' I asked.

'God knows. I've christened them the Happy Couple,' said Clover. 'They live opposite.'

I followed her gaze to the pavement below, where a young man and woman were stepping out of their front door.

'I've tried to talk to them about what's happening around here,' she said. 'They keep saying that they don't care where they are as long as they have each other and a good book. I mean *honestly*!'

I glanced down to the desk that sat in front of the window. On the top of the desk I could see a letter addressed to the Victorian Society. 'Dear Professor Pevsner,' it began. I jolted visibly at the sight of *that* name written down. Lucy followed my gaze – then looked at me.

'I'm sorry to be nosy, but are you writing a letter to Nikolaus Pevsner?' she blurted.

Clover looked surprised, then grinned.

'First, never apologize for reading other people's correspondence when they're stupid enough to leave it sitting on top of a desk in full public view. Secondly, yes I am.' She sighed. 'Four years ago, the Victorian Society was started in a house like this.'

'Linley Sambourne's place,' said Lucy quickly. It was as if she felt Clover was testing her, and that anything less than a first-class degree in Victorian Studies would be considered a terrible failure.

'That's right,' said Clover. 'The Sambournes were friends of my grandmother's. They were constantly dining together with the Great and the Good. Artists, politicians, layabouts with too much time on their hands, geniuses looking for the next play – Oscar Wilde and my grandfather were very close,' she added lightly, and dismissed the infinite number of possible questions that this statement raised with her next remark: 'I don't see why I shouldn't get Pevsner and Betjeman and all the others to do their bit and save us too. What makes my house less important than any other?'

'Of course they should save it,' said Lucy. She looked at her fingernails and frowned – at herself more than anyone else. I felt her brief stab of longing for Pa without her having to say a word. Mention of Pevsner always brought to mind Pa's face as he had handed over the Great Man's book on Cornwall to her all those years ago.

Clover shooed us upstairs.

'The drawing room,' she said, opening another door. 'It seems that in the past my family did an awful lot of stuffing their faces. There are records of thirteen-course dinners, and that's not including the fancy cakes and preserved fruit at the end. They needed somewhere comfortable to park their huge behinds once they'd finished.'

I stared at an entire wall dedicated to blue and white enamel porcelain.

'My great-grandfather's collection,' said Clover. 'This,' she went on, pulling a pink and white vase off a table and holding it up to the light, 'came from Paris in the summer of 1888. My grandmother records that it was purchased on the eighth of August.'

'Eight, eight, eighteen-eighty-eight,' said Lucy. 'I'd love to go to Paris.'

'Oh, then you shall,' said Clover immediately. 'It's the most disconcerting of places, somewhere that actually lives up to every-

240

thing written about it. Let me show your bedroom. You're at the top of the house in the old servants' quarters, I'm afraid.'

I laughed.

'I'm not joking, darling,' said Clover.

Indeed she was not. We climbed up four flights of stairs, surrounded by more walls covered with William Morris, and as we walked we caught fleeting glances of other rooms – Clover's bedroom with a huge free-standing bath in the middle of the room, another little bedroom that must have been a child's once upon a long ago, and was now stuffed full of boxes, clothes and old letters. Eventually we arrived at the top of the house. Clover pushed open another door. Despite the frugality of the room compared to the rest of the house, she had made it welcoming enough. There were two single beds ('Thank your lucky stars you're not sharing one like the chambermaids had to') and wooden floors, sparsely decorated with a couple of threadbare rugs. In the corner of the room was a little basin; on the other side, a mirror and a chest of drawers.

'I think it's a terrible error to give people too comfortable a room when they come to stay,' said Clover. 'If you do, they never leave. I learned that the hard way. Even when you're being paid, you need a break from the same faces at breakfast.'

I sat down on the bed, bouncing up and down.

'You're sleeping on one hundred and twenty years of history,' said Clover. 'So look after it, won't you?'

'Of course,' said Lucy, offended that Clover imagined for a moment that we might not. Then she couldn't help herself: 'Raoul would be bowled over,' she muttered.

'By me, or the house?' said Clover, grinning.

'Both,' said Lucy. 'He only fell in love with me because I described the interior of Bowood to him in graphic detail.'

'Lucy has a Photographic Memory for Houses,' I explained. 'Trademark.'

'Oh yes. I've heard about this from Matilda,' said Clover. I wondered what else she had heard – had Matilda told her how she and Lucy had fallen out and still hadn't stuffed everything back together yet? I doubted it. 'I imagine this place is perfectly easy to store in one's mind, but I shall test you on Digby O'Rourke's house after three glasses of whatever revolting concoction he dredges up to serve his guests tomorrow,' said Clover.

'What's his house like?' said Lucy, who always had to know everything before the event.

'Ravaged and badly kept,' she said. 'Not unlike him. He treats the place appallingly, and lives like a slut of the first order. He doesn't deserve a socking great house like that.'

'I expect he can afford not to,' said Lucy. 'His photographs are everywhere.'

'You'll work up here, too,' said Clover to Lucy. She removed a pile of old black lace from a dusty mahogany table in the corner of the room.

'Your desk,' she said. 'I'm afraid there's more to do than we can ever get done in time. I should have done all of this, years ago. There are seventeen boxes of letters and papers to go through, and we need to finish documenting every piece of furniture in the house.'

Lucy looked temporarily daunted.

'It makes a big difference to me to have someone helping,' she said. 'I expect Billy's told you you'll be paid, but I'm afraid you won't have much time to spend what you earn.'

'I'd do it for nothing,' said Lucy, 'if I could afford to,' she added hastily.

'Never do *anything* for nothing except fool around with unsuitable men,' said Clover.

Later we sat in the dining room drinking tea.

'Now listen,' said Clover, flipping open her compact and dabbing powder on her nose. 'While you're staying here, you're a member of an important and exclusive club.'

'What do you mean?' I asked, as ever full of suspicion. Lucy was so taken with Clover and Napier House, I don't think she would have cared if Clover had told us we were joining the Society of Ignorant Fools.

'It's called the Six O'Clock Club,' said Clover. 'Whatever happens during the day, you meet back here at six, in the dining room, for tea.'

'What sort of tea?' I asked.

'High,' said Clover firmly.

'You mean drugs?' said Lucy, not without a certain frisson of excitement.

'No. Good God, girl. Certainly *not*. I mean high tea, as eaten by the workers when they came home from the factories and fields. I'm not doing you thirteen courses, but what you get will fill you up.'

'Gosh. You mean, proper pies and puddings and suchlike?' I said in admiration.

'Precisely. Usually on a Friday it's fish pie followed by treacle tart.'

Lucy looked alarmed. 'I thought I might lose weight if I wasn't being stuffed every night by Imogen.'

'You'll run on adrenalin most of the time,' said Clover. 'And instructions from Madame Vernier,' she added to me.

'Who?'

'Your deportment teacher,' said Clover. She looked more than a little amused. 'Billy likes girls to be able to walk properly. He thinks it improves the voice. All his singers go to Madame.'

'It sounds rather last century,' I said.

'Nothing wrong with that,' said Clover promptly. 'Oh, and one more thing. Every time you make or receive a call, you must write down the details on the notepad beside the telephone.'

'Why?' I asked her.

'I'm compiling a history of this building so that we can look back and weep and gnash our teeth when it goes down. Part of that history includes any notable calls. It's a tradition that started when the telephone was first installed in the house, and it's not one I intend to break.'

'Not sure we're going to provide you with any notables,' I said. 'Unless Roy and Luke go on to win Wimbledon after all.'

'Well in that case I shall have to rely on Inigo and his mysterious American woman,' said Clover.

Lucy looked at me.

'Now, if you can indulge me for a moment, I'd like to show you both my egg-cup collection,' said Clover, deadly serious.

'Egg-cup collection?'

'Yes. Mostly early Georgian, but I have some wonderful later pieces too. My grandmother started it. As a little girl, she had nightmares about Humpty Dumpty and his grisly end. She claimed that she believed she could save him by collecting egg cups and spoons.'

She distracted Lucy from whatever she was thinking about by showing her things to marvel at. That was the glory of Clover. She was so unrepentantly excited about possessions, about *stuff*;

I would learn later that as far as she was concerned, physical objects healed emotional wounds. She utterly reversed Pa's lectures about material things being unimportant.

At six, we sat in the dining room and ate Clover's fish pie. It was remarkably good – the sort of thing that would have had Imogen reaching for a pen to take down the recipe. Lucy refused the treacle tart at first, but seeing me wolfing it down, changed her mind. Clover ate exactly half of what was on her plate, and talked to us about Charlotte Ferris and shopping, about Richmond Park in the autumn and how Billy had been teased when they were growing up because his mother kept his hair long.

'When does Inigo Wallace get here?' asked Lucy suddenly.

Clover laughed. 'He'll show up at Digby's party tomorrow,' she said. 'But he'll only be there in body, and very much not in spirit. When he's working, all he thinks about is when he's going to get back to the piano. You may hear him playing well into the night,' she went on. 'I find that a short, sharp bang on the door with Valentine Napier's hunting whip from the stand just outside the door usually tells him to shut up and go to bed. He has no concept of time.'

Sometimes I think about that first night at Napier House, the quiet of the drawing room after high tea, the peace of the red walls, the warmth of the night, and I think that of any of the nights that followed that summer, that would be the one that I would most like to relive. Because just a matter of hours later, we were thrown into the mayhem of modern London, all rocketing and crashing around as though the Victorians had never existed at all. Yet it was them who had put us there in the first place! Sitting in Chelsea, in Clover's Great-Great-Aunt Joanna's favourite armchair – itself a piece of art – made me realize how far from home I was, and how *little* I knew. It was as if opening up my eyes and coming to London had merely shown me how small I was. I looked at Lucy, and wondered if she felt it too.

22

Digby

We paraded in front of Clover the following afternoon, dressed in our new things.

'Sweet,' said Clover looking at me in my pink frock. 'Precisely what Billy likes his girls to wear.'

'I don't like it,' I said ungratefully.

'Why?' asked Clover patiently.

'It's scratchy,' I said, perfectly truthfully. I was agitated by the whole clothing palaver, and wished I had pressed harder for the riding habit.

'Alma would be proud,' said Lucy, in The Skirt.

'I'm too short for this,' I muttered. 'I look like a fool. I suppose there's no point in trying to compete with you,' I said. I didn't want to sound petulant, but it was how I felt. Lucy had come to London to *work*, not to wear the most fashionable new clothes and eclipse me completely. She did enough of that back at home.

'Billy likes his girls to look like girls,' said Clover. 'I'm just doing my job.'

She looked at me, registering my expression.

'All right,' she sighed. 'If you want, you can take your denims with you in a bag. If you're still at the party at midnight, I give you my permission to change. By that time everyone will be too drunk to notice or care.'

I ran upstairs, but couldn't find my denims; I had packed my jodhpurs by mistake. Still, even they were preferable to the get-up I was wearing now. I shoved them and a rather grubby white lace blouse into the bottom of the carpet bag that Clover appeared to haul with her everywhere she went.

The door to Napier House slammed behind us.

'Don't be alarmed by the state of some of Digby's acquaintances,' said Clover. 'He invites the most awful people to stay. At the moment he's got a tramp called Casper living in the basement. At least, he *looks* like a tramp, but like all the drunkest and most disturbed men in London, I think he's probably O.E.'

'O.E?'

'Old Etonian.' She grinned at me. 'As a result of a grim childhood, Digby needs to be looked after, but never given *too* much attention or he becomes ridiculous.' She lit another cigarette. 'Unfortunately he's so successful that no one can stop telling him how wonderful he is, so he's ridiculous *all* of the time.'

'You talk about him as if he's a child,' observed Lucy.

'He *is* a child,' said Clover. 'What's that guff from Corinthians they always read at weddings?'

'Chapter 13,' I said promptly.

Walking arm in arm, Lucy and I quoted it together:

> '*When I was a child,*
> *I spake like a child,*
> *I understood as a child,*
> *I thought as a child . . .*'

We stepped up to the front door of Digby's house and I shivered with nerves.

> '*But when I became a man*
> *I put away childish things—*'

'That's just it,' interrupted Clover, ringing the bell. 'He never
did put away his childish things. The camera's just another toy
to him.'

'*For now we see through a glass, darkly,*' I proclaimed.

The door opened.

'*But then,*' continued Lucy in little more than a whisper, '*face
to face.*'

She looked at me, squeezed my hand, and we breathed in as
the door opened.

'You've forgotten to get dressed,' he said. 'Very clever of you.'

He looked Lucy's legs up and down.

Lucy gasped in mock horror, clasping her hand over her
mouth. 'I *knew* I'd left something behind.'

'She's married,' said Clover crisply, kissing Digby on both
cheeks and pushing past him into the hall.

'So am I,' said Digby O'Rourke. 'To my art.'

He gave a low bow.

'Cherry Merrywell and Lucy Jupp,' said Clover, waving a hand
towards us.

'*Cherry Merrywell?* Come on, baby doll. You're not serious, are
you?' he drawled.

'Deadly serious,' snapped Clover.

She pushed past him into the house, and, shaking off her coat,
was immediately jumped upon by a man in a motorcycle outfit

and bare feet. In the far corner of the hall, two men dressed as red Indians were wrestling each other to the ground, helpless with laughter. Digby laughed, and looked at me for the first time.

'You're Billy's latest?' he asked, lighting a cigarette.

'I – uh . . .'

He looked me up and down as though I were a horse he was considering buying.

'Clover has a habit of depositing the most interesting-looking girls into the most uneventful clothes,' he said. Struggling to imagine whether this was a compliment or insult, I just stood there, staring at him like a prize imbecile.

'Still, I suppose Billy-boy's at the helm, isn't he? She has no choice, and therefore you don't either. Well, come in, then,' he said.

Conker-brown hair, odd socks and flinty green eyes like the pieces of glass that we used to find on the beach at St Ives after the summer, Digby was two parts Lost Boy to one part Captain Hook. The chaos that Clover had spoken of was so apparent, that even within thirty seconds of meeting him, it felt as though someone had slipped the floor at a forty-degree angle, turned up the volume on the record player, poured some lethal potion into our drinks and shoved us on a creaky stage to perform a monologue without giving us time to learn our lines. Looking back, I suppose that's a fair description of what *was* actually happening. He was short and stocky, lightly freckled and even-featured, resolutely *not* arrestingly pretty like Inigo, but there was a wildness to Digby that I had seen in my brother George before he had decided to follow Pa into the Church – repent or burn out. Digby was still burning.

Usually Lucy didn't entertain the idea of talking to men who were so much shorter than her, but for Digby it appeared she was going to make an exception. He led us through the hall, and on the way Lucy couldn't resist doing what she always did.

She glanced up the stairs. 'Four bedrooms?'

Digby's eyes gleamed at her. 'Five if you count the guest bathroom,' he said. 'Enough people have collapsed in there overnight to merit its inclusion, I think.'

'Kitchen in the basement?'

Digby laughed. 'I've never seen an estate agent as attractive as you.'

Here we go, I thought.

Lucy laughed and pushed her hand through her short hair. 'I'm sorry,' she said. 'I just can't help myself.'

'She has a Photographic Memory for Houses,' I said. 'Trademark.'

Digby looked alarmed. 'Photographic memory? Christ, rather you than me. I have an amazing talent for blocking out most of what happens to me on a daily basis.'

'How come everyone in this city has so much money?' demanded Lucy.

'They don't,' said Digby quickly.

'You and Clover both live in spectacular houses,' said my sister, without a shred of embarrassment.

'Of course. But that's nothing to do with us. We inherited them. Clover's doing her best to keep hers in amber, I'm doing my best to blow this place out in style. You want real Chelsea, doll? You need to visit my friend Elmo's flat down the road.'

'Elmo?'

'Oh, just call him Brian,' said Digby dismissively. He looked at me. 'I heard you sang at the Wedding of the Year.'

'In church,' I said. 'It was nothing, I was just doing a favour for Matilda.'

251

Digby laughed very loudly.

'Billy's gonna make a record with you?'

'Yes. Inigo Wallace is writing it.'

Digby grinned. 'Bloody hell. See you in the pop charts, baby.'

I laughed with the shocking realization that he was serious! And never before had the word that I had previously associated with my younger brothers making each other cry sounded so sweet. *Baby.* Suddenly I was Claudette and Peggy Sue and Little Susie rolled into one, and I might as well have injected liquid delight straight into my bloodstream.

Pulling myself together, I opened my mouth to say something about how the pop charts were probably too full already to accommodate little old me, but Digby had been grabbed by a girl with huge brown eyes and corkscrews of chestnut hair, wearing a tweed twinset and skirt. She collapsed into his arms, almost in tears. She could have been heard back at Napier House.

'All they gave me was three pages of editorial,' she was wailing. 'And the *pictures* they chose! You know, they picked the one of me wearing that awful pink and yellow blouse that, that . . . you know –' she gesticulated frantically around her chest.

'The blouse that squashed your tits?' asked Digby gravely.

'Yes!'

'With the mauve trousers that widened your hips?'

She took a gulp of her drink, grimaced and continued. 'And to *think*! We took all those shots outside in the park – with – with the ducks and the round pond and that homeless man with the dog and hardly any slap and everything – and you said they'd take *them*! You said *they* should make the cover!' Her voice was near hysterical now. 'But they were awful! Everyone at *Vogue* said so! They think you must have been drinking to have photographed me in that way!'

Digby appeared totally unfazed.

'They were great pictures,' he said unrepentantly. 'Listen, doll. That lot wouldn't know real style if it ran round their bloody office covered in red paint and bit them on the arse. All you need to know is that I was right. They *were* the best shots. If they don't choose to use them, that's their problem.'

'But it's *my* problem too! All I wanted was the bloody cover! I told Mum and Dad and everything! I wish you hadn't refused to photograph me in the lime-green and fawn tea-dress.'

'Believe me, you'll thank me for that in ten years' time.'

'But – but – but!' She was making so much noise now, it was impossible to pretend we couldn't hear. Thoroughly enjoying herself, Pa would have said.

Raising his eyes to heaven, Digby put his arm around her.

'I hear you, baby,' he said. 'The rest of the world can too,' he added gently.

'I just hoped for so much.'

'I know. And those bastards promised you the cover. I'll have words with Nicky,' said Digby, finally saying what she wanted to hear, more – I felt – to get rid of her than anything else. She fell into his arms again. Over her shoulder, Digby rolled his eyes at me and winked. I stepped back in surprise, and landed on Clover's foot.

'Oh gosh, I am sorry,' I gasped.

'Here,' Clover hissed, taking a bar of Cadbury's Dairy Milk out of its wrapper.

'Digby thinks that when you have a house this wonderful you don't have to feed anyone. He's wrong. Come on,' she added, handing a square to me. 'Keep your feet to yourself and suck on it when we walk in. It will enhance your cheekbones.'

The sprung wooden floor of the ballroom at Cheyne Walk

was almost entirely covered in what were probably priceless rugs, punctured with huge cigarette burns that somehow seemed only to add to their appeal. For a moment we stood in the doorway, out of anyone's sight, and watched everything. The curtains were closed, in what must have been an act of defiance against the summer, casting everyone's face in orange half-light. It had none of the efficient, self-conscious modernity of Billy's place. This house was all about the night-time, and the romance of ages past. It reminded me of Trellanack; the very air itself felt infected with the same effortless beauty, the same uniquely English magic. I wouldn't have been surprised to see owls flying around the room, cauldrons bubbling in the kitchen. Like Trellanack, it was alive. This was the centre of the universe, I thought; sparks seemed to be flying off the walls.

'Come on,' said Clover.

My ears were all of a sudden filled with the deafening din of the party. It was as thunderous and alarming as being pulled under by a wave and swallowing a mouthful of seawater. I gasped for air, and Clover looked around at us.

'Watch them looking at The Skirt,' she said happily. 'I hope Charlotte decides to show up – she can drown in the reflected glory. Come on. We're going to walk over to Billy.'

'Where is he?' I asked her. I felt I needed Billy all of a sudden, needed some sort of validation for being here.

'He's over there, in the corner of the room.'

'Can't see him,' said Lucy.

'Neither can I, but I know it's where he'll be,' said Clover.

So we walked. It was like that moment in *Gigi* where everyone goes silent for a minute, trying to work out who's turned up with Maurice Chevalier at Maxim's. It was as if I were viewing another species – these London creatures were tiny and skinny, eyelashes stiff with mascara, long fingers given purpose by cigarettes and cocktail glasses. There were plenty of girls dressed like me but no one, however alternative they looked, was wearing anything like my sister. Billy was exactly where Clover said he would be, laughing with two wild-haired boys in matching suits, smoking thin cigars.

'Theo, Daniel – this is Cherry Merrywell,' said Billy, 'and her sister, Lucy. They come from Cornwall.'

'Hellfire! What kind of a name is Cherry Merrywell?' asked Daniel.

He was distracted from my name by Lucy's get-up.

'Where did you get your skirt?' he asked her. 'Or lack thereof?' he added quickly.

'Cee-Cee's,' said Lucy.

'It was made for her,' interrupted Billy.

'I can see that,' said Theo.

Billy lit a cigarette and handed it to Lucy, then lit another for me. Then he walked off. But it was all he needed to do. Theo got the picture all right. That tiny gesture that lasted no more than a few seconds – it made everything quite clear.

It didn't matter if we were singers, dancers – gosh, girls selling matches on the street corner – the point was, we were *somebodies* suddenly. Billy's name didn't just open doors, it held them open for you when you were still half a mile down the corridor. Yet it was Lucy who still had the power. *She* was the one people wanted to talk to.

'What are you doing in London?' Theo asked her.

'Tara – I mean, *Cherry* – is making a record with Billy.' Sweetly, she directed the attention to me, which was embarrassing rather than helpful.

'Nice work,' sighed Theo. 'You must be good.' He turned to Lucy. 'You're a singer too?' he asked hopefully.

'Gosh, no. I'm working for Clover Napier,' said Lucy. 'We're trying to save her house, or at the very least, catalogue its existence into some sort of order.'

Theo looked horrified.

'You *like* that sort of thing?'

'You *don't?*' grinned Lucy.

'I went to Napier House last year, for one of Clover's extraordinary dinner parties,' said Theo. 'I swear to God the place is haunted. When I went to the bathroom, I felt I was being watched.'

'That's because you *were* being watched, darling,' said Daniel. 'You know perfectly well that Margot and Clive mistrust you after what happened in Puerto Banus.'

Suddenly, Theo's face fell.

'Bloody hell!' he whispered, handing his cigar to Daniel and rolling up his sleeves. 'That ghastly West Highland of Jennifer's is pissing on my coat! I knew it was a mistake leaving it unmanned. *Yves Saint Laurent!*' he cried, raising his fist as if rallying for battle, and shooting across the room, elbowing people out of the way. Daniel gasped, clapped his hand to his mouth and hurried after him.

Lucy and I looked at each other incredulously.

'I've always wanted to know whether men were as silly in London as they are at home, and now I know the answer,' she said.

'Do you wish Raoul was here?'

'With his leg in plaster? Certainly *not.*'

'I didn't mean that. Do you *miss* him?'

Lucy looked infuriated.

'Can't you stop for a moment?' she demanded. 'Perhaps all this has happened for a reason. Napier House and coming up

256

here, and everything . . .' She glared at me, as though she had said too much.

'What do you mean, *a reason*?' I asked her.

Lucy was saved replying by a man with a python around his chest filling up our glasses. I nearly leapt out of my skin.

'Oh don't be frightened,' he said in a heavy French accent. 'This is Bernie. She never 'urt anyone, even if she look like she might.'

I walked away from Lucy and the snake, fighting a terrible urge to cry. I would go out, I decided. Out into the London night. No one would notice, in any case. I stepped into the hall, poised to fling open the front door, when Digby appeared and spoke to me for the second time.

'You're very young to be prancing around at night on your own,' he said, handing me a full cocktail glass. 'How old are you anyway? Nineteen? Twenty?'

'Seventeen.'

He whistled. 'Billy's got a nerve, I must say.'

'I don't know what you mean.'

He looked at me, suddenly serious.

'Where are you going? You can't leave so soon.'

'Oh, I'm not leaving,' I said. 'I'm going to buy some cigarettes.'

'Good idea. I'm coming with you.'

I laughed, amazed.

'Let me just grab a coat—'

'I didn't mean you should come—'

But there was no stopping him – that was obvious. He shrugged on a long bright pink dress coat in shot silk.

'Is that yours?' I asked him stupidly.

'Course not,' he said, checking his reflection in the mirror and running his fingers through his hair. 'Come on.'

He snatched a tartan travelling rug from under a pile of shoes beside the stairs. I took a big gulp of the cocktail which tasted of orange juice with peculiar undertones of leather, and we stumbled out of Cheyne Walk and into the night. Digby walked fast.

'Diorissimo,' he said, pulling out a small bottle of scent from the pocket of the mystery coat. 'And a shopping list,' he added. 'I was under the impression they only existed in *Coronation Street*.'

'My sister Imogen can't go through a day without writing one.'

'Toothpaste, Pond's face cream, nail-varnish remover . . .' He laughed and sniffed the scent bottle.

'Kate Wentworth,' he said without hesitation. 'I shot her last week for the *Tatler* – some crap about people who are equally at home with city and village life, which was a bloody joke as Kate Wentworth's about as much as part of the country-side as that fucking ridiculous crane on top of that thing they're calling the Post Office Tower.' He looked at me. 'You know it's nearly taller than St Paul's now? London will eat itself, it really will. Not that I care as long as I'm the one taking the pictures.'

'My brother-in-law came to London last year to protest about them taking down the arch at Euston,' I said proudly.

'Good for him. How fucking pointless. Come on, we'll walk to the bridge.'

The pink coat looked absurd, especially when the person inside it was speaking with the sort of accent that made the Artful Dodger sound like the Prince Regent, yet the whole get-up gave Digby a strange, menacing charm. I felt suddenly glad he was with me. He felt strong, like London personified. He snapped his eyes away from mine and walked on.

'I hate giving parties,' he said. 'But always forget that I hate it, so end up giving them again and again.'

'If I lived in a house like you do, I'd feel guilty if I wasn't sharing it with everyone I knew.'

'That would be one thing. It's when it's full of people I *don't* know that it becomes a bloody pain in the neck.'

'I just followed Billy here,' I said.

'In love with him, I suppose,' said Digby, yawning.

'Don't be daft,' I said, nettled. 'He's just got married.'

Digby snorted. 'You know he dyes his eyelashes?'

'You can talk! You're wearing a girl's coat!'

Digby posed, hip jutting out towards me. 'To great effect, don't you think, Miss Merrywell?'

'Not from where I'm standing.'

Nerves were making me jittery and outspoken, just as they had in the old days when I had been caught stealing other people's ponies. Digby just laughed.

We walked in silence for some time, and I thought how odd it was to walk next to a boy who didn't make me feel small, dwarfed, and I liked the feeling more than I had thought I would.

'These shoes,' I said through gritted teeth. 'They're Clover's and they're too small. They're giving me blisters.'

'Take them off then,' said Digby.

So I took them off, and Digby wrapped them up in the travelling rug and threw them over his shoulder. He kicked his heels up like Dick Whittington and my bare feet padded along the pavement, which felt forbidden and was probably the best way possible of catching some rare waterborne disease, but I didn't care – nothing could have been as contagious as London that night. What I hadn't ever bargained for was London's prettiness. Albert Bridge stretched out before us like the backdrop for a Mabel Lucie Attwell illustration – surely there were fairies and imps dancing in the glow of the street lamps?

'Oh, London,' I said breathlessly, 'to think you've been here all this time and I never realized how lovely you are.'

'It's not really London, baby,' said Digby kindly. 'It's Chelsea. But take this image back home with you if you like. It's prettier than the underside of the East End.'

'Is that where you come from?'

He nodded. 'My dad's still there, working his arse off in Hoxton.'

'What does your father do?' I asked, hearing myself speaking like a debutante.

'He sells carpets. He thinks I'm a posh git now that I'm here.'

I laughed. No one could have sounded less of a posh git than Digby.

'*My* dad works his arse off too,' I said, blushing at the phrase, and feeling the thrill of echoing Digby's words stretch from my fingertips right through to my toes. 'And he's as stubborn as a donkey.'

'So where did you grow up?' he asked me.

I pictured the Rectory, crouching staunchly at the end of the village, blithely ignoring the relentless pull of time and progress, indifferent to the passing years.

'Cornwall,' I said. 'My father's a vicar, so we live at the Rectory.'

'A *vicar*,' mused Digby as though he had never heard the word before. 'The Rectory. I wish I was God-fearing.'

'I think God probably fears Pa more than the other way round.'

'Must be nice though. Knowing your boundaries. Living life by the Book and all that. Do *you* believe?' he asked me.

'I believe in my father,' I said. 'So yes.'

'I don't know,' said Digby. 'I'm not sure that's a good enough reason.'

'It is,' I said shortly. 'It always has been. What about your mother?' I asked him.

Digby stopped walking.

'Complicated,' said Digby. He hesitated, then said: 'She was killed, falling out of a window. She was twenty-four. I was five. Four storeys she fell.'

'*Fell?*'

'She was pushed.'

'*Pushed?*'

'It was my Dad's best mate, bloke called Alan James. He worked with Dad, selling threads. Well, Mum was knocking it off with him. I was only five but I bloody knew it − in the way that you always know everything you need to know when you're small and ignored most of the time. They had a fight, he shoved her, she fell through the open window. I was there, and I saw it happen. But it was my word against that of a grown man. He made out she'd topped 'erself. Got away with it. But I knew it was him. The bastard.' He shivered. 'Dad was so bad after she died, he couldn't work for two years. Just sat in the pub, drinking into oblivion and talking about Mum like she was watching over him all the time. My Auntie Jackie took me away from him after six months. Said the pub was no place for a small boy which was probably just as well. I could pour a pint by my sixth birthday and lived on crumbs from crisp packets.'

'Where did she take you?'

Digby grinned.

'Auntie Jackie worked for an old lady in Cheyne Walk. Old lady dies, Auntie Jackie inherits the place and everything in it. She wants me to stay, but I run back to my dad, and he's so happy I'm back he gives me an old camera for my ninth birthday. Ten years later, when I'm nineteen and trying to convince the world that I know what I'm doing with a fucking tripod and lens – Auntie Jackie dies. *I* inherit the house in bloody Chelsea. Some kind of strange justice, don't you think?'

'I'm so sorry,' I said. I felt unhinged by the story, half dizzied by it. 'My mother's dead too.'

He looked at me, and it seemed he was searching for something in my face that night give him a clue as to how we got to be where we were: slightly drunk, motherless strangers on Chelsea Embankment, listening to each other's stories.

'I don't know why I'm telling you all this stuff,' he said.

'Oh, don't worry,' I said quickly. 'Apparently I've got one of those faces that people can't help revealing their secrets to. My brother George says it's a great gift.'

'I can't stand people letting it all hang out. Keep it inside, where it's safe. I hate other people's dramas,' said Digby fiercely. 'Had enough of my own.' He laughed and pulled up the sleeve of the pink coat to reveal a scar above his left wrist.

'Auntie Jackie had a temper,' he said softly. 'She tied me up to the bathroom door one afternoon, and left me there while she went shopping for hats.'

I stared at him. 'That's *terrible.*'

He looked angry for a moment, then pushed his hands through his hair again.

262

'Not really,' he said. 'I mean, it was terrible at the time, but what of it now? What doesn't kill you makes you stronger, according to everyone I know who went to boarding school.' He glared at me. 'You know I never talk about any of this shit. Not to anyone. You want more stories, you'll have to ask the house. Houses always know the truth.'

Digby's face had altered completely, and he looked quite worn-out by the confessions of the last few minutes. He pulled on his cigarette and his green eyes became swampy; a cloud was passing over the rock-pools and I could feel him trying to get himself together again.

'The Rectory's probably bored senseless with all of us,' I said, gabbling now to block out the oddness I was feeling. 'I expect it's longing for some nice, sensible family to take it on. If I was a house like ours, I'd employ a few decent ghosts to whip us all out of the place as soon as possible, although even *that* wouldn't work. Roy and Luke would adore to live in a haunted house, and Imogen would most likely feel sorry for them and want to sit down and discuss how they died. Florence is never scared of anything, and Lucy would probably seduce all the handsome ones. Errant Jack wouldn't care one way or the other, and George would spend his whole time trying to exorcize them with verses from the book of Job.'

'Bloody hell! How many of you are there?'

'Eight children, if you can call us that.'

'Christ! And your father's a vicar!'

'I know.'

'I was at school with a vicar's niece. She was the first girl in our class to show me her tits. Susie Farriner. Still see 'er when I go home.'

'I imagine that "see" is a euphemism,' I said primly.

Digby grinned at me. 'You don't look like the type to flash your chest around without due cause.'

'I know,' I said despondently. 'I heard Inigo Wallace telling Billy that I looked like the sort of girl who wouldn't know what to do if a man so much as asked me out to tea.'

Digby's lips twitched – I could see he wanted to laugh.

'He doesn't know me,' I said savagely. 'Not one bit.'

'I'd take what he said as a compliment,' said Digby. 'He's said much worse stuff about me.'

I looked at him in surprise. 'Why?'

He didn't offer me an answer, but pulled a packet of Murray Mints from the back of his denims and offered me one. For a minute we sat and crunched, saying very little. Nothing ventured, nothing gained, I thought. Digby's strange stories of murder in the East End, and the irritation I felt towards Inigo Wallace had fused with the intoxicating *Carpe Diem* sentiment that had stalked me since Ma had died. A need to do something with this simple situation overwhelmed me. He was a boy, I was a girl.

'Would you kiss me?' I asked Digby quickly.

'What's that?' He turned to me and laughed, as though he had misheard.

'Would you kiss me?' I repeated.

I felt my heart beating into my mouth; I wanted to spit it out. Before I could think any more, I leaned forward, and touched my lips on to his. Digby looked at me; our foreheads were touching.

'Sweet thing,' he whispered. 'You know, I'm not very highly recommended as the ideal starter pack.'

'I don't care,' I said.

Pulling me into his arms, Digby made it perfectly clear that he didn't either. Half terrified, half delighted, my hands crept cautiously around his neck. He felt so strong – I was aware of the fact that he could overpower me within seconds if he chose to, and I had only just *met* him. Imogen would be horrified, I found myself thinking, then pushed her quickly out of my head again.

Digby knew what he was doing, that was certain. There was none of the inept clumsiness I would have expected from Lucy's tales of kissing the village boys. I had gone straight to the best, which was just as well, as I didn't have the slightest clue what came next. Drunk on my own champagne and my own cleverness, Digby could have taken full advantage of me then and there, but he was too astute for that.

'We should go back,' he said at last, pushing the hair out of my face. 'I don't want you to wake up tomorrow morning and regret anything.'

'Oh I couldn't regret it,' I said.

I looked into his green eyes, and was suddenly struck with remorse and shame. 'I'm very sorry,' I muttered. 'I shouldn't have asked you to kiss me.' I hung my head, suddenly seeing Pa's appalled face.

'Cherry Merrywell,' said Digby. 'You're not from round here, are you?'

I looked up at him, suddenly shy. He was used to models and actresses and society beauties. Who on earth was little Tara Jupp to someone like Digby O'Rourke?

'What you just did requires no apology,' he said, taking my hand in his and leading me back in the direction of his house rather quickly. 'And it has the advantage of being something that will irritate the hell out of Inigo Wallace,' he added. 'He hates being proved wrong.'

We laughed, from where we were standing, all the way back along the river to Digby's house.

23

Sit Down, You're Rockin' the Boat

We walked through the front door, with his hand still touching mine. We had been gone just over and hour, but it could have been three weeks. Once inside, Digby picked up a half-full champagne glass and handed it back to me. It was slightly warm.

'You better go and find your sister,' he said softly.

He lit a cigarette. At that moment, Inigo came into the hall. He stopped when he saw us.

'We popped out for some smokes,' I said defensively.

'Popped is hardly the word. You've been gone nearly an hour.'

Shrugging off Kate Wentworth's coat, Digby flung it back on to the pile.

'We lost track of time,' he said.

'Evidently.'

Digby grinned at me, lit me a cigarette and blew me a kiss before sauntering off.

'We didn't come here so that you could slope off with him,' said Inigo.

'I would have thought you'd approve,' I said. 'After all, Billy wants me to be associated with the great and the good.'

'Not *that* associated,' said Inigo. 'And whether Digby O'Rourke is either great *or* good is up for serious debate.'

'Billy says he's a genius.'

'If you believe that shoving a camera in someone's face and pressing a button constitutes art.'

'It's no more or less art than writing fifty identical three-chord songs about teenage love.'

For a strange moment I thought Inigo was going to throw something at me. Instead he laughed.

'Touché,' he said.

He took the champagne glass out of my hands and finished the rest of it himself.

'Hey! What did you do that for?'

'You've got to sing tomorrow. You shouldn't be drinking any more tonight.'

'Neither should you,' I said.

'I'm a good drunk. I don't shout at people, or try to kiss girls, or fall over.'

'What's the point in doing it then?'

'Takes the edge off.'

'Edge off what?'

'London.'

The doorbell rang behind us and we both jumped. For a second we stared at each other, as we had done back in the kitchen at Milton Magna Hall in 1956, when Inigo was the fifteen-year-old boy about to be taken out to buy shoes with his mother. I had seen that look on his face then, and it was there again now – that flicker of something – hope, fear – I couldn't place it then and I couldn't now. Not for the first time, I noticed the black rings under his eyes. His thin black jersey had slipped, revealing a jutting shoulder blade. He reached out and opened the door.

It was Matilda.

'Inigo!' She fell into his arms. 'Billy wanted me to stay in bed, but I couldn't *bear* to be away from everyone.'

Inigo looked startled by her, as though she were the last person in the world he had expected.

'Shouldn't you be resting?' he asked her. 'I thought most women seized the opportunity to throw in the towel once they're six months gone.'

'Gone where?' asked Matilda, confused.

She saw me and looked momentarily startled.

'I can't get used to seeing you in London, Tara,' she said. 'It's too peculiar and wonderful for words.' She smiled at me in delight, as though I had appeared by nothing less than magic. 'Where's Lucy?' she asked, as I knew she would.

'I was just going to find her,' I said.

'I'll come with you. And have you met Digby yet?'

'I have.'

'Oh, good. Billy *will* be pleased,' said Matilda, beaming at Inigo and me.

'Won't he just?' muttered Inigo.

She linked her arm in mine and we walked out of the hall and into the chaos of the ballroom. I wanted to find Digby again, but I was still floating on the power of the fact that he had kissed me. Dazed, I stood next to Matilda as people gravitated towards her, in that odd way that people do towards famous folk – with fake sincerity and badly disguised self-consciousness. No, perhaps that's unfair; there were plenty of people in that room who were perfectly sincere about their admiration for Matilda's dress, her shoes, her latest interview – but that wasn't *her* at all. They saw bits of her that had never even existed before. It was like they were admiring the new wing on a classical building – it seemed odd to me, who had only ever known what was there before. I wanted to go back to the kitchen to see if Digby was there, but she clutched at my arm.

'Don't keep walking *off*, Tara,' she hissed. 'Come with me and we'll get another drink. Lucy needs one too.'

'I don't even know where Lucy is.'

'Wherever she is, she needs another drink.'

We searched for my sister for a while before we found her kneeling on the floor flipping through records.

'I was wondering if you'd been sucked into a vortex,' said Lucy lightly. She handed a Humphrey Lyttelton record to the boy playing the music. 'I've been up to the top floor,' she said in an undertone. 'Couldn't move for the junk. You know Whistler and Emmeline Pankhurst used to live on this road? Not together,' she added hastily. 'Although that *would* have been something. We really should visit the Chelsea Physic Garden, by the way—'

'Girls, let me introduce you to someone,' interrupted Matilda. Her eyes had lighted upon a boy standing on the far side of the room, wearing – despite the heat – a black sweater with a high neck, black denims and hair as blond as my little brothers'. He was talking at great speed to the girl next to him, who leaned in to listen as though what he was saying was of the utmost importance.

'Who's he?' I asked.

'A friend of Digby's,' said Matilda. 'Calls himself Elmo, but really he's just plain Brian. He plays the harmonica – lives down the road, in total and complete mayhem,' she added, as though her own existence was one of quiet order and restraint.

As if drawn to the three of us, Brian, or Elmo, or whatever his name was, looked over suddenly, and seemed to do a double take.

'He'll come over,' said Matilda. 'He'll try and get you to go back to his house with him,' she said to Lucy quickly. 'You mustn't, of course. But he's rather dreamy, I think. You should just *hear* him—'

'I'm married,' said Lucy simply.

'But Raoul doesn't deserve you,' said Matilda. She actually tugged at Lucy's sleeve. 'He hasn't looked after you like he should have.'

'What do you know?' Lucy laughed out loud in surprise.

Matilda leaned forward and spilt some of her cocktail.

'You're drunk,' said Lucy.

Matilda looked confused. Her lipstick was starting to smudge and she rubbed her eyes suddenly, encouraging a great blob of mascara to streak under her eye.

'That little world in Cornwall,' said Matilda. 'You were meant for more than that. You could have had anything – anyone.' Matilda sloshed her glass towards the crowd. 'You still could,' she added.

Lucy walked off, leaving us staring after her.

'Raoul used to say that he loved big English houses because they were all about fantasy,' said Matilda, watching her. I don't think that she was really speaking to me at all. 'You know – design your own castle of destiny. That was what he liked about Capability Brown.'

'You remember all that stuff,' I said. 'You remember everything he said.'

'No,' said Matilda. 'I remember everything *she* said.'

A second later the model with the tweed skirt whom Digby had placated at the beginning of the night, took the plunge and came up to us, face flushed, claiming to have shared the Dior catwalk with Matilda the previous spring. Gratefully, Matilda fell into conversation about Paris and Milan and didn't so-and-so look awful in those shots for French *Vogue*, etc. And all the while, she was being looked at. I don't mean stared at, because people were far too cool to be that obvious, but she was being glanced at, sidelong, which was, I decided, the fate of the famous. Famous – Matilda Bright was famous. And to think she used to cry when she was plonked on a pony! I simply couldn't get used to it at all. It had been one thing seeing her in magazines, another thing to see her getting married, but it was quite another seeing it really, *really* happening in front of my very eyes. People we had grown up with weren't supposed to end up like this. It simply didn't happen.

The party had scattered into pieces now – little groups of people were all over the house, standing on the landing between staircases, sitting in a circle around the kitchen table. I wanted to take off my shoes again, but suddenly recalled Clover's promise. I glanced at a plastic Mickey Mouse alarm clock on the red and white marble fireplace. *Five to midnight!* Hurrying into the hall, I found Clover's bag under a pile of discarded coats. Pulling out my jodhpurs and blouse, I shot upstairs to find somewhere to change.

There was someone – or perhaps more than one person – in the upstairs bathroom. I pushed open the door next to it, revealing a blue and white papered bedroom in a breathtaking state of disorder. I couldn't even see the bed for the stacks of clothes, records, magazines, cigarette packets, books and unopened letters. The window was wide open, yet the night was so still it didn't appear to offer any relief from the heat at all. I steadied myself by leaning against a huge wardrobe and taking three deep breaths. Thanks to the champagne and the general sense of altered reality pervading that night, I couldn't get my dress off very quickly, and looking in the filthy mirror at my reflection as I fiddled with the zip only confused me further. Eventually I prised myself free and stood dressed in nothing more than Clover's push-up bra and my knickers and stockings. It was so hot, and the relief of being out of that itchy dress was so intense, that I stood for a moment by the window, my eyes closed.

I don't suppose that I locked the door to change out of my clothes, because I never did at home, and I don't think there *was* a lock on Digby's bedroom door, and more to the point, even if there *had* been a key, I was too drunk to have thought about using it. When I heard the sound of the door handle turning, I darted behind the curtain, just like Roy and Luke liked to do at home when exciting people like Errant Jack and his wayward French girls entered the Rectory. Hidden, I held my breath. Digby lit a cigarette, lay down on the side of the bed not occupied by clutter, and – to my astonishment, opened *The Times*. Stretching under the bed, he retrieved a pencil, turned to the back page and started doing the crossword.

I could have been there five minutes, I could have been there for twenty. Time itself seemed irrelevant – what was possessing me was the complex question of how to extricate myself from this situation with something resembling my dignity intact. On the one hand I imagined that he wouldn't remain up here very long – he was the host, after all – yet on the other hand, the brief amount of time I had spent with him had alerted me to the fact that Digby didn't operate according to normal rules. He stretched out his legs, opened a bottle of something indistinguishable beside his bed and poured several inches into a tooth-mug. He appeared to be settling in for some time; there was nothing for it. I would have to reveal myself.

Without allowing myself to think further ahead than the next few seconds – I stuck my head out from the curtain and waited. Still he didn't appear to notice. Keeping the material wrapped around me, I coughed.

Digby looked up at me and grinned, the cigarette clamped to his bottom lip.

'I was wondering when you were going to get bored behind there,' he said.

'What do you mean?' I asked him ludicrously.

'I saw you coming upstairs. I followed you in here.'

'Why?' I asked.

'It's my bedroom. Don't you think I should be the one asking the questions?'

'That's not fair!' I said weakly. 'Could you pass me my clothes, please?'

He looked at the dress, discarded on the floor.

'Quick work,' he said. 'Who else is in here? Please, dear God, not Casper—'

'No!' I squeaked. 'Clover gave me permission to change at midnight. I can't *stand* that dress.' I kicked it with my bare foot.

'That makes two of us,' said Digby. 'Billy likes girls dressed like their mothers. Or more specifically, like *his* mother. If ever there was a candidate for Dr Henry Wright's investigation, it's him.'

I looked at him blankly.

'It's all right,' he said. 'Get changed. I won't look.'

Half a minute later I was dressed. I stood beside the bed, trying to look defiant. Digby narrowed his eyes.

'You're much improved,' he said. 'Where's your horse?'

'Never had one,' I said truthfully.

He stretched out a hand and touched the ripped material of my blouse.

274

'You're like Cinderella in reverse.'

'I don't want to be like everyone else,' I said. What a bloody asinine remark – but there it was, and I couldn't take it back now.

'Here –' Digby handed me the tooth-mug – 'get that down you.'

I pulled a face. 'I'm certain I've had enough of whatever that is.'

'No, you haven't,' said Digby. 'I'm about to ask you to do something that will require at least another three shots.'

'What is it?' I demanded.

He climbed off the bed and took my hand.

'Come on,' he said. 'Let's see if you're as good as Billy Laurier says you are.'

'What are you talking about?'

'The voice, baby. That's what you're all about, isn't it?'

I looked at him and laughed. 'You want me to sing? *Now?*'

'But of course!' He took my hand and led me downstairs. Clover was standing in the hall, holding court with three girls with wafer-thin smiles and lines of pearls around their white necks.

'Why did you chuck Henry out?' one of them was asking. Clover took a big gulp of wine.

'Henry told me that my desire to hold on to Napier and preserve its contents was based on insecurity stemming from a childhood without maternal love. I mean, the man charges people vast sums of money to listen to this twaddle. I said to him, "My dear man – couldn't my need to keep the house stem from the very simple desire not to be homeless?" He's a *ridiculous* person.'

Clover stopped short when she saw Digby and me. She looked at me and my get-up, and shook her head.

'You can take the girl out of the Pony Club, but you can't take the Pony Club out of the girl.' She sighed.

'It's midnight,' I said. 'You said I could change at midnight.'

'I didn't for one moment expect that you would still *be* here at midnight.'

'Who are you? Her fairy godmother?' asked Digby. There was an edge to his voice.

'If I am, then that makes you the rat,' said Clover sweetly.

She flicked her cigarette ash into an upturned top hat on the hall table.

'I'm sorry I asked you to kiss me,' I said to Digby as he led me into the ballroom. 'I won't do it again. And even more than that, I'm sorry that I used your bedroom to get changed. I should have asked you—'

Digby put his arm around my shoulder.

'Sing,' he said.

'Oh gosh, please, no,' I muttered.

I stumbled forward and he caught me.

'Come on. I want to hear you. Sing something.'

I looked around wildly, the room spinning.

'Pass me the piano,' I said.

There it stood in the far corner of the room, an elegantly wasted Baldwin Acrosonic – a very beautiful piano that had been badly treated.

'Nice,' I said admiringly. 'Or at least it was once. Pity it's so wrecked.'

'Do you mean me or the piano?' asked Digby, lifting the lid.

There must have been at least forty people still throwing drinks down their throats and shouting loudly at each other. Somewhere deep inside me there was someone shaking a disapproving head and putting one hand over their eyes in horror. But there was a far bigger force, fuelled by cocktails and the drunken effects of walking the streets with Digby, that wanted me to carry on talking in such a fashion. It is true to say that for the first time in my life I was too far gone to know that I had had enough.

I sat down on the piano stool with a thud, nearly missing it completely. Digby stopped me from falling. Laughing, he took my cigarette from me and rested it, burning, in an ashtray on top of the piano. I could see Billy and Inigo talking in the hall, neither of them aware of what I was about to do.

'Hey, Mick!' shouted Digby. 'Cut the record, will you? We're going to have some musical entertainment from Miss Merry-well here!'

I was aware of Lucy standing near the harmonica player – near but not too near. There was no time to think any further.

At once, the music stopped. Next, Digby gave a high, piercing whistle, and to my amazement, everyone stopped talking and turned his way.

'Speech!' slurred someone from the back of the room.

I looked down at my legs in my jodhpurs.

'Go on, baby,' said Digby.

He was so sure, so confident that I was going to be all right. What did he know about me, other than the fact that it was Billy Laurier who had got me here? But that was enough, of course. That was enough for him to be sure that I wasn't going to fail him.

My mind fizzed. I needed something to sing – but what? For a second I thought I would have to stand up and walk out of the room again having failed this little test completely. But I couldn't! I couldn't fail in a house like this. I coughed. What had Inigo said about New York? There was a Nathan Detroit on every street corner. There was the answer! I would serenade

Digby and his terrifying friends, and Billy, and bloody Father Hit-mas himself with "Sit Down You're Rockin' the Boat" It came to me as a Great Epiphany, I could have roared out loud at my own genius! It was a song I knew backwards – Ma had been near-obsessed by it. I could see Lucy moving closer, and in the reflection in the piano I noticed Inigo and Billy coming into the room from the hall to see what was going on. I cleared my throat. 'You might know this one,' I said. 'And if you do, you may as well join in. It sounds better with lots of voices. Especially drunk ones.'

The room had fallen deathly quiet. Digby handed me a glass of champagne. I drained it in one gulp and handed it back. Someone cheered from the stalls. I cleared my throat and plunged my hands onto the keys for the first verse of a song that took me straight back to the piano at home, to Ma, eyes closed, while her children giggled and clutched each other, spark-eyed with delight, waiting for the thrill of the ensemble moment – those sacred seconds where we would all dance and shout the words *together.* Now here I was, dice-rolling on that boat to heaven, and although I knew it was my own voice singing the words, it was Ma that I heard, not me. Several people in the room whistled and clapped as I sang; I was, as ever, dimly conscious of catching them by surprise – 'the little slip of a girl with the big voice strikes again' – and yet a great part of me wasn't in the room at all.

I paused, as Ma used to do, before I jumped off that cliff into the chorus. I swung round on the piano stool and in that split second, caught Inigo's eye. He looked at me, and bit his bottom lip and tried to hold back a grin. I turned back to the piano, and *bang!* There came the title of the song, in a frenzy of ivory and alcohol.

Ma can't have been the only one who loved Nicely-Nicely. Digby's crowd needed no further cue. The whole room shouted the refrain back to me, and as I laughed out loud, Inigo ran up to the piano, jumped onto the chair next to it, and joined in. Now Matilda was up beside the piano, waving her arms around, her blue eyes full of delight at what was happening. All three of us, plus a skinny-legged boy with horn-rimmed glasses and his blonde, drunk companion sang the next verse together, while Inigo lit a cigarette and poured himself another shot of whisky. When he had taken a drag, he sat down beside me and shoved me up the piano stool. His hands took the top half of the piano from me, and mine ran down to the bass.

We played on, singing those choruses faster and faster, while the crowd got louder and louder. Digby, now up on the sofa that straddled one side of the room, was conducting his guests into each other's arms for a dance.

'What the *hell* key are you in?' demanded Inigo, watching my fingers shooting all over the place, and laughing.

'I don't know,' I shouted. 'But whatever I'm in, you're not.'

'And what do you think you're wearing?'

'Something that bird Cherry Merrywell wouldn't be seen *dead* in!' I yelled, and jammed my fingers down on a D chord at the same time as he did. We laughed — half collapsing with the silliness of it — but then he could have been laughing *at* me, rather than with me. By that stage in the evening, it was hard to tell.

The smell of smoke and whisky filled my lungs — a green glass lamp, standing beside the piano, crashed to the floor, to a cheer from several of the gathered throng. I didn't stop. When the song should have ended, we sang the first verse again. I can't think what anyone walking past the house must have thought.

To me it sounded like the greatest interpretation of the song that had ever been achieved, even though I knew that I was only thinking such nonsense because I had drunk too much, and Digby had kissed my cheek, and Inigo had actually treated me like a human being. When we finished, the shouting, clapping and cheering could have been heard in Bodmin.

'More! More!' shouted old Theo, from the early stages of the night.

'More! Encore!' yelled Matilda in agreement.

'Thank you very much,' I said, like Elvis, for crying out loud! 'For my next song, I'm going to—'

But I never got to the next song. The last thing I recall with any clarity was observing that someone had drawn a cartoon face wearing spectacles on the wall in the corner of the room, and that the zip on Digby's trousers was undone. I don't think these two things were connected in any way – they just both struck me at the same time. Then I fell off the piano stool and on to the sprung floor with a thud.

24

Ingénue

I woke up the next morning, back in Clover's house, still spinning and rummaged on the floor for my watch. It was Sunday, I thought blearily. Ten thirty. Pa would be warming up for his second service by now. Lucy was sitting on the bed with her back to me, unaware that I had woken, applying mascara.

'I think I'm dying,' I said.

'Hurry up about it,' said Lucy briskly. She peered at me. 'You look awful.'

'Thanks. For a moment I thought you were going to pay me a compliment.'

'Hardly. You were *way* over the top last night.'

Lucy was a great fan of people making exhibitions of themselves – I sensed her glee.

Clover came into the room.

'Good. You're alive,' she said.

'I don't think I am.' I sat up. 'Everything's spinning. *Still.*'

'Oh dear,' said Lucy kindly.

'I think I'm going to be sick—'

'Oh no,' said Clover. 'Not in my great-grandmother's chamber pot.' She shoved it under the bed in haste. 'Get thee to the bathroom. It's nearly eleven o'clock. We're having ham and scrambled eggs.'

'Oh, please, no.'

'Digby's rung twice today to check on you,' said Clover, ignoring my plight. 'I must say, it was a very impressive show – singing like you did, then falling off the chair. I *warned* you about those *hideous* cocktails.'

A great grin spread across my face; I couldn't help it.

'He called for *me*?'

'You must have made quite an impact,' said Lucy.

'On the floor of his ballroom, perhaps,' I said. 'I can't think he'd care about me otherwise.'

'Did you kiss him?' demanded Lucy.

'I might have,' I said.

'Are you lying?' said Lucy suspiciously.

I didn't answer. Let them think what they like, I thought delightedly. The only thing that mattered was that he had called me! There it was, that shot of bliss, pure, unadulterated bliss, straight out of the bottle and swallowed in one intoxicating shot. He had rung. He had remembered. It had *happened*.

'I saw you disappearing into the night, with him wearing the Wentworth girl's pink coat like Noël Coward,' said Clover disapprovingly.

'We went to get cigarettes,' I said weakly.

'Save all that for *Woman's Own*,' said Clover drily. 'I must say, he acted fast, even by his appalling standards.'

'Really, *nothing* happened,' I insisted, but Clover wasn't listening.

'How did I get back here?' I asked, desperately trawling through the spectrum of possibilities.

'Inigo ordered us a cab and we all piled in.'

I sank back into the bed. '*Inigo* did?'

'Yes,' said Lucy.

'Gosh,' I said.

I reached for the glass of water beside the bed and raised it to my lips with a shaking hand. 'I fell off the piano stool,' I recalled with grim horror. 'I think there was something in the cocktails.'

'Where Digby's concerned, there usually is. It's called vodka. V-O-D-K-A. It's a Russian spirit – not much flavour but lethal kick.' Clover grinned at me. 'Combined with champagne, it's even more potent.'

I sank back into my pillow.

'Billy told me not to drink too much, and that's just what I *did*. He must be furious with me. Why didn't you *stop* me, Lucy?'

'Impossible,' said my sister. 'You know what you're like when you've had a drink and someone shows you a piano. Wild horses wouldn't have got you out of that room. Although, no,' she reflected. 'That's the only thing that *would* have worked.' She looked at Clover. 'Pianos and ponies,' she said. 'If she's anywhere near one or the other, you can be sure she won't leave until she's had a go.'

'Was Billy furious?' I asked hopelessly.

'He doesn't get furious,' said Clover. 'It's not his style. In any case, Matilda kept telling Billy to go easy on you – that surely he could forgive you for drinking too much, because you'd kept the crowd jumping better than Little Richard. He kept saying, 'But why did she have to wear *that*?' He said that if he'd wanted a girl dressed like they were about to enter the show ring, he'd have hung around Olympia at Christmas and kidnapped the winners of the Prince Philip Cup for gymkhana games.'

'He'll never forgive me!' I wailed. 'What if he packs me straight back home on the next train west?'

'No chance. If Digby thinks you're the sweetest thing since iced gems, then you're all set.'

'What do you mean?'

Clover looked at her fingernails and frowned.

'Billy may have told you not to drink for fear that you were going to make a goof of yourself,' said Clover. 'In fact, you did drink too much, but it worked. If the most famous photographer in London thinks that you're worth loafing around SW3 with for an hour at one of his ridiculous soirées, then that's quite something.'

'It is?'

'Yes,' sighed Clover. 'And for Billy, it means there's much less inventing to do.'

'Inventing?'

'You're making a record, aren't you? If you're seen around with Digby, it *accelerates* things somewhat. Makes you someone worth reading about, as well as someone worth listening to.'

'Inigo doesn't seem to like Digby very much,' I said, recalling our conversation in the hall.

'Men generally don't,' said Clover. 'And those two in particular don't have a very good history.'

'Why? What happened?'

For a moment I think Clover considered telling me, but then she decided against it.

'Nothing. Nothing important at all. What I mean is that they're a difficult combination. Fire and ice.'

'Which one's which?'

'You tell me,' said Clover crisply. 'Now, much as I hate to be the bearer of bad news, I think you should know that you've got to be in the recording studio in one hour and fourteen minutes.'

I turned even paler, if such a thing were possible.

'How am I going to sing when I can barely even talk?'

'You'll be perfectly all right,' said Clover. 'If Dean Martin can drink what he can drink and sing how he can sing, then so can you.'

'But what if I can't?'

'I suppose they'll give the song to Helen Shapiro,' said Clover without the slightest ounce of sympathy. 'Tara Jupp may be dying in bed, but Cherry Merrywell's quite capable of staying out all night and singing her heart out the next day. Get a grip on yourself.'

With that, she turned and stalked out of the room.

'Hellfire!' said Lucy admiringly. 'She can be very scary when she wants to be.'

'What are you supposed to be doing today?' I asked her. I pushed the thought of Raoul, lying on his hospital bed, out of my head.

'Starting work here,' said my sister. 'There are twenty-five boxes to sort through in the attic rooms.' She suddenly went down on to her knees.

'What are you doing?' I croaked. 'Praying for our lost souls?'

'No,' said Lucy, lowering herself into a horizontal position. 'It's far too late for all that now. But not too late for *this*.'

She pulled the chamber pot out from under my bed and stared at it in awe. 'I *thought* so,' she said in triumph, squinting at the mark on the underside of the thing. 'I think this is a Port-meirion original.'

'That means nothing to me, and you know it.'

'Well, it could mean something to the auctioneers at Sotheby's. This is worth something. I ought to list it in the records.'

'You're beyond strange,' I said, because sometimes Lucy's

encyclopedic knowledge of such items was just plain infuriating – particularly on a morning such as this, when my vision was so blurred that I felt incapable of identifying my own face in a mirror, far less the origins of a vessel that someone used to pee in midway through the last century.

Lucy was hunting for a pen.

'Have you called Raoul?' I croaked.

'No.'

'Although,' said Lucy, after a pause. 'Matilda's harmonica player gave me his number.'

I opened my mouth to ask her what she intended to do about that, but she delayed any further interrogation by walking out of the room. Was she telling me these things to upset me? Or because she didn't know how she felt about them herself?

Seeing inside a real recording studio was enough to justify the whole trip up to London, I thought, as Billy pushed me through the door and led me into a room about the size of the study at home, surrounded by glass panels and overlooking a second room joined to it containing a piano among other things. I picked up a set of headphones and put them over my head like I had seen Alma do on television. The smell of that room – that industrial, electric scent of wires and hot tape mixed with new carpet and strong coffee – was about as intoxicating as it gets. I walked into the room and stared at the huge desk in front of me – all those buttons, all those channels, all this difficult, technical grey and black mass of technology to create something as fluffy, as light and as pretty as a pop song. It seemed like a miracle to me; it was as though I was peering in through the backstage door to heaven itself.

'Make yourself at home,' said Billy, opening a box of sugar

lumps and squinting into a red and white teacup.

'I'm sorry,' I began. 'About last night, and falling off the stool, and not remembering what happened after we sang . . .' I tailed off. Billy smiled at me.

'We'll say no more about it,' he said. 'You certainly introduced yourself to London, although perhaps not quite in the clothes that I had in mind.'

'I'm sorry.'

'Cherry, we don't need to talk about it,' he said. 'Digby was very impressed by you. That's all that we need to know.'

Clover had been right, I thought. He was happy because Digby had noticed me – not just because he had been told to, but because he was actually interested.

I nearly jumped out of my skin when a man wearing a crumpled grey and black suit stood up from behind the big desk.

'Oh, you're here,' said Billy, shaking his hand. 'Thank God you could make it. We had Ian last week. That guy couldn't mix his way out of a cake bowl.'

The man in the suit smiled and pushed his glasses back on to his nose. I wanted to speak, but felt as though I couldn't say a word, not even hello. I felt static, incapable of normal speech. My mouth had gone dry.

'William Moore-Jones,' said Billy, watching us shake hands. 'William's going to engineer today.'

'Engineer?'

'He'll shove the whole thing in the right direction and make it sound like it belongs on the radio.'

'The others have been here for a couple of hours,' said William. 'They're due a bit of a break. So there's a bit of time for you to go through the songs when Inigo arrives.'

'The others? Where – *who* – are they?'

Billy pushed me forward. 'Down there,' he said.

And they were. Three boys playing variously the drums, the bass guitar and the acoustic guitar, and six girls sitting in a huddle with stringed instruments about their persons.

'Inigo likes a bit of an orchestra in the instrumental section of his songs,' said William. Misreading my expression, he said, 'Oh, don't worry. They're absolutely the best.'

'I don't even know the songs,' I muttered.

'For the B-side, we'd like you to sing "Over the Rainbow",' said Billy.

'"Over the Rainbow"? As in Judy Garland?'

'Precisely.'

'But why would I do that?'

Billy looked puzzled. 'What do you mean?'

'Why would anyone want to listen to me singing it when she's already done it in a way that can't be touched?'

'We won't do it the same,' said Billy patiently. 'Your recording will have a different feel. It's a classic, beautiful song,' he said. 'You can't go wrong with it.'

'What about the third song?' I asked.

'Inigo has something,' said Billy vaguely. He looked at me. 'You're a little pro, Cherry Merrywell. This will not be difficult for you. My God! I've never known a girl ask so many questions!'

Billy pulled up a chair for me and sat down on the sofa. I strained my eyes towards the small window in the corner of the room, doubting that the real world existed any longer.

'Can I smoke?' I asked pointlessly, as everyone else in the room was.

Billy frowned. 'I don't like you smoking,' he said.

I gave an apologetic shrug and lit up anyhow. A powerful part

288

of me felt as if I had to go against Billy– which wouldn't amount to much. I had to rebel where I could. Billy ignored what I was doing anyway, and stood up.

'Inigo should be here in five minutes,' he said.

'Where are you going?' I asked, panicked.

'I've got a new group recording in the studio next door,' he said. 'I told them I'd be in to say hi. I'll be back. William, get the girl a glass of water, would you?'

He actually patted me on the arm.

'William went to Eton – he knows how to look after girls,' he added.

'Oh! Does that make you an Etonian?'

'An old one, I suppose,' admitted William.

I drank nearly the whole glass in one go, still feeling as though I needed to slosh the vodka out of my body.

'Have you worked with Billy before?' asked William, stubbing out a Lucky Strike.

'No,' I confessed.

'You'll be all right. If Inigo Wallace wrote the A-side, and Billy's in charge,' he said, 'you could sing "Three Blind Mice" and it would be a hit.'

'I fear Inigo would consider that far too downbeat,' I said.

'Perhaps you're right. I don't know where all that lyrical exuberance comes from. He's a miserable sod most of the time.'

William grinned at me, and I knew he was on my side. I felt a great wave of nausea, compounded by a flash of regained memory; I had fallen off the piano stool in front of not just Digby O'Rourke but Inigo too.

'I think I need to go to the . . .' I muttered. I didn't finish the sentence. William knew what I needed.

'Down the corridor, turn left.' He looked at me, observed my still-shaking hands, my black-ringed eyes.

'Are you all right? I'm not sure if it's just the lighting in here, but you look – well – *green*,' he said, frowning.

I ran to the loo and threw up, washed out my mouth, downed two more cups of water, found a stick of chewing gum in the bottom of my bag and returned to the studio considerably revived. I was just in time. Inigo came into the studio thirty seconds later, dressed in his customary black jersey, and holding the remains of a bacon roll.

'You're alive then?' he said to me.

'Apparently.'

'Good.' He smiled suddenly, which unnerved me. 'Well, that was fun,' he said.

'What was?'

'Last night.'

'I made a fool of myself,' I said. 'I know.'

'Actually, I thought it was rather interesting.'

'What does that mean?'

'I didn't have you down as someone who would do that sort of thing.'

'What sort of thing?'

'Oh, you know. Playing to the crowds, chucking back vast quantities of vodka and champagne, showing up halfway through the party in those extraordinary clothes—'

'Oh, I know!' I interrupted him. 'And it's all the more odd, isn't it, because after all – I'm no conventional beauty, and I'm far too short, and I don't look as though I'd know what to do if a man so much as asked me out to tea!'

To my fury, he laughed.

'I couldn't have put it better myself,' he said.

'Well, that's because you said it all in the first place!'

He didn't miss a beat.

'Ah. You overheard me talking to Billy that night in Corn-wall?'

'Yes,' I said defiantly.

'I see,' said Inigo. 'That explains the cold front.'

'Or no front at all, according to *you*.'

Inigo took a seat and stretched out his legs in an irritating gesture of relaxation.

'I'm sorry you heard that,' he said. 'But I have to tell Billy what I think about his artists. I wouldn't be up to much if I didn't.'

'But what about me and my feelings?' I demanded.

'I didn't know that you were lurking around in the passage. I thought you'd gone home.'

'Well, I hadn't. I came back into the house to – to – to see if there was dry rot in the Yellow Room.'

'Dry rot? What are you? A plumber?'

'My brother-in-law needed to know,' I said with dignity. 'He loves Trellanack.'

'Right. You've lost me now, Miss Merrywell.'

'I wish people would stop calling me that.'

'Not when you've read this, you won't,' said Inigo.

'What is it?' I asked suspiciously.

He pulled out a newspaper from the pocket of his denims and unfolded it.

'It's the late edition of the *Sunday Express*,' he said. 'Listen.'

'"Photographer Digby O'Rourke – well known for discovering models Matilda Bright and Caroline Sinclair – held a party for Miss Cherry Merrywell, his latest ingénue, in his Chelsea town house last night",' he read.

'Held a party for *me*?' I gasped. 'That's not true! And what's an ingénue anyway?'

'Well, precisely, darling,' said Inigo, in that voice he used that veered somewhere between horribly sarcastic and desperately condescending.

'Go on, then,' I urged.

'It says, "Miss Merrywell, 17, from Dawlish, Dorset, dressed in jodhpurs, wowed those privileged members of London's perpetually high society with a selection of songs from the musical *Brigadoon* banged out on the piano at midnight. Neighbours of O'Rourke, 26, were forced to complain when the singing continued well into Sunday morning".'

'Don't joke,' I said crossly.

'I should tell you, Miss Merrywell, that my mother recommended that one should never make jokes before four thirty in the afternoon. Apparently to have the presence of mind for wit before such a time is a sign of bad breeding.'

I was unable to think of a reply to this.

He tossed the paper to me. There it was, exactly as he had read it, in black and white. There was also a photograph of Digby standing next to Matilda, outside a cinema.

'There's more!' I whispered in astonishment. '"Also present was Miss Merrywell's sister, Lucy, 23, childhood companion of Matilda Bright and currently working for Clover Napier. Wearing a revealing skirt fashioned by designer of the moment Charlotte Ferris, she held the party in her thrall. 'Lucy and I grew up together,' says Miss Bright. 'She is without a doubt one of the most intriguing young women of our generation.'"'

'When did she talk to them?' I asked. 'She must have planned what to say! Matilda doesn't speak like that!'

'What – in complete, coherent sentences, you mean?'

'*Brigadoon?*' I said slowly. 'But I didn't *play* any songs from *Brigadoon*. Did I?' I scanned the paper again. 'And I didn't know that the neighbours had complained. And I'm not from Dorset,' I concluded indignantly.

'My dear Cherry – as if anyone cares about any of that,' said Inigo. 'The point is – you made it into the paper. I mean, I must admit we're talking about the *Express* – a rag that the Duke of Edinburgh himself said was full of lies, scandal and imagination – but still. The papers are the papers. Billy will be *thrilled.*'

There was a silence. I didn't know how to react to all this: I wanted to be cross, but there was something grimly, disgustingly thrilling about it all too. I looked at Inigo.

'*You* don't sound very pleased,' I said eventually.

'Oh, I am. The more publicity you get, the more copies the record will sell, the more money I'll make. Everyone's happy.'

'I didn't know anyone was going to write about me,' I said.

'Well, they have. Isn't it marvellous?'

Inigo took the paper in his long fingers, tore the article out and handed it to me.

I read it again, turning it over in my hands as though it might self-destruct at any moment.

'It seems rather silly,' I said at last.

Billy came back into the room and there was a great deal of hoo-ha about the newspaper again, and wasn't it good that Lucy and I had gone to the party, and he knew it was the right place for us to get seen, etc. Then he started to talk about me as though I weren't in the room.

'She should see Digby again,' mused Billy. 'Perhaps tomorrow night? The cinema – then something to eat? Nice to get them photographed doing something – I don't know –' he cast around for the word – 'ordinary,' he concluded.

Movies and restaurants with Digby O'Rourke weren't my idea of ordinary. I coughed. 'He might not want to see me,' I said. 'He's probably busy—'

'Did you like him?' asked Billy, ignoring my point.

I laughed, embarrassed.

'He seemed – nice.'

'*Nice*,' repeated Inigo. 'Very useful word, nice.'

'What do you mean?'

'It actually translates to mean either absolutely awful or completely wonderful.'

Much against Cherry Merrywell's wishes, I felt Tara Jupp blushing scarlet.

'Stop embarrassing her,' said Billy.

'I don't even *know* him.'

'He's *exactly* the right person for you to be associated with,' said Billy. He looked at my face, and his expression changed. Misreading me, he said, 'Look, Tara, I'm not suggesting that you go out and start choosing curtains with the guy, or anything.'

'On the other hand, you could,' said Inigo. 'By all accounts, he'd make a wonderful husband. Reliable, clean-living, faithful . . .'

'Oh, please be quiet,' I muttered. 'Shouldn't I be learning this song?'

Inigo opened the studio door that led back out to the corridor. I swear I heard Adam Faith talking outside. Billy put his hat back on, grinned at me, clicked his fingers and said, 'I'm taking Matilda on a little honeymoon this afternoon. Just Paris.' He spoke as though it were Blackpool.

'What about me?' Billy smiled as though I were joking. 'When I come back, I want a number-one smash, kids.'

The door closed behind him.

I laughed because I couldn't help it.

'I didn't think people actually said that sort of thing in real life,' I said.

'They don't,' said Inigo. 'This *isn't* real life, and don't you forget it.'

He sat down, took his guitar out of the case and sighed.

'I can see that you're still harbouring terrible grudges against me for my comments in the room with the collapsed ceilings.'

'Actually the ceilings weren't any worse than they used to be,' I conceded. 'That was the one good discovery I made that night.'

'Saints be praised,' said Inigo. 'Look, I can't make any apology for talking about you like I did. But now that I've seen you in action, I suppose I was wrong about a couple of things. Certainly, you *can* play,' he said. 'And you know how to sing to a crowd. You were good.'

'Thank you, sir,' I said.

'That's enough of that,' said Inigo crisply. 'Can we agree to some kind of truce?'

'Of course,' I said. 'Why not?'

'And just for the record,' said Inigo, twanging the A-string of his guitar and frowning at the tuning, 'it's "Your Royal Highness" to you – if you don't mind.'

I laughed. I couldn't help it, even though he was still nothing how I wanted him to be.

For five minutes, neither of us said a word. It was strange how we could go from all that conversation to nothing at all, and I didn't like silences between us; they hung louder than they did with anyone else.

'So where's this song, then?' I asked him.

Inigo picked a record out of his bag.

'"May to September",' he said. 'This is Susan's version.'

He moved towards the record player and took the thing out of its sleeve.

It was instant – I'll certainly give Inigo credit for that. The melody was as light as icing sugar, and Susan Vaughan sang with a sweet, innocent sincerity – I could see immediately why Billy had loved her voice so much; it was right up his street.

'It's a good tune,' I said, as the first chorus ended. There was no sense in not saying it.

'Thanks,' said Inigo.

'I take it you played it?'

He nodded. It was a song for little girls to chant together in the playground or at the bus stop – demanding nothing of the listener but the ability to believe the story. *Girl meets boy, girl loses boy, boy comes back, girl and boy get married in Malibu, and all is well with the world.*

'Not exactly singing the blues, is she?' I said when the song ended. I wanted to tell him how good it was, but I couldn't bring myself to do it. Those overheard words still stuck with me, however hard I had tried to push them out of my head. *He didn't think that I could do it.*

'No,' agreed Inigo. 'It's about as far from the blues as it's possible to be.'

'And where is Malibu anyway?' I added, sounding suspicious – as though he had invented the place for the sake of the song.

'More than five thousand miles from here,' said Inigo. 'On the west coast of America.'

'Isn't that going to make it hard for people over here to understand?'

'If you want to change it to Sunderland, be my guest.'

'Play it to me again,' I said.

He picked up the needle on the record, but I said, 'No. I mean *you* play it. I want to hear how it sounded when you wrote it.'

It was a direct challenge. Inigo looked surprised. 'All right,' he said calmly. He nodded down to the now empty live room. It was Sunday. They had gone for lunch, I thought, suddenly picturing Imogen batting Roy and Luke's greedy little fingers away as she struggled to carve a roast chicken in time for Pa's arrival after church.

Inigo loped across the room and lifted the lid of the white baby grand in the corner. Lined up in front of their chairs sat the instruments of those who were being paid to play for me that day. Inigo sat, fingers hovering above the keys for a moment. His hair fell forward and he closed his eyes; deep in concentration, he lost the wariness that stalked him the rest of the time.

'All right, I've got it.'

Off he went. Left hand pounding the bass line, right hand skittering over the tune, grabbing gulps of coffee between verse, chorus and key change and still keeping it going, I could see precisely why he had become as successful as he had. Just like that afternoon at Milton Magna, he had that effortless way of playing and injecting the most innocent, almost childlike words with that *one thing* that I *knew* was out there, but had never tasted first-hand. When he had finished, he looked at me and pushed his hair back.

'All right?' he said. 'A singer like you can do this standing on your head.'

'Do I have to sing with an American accent?'

'Yes,' said Inigo shortly.

'What does it mean?' I asked him.

'What does it sound like? She wants him, she loses him, she's sad, then he comes back, she's happy.'

'Does she *have* to get him back?'

'What do you mean?' Inigo lit a cigarette and looked up at me sharply.

'Well – why *should* she get him back? I mean, it says in the second verse that he's found someone new. When he *does* come back at the end of verse three, the chances are that she's always going to be suspicious of him. Gosh, it stands to reason, doesn't it? *I* wouldn't want him back if I were her.'

'You *are* her, so you'd better get used to it,' said Inigo.

He pushed past me, and for a moment I thought, *Help! I've blown it now!*

'Why don't *you* play *me* something while I set up the microphone for you,' he said.

'What do you mean?'

'Go on. Anything at all.'

He made a shooing gesture towards the piano.

'I don't want to.'

'Don't be so babyish.'

'You're not interested.'

Inigo shrugged. 'I'll decide whether I am or not after I've heard you.'

'All right,' I said.

As soon as the words were out of my mouth I sat down at the piano, knowing that if I didn't play right away, then I would be too afraid.

'Promise you won't say anything afterwards.'

He dropped three lumps of sugar into a teacup and looked at me as though I were a complete idiot. 'All right. I promise.'

So I played a song I had written back at home – a song about losing someone and wishing they were there. A song about my mother, that I hoped would make Inigo think about his father. I'd love to say that as I sang the whole world sighed and everything stopped – stock-still – for a moment to contemplate the brilliance of what I had created, that Inigo promptly announced that he might as well give up because he couldn't compete with me. I *wish* I could say that. But that's not how it was at all. At home it had made sense to me, and Imogen had been on hand to run into the room and tell me how wonderful I was. Here, in a recording studio in the capital city, in front of Inigo, it was suddenly too small. I was aware of the basic lack of originality in the melody – a tune that I had really just adapted from a song on a Nina Simone record of George's. My fingers stumbled over the notes and I hesitated to remember the words to the second verse. It felt too slim, too amateur, too babyish. I was just a little girl singing – but without emotion, because I was too busy trying to make it sound more than it was. I pushed my voice to its limits, knowing that the voice would have to remain my calling card if the song wasn't working. *Oh Lord*, I thought. *Save me from this. He's too good for me.* I didn't want to admit it, but hearing myself, and my songs, made it oh, too clear. What he did required far more talent than I had imagined.

When I finished, I turned to Inigo. He was standing, leaning on the door, impassive, impossible to read. He said, as promised, nothing at all. He didn't know me, I realized. It hadn't been to him what it had been to me. Lucy hadn't been right about That Thing.

'Shall we press on?' I asked him irritatedly. I wished, as soon as I had finished playing, that I hadn't done it. I never played my songs to anybody; I would have felt less violated had I danced naked around the microphone stand.

He nodded.

'Well?' I said.

'Well what?' He was adjusting the height of the microphone so that it was level with my face.

'Did you like it?'

'I thought you didn't want my opinion?'

'No. You're right. I don't.'

There was thick silence between us for at least a minute, there in the padded womb of the studio, and I stood still, staring at the unreal world around me, feeling nothing from outside, knowing nothing. He was down on his knees now, plugging things in, pulling wires out. At last, he stood up. His face was as impassive as ever. 'It was nice.'

I said nothing.

'Now shall we do what we came here to do?' said Inigo. 'Before one of us loses the will to live?'

I looked at him. 'Of course. And you want me to sing it exactly like Susan?'

'*Exactly* like Susan.'

'Because that's how Billy wants it to sound?'

'Because that's how Billy wants it to sound.'

I hesitated. 'And we always do *exactly* what Billy wants?'

Inigo sighed.

'Billy heard you, and he knew that you could do this. But there are other girls out there who could do it too. If you don't sing this, then one of them will.'

'It just doesn't feel like *me*.'

'Do you think Alma believes every word that she sings?' asked Inigo.

'I don't know,' I confessed. 'I like to believe she does.'

'Exactly,' said Inigo. 'You're selling a dream here, and one that everyone listening wants to believe in.'

300

'But what if *I* don't believe it?'

'Baby, you're going to get paid, and if you play your cards right, you get to be on the television and the radio. You get to stand on your own two feet and say that when you were seventeen, you were *there*. That's all you need to believe in.'

He lit a cigarette.

We left two hours later. I sang with the band and the orchestra playing as though I were singing along to a record at home. I wanted to feel the thrill of it all, but it was dulled by knowing that I was merely copying someone who had done it before me. I never wanted to copy *anyone* again. Then we recorded 'Over the Rainbow', and a second song that Inigo had written called 'Paint the Clouds'. He handed me the lyrics, typed on a piece of paper, and it was all over in what felt like minutes. But I saw myself as I knew I was: a puppet for him and his talent – that was all. And I knew that I had made a mistake by playing my song to him: I felt like a fool who had exposed too much, given too much, revealed all her cards, only to realize that there were no aces there at all.

Inigo dropped me back at Napier House; he was going off to meet his sister in Mayfair before the Six O'Clock Club.

'Digby will call you in the next hour,' he said, as I stepped out of the car.

'How do you know?' I asked, wanting assurance that what he was saying was actually going to happen.

'I just know. But for God's sake, be careful. I know that Billy thinks that you being seen prancing around with him is the best news since rationing ended, but you shouldn't let him take you too far.'

'How far is too far?'

'You'll know,' said Inigo.

Putting his car into gear, he sped off. It was, I reflected, a good thing that he hadn't waited for my reply. I wasn't sure that either Cherry or Tara knew how to respond to him at all.

That evening, Clover served Welsh rarebit followed by trifle. Inigo came in five minutes before we all sat down, and grinned at Lucy and I, jittering at the octagonal oak table.

'Anyone telephoned?' he asked Clover casually, lighting the candles on the dining room table.

'No,' said Clover. She looked at him curiously. 'Are you waiting for a call?'

'Perhaps,' said Inigo. 'Perhaps not.'

We sat down as the clock struck six. The room was so quiet; I shuffled on my green leather chair, and wondered what Digby was doing. On the sideboard, Clover had placed a vase of blue and white hydrangeas, and in doing so, lightened the room both physically and figuratively. This act, combined with the invasion of hot food, salt and pepper shakers, clean, freshly ironed napkins and *people*, made it as operational and real as it had been when it was first decorated. We were eating as they had eaten; they were not so very far away from us.

Lucy, who had changed into a long skirt as though she felt herself too modern without it, had Colette Napier's diary in front of her, and was carefully studying her kitchen notes.

'It says here that she dismissed a servant called Emma because she mistrusted the way she handled the gammon steak at luncheon,' she said.

'Oh, Emma's in and out of her good books all the time,' said Clover, spooning mustard from a silver dish. 'At one point Colette spends two hours in the kitchen, arguing over Emma's refusal to salt the parboiled potatoes for Sunday lunch. She says that her husband and his friends smoked cigars, drank his best wine and bantered cheerfully while this sorry row was happening. By the time Colette got the potatoes on the table, half the party had passed out.'

'Jeez, I lived in the wrong century,' said Inigo.

'She seems to be "much vexed" a great deal of the time,' said Lucy, turning over a page and frowning.

'That's something else she and I have in common,' said Clover.

Lucy spooned a heap of spinach on to her plate and reached for the delicate butter dish, no doubt dating back to 1870. Such an item would last ten seconds at the Rectory, I thought, thinking of Roy's flying bread rolls and Florence's over-zealous handling of the washing-up brush.

'Did you have a good day?' Clover asked Inigo and me. Whether or not she cared either way, I couldn't tell – her concentration was somewhat erratic. Clover always appeared to have half a mind back in the mid eighteen-hundreds.

'Oh we had a blast,' said Inigo. 'Cherry's been written about in the *Express*, and she's managed to go at least half an hour at a time without arguing with me over the quality of my writing. We recorded three songs, and no one was sick. Actually, I don't know if that's true?'

He looked at me frowning.

'I refuse to answer any—' I began, but stopped sharply. The telephone was ringing in the hall.

'Carry on,' said Clover briskly. 'I don't answer the telephone during the Six O'Clock Club. Whoever they are, they can wait.'

But Inigo stood up.

'Excuse me,' he muttered, loping out of the room.

Clover looked at us.

'I must get the double cream,' she muttered, speeding after Inigo.

Lucy looked at me.

'How was he?' she whispered.

'Tricky,' I said. 'I made myself look a fool.'

'After last night, I can't think how,' said Lucy, grinning.

'How about you?' I asked her. I didn't want to talk about me and Inigo in the recording studio any more than was necessary.

Lucy took a poached egg from the tray in the middle of the table.

'It's good to feel useful. Makes a change from perms and the same old mindless gossip. Although I spent the afternoon in tears.'

'Why?'

'Colette Napier's estranged Aunt Jessica comes back to see her after three years in exile. Then two weeks later, she drowns herself in the Thames.'

'You'll be a basket case by the time this job's over,' I warned her.

Clover came back into the room, lips pursed.

'It's America,' she announced. She looked at me and smiled wickedly. 'I heard him drop his voice so low I couldn't hear a damn word he was saying, but it's *her* all right. Female from across the Pond. Father Hit-mas is in love,' she sighed, hand to her chest.

Lucy looked at me.

'Where's the cream?' she asked Clover.

Later that night, I padded up to the telephone book and flipped it open.

America called Inigo Wallace, he had written in his big, spidery hand. *Purpose of call: None of your bloody business. PS Listening in on other people's telephone calls is a sign of imminent insanity.*

Standing by the telephone, I nearly leapt out of my skin when it started to ring again.

Nervously, I picked it up.

'Hello?'

'Who's that?'

'Tara, I mean – Cherry.'

Digby laughed. 'You need an early night, Miss Merrywell,' he said.

'How are you?' I asked him nervously. 'Thank you for the lovely party—'

'Sweetheart, you mustn't thank me. Who do you think I am, Princess Margaret? Listen, I'm only calling to tell Clover to bring some decent threads for you. You don't suit all that rubbish she had you strung up in the other night.'

'I don't think I can tell her what to bring,' I said delightedly.

'Well just pack your jodhpurs and hide them under your skirt,' he said promptly.

'I don't know that Clover wants me photographed in my jodhpurs.'

'Of course she doesn't, darling. That's exactly why we have to do it.'

'Billy wouldn't think it was right.' Down the end of the line, I heard the sound of breaking glass.

'Bloody hell,' swore Digby. 'Look, I've got to go, angel. Caspar's just walked in. I'll see you tomorrow. Sleep tight and for God's sake, don't let her boss you about.'

I replaced the receiver.

Digby O'Rourke called for Clover, I wrote. *Spoke to Cherry Merry-well. Purpose of call: sartorial enquiries.*

I ran upstairs and put my jodhpurs into a paper bag.

25

How It Was Lost and Why

'Dear girl, haven't you anything else to wear?' Clover and I were walking to Digby's house two days later.

'Nothing clean,' I admitted.

Clover sighed. Earlier that morning, she had taken delivery of a whole load of dresses from a French designer she once slept with and who owed her because she promised to keep it a secret from his wife. She had packed them into a suitcase with wheels and pulled it behind her down the street like an air hostess – but that's not giving her enough credit. With her sunglasses, her heels, her blue-black fringe and her frightening efficiency, she looked ready to land the plane single-handedly.

We had left Lucy working through trunks of papers at Napier House, but there was a distance between she and I that morning. The harmonica player had telephoned for her at eight o'clock in the morning; I had seen Clover's entry in the book. I didn't know what Lucy was going to do, but when boys had run after her in the past, she had usually caved in at some point, if not for anything more than the chance of getting out of Pa's clutches for a night. I couldn't think about her now – not when I had to concentrate on trying to remain cool in front of Digby.

When we got to Cheyne Walk, Digby answered the door wearing blue jeans and no shirt, while holding a bowl of plovers' eggs like Sebastian Flyte. His goblin's eyes narrowed at Clover's suitcase.

'You're moving in,' he said with a sigh. 'You'll have to share with Caspar. He doesn't look too hot, but he's definitely got something about him.'

'Syphilis, I imagine,' said Clover, pulling the case into the hall.

'Don't worry,' said Digby. 'I know what Billy wants more than he does. I work best with a splitting headache.'

'Good, because I'm about to make it an awful lot worse,' said Clover.

Digby grinned at me.

'Hello, baby,' he said. 'Come in. I don't think I had the chance to tell you that you certainly *can* sing. You were bloody brilliant.'

'I really don't think I was,' I said. I felt myself burning red, but Digby held my eyes in his and laughed.

We walked up the stairs to the top floor of the house, Digby staggering under the weight of Clover's case. He looked at me, carrying my paper bag and raised his eyes questioningly. I nodded.

'Good girl,' he said softly.

'What are you whispering about?' said Clover, irritated.

We spent an hour trawling through all the clothes, dresses straight from the catwalk in Paris, hats, gloves, beautiful scarves, exquisite blouses, and I tried them all on, getting hotter and hotter and more and more worried. Digby made a mockery of much of what Clover had been sent, pulling out priceless items and putting them on himself, or fashioning them into even odder pieces than they already were.

'We want thousands of teenage girls to go out and imitate her look,' said Clover, losing patience as Digby tied a red and blue striped scarf around my head like a pirate.

'The trouble with Billy-boy,' said Digby, under his breath, but loud enough so that Clover and I could clearly hear him, 'is that he doesn't like anyone being themselves. It frightens him. He can't control it.'

'He knows what works,' said Clover.

'Up to a point,' said Digby.

As Clover sat on the floor, sighing and taking up the hem of a shot-pink taffeta ball gown, Digby touched the back of my neck, sending shots of adrenalin up my spine. It was his lazy, Puck-like confidence, the blatant pull of his flinty eyes, that rendered me pretty much done for. No doubt thousands of girls had fallen for all of it before, I told myself, but didn't those statistics speak of supreme talent? If a job's worth doing, it's worth doing well, as Imogen had always said.

'Come out with me later,' muttered Digby.

'I heard that,' said Clover. 'Tara, if you want my advice, you'll do nothing of the sort.'

I bit my lip and tried not to grin.

Even through my days of equine infatuation, I had allowed myself the odd moment of Cinderella reverie – these hopeless, soupy dreams that one day someone like Clover would pick up a stick of mascara and a pot of Elizabeth Arden face powder and trans-form me – Eliza Doolittle style – into the sort of society beauty that could stop traffic. But real life doesn't work like that. Clover had painted my face as beautifully as anyone could, but I looked alien, utterly wrong. Pink lips, pale blue eyeshadow, high blusher and my hair huge and pinned up in a diamond clasp – I had become just like Alma, only without the authenticity that made Alma real to me. I was clownish, absurd. Alarmed, I stared at myself in the mirror.

'I don't look like me,' I said.

'That's the whole idea,' said Clover, not unkindly.

'I suppose so,' I said. Some of the pink lipstick had come off on my front teeth. I rubbed it away.

'Stay very still and do exactly as Digby says,' said Clover.

You know, I really didn't need to be told.

He took my photograph, talking to me all the time. He threw out superlatives like he was handing out liquorice allsorts at the school gate – and for that I was extremely grateful – but there was a distractedness in him, a sense that he had said it all before, that I was in a long line of girls Clover had provided him to photograph, which of course I was. We changed outfits three times, but never into any of the clothes that *I* had picked out.

At one point, Digby put down the camera, frowned, looked at Clover and said, 'I don't like the skirt.'

'It was made in Milan,' said Clover, as if that settled it.

Digby shrugged and carried on. I rather agreed with him. I don't think that I would have chosen to wear that skirt had Clover not been so utterly convinced that it was exactly what Billy wanted.

'I don't see why he should dictate absolutely *everything*,' I said. 'He's a man, after all. Do most men have the right idea about girls' clothes?'

'He's not most men,' said Clover, looking at Digby.

'Do you think you're getting there?' Clover asked him an hour and a half later. I had escaped to have a sandwich, kindly provided by Digby's long-suffering cleaner – and could hear them talking in the next room. Clover was trying to hide the

310

anxiety in her voice, and I realized that she, more than anyone, needed this to be right. If it didn't work, Billy would blame her, not me.

'It's what Billy wants,' said Digby. 'I'm only the bloke pressing the buttons.'

'Billy wants her to look "innocent yet knowing",' said Clover, ignoring him. 'Do you think we've captured that?'

'No.'

'Why not?'

'What's the sister called again? The bird with the legs?'

'Lucy.'

'She could pull off "knowing". But not this one. She's a sweet little virgin from Devon, for Christ's sake.'

'Cornwall,' corrected Clover.

'Same thing, isn't it?'

'Not for those who live there,' said Clover stiffly. 'And I suggest that you'd better not let her fall too hard—'

'Piss off. I like her,' said Digby. 'What does it matter to you, anyway?'

I had to push my hand into my mouth to stop myself from laughing out loud with glee.

Clover opened the door and smiled at me.

'I've got to go,' she said. 'I've got a meeting,' she explained briskly. 'Digby will walk you back when you're finished.' Clover pressed a pound note into my hand.

'Emergencies,' she said. 'And if you were wondering – being jumped on by photographers with more money than sense certainly qualifies. Billy may like the idea of having you two pictured together, but it's a dangerous thing.'

'What is?' I asked.

'Doing what either of those two men expect. They both get

their own way all the time. It's not always the best idea to give them what they want.'

She left, and suddenly we were on our own. I wondered if Digby wanted me to go right away, but I couldn't bring myself to move.

'I've got nothing to eat,' he said, opening a cupboard, shutting it again and opening it once more, as though repeating the action might encourage a roast chicken or jacket potato to materialize out of nowhere. 'Peaches,' he said, picking up a tin and looking at me regretfully. 'Do you like peaches?'

Miraculously he found a bottle of white wine and we stood outside on the balcony and looked over the river. I couldn't think of anything to say. He looked at me thoughtfully – as though I were a painting he was halfway to completing.

'Will you come to the ballroom with me?' he said.

I walked down the stairs in the red heels, slowly, for fear of falling, and Digby and I stepped inside the room with the piano. Everything was still shut – there was the smell of old cigarettes and perfume and, in the corner of the room, a steel-grey Siamese cat looked up from a cushion upholstered in faded pink parakeets.

'Most of the people who enter this room need the dark to feel safe,' said Digby. 'Not you, Miss Merrywell. You need light to survive.'

Then he opened the curtains so that the July sun bombarded the room, and I flinched, putting my hand up to my eyes like a visor. He smiled at me, half triumphant, as if he had a plan and he was going to carry it out. Then, just as I imagined he was going to take me in his arms and resume where we had left off on the embankment, he looked thoughtful.

'Your riding things,' he said. 'Where are they?'

I pointed to the bag by my feet.

'Would you put them on for me? Please?'

'I can't just change here . . .'

'Why not? You did it before, remember?'

I took a deep breath.

'If I get changed, would you kiss me again?' I asked him.

He laughed. 'I'll do *that* even if you stay dressed in that awful get-up of Clover's. But you're far lovelier without all that slap. Come here.'

I walked across the ballroom to him, quite out of step with my pounding heart.

Digby took my hand and led my upstairs. Our feet made little noise on the carpets; on the landing there was an overflowing ashtray. *Peter and the Wolf* played on from the record player in the room where he had taken my picture.

It's going to happen! I thought in terror. Digby raised his eyebrows and grinned at me, then opened the door of the bath-room and ran the hot tap. I stood next to him beside the basin; we looked at each other, side by side in the mirror. My hair had come free of the diamond clasp Clover had lent me; some of my mascara had smudged. Digby looked at me as though we were about to fill a couple of balloons with water and surprise the maths teacher.

He found a clean flannel and a bar of Pears soap – which, I might add, reminded me *most* unfortunately of Imogen – and left the room while I wiped all of the make-up from my face. When I had almost finished, he knocked softly on the door.

'Do you think I'll ever get all the pink off?' I asked, biting my bottom lip and rubbing my mouth with my hand.

Then he kissed me, right there in the bathroom, and even

though I closed my eyes, I knew that our reflections were kissing too, and that doubled the weightless feeling, the sensation of falling into something I couldn't begin to have understood before that afternoon.

'I think we'd better move into the bedroom,' he said. 'That is – if you want to.'

Nice that he suggested it, but we didn't make it out of the bathroom in the end. I felt the cold floor on my back, heard the buzzing of some lucky fly around the light bulb over the mirror, and closed my eyes to everything except the warmth of this stranger under my skin. It was his strength that had me so completely, the feeling that he could lift me up and place me exactly where he wanted to and that I would be powerless to resist him. I put myself in his hands, and gave it all up for him.

'Are you all right?' he whispered when it was over. He touched my spine. 'Your back . . .' he began.

'Funnily enough, I never went away.'

The sun was setting by the time I had changed into my riding clothes as he had asked me to. We were back in the ballroom, Digby wearing just his denims; I could feel a sweet, intense stinging between my legs, and in the back of my mind – where there was the tiniest bit of space to think about anything other than him – I knew that that afternoon had changed me forever – only I wasn't ready for forever to start just yet. I wanted to hold on to it for as long as I could. I had unbuttoned the top of the blouse, pulled it down a little so that he could see something of my chest, but Digby crossed over to the piano and, staring me right in the eye, he did it up again. I looked down, embarrassed.

'Better to leave everything to the imagination,' he said.

I sat down at the piano, and he took just one roll of film, very fast, without saying a word. Then he put down his camera and looked at me.

'Play me something,' begged Digby. 'Please.'

'All right. What do you want?'

'Something for my head,' he said.

I looked down at my hands, and began to think about Ma and what she would say if she could see me now, and I thought about Imogen and Florence and what they would feel if they knew that I had just *had* a boy on the blue and white tiled bathroom floor of his house in Cheyne Walk, Chelsea, and suddenly I found I was crying.

Digby sat down next to me. 'What is it?' he asked.

'I don't know,' I said. 'I just didn't expect all of this to happen. I didn't think that anything could happen so fast. Especially – especially what just happened now.'

'Was it too fast?' he asked me, his hand on my leg.

'I only met you two days ago,' I said. 'And now I've let you do what you did to me, and I can't *ever* get it back!'

'Come here,' he said. He took me in his arms. Already the smell of him was so familiar!

'Don't regret it,' he said. 'I certainly don't.'

'I'm sorry,' I said. 'It's just that I've got to be the one who's all strong and cool and distant and happy to walk away and say thanks for the good time, and see you next time I'm in town . . .'

Digby laughed. 'If it's any consolation,' he said, 'I don't know anyone who speaks like that.'

I smiled weakly.

'You're just so unlike every other boy I've ever known, and I'm scared that you're not going to hang around for very long.'

Being this close to Digby was having the appalling effect of a truth drug – once I had started I simply couldn't stop. All my feelings for him were thundering out of my mouth without my being able to help it.

'Cherry,' he said. 'Stop. Don't say any more. It's all right. You don't have to *worry* about anything. Just let things happen.'

'What do you mean?' I asked him, confused.

'I mean, don't plan it. Don't think about it. Just live it, just *do* it. You don't have to have explanations for every bloody emotion you're feeling. No one can. Most of the reasons why we do things are a mystery. That's what makes us real.'

He looked satisfied with what he had said to me, and warmed to his theme. 'You know, people pay big money for this sort of chat. Clover's bloke, Dr Henry Righter-than-Wright, makes a fortune telling rich birds to think more. Fuck it, I say. Think *less. Be* more.'

'It was my first time!' I said to him in a violent little whisper – my hands trembling as I accepted his cigarette.

'You're seventeen and your dad's a fucking vicar. I should bloody hope it was.'

'But the trouble with the first time is that you place too much of *everything* on it.'

'Oh, Christ. Are you trying to tell me that it didn't live up to expectation?'

He still looked amused, as well he may.

'No,' I said quickly. I hung my head. 'It's just that it's not *your* first time, is it? It's not going to mean the same thing to you. I mean, you never hear of anyone saying they want their *ninth* time to be the greatest thing that's ever happened, do you?'

Digby laughed.

'Yes, you do,' he said.

'When?'

'Right after the crushing disappointment of their eighth.'

I laughed weakly. He opened a can of Coca-Cola.

'Can I make a suggestion to you, Miss Merrywell?'

'All right,' I said.

'Stop worrying and play me something.'

I sang an old blues song that should have reminded me of home – but thought of nothing more than how his body had felt lying next to mine and how I never wanted to leave him ever again. Without exaggeration, you could say that I gave him everything that afternoon. When I had finished, I turned around, half smiling, but Digby was frowning; he looked – God help me – *concerned*.

'Hey,' he said, 'that's – that's not what you recorded with Billy and Inigo, is it?'

'No. Nothing like it.'

'Thank God for that,' said Digby with relief. 'Because that shit you're playing now . . . is *weird*, baby.'

'Weird but good?'

'Weird but good.' He looked at me. 'Like you,' he said.

We didn't get back to Napier House until five to six. I stepped out of Digby's car, carrying my shoes, my fringe covering my eyes. Even walking up to the front door I felt nervous – as though anyone going past would see me very clearly as the little harlot that I felt I was. It was all right when it was just him and me, but now that I was out of the warmth and shelter of his arms, I felt certain that the whole world would be aware of the swell of my lips where he had kissed me, the high colour in my cheeks, the just qualified, delightfully violated little Tara Jupp, who didn't know what she was doing, only that it felt right. It

317

was something of a torment to me – the luxury of being with Digby, combined with the sneaking suspicion that I might very well be damned for all time.

There was roast chicken and apple crumble at the Six O'Clock Club, but I barely managed a thing. I don't think I noticed what anyone spoke about.

'What's wrong with you?' whispered Lucy, putting down Colette's diaries for once and looking at me curiously.

'Just tired,' I said.

But Lucy looked at me, and she knew.

'I suppose I should tell you to watch out,' she said, forking up the remains of my green beans.

'I don't know what you're talking about,' I mumbled.

'Two pieces of advice,' said Lucy calmly. 'Don't make anything too easy for him, and don't tell him all your secrets.'

Scrubbed and washed and ready for bed at half past nine that night, my face in the bathroom mirror looked resolutely naïve. But he *knew* me now, I thought, pulling my nightdress over my head. I had already messed up that first rule from my sister. I had made it too easy for him.

'I wanted to do it,' I said defiantly to my reproachful reflection.

I stayed awake in bed for two hours listening to Inigo playing the guitar through the walls, and ran over and over the day's events. Imogen wouldn't believe it, I thought.

Lucy came to bed as the clock struck a melancholy midnight. She had been making notes on the contents of Colette Napier's writing desk. I watched her undressing – stepping out of her clothes and leaving them on the floor as usual, and running a

318

flannel over her face – not even bothering with the face cream that Imogen, and even Florence, thought so important.

'You awake?' she whispered, climbing into bed.

'I don't know,' I replied.

There was a pause.

'I've got a third piece of advice,' she said, staring up at the ceiling.

'What is it?'

'If you want to stay happy, don't get married.'

I sat up in bed and looked at her.

'And don't ask me any more questions,' she added. Switching off the light, we lay in darkened silence.

Digby, I thought, my face burning. I didn't want to marry him, but I wanted to be with him more than anything. I needed to know that what I had done had not been in vain.

26

Me and Mr O'Rourke

The next morning Clover announced that we had some time to do what we wanted. For Lucy, this meant a trip to the Coal Exchange to beat herself up over its shaky future – now she was in London, she intended to be one of the number who had made it their mission to stop it from being ripped down – but Clover could see that for me a free day meant something very different. I raced back to him. I didn't call – I simply imagined that he would be as delighted to see me as I would be to see him. I knocked on the door, breathless.

'Oh, it's you!' he said in surprise. 'How nice.'

'I had some time off. I thought I'd come and see if you wanted to – er – go to the pictures or something?'

Clunk! I thought. How silly I felt.

'I'm just learning my way around London,' I said. 'Clover says if I carry on walking the streets at night I'll be ready to take the Knowledge and become a taxi driver if it doesn't work out with Billy and the selling-records thing . . .'

He laughed. That was the thing about Digby – he always laughed at the right time.

'Come upstairs,' he said, probably to stop me from talking

more than anything else. 'I'm doing the crossword.'

Yet upstairs I had quite the opposite problem. Back in his bedroom, I felt ridiculous, as though I had invaded something quite private – and anyway, I hardly knew Digby O'Rourke. Bowling along the road towards his house on the strength of my romantic ideals alone seemed *too* silly. What was I *doing* here? Words seemed impossibly difficult suddenly – where to *go* with them? Was I best seen by him in the style that he had left me after his party? Or should I be darker – perhaps more unexpected? What would hold him, damn it? I shuffled in the doorway of his room. Digby lay down on his bed.

'Can't you sit down? You're making me nervous, standing by the door like you're about to make a run for it.'

I kicked off my shoes and sat down beside him. The bed creaked. To my surprise, Digby put on a pair of glasses.

'They suit you,' I said.

'They create the illusion of intellectual intelligence, a quality that I am sorely lacking,' he said. 'Lie down. Come on, baby. You're here, aren't you?'

'What do you mean?' I asked, understanding exactly.

He hooked an arm around me, and picked up the paper with his free hand. He was as relaxed as I was terrified – there was clearly nothing remotely odd for him in a girl like me showing up at his door having fooled about with him after a couple of cocktails. I was horrified afresh by my own newness, my lack of sophistication. How could I *hold* someone like him? How was it *possible*? I felt my stomach rumbling, and loathed it for betraying me. He appeared to notice nothing, but frowned into *The Times*, all absorbed.

'It's a good thing you're here,' he said after a bit, chewing the end of his pencil. 'You can help me with this one. Six down.

Six letters. "Prophet whose associates are thrown into the fiery furnace."'

'Daniel,' I said automatically.

'Of course,' said Digby, 'Daniel.' He wrote the six letters in, with childish glee. 'The fiery furnace,' he repeated. 'Give me the low-down on that one. What happened?'

'Three of Daniel's gang refused to worship at the feet of a golden statue. Into the flames they went.'

I didn't really want to talk Old Testament with Digby; it reminded me too uncomfortably of home.

'Yikes,' said Digby. 'And I thought *I* had it tough.'

'God saved them though.' I pointed out. 'He generally looks out for the good guys.'

'And the bad guys?'

'Straight to hell.'

Digby threw the paper on to the floor and pulled me to him. We abandoned the cinema. Digby said that old Liberty Valance was probably overrated anyway, and that John Wayne was enough to give any man an inferiority complex.

At two thirty in the afternoon we left the house together, and within a very short space of time it became clear to me that wherever Digby went, camera slung over one shoulder, eyes hazy from cigarette smoke and lack of sleep, people knew him. Not caring about 'cool' made him the hippest person in the room; his association with the fringes of society – with tramps and druggies, with elderly schoolteachers, fat waiters recovering from heart surgery, builders on his street – made him close to Jesus in my eyes. Nobody I had ever met would have been capable of pulling off such behaviour – Digby simply didn't appear to care.

At four o'clock, he hailed a cab.

'Where are we going?' I asked him.

'Jump in,' he ordered. 'Hoxton, mate,' he said to the driver. 'No, don't panic,' he added in my direction. 'It's all right. You can't come to London and not visit the East End. It's fucking *illegal*, baby.'

'Hear, hear!' guffawed the cab driver.

'What about Clover? We must be back by six,' I said. Not usually given to following rules, my need to stay in Clover's good books was startling, especially to me.

'Oh she'll be all right,' said Digby. He noted my expression. 'I'll call her. I'll tell her I've kidnapped you and that you'll be back late. She'll be fine.'

'How do you know?'

'She has no choice,' said Digby.

In the hour and a half that followed, I quickly twigged that everything that Billy had said was right. Digby had an extraordinary way of making one afternoon feel like a whole week, and making me feel like the only lover who had ever mattered to him, and that afternoon, I was quite happy to believe it. He could have taken me anywhere and it would have lit up for me that afternoon, but we ended up in a little café called Harry's Place, deep in the wounded heart of the East End, eating chips and peas and watching the locals piling into the pub on the opposite side of the road.

Seeing Digby in the window, people stopped in to say hello – big-armed men smelling of the sea who had been selling cod all day at the market, sweet-faced women with creased foreheads and fat babies on their hips, and Digby's nephews, Tom and David, carrying bottles of ale to their father who was shutting up the shop on the corner for the night. *He had taken me to see the cast he had left behind!* I thought in ecstacy, several drinks later. *He believed that we would be together forever, which was why I was here with him now!*

'Sorry I've dragged you here under false pretences. I borrowed some bread off Jimmy a while back,' said Digby, shattering my dreams in one fell swoop.

'It's all right, I like seeing where you're from. Gosh, that's a lot of money for a loaf of bread,' I said, watching Digby handing a ten-bob note to the harassed man in the dirty apron behind the counter.

Digby laughed. 'Bread and honey, baby. *Money.*'

For the next hour, we did nothing but smoke and eat chips and talk and rather like playing tennis against a strong opponent forcing the standard of your own game higher, I found that being with Digby made me glitter in a way that I never had before. There was nothing, nothing stronger than the hit I got from being seen out with him – the hit I got from knowing that I had been naked with him. I had been naked, in a bed with a man! I groaned inside with the horror and the delight.

'This is Cherry,' Digby kept saying to everyone who came up. 'You better remember her name because she's sure as hell going to be famous.'

Somehow, he threw out these words in a way that avoided being saccharine, and in doing so, he hoisted me up somewhere way out of reach of anyone else. I ached with wanting to do what we had done together one more time. He had freed me, and trapped me all at once.

'Nice face,' said a pale girl, nodding at me and glaring at Digby. 'Where d'you pick this one up?'

'This is Susie,' said Digby. 'Susie, this is Cherry.'

'Charmed,' said Susie. She rummaged in her bag for something.

The one with the tits! Digby mouthed at me, cupping his hands up to his chest to illustrate the point. *The vicar's niece from school,* I thought, trying not to giggle. Susie looked up.

'Where are you from?' she asked me, looking me up and down.

'The midde of fucking nowhere,' said Digby.

'Cornwall, actually,' I corrected him.

'That's C-O-R-N-W-A-L-L,' said Digby.

'Bugger off,' said Susie. She looked at Digby. 'Your Dad's over the road. Shall I tell him you'll be over?'

'Christ, no,' said Digby in horror.

'Oh shouldn't we say hello?' I asked quickly.

'*Absolutely* not. We'll never get away. Tell him I'll see him Sunday.'

'My mum says 'e's drinkin' again,' sighed Susie. 'You know, if it weren't for 'er lookin' after 'im, I don't know what'd 'appen to 'im.'

'I don't know why she does it,' said Digby.

'Cos she bloody loves 'im, that's why,' said Susie gloomily. 'If 'e could just shut up about your bleedin' mum for more than ten minutes, they could be all right togevver. You know that, Camera Boy?'

'Yeah,' sighed Digby. 'I know that.'

Susie was on a roll now.

'That weasel from the council was over this week talkin' about *you know what.*'

She looked meaningfully from Digby to me and folded her arms over her vast boobs in her tight brown sweater. Digby took another gulp of Guinness.

'What's *you-know-what*?' I asked cautiously.

'They're going to pull his house down,' said Susie promptly. "Aven't you told your girlfriend, Digby? Suppose that sorta thing don't matter to you in bloody Sloane Square.'

I giggled with the thrill of being called his girlfriend. I was rather warming to Susie.

'You're getting ahead of yourself,' said Digby – to which one of us, I did not know.

'Yeah, well you just keep yer lens-cap on,' she said pertly. Sticking her tongue out at him, she walked off.

'What was she talking about?' I asked, watching her leave the café. 'Why is your dad's house coming down?'

Digby looked agitated for a moment.

'Fuck knows. The council is demolishing every house in the street because they say they're not safe to live in any longer. At least that's their excuse – but really, these people just like the sound of bricks falling. Makes them feel like they're doing some-thing, you know – something useful. They want to modernize the whole area. Dad says modernize is another word for kill – and in this case, I agree with the old soak.'

I thought for a moment.

'Could your dad come and live with *you*?' I asked.

'No.'

'Why not?'

'What use would he be on the King's Road? He's East End born and bred. He says it's about more than money. I tried telling him that there's no such thing, but he won't listen. He'll be in his kitchen till the first bite of the bulldozer, God bless his woollen socks.'

'Like Clover,' I observed.

'Yeah, except no one's going to make her go and live in a

paper-thin tower block for the rest of *her* days,' said Digby bitterly. 'Come on. Let's get out of here. I'm starting to get the bends.'

Half an hour later, we were back in Chelsea. We jumped out of the cab, and walked side by side, rather quickly towards the front door of Napier House. I tripped on an uneven paving stone and almost fell to the floor; Digby held my arm. When we were outside, he turned to face me, flicking a glance up at the building that I was at a loss to decipher.

'Thanks for coming East,' he said.

'Thanks for having me.' I blushed at my choice of phrase. 'Will I see you again?' I asked. I could have cursed myself for opening my mouth and saying exactly what I was thinking – honesty was a terrible burden, Errant Jack used to say, and now I knew what he meant.

'I'm not running off to fight in any war,' said Digby. 'Of course you'll see me again,' He pushed my fringe out of my eyes.

'You'd better get in,' he said. 'Clover doesn't like people sneaking in late. Go as quietly as you can.'

I nodded, and opened the door. It wasn't until I had crept up to the top floor that I wondered how he knew that Clover didn't like people coming in late. How many other guests had he entertained in the past year? I didn't want to know the answer.

Lucy was asleep, tucked under the sheets with just her right foot sticking out of the bed – she wouldn't have woken if the nuclear war had cranked up in the next-door room. I took off my clothes, and lit a cigarette beside the open window. I wondered how it was possible for somewhere to feel so foreign, yet at the same time so familiar. I had been here such a short time, and yet if I had left Napier House that night – never to return again – it would have held part of me in its thrall forever.

Every morning in the week that followed, I had breakfast at Napier House with Clover, usually before Lucy had woken up. Clover banned any conversation until we had finished two cups of tea, which I have to say suited me down to the ground, as at home I spent the first hour of the day wondering how on earth Imogen could be so awake and available for comment before she'd so much as spooned golden syrup into her porridge. Clover and I wished one another good morning, then sat quietly while she read the paper and I stared at the back of the corn-flakes packet, listening to the wireless. After breakfast, I would attempt to do something with my hair, fail, and make my way to Cheyne Walk. Expecting Digby to be out for the count, and that I would have to climb in through a window, I was amazed to find him up and dressed every single morning. Seeing him loading up his bags for a job was somewhat humbling. Here was the most successful photographer of the moment, and he wanted to spend time with *me*. The ballroom was filled with film from his cameras and the smell of sunlight on dust.

We had more tea, and he would kiss me, make telephone calls, burn toast and marvel at the vocal range of Gene Pitney. Then we would walk together to Sloane Square, where he would drop me off at my deportment class, before going to shoot some ten-foot model standing in front of the Houses of Parliament or the market in Portobello Road. As soon as we were apart, I felt dizzy with wanting to see him again. Madame Vernier – short, stout, French and terrifying – was just as Clover had described her. Seeing who had dropped me off – and noticing my flushed cheeks and inability to concentrate – she spoke to me about Digby as though he were a tiresome but treatable medical condition that required immediate attention before it got any worse.

'How long have you known him?' she asked me on Friday morning, balancing a copy of *Ruff's Guide to the Turf* on my head.

'A few days,' I said. Resistance seemed futile.

'Ah,' said Madame Vernier. 'I thought so.'

'I like him,' I said defiantly.

'Of course,' she said. 'He is brilliant, and he knows what he is doing. Why on earth *wouldn't* you like him?' She looked at me. 'And you are seventeen. How one *forgets*,' she said, stepping towards me and tilting my face up to the light. 'Youth,' she declared, as though heading an essay. 'Seven years ago you were but ten years old!'

She laughed loudly and gave me an unexpected squeeze around the middle.

'Little thing,' she said. 'You're too thin. You must remember to eat. The force of these awful infatuations girls get at your age flattens the appetite, but not eating the right food at the right time of day can be as influential on the brain as opium. You don't eat, you can't think straight, you make the wrong choices. Before you know it, you've lost. Keep eating.'

'My sister back at home says the same thing,' I said, with one of my regular Pangs for Imogen. 'She always says you should never decide anything without first having a cheese-and-tomato sandwich. Or at the very least a bowl of Weetabix.'

'I would suggest a salad *parisienne* and steak Béarnaise, but yes, the point stands.'

She frowned at me. 'The limp when you walk,' she said suddenly. 'How did that come to be? Did you suffer from polio, dear thing?'

Despite the fact that everything that I did with Madame was focused on posture and movement, I felt jarred by the directness of the question. She had not mentioned my limp before. Polio, I thought savagely. I wished it had been. That one word would have obliterated all further explanations, all need for me to cast my mind back to Ma's death.

'My – my sister and I fell off a bike. We were riding it together. Silly, I suppose.'

Madame stayed quiet. 'It was just after my mother died,' I added unwillingly, yet unable not to say it. I always had to say it when people remarked upon my limp. It was part of why it had happened. Madame placed her hands on my abdomen. 'Breathe,' she said. 'As we did yesterday.'

I closed my eyes and did as she requested.

'All right,' said Madame, holding up her hand with a cacophony of jangling bracelets. 'Keep it.'

'What?'

'The limp. It is characterful. But I suppose you know that you needn't have it any longer. You have kept it because you *wanted* to.'

'I – what?'

'The time that it 'appened, it was important to you. That is why it is still with you. It takes you back to your mother.'

'Yes,' I whispered.

I didn't want to talk about it any more. Speaking about Ma was jarring, wrong. It was too bright now, too sunny to be reminded of the agony of that first week without her.

After seeing Madame, I would walk back down the King's Road – thinking every street name more romantic than the one before. *Radnor Walk, Shawfield Street, Flood Street, Oakley*

Street. Arriving back at Digby's at the same time as him, he would be crazed with hunger, so we would go out for lunch, or tea, or just cigarettes and endless rounds of sandwiches at the Chelsea Kitchen. He was light with me when we were out, as uncatchable as ever. Yet when we were horizontal, the whole world seemed to turn in on itself. Nothing meant anything if it wasn't in his bedroom. I didn't think that it would happen to me like this; it *did*. I didn't think that I would give myself like this; I *did*. Before, I had needed something else for my kicks – a horse, a piano, a ticket to the cinema, a new record. Suddenly, all of that fell away with the thumping realization that the sensation of someone else's hands on my skin could actually mean more than any of that – and for *free*! It was almost as if I expected someone to walk in and stop it from happening – it felt far too powerful – too insanely powerful – to be allowed.

And it *was* quite something – that thrill that seemed to come with the simplest of things: lying naked, drinking tepid mint tea in his bed, having cool shallow baths at five in the afternoon on Sunday, with the window slightly open so that I could hear the world going on outside as if listening to a radio play. Did I love him? Certainly, I presumed that I must. I didn't want to be without him. Despite Clover's words, Digby was the ideal starter pack. He was a shot, a surge of something new and vital. I didn't want that to end, but I knew that it couldn't go on like this forever. No one was entitled to this much bliss, to this much of *anything*. Or were they? It felt at once like the antithesis of everything Pa stood for and everything anyone could ever want.

When those seven days were over, I waited for Billy and

Matilda to return from Paris. I knew that once they were back, the spell, the freedom, the luxury of it all would be splintered.

27

The Sound of the Week

And I was right. Billy came to Napier House just a few hours after his plane landed. I was sitting in the drawing room, helping Lucy and Clover go through a pile of old photograph albums from Napier's past. My lesson with Madame was an hour away, and Digby was out of town taking pictures of a politician for *The Times*. Clover insisted that while we were working the conversation stayed strictly nineteenth century.

'Look at her,' said Lucy, pushing a picture of a terrifying-looking woman in a huge fur hat in front of us.

'My Great-Great-Aunt Joanna,' said Clover. 'You can always tell her by the expression of perpetual disdain.'

'Can't we summon her up and persuade her to haunt those who plan to destroy the house?' suggested Lucy.

We were all so engrossed in what we were doing that we didn't hear the doorbell at first.

'That will be Billy,' said Clover eventually.

'How do you know?'

'He telephoned from Paris last night and said he was coming straight over.'

Billy looked uncomfortable in Napier House; it seemed to

depress him. He stood above us, beautiful, manicured Billy Laurier, in a pale grey suit and yellow tie. He was so immaculate, so perfectly modern, that I felt nothing more than a worthless little scruff beside him. I hadn't brushed my hair for days, my face was white from lack of sleep. There were holes in the toes of my socks that I hadn't darned – I sat on them to hide them, but I don't think he would have noticed anyway. He was too caught up in the magnitude of what he had to say to me.

'Cherry Merrywell, I've got some news for you,' he said, brushing away our questions about his stay in France and comments on the hot weather. He accepted a cigarette from Clover, which was rare, and pulled off his tie, which was rarer still.

'What is it?' asked Clover, Lucy and I all at the same time.

Billy laughed at our expectant faces. 'First, have a look at this.'

From his bag he pulled a record in a red sleeve. He handed it to me, grinning. It was warm.

'Mine,' I said stupidly. 'Gosh, it's me. This is my record.'

Nothing could have been less ordinary, and yet all I could think was that Cherry Merrywell wasn't me at all. I felt more of a fraud than ever. I stared at the name, then at the song titles, with Inigo's name in brackets after "May to September". Flipping it to the B-side, I read "Over the Rainbow" and thought back to the fleeting minutes in which I had sung that famous song while the orchestra swelled around me. I smelled it. It smelled like a record, it looked like a record – holy smoke, it *was* a record – only it felt like a plaything, no more real than the sleeves I used to design at home. There was the large 'B' for Bilco in the middle of the thing, putting me in the same club as all the girls and groups that had gone before me.

'It can't be!' said Lucy, taking it from me gently and inspecting it as though it were an egg about to hatch.

'Whaddaya think?' asked Billy.

I grinned at him. 'Does it play?'

'Of course! And now for the good news, babies. Our little record's going to be played on Radio Luxembourg next week. They love it. They're going to play it on *Rockin' To Dreamland*.'

'Oh my God!' shouted Lucy.

'No!' I said in disbelief.

For we who had spent feverish nights under the bedclothes tuned into this programme, it seemed nothing short of a miracle that *my* voice would be heard on radio-sets tied to bed-posts around the country. I felt a sudden surge of pure terror.

'That's wonderful,' said Clover, who very sweetly looked thrilled, despite the fact that she had obviously heard words such as these from Billy on several occasions before. 'Shall we have a drink?'

'Of course,' said Billy.

I was staggered. '*What?*' I asked. 'But it's so *soon*,' I began. 'I haven't even heard it! How can they have heard it when *I* haven't heard it?'

'Oh, that's nothing,' said Billy dismissively. 'I know several groups whose drummers have never even listened to their finished records when they had copies in their hands!'

'But how did you do it so *fast*?'

'I always get the records I'm really happy with to the radio as soon as I can,' said Billy. 'We did it,' he said softly.

'You mean, they've already *heard* it?' I asked. 'They've heard it, and they *like* it? They actually like my *voice*?'

'They love the whole thing,' said Billy. 'Your voice, the song, the story . . .'

'The *story*?'

But Billy was shaking my hand now.

'Congratulations,' he said. 'Didn't I say, as soon as I heard you, "That girl needs to make a hit record?"'

'It isn't a hit *yet*, is it?' I looked at him in confusion, as though perhaps I had missed out on my own rise to fame. 'I mean, just because they're going to play it—'

'If Billy feels like this, it's a hit,' said Clover. 'You needn't complicate the issue with small matters like the fact that it hasn't actually been pressed, or placed in any shop windows yet.'

I couldn't tell whether she was being sarcastic or not; it was one of the most bothersome things about Clover.

'Tara,' said Lucy, 'your voice on the radio.' She grinned at me. 'What *will* Mr Bell say?' She grinned at me and left the room, blowing me a kiss and executing a perfect pirouette on the way out of the door.

Clover handed me a full glass of champagne, which really, I didn't need.

'I never thought it would be so . . .' I stopped, unsure of what I was going to say next. 'I never thought it would be so *easy*. It was an impossible dream – now it's happening. I almost don't know what to do with myself.'

'How's Digby?' asked Billy, jumping on to my train of thought.

I blushed. 'I think he's all right.'

'When d'you last see him?'

'Yesterday.'

'Good,' said Billy. He looked at Clover. 'But she hasn't missed the Six O'Clock Club?'

'Not once,' said Clover. I didn't dare look at her.

Inigo came into the room holding a bottle of beer.

'How's it going?' asked Billy, shaking his hand.

'It's like Morocco out there,' said Inigo. 'The only time I can write is after midnight when the house cools down for a couple of hours.'

'As long as you're writing, I don't care what time it is.'

I was aware of Inigo looking at my unkempt hair and vampire-white face. I hadn't seen him all week. I wondered if he knew how much time I was spending with Digby.

On cue, the doorbell rang.

'That will be my wife,' said Billy. 'I'll get it.'

'I'll get coffee,' said Clover.

They left the room. Inigo and I looked at each other.

'He can be so ridiculous,' he whispered, although there was no chance that Billy could hear us now.

'Who?' I demanded. 'Billy or Digby?'

'Oh God, Tara. Both.'

I could hear Billy opening the front door. Hesitating, then deciding that he may as well make conversation with me, however tedious that may be, Inigo crossed the room to where I was leaning against the wall, and stood next to me. He took a gulp from his beer and handed it to me.

Saying nothing, I took it from him and finished it off. I handed the empty bottle back to him.

'How is he?' he asked me.

'Who?'

He grinned. 'The boy with the camera.'

I looked at him and he seemed extraordinarily different to when I had last seen him, though I knew it was me who had changed – not him. After the familiarity of Digby's solid, boyish features, he seemed unbelievably feminine.

'I expect you're wondering why Digby wants to hang around with a little snip like me from the West Country when he could be fooling around with the entire editorial content of last month's *Vogue*?' I said.

'Oh, not at all,' said Inigo. 'I absolutely understand precisely why he's hanging around with you.'

'W-why?' I asked defiantly.

'Novelty,' said Inigo. 'You're not like any of those girls. For all that I don't like the bloke, he always picks out the most interesting person in the room for his undivided attention. He wouldn't be where he is if he didn't.'

It could have been a compliment; coming from him it felt like anything but.

He crossed the room to the window and looked at me. I wanted to give him an Estella-from-*Great-Expectations*-inspired look of chilly dislike, but he threw me by snorting with laughter. Furious, I turned on him.

'What does it matter to you, anyway?' I said. 'You said that I wouldn't know what to do if a man so much as asked me out for tea!'

'I wish you'd forget about that, for God's sake,' he said. '*Jeez*, Tara.' He pushed his hands through his hair. 'You know, where he's concerned, you should never listen to anyone. Just do what the song says: follow your heart.'

'Follow my heart?' I laughed, embarrassed and wrong-footed.

'If he rocks your boat, you've got to make him yours for as long as you want him.'

I took the empty bottle back from him and squinted into it, just for something to do. It was terribly uncomfortable, hearing Inigo talking like this – encouraging something that I had been so certain he would find deeply silly.

'I thought you said you didn't like him.'

'I don't. But telling girls whom they can and can't fall in love with is one of life's more futile ventures.'

'You speak as if you know what you're talking about,' I said.

'Oh, I don't. I just pretend I do.'

I laughed. 'No one can write like you do and not know anything about girls.'

'I make it all up and hope for the best,' said Inigo. 'All I learned about the female of the species came from my mother and my big sister. The more you tell them that someone's wrong, the more they're going to think they're right. So there's no point. If you want my advice, don't go and see him tonight.'

'Why? He's expecting me.'

'All the more reason not to go. Keep your distance and he'll never lose interest. Really, Tara, this is basic stuff. They should teach it at school.' He sighed.

'He's expecting me. He's going to think it very odd if I don't show up.'

'He'd also think that you had something better to do than flap around him all night.'

'I don't flap, and I certainly don't stay there all night,' I said, with very little conviction. For the past three nights, I had let myself into Napier House just as the birds started singing.

'Listen, this makes no odds to me. I'm just throwing out suggestions to you, but the one thing I *do* know is how a mind like Digby O'Rourke's works.'

'How? He's about the most complex person I've ever met,' I said defiantly.

'Well, he's not. He's about as simple as they come.'

'How can you say that! He's had such a strange upbringing—'

'Christ! Show me someone who hasn't! You've grown up with no mother, and a father in constant dialogue with the Almighty. I grew up with no father, and a mother who ran off with an American – who was pretty much *her* idea of the Almighty actually,' he added, reflecting briefly. 'There's no such thing as a normal childhood. End of story.'

He lit a cigarette and handed it to me.

'Why do you always have to talk like this?'

'Like what?'

'As though everyone around you is an idiot without a clue.'

'All I'm saying is that if you want to stay in with him, then I'd stay in tonight.'

We heard the sound of footsteps coming back up the stairs. From outside came the unexpected cries of seagulls.

As the door opened again, he moved away from me, towards the window; it was as if the last few minutes had never happened. Inigo was very good at acting with blithe serenity when the scene had to change again.

For all that I didn't want him to know that I had listened to him, I took Inigo's advice and had an early night. I telephoned Digby to tell him that I wasn't going to be seeing him.

'That's all right.' I heard him yawning.

I wanted him to try to persuade me to change my mind, but he didn't.

'You sleep well.'

'Tomorrow night Lucy and I are going to Claridge's with Matilda.'

'You'll love it,' said Digby. 'Have the avocado soup.'

Avocado, I thought. Raoul had brought us avocados at Trellanack the first time he had met us. How was he? I was shocked by how much I missed him.

When I put down the phone, I entered my conversation in Clover's book. *Tara Jupp to Digby O'Rourke. Duration: three minutes.* Then I scribbled out *Tara Jupp.* To Digby, I was always *Miss Cherry Merrywell.*

As I climbed the stairs, I could hear Lucy, Clover and Inigo playing Scrabble and drinking Scotch. Lucy was bellowing about the authenticity of the word 'populatory' and how Clover's Victorian dictionary ought to be outlawed.

I slept for twelve hours, and when I awoke Clover dispatched me to Billy's house for a meeting about an interview for *Woman and Home* magazine.

'You can talk about all the sorts of things that girls like to hear about,' Billy said. He was sitting behind his desk, actually smoking a cigar. I breathed in the heavy smoke and closed my eyes.

'What's that?' I asked him. 'I mean, what do girls *like* to hear about? I don't know any girls who like the same thing as the next.'

'Oh, come on, Cherry. I'm talking about your clothes, your make-up, what you like to cook . . .'

His confidence faltered as he looked at me.

'Who are we fooling?' he said with a sigh. 'Listen. *We* both know that you don't care about any of that shit, darling, but the rest of world doesn't need to know that.'

I felt a wave of pity for Billy – how awkward that he had selected such a hopeless case in me.

'Can't I talk about other stuff?' I asked. 'You know – the fact that we're all on the verge of war and destruction, or something?'

'Good God, no,' said Billy, alarmed. 'This is a magazine for women, Cherry. They don't want to read about that sort of thing. And in any case, it won't happen.'

'What won't happen?'

'Nuclear war.'

'What makes you so sure?'

'Well, we haven't got time for it, of course.'

He looked at his diary and flipped through a couple of pages. 'I suppose I *could* squeeze it in between my meeting at Decca next Wednesday and lunch with Hank Marvin on Friday, but it *will* be tight. It'll have to be over by Thursday morning for sure – I'm having breakfast with my accountant.'

I smiled weakly.

'And there's another reason of course,' he added. 'You and Lucy are having dinner with my wife tonight.'

'Yes,' I said, as brightly as I could. 'I hadn't forgotten.'

'She needs her old friends.'

'Everyone needs their old friends,' I said blandly. To be quite honest, dinner with Lucy and Matilda was only fractionally less terrifying than nuclear war, I thought. I had no idea what to expect from it at all.

Billy took a record off the gramophone and looked for the sleeve. He didn't like talking about Matilda unless he was pre-occupied with something else.

'It was always going to take time for Matilda and your sister to regain what they had, but I know it will happen. I just know it. You understand how much it means to her, don't you?'

'I don't know,' I said.

'I think if we could just get them back on track—'

'You can't expect Matilda becoming friends with Lucy again to return everything to how it was. She was never normal in the first place.'

'She wants to tell you both something,' said Billy. 'Something that's important to her. Please, Cherry.' He stopped suddenly.

342

'All right,' I said uncomfortably. 'I didn't say I wouldn't go.'

Billy sighed. 'You need to hear her out, all right? When you're as famous as she is, no one really listens to you – they just *look*.'

He clicked his tongue, appearing suddenly irritated with himself for saying this, and changed the subject swiftly.

'I think you should go back home with your sister this weekend.'

I thought I had misheard him.

'Back *home*? To Cornwall?'

'Yes.' Billy smiled at me. 'Back home, to Cornwall.'

'I don't understand. Is it over already?' I looked at him in confusion.

'No, Cherry. It's just beginning. This is the calm before the storm. Take this chance, while you can. Now that the first song is being played on the radio, we need to move everything on again. Get back into the studio. I'd like you to have a break first. I've spoken to Inigo,' he went on. 'He'll drive you both back.'

'Inigo?'

'One of the things you'll have to learn about me is that I don't like keeping people away from the places where they feel safest. If I ever feel that you need to go home, I shall send you back right away. This isn't boarding school.'

'But I wasn't expecting to go home so soon!' I looked at him, suddenly taking on board what he had said. 'And with Inigo! He won't want to come—'

'Why on earth not? I rather think he likes getting back to his roots.'

'He's not from Cornwall,' I said. 'His parents' house was in Wiltshire. That's at least four hours away.'

'Four hours? That's nothing,' said Billy. 'Travel the length and

343

breadth of the United States, and you won't think like that any more, Cherry.'

'Where will he stay?' I asked. 'He can't stay with us!'

I felt a wave of horror at the mere thought.

'No, no, no. He shall stay at Trellanack. He can do a little work there – put the piano to good use – then return with you after the weekend.'

'Gosh,' I said. 'It sounds like you've got it all planned. I'm still not sure that he'll be all that pleased.'

He ignored me.

'You and Lucy should both be back in London on Tuesday afternoon. That gives her plenty of time to visit her husband in hospital.'

Thank God, I thought. *She would have to see him again.*

'You want Lucy back again after that?'

'Clover says that your sister is unrivalled in her knowledge of what the Victorians got up to, and she can't think of a better person to be campaigning for Napier. But she must go home this weekend and talk to Raoul about it. She could be up here for another three months. She needs to speak to him about taking the job.'

God in heaven. I felt a chill inside. For whatever he claimed, it felt as though he was sending me and Lucy back to say goodbye. Now that the record was made, and was going to be played, he needed to have me at the snap of his fingers. What would Ma have done? I wondered. But as soon as I had asked myself the question, I knew the answer. Ma wouldn't have wanted to be home again. For her, this would have been the beginning of the dream.

That fact reinforced itself when, crowded around Clover's wireless, we listened to the song on the radio for the first time.

When it started to play, I stared dumbly at Lucy, frowning. Despite the fact that I knew that I had sung it, a part of me was terrified, as I listened to my voice throwing out Inigo's melody to the universe and beyond, that I may suddenly stop singing, or forget the words, or ask to start again. Lucy went bright red and started to shake as the chorus started. Clover smiled – she had seen and heard people she knew on the radio before of course – but she was not unaware of the impact such an event was having upon two girls from west Cornwall, who but a few weeks ago had been imagining a summer filled with nothing more than cutting hair and riding unfit ponies up and down dusty bridle paths for barely any money.

'Is that *you*?' asked Lucy. She was incredulous. 'It *can't* be you!'

'I don't know,' I said. 'I can't believe it is either!' I put my hand up to my mouth to hide the grin. It wasn't that I loved the song any more than I had when I had sung it – but there was a triumph in all of this that I would have been foolish not to appreciate, and I knew that.

'You sound like . . . you sound like a proper singer!' said Lucy, craning forward towards the wireless as though she expected another version of me to pop out from the speakers and start dancing around in front of her.

'Father Hit-mas has done it again,' sighed Clover. 'This will be going round and round in my head all night long.'

Just to be sure that it was me, just to be sure that there wasn't some mistake, I sang along with the last verse – and as I did so, I suddenly saw myself as the ten-year-old girl who had listened to Alma Cogan and vowed that one day I would be just like her.

'Ma wouldn't believe it,' Lucy said in a shaky voice. 'She really wouldn't believe it.'

'What will your father think?' asked Clover. She picked up the paper and flipped though until she hit the social pages.

'I don't know,' I said. 'Hard to say.'

'He'd be proud,' said Lucy without looking at me. 'Like I am.'

Then all three of us sang along – even though neither Lucy nor Clover had ever heard the song before – right through to the very end of the record, when they announced that it was me, and I hadn't expected to know so soon, but I did. Cherry Merrywell was going to make it, but it was nothing to do with me. It was Clover and the clothes, and Billy and knowing the right people, and Digby and his pictures, and Inigo and his song. It was everyone except me – and the only thing that I had to do was not mind about that. Soon I would be back in Cornwall, I thought, and it seemed further away than Neptune.

28

Claridge's for a State of Mind

After listening to the song, and knowing that what I had come up to do had actually *happened*, I had a terrible desire *not* to see Matilda for dinner, and I disliked myself for it. I wanted to be with Digby – I felt that I needed him to tell me that nothing had changed. Hearing the record had made me feel lost, almost jealous of myself, if such a thing were possible. Where was I now? If I had been a girl listening at home, I would have imagined Cherry Merrywell to have the most enchanted life. She would be out at parties, or meeting new people who would be dazzled by her, or singing new songs, or charming boys everywhere. I was going to Claridge's, but not in the golden coach to meet princes from other lands. I was going to see my sister's old friend, who couldn't stop drinking, and if this was what became of you when you made money and became known to the masses, then what on earth was the point! Yet Lucy and I had known her before all of this. I had known her in that far-off, distant country called happiness, and that was why she was so desperate to see us. In any case, not seeing her was simply not even an option. Billy had booked the three of us a table at the most alluring place in the whole city. I could see why he was doing it; most of what Billy did was fairly transparent. I think that he assumed that by putting us in the most beautiful restaurant in the whole of London, and telling us that he would pick up the bill, some sort of alchemy would be take place, some kind of marvellous resolution to everything.

Lucy and I had expected that Matilda would be late, but I knew that it was my business to arrive a little early. Clover booked us a taxi from Napier House, and I resisted the smell of roast chicken and apple pie destined for the Six O'Clock Club. Clover had several friends joining her for supper – Charlotte Ferris would be among their number; I think she may have been pleased to be ridding herself of us for the evening.

'You'd better smarten yourself up a bit,' she advised, opening a box of brown sugar with a bread knife. I must have gone a bit pale, because she took pity on me and said, 'Go up to my room. Open Lady Louisa's wardrobe. There's a black lace dress near the back. Billy would say it was horribly funereal, but since this place is heading for destruction I've come to the opinion that there's no such a thing as looking too haunted. Try it on.'

I could have stayed all evening in Clover's bedroom, but its immaculate tidiness gave a frosty reception to one as scruffy as I was. In the middle of the room, between the two windows, was her dressing table, and upon it her endless creams and pots and jars, perfumes and brushes. I wanted to pick up each and every one, smell them all, roll in Clover's unique brand of magic and hope that it would give me her power, her cool. Instead, and slightly fearing that she was timing me from the kitchen, I hurried to the wardrobe and found the dress. Stepping out of my green skirt and blouse, I pulled it on and stared at myself in the mirror.

For the first time since I had arrived in London, I looked

348

like I had always wanted to look. For the first time in my life, I was wearing black. It was long – too long really for someone as short as Clover and I were – and high at the neck. Black lace fringed the edges of the sleeves and the hem; it took a while to do the wretched thing up as it was all hook and eye fastenings that had stiffened and warped out of shape with age. Terrified that I would tear it, I walked downstairs with deliberate slowness, the rustling of the material adding drama to my movement. Inigo was standing at the bottom of the stairs, kneeling down beside his guitar case. He looked up at me without missing a beat.

'You've been in Clover's dressing-up box,' he said. 'Very Mrs Danvers.'

'I'm going to Claridge's,' I said, registering the snub.

Inigo whistled. 'Digby's taking you to Claridge's?'

'No,' I said, irritated. 'Lucy and I are having dinner with Matilda.'

'Ah,' he said. He paused. 'Don't order duck.'

'Duck?' I laughed. 'Why ever not?'

Inigo looked at his hands.

'My mother used to force duck upon us when she wanted to make dramatic announcements. Duck for supper always boded badly.'

'Was your mother a terrible cook?'

He looked up at me, as though the question had never occurred to him before, which I imagine it hadn't.

'No idea,' he said. 'I don't think she's ever looked at an oven in her life, except perhaps to check her reflection.'

'Who cooked for you?' I felt my heart speeding up.

Inigo looked puzzled.

'Sweet old thing called Mary,' he said, picking up several

packets of guitar strings from the case. 'Unfortunately she only had one setting in her repertoire.'

'What was that?'

'Boil. She boiled everything.'

'At least you had someone to cook for you,' I said. *And that someone was my aunt!* I wanted to yell. Even though I whole-heartedly agreed with his assessment of her skills, I felt fury rising inside me.

'Mary was a great cook in the same sense that Digby is a great photographer,' said Inigo.

'I don't know what you mean.'

'She *wasn't*, but she did what any old fool could do, simply by being in the right place at the right time with an odd charm, invisible to many, but powerful to the chosen few.'

He wrong-footed me utterly with what he said next.

'I used to love the kitchen at Magna. Mary never minded me practising my guitar in the pantry, God rest her soul.'

For the second time in as many days, I fought back a terrible urge to cry.

Inigo closed his guitar case and stood up.

'You're wasted on Matilda,' he said, and walked off. He stopped outside the library and turned around again. 'And Digby,' he added.

No amount of imagination could have conjured up a place more arresting than Claridge's – it was the closest I had ever been to entering a palace. I very nearly fell down on my knees in grati-tude to Clover for allowing me to wear Lady Louisa's dress. The thought of appearing in anything else was appalling – I shuddered at the image of little old me in an alternative universe, standing doltish in my linen smock, waiting for Matilda with my knotted hair and scuffed knees, like a child. Lucy was attempting calm and failing somewhat.

'We must see if we can get into one of the bedrooms,' she said.

'More your area of expertise than mine,' I said, with perfect truth. Lucy laughed. I wanted to ask her if she was missing Raoul, if she had spoken to him, and if the harmonica player had tracked her down, but I found I couldn't say anything, the words stuck in my throat. There was something unknown about Lucy now, and all I knew was that she wanted it to stay that way. I squashed down my questions.

I could have stood in the entrance hall for at least half an hour, watching people slide in and out of the building like extras on a film set, their footsteps perfect on the black and white marble floor. How could anyone walk through such a building without conviction, without knowing where they were going, without falling in love? It was impossible. They were like toy people to me. I shook my head to rid my thoughts of Luke's account of Jesus's temptation by the devil in the wilderness: *All This I Will Give To You.* Pa would be shocked by such extravagance. Needless to say, I was completely in its thrall.

Lucy and I were taken to the bar to wait for Matilda, where we were asked what we wanted to drink.

'Oh, what would *you* have?' Lucy asked the man wielding the cocktail shaker.

He looked at her with some satisfaction.

'Cosmopolitan, of course,' he said.

'Thank you. That is, of *course*, what I wanted you to say.'

Oh, if Imogen could see me now! I should have asked someone to take our photograph, to preserve the Jupp sisters in this place for all time.

'Here goes nothing,' said Lucy, grinning and taking a big gulp. Lucy could never do moderation when standing somewhere as beautiful as this. She was already drunk on the magic of the place, and just the smallest sip of the concoction I was handed two minutes later was enough to send my head spinning.

'I'm going to the Ladies' Bathroom,' announced Lucy. 'Clover said it had to be seen to be believed.'

'Don't be too long,' I bleated. Lucy was forever vanishing like this – she would become distracted by everything.

Five minutes later I glanced at my watch, or at least I would have done had I been wearing one. Actually, I think I asked what the time was and, on hearing that it was ten past eight, realized that I could be waiting a good deal longer. It was then that a woman walked in on the other side of the bar, registered my lonely state and asked if I would like to join her. She looked young – older than me but younger than Lucy – and was dressed to kill, as though her life depended upon the perfection of her eye make-up.

'Come and have a drink with me,' she said. 'While you wait for your lover.'

I almost choked. 'Gosh, I don't have a lover.' Then I thought about Digby, and added, 'At least, I'm not meeting him this evening.'

I should never have had the nerve to say such things without the cocktail. I was shocked at myself, and delighted at the same time. I grinned at her from under my fringe.

'Actually, my sister's here somewhere,' I said. 'And we're meeting a very old friend.'

Juliet, as she was called, had tight blonde curls and thick layers of black eyeliner that gave her the look of a friendly panda bear. She accented her sentences with excited gasps.

'I've never been here before,' she said. 'It's like steppin' inside a box of chocolates. Isn't it just the *end*?'

'The end is *certainly* what it is,' I said. 'We should be making the most of this.'

'Are you talkin' about the nuclear war an' all that?'

I nodded.

'Oh, right. Only, no, that won't 'appen.'

'How do you know?'

'Too much love in the world, in't there?'

She went off into a great peal of laughter. The barman raised his eyes at us and smiled.

Lucy returned and there was all the hoo-ha of introductions. Lucy, I could tell, wasn't impressed by the fact that I had become embroiled in conversation. I could see she was bursting to talk about the gold taps and the scented towels in the bathroom, and now couldn't. For another ten minutes Juliet and I talked – two people with absolutely nothing in common except for the fact that we were both in the bar at Claridge's for the first time, and really, that was enough.

'Do you have children?' I asked her, by way of filling the space. Surely Matilda would be here soon. Lucy's eyes were on the ceiling now, assessing the paintwork, calculating the hours of labour involved in achieving such a feat.

'Four,' she said.

Even Lucy looked shocked. 'You look too young,' said Lucy.

'Probably because I left my husband last week.'

'I thought you were waiting for your husband.'

'No one comes to Claridge's with their husbands, do they? Actually, he's my husband's best friend. We're having the most monumental affair.'

She stared at us both for a moment.

'Gosh,' I said. 'What a thing!'

'Yes, isn't it?' She took a great breath in, as though she needed more air, then finished her drink, her hand shaking. 'It feels wonderful to tell someone. I just *had* to tell someone. I saw you and I thought, I'll tell *her*. The sweet, pretty thing in black. I'll never see her again, so it may as well be she who knows.'

Lucy was very still beside me. I think she was waiting for Juliet to pass some great pearls of wisdom to her, some wondrous piece of advice that would see Lucy through the next year of her life.

'*Affair!*' I repeated. I sounded ridiculously bright, as though we were talking about a holiday destination. Oh, I've heard about Affair – it's supposed to be wonderful at this time of year!

'We'd known each other for some time, of course,' Juliet went on. Now she'd started, she didn't want to stop. ''E always used to flirt a bit, you know, tell me I looked lovely, that sort of thing. Then one day, he turned up out of the blue. It was rainin' and I was at home on my own. The kids were at school, my 'usband was in a meetin'. He just pulled me into his arms and that was that.'

'Jeepers,' I said. 'I didn't think that sort of thing happened in real life.'

'We went on like that for a while,' said Juliet. 'You know, sneakin' round everyone. But it was too difficult. I couldn't contain all this –' she opened her arms wide, jangling her bracelets – 'all this blinkin' *love*. I told my 'usband that I was very sorry, but I was leavin'. He didn't believe me, but 'e 'ad to when I started packing up bags.'

'How did he take it?' asked Lucy, in spite of herself.

'I don't know,' said Juliet. 'He'll find someone new.' A flare of bitterness crossed her face for a moment. 'They always do.'

'Don't you miss your husband?' I sounded accusing.

'No' She looked at me and grinned. 'It turns out, after all those years, I wasn't in love with him after all.'

I didn't want to look at Lucy. I wanted, very much, to get away from Juliet and everything that she was saying. Why was it, that everywhere we went, there seemed to be nothing but people encouraging Lucy to leave Raoul? Lucy was going to say something, I could tell she was, but fortunately it was at that moment that Matilda entered the room.

She was wearing black, like me, but her dress was see-through, and underneath she was wearing what looked like pink silk. Her hair was loose around her face, vaguely curled, as though she hadn't quite shaken out the results of her last photocall. She wasn't wearing heels, but little black ballet pumps, and around her neck there was no jewellery. She looked plain, undecorated, but still there was that great surge of energy that entered the room with her, whether she wanted it to or not: the fame thing, knocking everyone for six, giving them all something to talk about for weeks to come. When she saw me, she waved briefly and struck out across the floor towards us.

'Don't look,' hissed Juliet. 'But Matilda Bright's comin' this way. A friend of mine saw her at the theatre a while back, said she was dead drunk. I think all those cameras probably set your head spinnin', don't they? Prob'ly she's gone a bit doolally.'

The next moment, Matilda was standing right next to us.

'Have you been waiting forever?' she asked me, rubbing my arm up and down.

'No,' said Lucy quickly.

'Delightful to have met you both,' said Juliet, backing away, her face crimson.

'Oh, have you made friends?' asked Matilda, beaming at her.

'We were just passin' the time of day,' said Juliet.

'I love your blouse,' said Matilda, reaching out and stroking the collar. 'I can't wear peach. It drains me so.'

Juliet stared at Matilda.

'You're far, *far* more beautiful in the flesh,' she said.

'Aren't you sweet?' said Matilda. She had heard it a million times before; it had ceased to register, but she knew to react as though it were the first time anyone had paid her such a compliment. Juliet blushed and bowed her head slightly, as though she were meeting royalty.

As we were led to our table, I saw a man entering the bar, looking around. He was anxious, sweating, carrying *The Times* under one arm and an umbrella under the other, and smiled, relieved, when he saw Juliet. The most ordinary of men, I thought, were capable of starting unstoppable fires. I wished we hadn't talked to Juliet; I knew that Lucy had taken all of what she had said on board. I could practically feel her edging closer and closer to the damned harmonica player.

Matilda parted diners like Moses through the Red Sea, and we sat down to dinner. It was only then that I realized how much she had already had to drink. Lucy caught my eye and shook her head. The night had only just begun, and already I felt as though we had been there a week.

'Here goes nothing,' I muttered.

29

Us and the Famous Girl

From the moment that we sat down, it was obvious that Matilda was flying. The table, immaculate, glittering crystal, white and silver, lurched in front of us as she sat down.

'There are wine glasses here fearing for their lives,' said Lucy cheerfully.

Thirty seconds later, the first of these unfortunate glasses went over. There was nothing in it to spill, but the glass smashed over everything. The waiters rushed up, horrified that such a celebrated guest was enduring such a thing; it had to be their fault, not hers.

'Miss Bright, may we move you and your guests to another table?'

Lucy and I stood to move, but Matilda stayed put and lit a cigarette.

'We're fine, thank you,' she said. 'Gosh, now I've sat down I really don't think I could possibly stand up again.'

'Of course, Miss Bright.'

While he picked little pieces of glass from all around us, Matilda talked, loudly.

I'm so happy that we're all here,' she said. 'It means so much to me. You'll never know how much.'

'What were you doing today?' I asked her. I didn't want to hear her dissolving into sentimental talk just yet. Surely that could be staved off until we had finished eating.

'Standing around in Dior, surrounded by deer.'

'Really?'

'I was in Richmond Park,' she said. '*Woman's Own*. They can only employ me for beauty pages now because of the bump. It was terribly hot. I lay down at one point and fell asleep. They actually poured water over me to wake me up.'

'I think you should stop working,' I said. 'It can't be good for the baby, standing around all day.'

Matilda said nothing, but stuck her hand into the wine bucket and pulled out the bottle. Taking out the cork, she sloshed more wine over the table than into her glass. 'The baby's *fine!*' she said suddenly.

Her voice was too loud, and now even she knew it. Hunching her shoulders, she looked at Lucy and me with her chin almost touching the tablecloth.

'All I wanted to do tonight was see you both. Talk to you. And now here we are. It's nice, isn't it?'

Lucy said nothing.

'It's lovely,' I said firmly. 'What are you going to have to eat, Matilda? What do you recommend?'

'God in heaven, Tara, I'm not the Head Chef! How on earth should I know?'

She scanned the menu, frowning and blinking at it. I switched it around the right way for her.

'How about fish?' said Matilda. 'We should all have fish. It's Friday, isn't it?'

'No,' I said.

'Mother always insisted on fish on a Friday,' said Matilda, not hearing me. We should have fish in memory of Mother. Wouldn't that be nice? You loved Mother, didn't you, Lucy? She loved *you*. She thought you were the bee's knees. She thought you were wonderful because you wanted to be my friend, and no one wanted to be my friend before you came along.'

'That's not true,' said Lucy without sentiment.

'It is.'

'No one knew you. You weren't let out of the bloody cage until you met me.' It was the first time that Lucy had observed anything about their friendship since they had met again. Matilda looked at her in awe.

'Yes. That *is* true,' she said.

The waiter buzzed over us, refilling glasses, asking if we were quite all right, swiping more glass from under the table. Those on the table next to us were talking too much – an infinite deal of nothing – so that they could listen to us at the same time. I was clued up to all this now; I could see how it all happened.

'What's happening?' Matilda said, suddenly bewildered. 'Where's our man? We need to eat. Tara, you look so tired. Billy's been working you too hard. Are you all right? I think you need water. A glass of water!'

She actually snapped her fingers at the waiter, an act that probably inspired secret admiration from Lucy, who longed to be the sort of person who could assert dominance over the serving classes.

'Miss Bright. What can we get you?'

'Water. For this poor child,' said Matilda. 'Can't you see she's wilting away? Oh, and dear man, we'll have the fish. And some roast potatoes.'

'We have no roast potatoes tonight. Perhaps Miss Bright would care for a little creamed potato?'

'No, she would not.'

'I will see if I can arrange for roast potatoes.'

'We don't need roast potatoes, Matilda, for crying out loud,' said Lucy.

'We do. I should like spinach too. It's good for the baby. Oh, and carrots. Don't they help you to see in the dark? I'm always in the dark.'

Our waiter scribbled frantically.

'I tell you what,' said Matilda. 'Just bring us everything.'

'Everything?'

'Every vegetable you have. I think we all need vegetables. Tara looks as though she hasn't seen anything green for weeks on end, except perhaps her own reflection. I know what Digby's like. Nothing but cereal and tinned peaches. He's famous for it.'

I laughed out loud; I couldn't help it. Matilda's sudden detour into lucidity was as surprising as it was accurate.

'You'd like me to bring every vegetable we have? The carrots, spinach, beans, peas, cabbage in butter, asparagus spears, broad beans and three different potatoes?'

'Yes,' said Matilda.

'No!' insisted Lucy and I together.

'It will go to waste, Matilda. You never eat very much,' I said.

'We can take it home if we don't finish it. Have it tomorrow. You can take it to Digby.'

Lucy sat back in her seat and took out her cigarettes.

For forty minutes Matilda talked at us. Lucy didn't want to talk – it was probably a relief to her that she wasn't required to. When I tried to speak, Matilda didn't listen – I don't think she was capable of listening. She screwed up her eyes as though trying very hard to, but it was too much effort, too hard to hold on to other people's words. I had never seen someone drink as much as she did. Twice she announced that she needed to go to the ladies' room. When she stood up, the whole room seemed to intake breath. How she got from one end of the room to the other, I don't know. She carried her pregnancy so oddly; there was no protective hand over her bump as she crashed across the room – it was as if she were entirely unaware of its presence. The first time that she left the table, Lucy leaned forward.

'Dear God! We have to leave.'

'We can't! She's ordered every vegetable on the menu! If we go now, it will look terrible!'

'If we stay, it looks even worse.' Lucy sighed with frustration. 'Why does she have to be like this anyway? What the hell is *wrong* with her?'

'I don't know.'

I took a piece of bread from Lucy's plate, although I had no desire to eat now. Matilda's behaviour was too unnerving to concentrate on anything other than her. When she came back, she had water splashed down the front of her dress. Her hands were still wet. She crashed into her seat and reached for her wine glass.

'We should have cocktails,' she said. 'I'd like a whiskey sour.'

'Don't you think you've had enough?' I said.

'Me? I'm celebrating! We're out together again, aren't we? And anyway,' she went on, 'it was you, Lucy my dear, who – who . . .' She stopped, swallowed, regained control of herself and went on: 'It was you who first introduced me to wine. Communion wine. We snitched it from the vestry. Remember?'

'And all the time Pa blamed poor Sarah Cartwright,' drawled Lucy.

'She was a drip. She deserved to take the blame,' giggled Matilda.

I saw Lucy stifle a grin.

The waiter returned, weighed down with vegetables. There were too many to set down on the table, so he put them on a smaller table beside us. Then, with a flurry of silver platters and steam, came the fish. Matilda squeezed her quarter of lemon on to hers, then threw the lemon across the table at me, where it landed in the lap of the black dress. Following this, she tipped half a ton of salt on top of her food, and ground enough black pepper to bring on a week of sneezing.

'Darling!' she shouted, waving at our waiter. The people on the table beside us shot glances at one another. They were drinking coffee by now; I felt certain they had only ordered it so that they could stay and watch the scene unfolding. Our poor waiter returned to us. If he could have wrung his hands without fear of losing his job, I think he would have done.

'My dear man,' said Matilda. 'We need something else. The chicken, perhaps. Something less –' she paused – 'fishy.' She delivered this last word in deadly serious tones, then, looking from my anxious face to that of the waiter, dissolved into helpless laughter. The waiter, relieved that she was laughing rather than shouting, giggled gently, a little echo of the torrent of noise coming from Matilda. Lucy, unsmiling, spoke over her howls of mirth.

'We don't need any chicken!' she hissed. 'We're quite all right, thank you,' she added to the waiter. But he was programmed towards Matilda, and only Matilda. We were as good as invisible. He turned back to her.

'You'd like to have the chicken? I can arrange that for you.'

'Yes, please. And while we're at it, I don't think we want all those vegetables sitting there. I don't like the shape of those carrots. So helpless, chopped up like that into those little round pieces. No, no. It won't do at all. Sorry. Take them away, won't you?'

'Yes Miss Bright. Right away.'

He piled the bowls up again, and off he went.

That set the pattern for the rest of the evening. Nothing was good enough for Matilda, and her agitation was infectious; I was unable to relax, so nervous was I that she was about to explode. It was like dining with a wound-up toy, pieces of it falling apart in front of our eyes.

'Lord,' said Matilda, turning to Lucy. 'I must go to the bathroom again. Never needed to pee so much in my life. It must be the baby.'

'No,' I said to her departing back. 'It must be the drink.' I looked at Lucy. 'Right. What do we do?'

'What can we do?' said Lucy. 'She's beyond comprehension. Pass me some of that rejected duck. It looks delicious.'

'Don't eat the duck!' I hissed.

'Why not?'

'Just something Inigo said. Eating duck at supper. It bodes badly.'

Lucy laughed, very loudly.

'Firstly, how on earth did you and Inigo start talking about superstitions involving *duck*? And secondly, it's a damned waste, Tara. She may be treating this place like the Bull, but I'm certainly going to make the most of it.'

Lucy stretched over and took the rest of the duck from Matilda's plate.

'She needs our help,' I said flatly.

'We can't help her – don't you see that? No one can help her but herself.'

363

'I don't think you're being very Christian,' I said. I pulled *this* one from out of nowhere.

'No,' agreed Lucy. 'But neither was she. *Neither was she!* And now she just waltzes back into our lives and tries to act as though nothing had ever happened! Do you have any idea how much she hurt me? *Any idea?*'

The room seemed to swim in front of me. The Cosmopolitans, the odd exchange with Juliet, the horror of Matilda's state and the realization that Lucy had not – and would never forgive her – crashed against my ribs in uneasy waves. Then, without warning, my thoughts swam frantically to Digby. I don't know him, I realized, with sudden despair. I don't know him, because I wouldn't know how to tell him about tonight. Digby wasn't about difficulty and falling apart; he hated other people's dramas, didn't he? Frantically I pulled myself back to the moment.

'We've got to get through this,' I said. 'Just for another hour or so. I need your help.'

'What do you mean?'

'Matilda wants to tell us something. She's been building up to it.'

'How do you know?'

'Billy said so.'

'Well, what is it?'

'I don't *know*. All I know is that she's not capable of saying anything at less than two hundred decibels. Whatever she has to say needs to be kept in until we're somewhere without the rest of the nation listening in. Surely you agree with that? Gosh, for everyone else's sake, if not for hers.'

Lucy shrugged. 'All right.'

'Right,' I said. 'For the next hour we shall talk about the

following things: the weather, the traffic, who designed Lady Louisa's wedding dress. Anything.'

'Fine. You take the lead, and I'll follow.'

I was very aware that this was the first time that I had ever taken the lead on anything concerning Lucy, but there was no time to dwell any further on this novel turn of events. Matilda was coming back towards us – at least she was trying to. She kept heading in the wrong direction, and twice had to be redirected to our table.

'Poor Matilda,' I said loudly, so that Those With Ears next to us could hear. 'She's been working too hard. She needs some rest.'

Matilda sat down.

'You know there's something I want to talk to you two about,' she said.

I glanced at Lucy, then smiled blithely at Matilda.

'That's lovely, Matilda, but first of all, couldn't you tell me where did you get those wonderful shoes? Clover had a pair very similar, only in fawn.'

Matilda was bemused.

'They're Chanel,' she said. 'I was given them. You can try them if you like.'

'What a pity I have such large feet,' I said. 'You know I won't fit into them.'

And so it went on. Every time Matilda attempted to speak, I talked over her, didn't let her finish a sentence. Of course Matilda was still drunk, but there was no outlet for her behaviour now; we simply didn't allow there to be. Every time she tried to change the subject and talk about anything other than the most banal of topics, we cut her right down. It was exhausting; I felt as though we were herding a stubborn cow down a lane, running ahead of her all the time to stop her from straying into the neighbours' gardens. Eventually, and despite her alcoholic daze, Matilda actually complained.

'Why aren't you letting me speak? I came here to tell you something! Something *important*!' She looked ready to stamp her foot like a little girl.

'Wait!' I looked thunderstruck. 'I can't remember the name of your mother's horse! You know, the one who used to come inside the kitchen at Trellanack while you were having breakfast. What was she called? She was beautiful – chestnut, I think . . .'

'Tempy,' said Matilda. 'She was called Tempy.'

'That's right,' said Lucy.

Matilda ordered three puddings, then sent them all back. She claimed that the vanilla ice cream tasted of coffee, and that the strawberry tart (possibly the most delicious thing I had ever encountered) was too sweet.

'You know, you have to keep a place like this on its toes,' she said. 'They think they're beyond criticism, but actually they're not.'

'Reminds me of someone,' said Lucy, glaring at Matilda, who didn't notice.

It was past midnight when we left. We walked out of Claridge's on either side of Matilda, for fear that she may fall over. Being Matilda, she managed one trip, just as we stepped outside into the street again. The manager of the hotel caught her arm, and she laughed and thanked him, and he smiled – delighted.

'Have a very good night,' he said. 'May I find you a taxi?'

'Yes, please.'

Suddenly something seemed to click in Matilda's brain. She stood and stared at the manager as he waved to the doorman and instructed him to hail us a cab.

'Oh no!' she wailed.

'What is it?' I hissed.

'Oh no! I said terrible things to that poor waiter. I was awful, wasn't I?'

'You weren't easy,' said Lucy.

'I need to go back,' said Matilda. 'I need to go and say sorry to him.'

'No need,' I said. 'You can drop him a note. Don't go back in there . . .'

But she was off. For someone who had consumed the amount of alcohol that Matilda Bright had, she set off with considerable speed.

'Don't!' I tried to pull her back. 'You don't need to!'

'Of course I do, Tara. Don't be ridiculous. I was awful. So rude!'

She pulled herself away from me, and strode back into the dining room. Seeing our waiter, she paused for a moment.

'Stay here,' she ordered me. 'Just let me do this.'

I could do nothing but watch. I wanted to put my face in my hands, but I assumed an expression of serenity – a mother watching her daughter thank her teacher for a sugar mouse at Christmas. Matilda pulled it off, of course, and I can't believe that I doubted her for a second. She walked up to the waiter, held his arm, whispered something in his ear that made him laugh, and then stood next to him for another two minutes, talking and listening, laughing and nodding. Finally she took a piece of paper from his notepad, borrowed his pen and wrote something down. When she left the room, all eyes were on her – but this time she was almost ready to bow. She walked, fashion-model perfect, back to me.

'Right,' she said, straightening her skirt. 'Shall we go? Don't look so thunderstruck, Tara. He asked for my autograph. His wife never misses an issue of *Woman* magazine.'

How she pulled it off, I don't know. It was as if there was some switch in Matilda's very being that, when activated, meant that she was able to act like the star she undoubtedly was. All that falling apart, and drinking, and odd half-finished sentences could be smoothed over with just a smile and a stroke of the pen across the page. It was practised, perfectly executed. It was superb.

30

True Fire

Lucy and I were ready for the night to finish. We felt, once inside the taxi, that we were safe, crossing the finishing line. With Matilda, however, there was no such thing.

'I need to come in for a bit,' she said as the taxi pulled up outside Napier House.

'I think you need to sleep.'

'No!' said Matilda. She looked distressed. 'No! I need to talk to you. Please, Lucy.'

Lucy looked at me anxiously, as though I would come up with an escape route for her. She didn't want this, but she was trapped.

'Come in then,' she said. 'But if you wake up Clover, she'll go spare.'

We settled in the drawing room with cups of tea, but Matilda moved towards the drinks cabinet.

'You don't need any more,' I said.

'I most *certainly* do.'

She sat down and closed her eyes, crossing her legs in front of her.

'If you're just going to sleep, there's no point in you being here,' Lucy began.

Matilda kept her eyes tight shut.

'I just wanted a moment to lie here and breathe.' She wasn't asking for much. We sat in silence for nearly three minutes, which was the length of "May to September" in fact, yet silence felt much longer than Inigo's cheery little pop song. How was Matilda still so incapable of gauging mood? It wasn't merely that she had drunk too much. She had always had no awareness of such matters.

Slowly, she opened her eyes.

'It's always going to be hard, today,' she said.

I looked at Lucy who looked down at her hands, quietly handing the baton to me. I would have to guide Matilda through the next few minutes, there was no way that Lucy was capable of doing so.

'Why?' I asked her.

Matilda squinted and raised her left hand over her face, as though blocking out some invisible light shining too brightly in her face.

'It's Paul's birthday.'

'Paul?' Whatever I had been expecting to hear her say, those words were not it.

'Paul Warren,' she said, keeping her eyes shielded. 'Paul Warren,' she repeated.

'Who's he?' I asked blankly. Then, remembering that night at Trellanack when I had seen Inigo again for the first time, some-thing clicked.

'The singer,' I said. 'The one Inigo wrote for.'

'He only had hits in America,' said Matilda. 'You wouldn't have heard him. He hadn't made it over here yet.' She spoke

370

this jealously, as though she didn't *want* us to hear him.

When she lit a cigarette I saw that her hands were shaking. I had a desire to push her out the door, and to shut it behind me. I didn't want Matilda and her strange behaviour here in Napier House – it should be safe from all that – but it was impossible. She had started now; she was going to finish.

'Billy managed him,' said Matilda. 'He discovered him.'

'Must have been good then,' I said.

'He was better than good,' whispered Matilda.

Now she wasn't looking at me; she was speaking as though someone had put her into a state of hypnosis. I glanced at Lucy, who was listening, I knew, but not watching her.

'He was such a sweet boy,' said Matilda. 'And so good-looking. The kind even *your* father would have approved of.'

'I sincerely doubt it,' I said. Matilda laughed, sadly.

'He had the purest heart of anyone I've ever met. He was one of those rare people who walked into a room and lit it up just by being himself.'

'I'm always suspicious of people like that,' said Lucy suddenly.

'Well, you *shouldn't* be, because *you're* one yourself,' snapped Matilda. 'And anyway, Paul was funny and kind and beautiful and you would have fallen flat on your face for him if you'd ever met him, so – so *there!*'

This was the first time that she had turned on Lucy since her quest to win back her affection had begun. Lucy looked surprised, to say the least, but was, I felt, just a little bit impressed. I don't think that she thought that there was any fire left in Matilda – she had assumed, as I had, that any spark of it had been extinguished by fame.

'Today he would have been twenty-two years old,' said Matilda.

'*Would* have been?'

371

'Yes.'

Matilda looked at me, her eyes pleading with me to understand, to finish off the story so that she wouldn't have to; I couldn't of course. She took another shaky breath, and when she next spoke, she was suddenly all clarity, her hands quite steady as she plaited the tassels on one of Clover's cushions.

'He was the first boy Billy cut a disc with. Back in 1956, before any of us had even tasted our first cider.' (That was debatable, I thought, remembering Pony Club camp from that year.) 'He was just this sweet boy from Kentucky, Illinois, with this *lovely* voice.' Matilda sniffed, and took another gulp of tea. 'Billy heard him playing at some barn dance, and couldn't believe his ears. He had the looks, the way of talking, *everything*.' Matilda unthreaded the tassels and started plaiting them again. 'Inigo wrote for him,' she went on, looking up at me as she said his name. 'His first two singles went to number one. Billy says it was one of those rare occasions when everything goes right in the studio. It just worked, that was all. Inigo played guitar and drums on the recordings,' she added. 'They were *joyful*.'

Her face crumpled again. She blew her nose into her hanky and grimaced.

'What happened?' I asked, glancing at Lucy who was staring out of the window, her face set.

'What happened was that I loved him too,' said Matilda. 'One night I went and told him how I felt. Silly me, but I never could keep that sort of thing to myself, could I?' She paused, as though half expecting someone to fill in with a response of some sort.

'Anyone would be flattered to hear that you—' I began.

Matilda put up her hand to stop me.

'I believed him when he said he loved me too for a little

while, but when he kissed me I had this terrible feeling that he wasn't all there, like a part of him was missing.'

'He was your – your *boyfriend*?'

'Yes,' said Matilda. 'He was *my* boyfriend.'

She laughed, a little burst of delight, as though in saying it, it became real. In sharing it with us, it had actually happened. But just as quickly, her face clouded again.

'The truth is,' she said quietly. 'The truth is that he . . . he loved Billy. You know? He *really* loved Billy. He couldn't tell me, but there it was, all the time. I suppose I knew it.' She sat on her hands. 'One night I confronted them both about it, and Paul broke down and told me that I wasn't going out of my mind. He told me I was right.'

She looked blankly into the middle distance; I don't think that she was hearing herself speaking at all; it was as though she were listening, expressionless, to someone else's story.

'Gosh, Matilda—' I began.

'I know what you're thinking,' she said. She was looking at Lucy.

'You don't,' said Lucy.

'What happened?' I asked. I sat on my hands to ground myself.

Matilda cleared her throat. 'Paul was so distraught, so terrified of his parents finding out, of losing Billy, of hurting me, that he drove off the road,' said Matilda. 'He drove right off the road.'

'What do you mean?'

'What do you think I mean?' said Matilda. 'He drove his car into a tree. He was killed.'

'*Killed?*' I gasped. Despite her tears, despite knowing that the unhappy ending to the story was coming, this was not at all what I had expected her to say; the word jarred around the room, setting everything off balance.

'He was only twenty-one.' Matilda sloshed her tea around the cup.

'How awful,' said Lucy quietly.

'Inigo played the guitar at his funeral. His parents wrote to Billy the week afterwards. They didn't know that he loved Billy in – in *that* way of course, and they never will.' She looked up, defiant, as though one of us might run off and call them that minute. 'Billy keeps the letter inside a copy of Paul's first record. Today I found him reading it, crying his eyes out like a little boy of six. He couldn't speak. Not for a whole ten minutes. He just stood there, crying and holding me.'

Matilda rubbed her bump, and as she did, her tears drained blue-black mascara from her eyes, down her rouge-powdered cheeks, making her clownish, absurd.

'He loved him,' said Matilda. 'More than anything before, and probably more than anything ever again.'

'Not more than you,' I said automatically. 'He couldn't.'

'Why? Because I'm a girl, and that's the way it's meant to be? Don't be so childish, Tara.'

I didn't blame her for her anger. I was angry with myself for my incredulity.

'But you married Billy knowing all of this!'

'I know.' She looked up, suddenly defiant. 'Billy's got the truest heart of anyone I know. He rescued me, you know.'

We listened to a police car belting out its siren in the distance.

'You found each other because you had both lost Paul,' I said slowly.

'Yes,' said Matilda. 'We had both lost Paul. A month after he died, I realized I was pregnant.'

She said no more, just looked right at us, waiting for the reality of what she was saying to hit us. I felt Napier House

374

breathing in and out all around me, listening carefully.

'The baby's Paul's,' she said simply. 'I'm having *his* baby.'

'Oh, Matilda,' I heard Lucy's voice sounding as it had done in days gone by, perhaps when Matilda had knocked over her mother's teacup or tripped over the rug in the hall.

Matilda folded her hands in front of her bump.

'Billy knows, of course,' she said. 'He's going to bring the baby up as his own. He'll be the most wonderful father,' she added defiantly.

'What about . . . ?' I gulped. 'What about Paul's parents?'

'They know that part,' said Matilda calmly. She looked at Lucy. 'So you see, Billy saved me from all of it – from being a mother on my own. And you can think what you like about me – call me a victim if you like. Life doesn't always work out the way we've planned it, but I don't imagine you'll ever find that.' She was angry now, her face looked pinched and pale in the half-light of the drawing-room lamps. 'Well, I just wanted you to know that I'm going to get through all of this. I *will.*'

Lucy pushed her hair back from her face and looked at Matilda.

'I know you will,' she said. 'You've always been far stronger than you give yourself credit for. That's one of the odd things about you, Matilda.' She stood up; I could see that her skinny, long legs were trembling.

'I'm going to bed,' she said. 'But I think you should know that I'll never say a word about this to anybody. For what it's worth, I understand. All right? I understand.'

She said it sharply because I don't think she knew how else to put it. Not after all that had happened, after all the time that had passed. A moment later, and she was out of the room, leaving us nothing more than the sound of her feet padding up the stairs to our bedroom.

Matilda smiled at me, and without saying another word, put her head down on a cushion and fell asleep.

I sat in the dark, letting what she had said wash into my head. Half an hour later I heard the telephone ring, then Clover came into the room in her dressing gown.

'That was Billy,' she said. 'Wanting to know where she is.'

'She's here.'

Seeing Matilda lying on the sofa, Clover shook her head.

'I'll tell him to come and fetch her,' she said. 'I don't think it would be wise to put her into a cab in this state.'

He arrived twenty minutes later, and came into the drawing room without noticing me, curled up on the other side of the room. I had never seen Billy look concerned, worried about anything that didn't relate to music or records, but seeing Matilda on the sofa, a tartan blanket over her bump, he looked like a vulnerable little boy, not quite knowing what had happened.

'She should have come straight home,' he whispered to Clover. 'The baby . . .'

He reached out and touched the bump, pressing his big hand on to Matilda's tummy. Opening her eyes slowly, she smiled at him.

'Oh, good, you've come to get me,' she said, struggling into an upright position. 'I should have hated to have to get a taxi now. We had such a lovely night at Claridge's. Terribly sweet waiters. So lovely to spend some time with little Tara. I do adore her, you know. She reminds me of how it was before. She reminds me of Mother.'

I was going to cry unless I got out of there quickly. I coughed and tried to smile.

Both of them turned and saw me.

'Cherry Merrywell, what are you doing still awake? You need sleep,' said Billy softly.

'I know,' I said. 'I was just waiting for you to get here, that's all.'

Did he know that she had told us? It was impossible to say. I was struck by how knowing what I now knew about him changed nothing; he was still the all-powerful force behind everything that was happening to me.

Matilda looked at me and remembered something.

'Oh,' she said to Billy. 'I don't think I told her.'

'Told me what?' I asked. I couldn't take any more revelations now. I just wanted to be upstairs and in bed and going home tomorrow.

'When you go back to Cornwall tomorrow – I've asked Digby to go with you.'

'What?' I whispered.

'I want him to take some pictures of the house. You know, before it goes.'

'Matilda wants to remember the place as it was,' said Billy.

'*Digby's* coming to Cornwall?'

'And Inigo of course,' said Billy softly. 'He'll be driving you all. I certainly don't want Digby at the wheel.'

'But they don't like each other! He won't want to come—'

'Trellanack is a big enough house for two people who dislike each other to live in for a weekend,' said Matilda. 'My parents managed it for a whole lifetime.'

I was floored by how I felt. If he were in the village, it would be too much, too close. He would *know* everything.

'It's important that he takes photographs,' said Matilda, reading my mind. 'He can keep out of Inigo's way and do his job without disturbance. They can both return with you after the weekend.'

She smiled at me. 'Isn't that a nice little present for you, Tara? Oh, and you can ride Hester again. Take her out. Like the old days.'

'Oh I couldn't,' I said quickly. 'Not without your mother's permission.'

'You can take her out,' said Matilda again. '*I* say so.'

I nodded, but I knew that I wouldn't. I had been disobedient enough to Lady W-D in the past. I wasn't going to let Matilda overrule her on that one, however much I would have loved her to.

I climbed the stairs and took off Clover's dress and lay in my knickers on top of the bed. It was a hot, still night. Where was Digby? When I wasn't with him, he felt as far away – as impossible to hold – as water in a cupped hand. And Matilda and Billy – how could they carry on as normal when both of them carried this secret with them? Surely things like this were so big they trampled over everything else?

I could hear Inigo in his bedroom. I heard him playing the guitar for another hour, so softly, so softly. There was a part of me that wanted to run downstairs in my nightdress, holding a flickering candle, and sit huddled in the corner of the room listening to him forever. I lay awake until four in the morning, thinking about Paul Warren, Matilda, Billy and Inigo, all linked together forever through a black circle of vinyl.

31

Home

The thing about going home after being somewhere extraordinary is that one slips back into life as it was before far quicker
than one would ever have considered possible. Nothing had
changed in the Rectory – and yet *everything* had. Cornwall itself
felt exaggerated: the sense of salt and sand under the fingernails,
the eternal drag and crash of the Atlantic from the attic windows.
I was seeing the house and the village for the first time through
the eyes of someone who had not been here before. Lucy and
I walked into the kitchen and sat down as though we hadn't
been away. When Imogen appeared, the first thing that I thought
were how old her clothes looked. I wanted to cry.

'Tell me again about the night that you had dinner at Claridge's,' she begged, cutting me another slice of Victoria sponge.

And Lucy and I did, although we didn't tell her how drunk
Matilda had been, or about how she was carrying Paul Warren's
baby, we spoke only about the crowds who recognized her. That
was the thing about telling stories. It was really more about what
you left out than what you said out loud to other people.

I regaled them all with tales of Clover and Charlotte, of the
cafés on the King's Road, of Digby's parties and of recording in

the studio. Pa, sitting at the head of the table, said not a word. He pretended not to be interested, but every now and then I noticed him opening his mouth and closing it again, like a chorister, unsure of when to start singing.

'Pass the lettuce, Tara,' he barked at the end of my story about being photographed by Digby (actually, not *quite* the end – I was saving that for Imogen and Florence later on).

'I feel a bit like Errant Jack,' I said. 'I never realized that going away would make me so popular back home.'

'You should go away more often then,' said Florence, grinning.

'The choir,' said Imogen. She turned pink. 'Matthew – I mean, Mr Bell. He was hoping you might want to listen to the choir on Sunday morning. They're doing *The Magic Flute*.'

'But are you doing *his* Magic Flute?' I muttered to her. She turned crimson.

'What was that, Tara?' demanded Pa.

'Nothing. I just said that I hope Matthew Bell is behaving in an honourable fashion towards my sister.'

'He took me out to the pictures last night,' she said in a high voice.

'Hot stuff,' I said to her. 'Antonia Jones will kill you.'

'Well,' said Pa, standing up, 'I've packing to do. Imogen, can I rely on a lift to the station from you in the morning?'

'The station?' I asked. 'Where are you going, Pa?'

'Glasgow,' he said. 'I shan't be back for ten days.'

'Ten days? But we've only just arrived home!'

'I imagine my departure won't cause you too much pain,' said Pa drily. 'I saw those two young men driving up to Trellanack on my way back from church.'

'What?' demanded Imogen and Florence at the same time.

'That's right,' said Lucy. 'We drove down with them.'

'Who are they?'

'One of them is Digby O'Rourke,' I said. I didn't want them knowing that Inigo was here too. It would be too complicated if Pa started putting two and two together.

'*Digby O'Rourke* is at Trellanack?' spluttered Imogen.

'Matilda's asked him to take photographs before the place is sold,' I said.

I chewed hard on a piece of toast to stop myself from blushing. Florence grinned at me.

'I sincerely hope I can rely on your good judgement and good upbringing in the following days,' said Pa. 'I wasn't expecting half of London to follow you back to Cornwall.'

'They're hardly half of London,' I protested.

'I'm not here to keep an eye on you, so you'll have to keep eyes on each other.'

'Of course, Pa.'

With that, he shot us one of his remarkable, eyebrows-in-the-air looks, and pushed off out of the room.

'*Well!*' said Florence. 'You've certainly lucked out there. No Pa lurking around to pounce on you, and real, live *boys* up at Trellanack.'

'Gosh, Tara,' said Imogen. She looked terribly worried. 'I hope you *are* going to behave.'

'I certainly hope she *isn't*,' said Florence.

Trellanack with Inigo and Digby within its walls had become a different island overnight. Digby's remarkable talent for mess and disorder had succeeded in turning the sparse, half-emptied rooms on the ground floor into places of vampish colour and light and thoroughly modern mayhem. Cameras lay at angles on the brocade sofas, half-finished bottles of beer stood on the side tables next to a deeply sinister photograph of Sir Lionel in the arms of his nanny, taken three days before he boarded RMS *Titanic*.

'Lady W-D would go spare if she knew what was happening,' I said.

'Why?' demanded Digby. 'I'm treating this pile as if it were my own home.'

'That's exactly what's worrying me.'

Digby grinned. 'Matilda told me that you would show me around and help me make sense of it all. I've got a list here of places she wants photographing. Really it would be more helpful to have an Ordnance Survey map. Where the hell's the Violet Room?' he demanded.

'The East Wing.'

'Where's that?'

I grinned. 'The other end of the house. Practically in Devon.' 'Shall we go outside first?' I suggested. 'It's supposed to rain later. We've only got three days,' I added. I kept saying it, kept thinking it. *We've only got three days.*

We took Digby first to the walled garden, where Lucy, Matilda and I had spent many afternoons that first summer that they became friends. The air was weighed down with the smell of warm roses and the drowsy hum of bees. If Matilda was here, she would be sneezing for Britain, I thought. Like Digby, the walled garden now contained an atmosphere of barely contained disorder – and like him, this only served to enhance its appeal. He pulled up his camera from around his neck.

'Stand under that tree,' Digby instructed me, pointing to the little cherry blossom where Matilda had first announced her adoration for Raoul.

'Oh! First let me show you the bamboo garden,' I said. 'Then we should look at the rockery, and the Chinese garden. I suppose they're all looking a bit shabby without Lady W–D's iron fist, but perhaps that doesn't matter . . . Everything looks out of control,' I continued. 'It was never like this before. It was *ordered*.'

Digby was fiddling with the lens of his camera.

'It doesn't matter if everything's out of control as long as it's pretty,' he said.

We walked to the west of the garden, where the two glasshouses stood. One of the panes had been smashed, and there was a long vine creeping out of it from the inside. I was shocked; I had only seen this part of the garden at night. By day, it looked as though it had been assaulted.

'It's terrible, what's happened to this,' I said – but even as I spoke, I knew that Digby wasn't really listening. 'This was built to mark the King's coronation . . .'

'But look at this *light*,' murmured Digby. He stepped forward and pulled a little more of the vine out through the window and picked up his camera again.

It soon became quite plain to me that Digby didn't care what he was looking at, so long as it made a good picture. We could have shown him pyramids or koala bears and he wouldn't have questioned it. He simply set up the photograph and pressed that little button and there it was, frozen in time forever – or at least until the picture faded – and if it gave him pleasure, then he needed no definitions, no dates. He cared about the instant reaction to seeing something pleasing, something enter-taining or something beautiful. The facts were of no interest to him whatsoever. In that sense, he was the very opposite of Raoul. After a while I felt that desperate feeling again; I sensed him slipping out of my grasp and I needed to haul him back on to dry land.

'Can we lie here for a while and feel the sun on our faces?'

Digby always responded how you wanted him to when asked if he wanted to lie anywhere. He collapsed on to his back. I lay down beside him.

'Do you like it here?' I asked him cautiously.

He didn't even answer. 'Sing me that blues song,' he said. 'That weird thing you sang for me that afternoon in Cheyne Walk.'

'It's not an afternoon for the blues.'

'It's *always* an afternoon for the blues,' said Digby.

He turned and lay on his side so that he was facing me. 'Go on,' he urged. 'Sing me something I know.'

I sang him some old spiritual from the Deep South that Ma used to sing to us; something far from modern, but something that reminded me of where I had been when Trellanack had been our playground. It wasn't really any more. Too much had changed now – we had passed the point of no return.

Later that day, we had tea in the garden. It was still warm, and we had laid out the blankets in the shade, but there was a lively breeze spinning our hair around our faces, keeping the wasps away.

'How's your writing going?' I asked Inigo. Here in Cornwall I felt as though he had closed up more than ever. I was acutely aware of the extent of his dislike for Digby, and knew that he was here simply because Billy wanted him to be. He spent most of the time alone in the Violet Room, and when he joined us for lunch there was the sense of his having sent only a part of himself, that was all. His head and his heart were somewhere else.

'I don't like writing in the country,' he said.

'Why not?' I was shocked – not just by the fact that he had answered me, but also by the concise nature of his response.

'This part of England – everywhere west of London, in fact – just reminds me of home.'

He picked the stalk off a grape.

'You mean the house that burned down?'

He looked at me, half annoyed.

'Yes,' he said. 'The house that burned down.'

Was now the moment to tell him? I didn't know. It never seemed to be the right time.

'Would you ever live in England again?' I asked. I knew I wouldn't be able to question him for long – I could see Digby coming back towards us, and anyway, Inigo didn't like coming up with answers.

'I can't,' he said.

He pushed his hair out of his eyes. For a minute we sat saying nothing; I marvelled at that exquisite profile, the pale skin unblemished by freckles, the dark hair falling over those eyes that had met mine when I had stolen the elephant, when I had sung to him in the kitchen.

'The thing is,' he said suddenly, 'you don't really get over a house like that.'

I stared at him, shocked by what he was saying. Was he actually offering me *information*? Seconds later, Digby flopped on to the rug.

'Your sister just telephoned the house,' he said. 'She wants to know if you want to go and see Raoul this afternoon.'

I wrenched my mind back to the present and stood up.

'I must go,' I muttered.

'Oh God,' said Digby, closing his eyes. 'You'd better not leave the two of us together.'

He looked at Inigo on the red and white rug, cigarette in one hand, staring over the orchard. 'On second thoughts, stay right where you are,' he muttered. Picking up his camera, and pointing it at Inigo with absolutely no apology, he took several photographs in rapid succession.

'I'd save your film if I were you,' said Inigo, without moving.

'In fifty years' time I'll send you a copy of this, and you'll thank me for putting aside our differences long enough for me to capture your indisputable beauty for future generations.'

Digby pulled the film out of his camera and bowed at Inigo. Shoving the cartridge into his pocket, he lay back on the rug.

It was at this moment that I saw the horses. Beautiful Hester – whom I had loved in the days when I was allowed to ride at Trellanack – stood still as a statue in the entrance to the orchard, and behind her – squealing loudly like overexcited backing singers – were two of the stoutest of the Shetlands in Lady W-D's collection. Pamela the groom – left to her own devices so often now – was plainly not keeping these ponies in order; they were terribly overweight.

There had always been a danger of horses getting out of the park at Trellanack through gaps in the fence or hedge – I was forever leading them back to their rightful positions when I was little – but seeing them out today brought a lump to my throat. Hester had seen me on my way down the drive, and had come looking for me – I was *sure* of it.

'What's going on here?' asked Inigo, following my gaze.

'*Gunfight at the OK Corral,*' I muttered. 'We must catch them.'

Digby had scrambled to his feet.

'What's going on?' he demanded. 'Why are *they* here?'

'It's all right,' I said, laughing at the anxiety in his voice that I had never heard before. 'I know this lot. They've got out some-where. I need to get them back.'

★

Slowly, I approached Hester as I had done in the early days, holding out my hand and trying to fool her that I had something to give.

'Come here,' I said softly. 'Here, Hester.'

But even if Hester *had* been missing me, she wasn't prepared to give herself up without a fight. Her tail high, nostrils flaring, she trotted off towards the back wall of the orchard.

'Bugger,' I said in irritation.

The Shetlands had put their heads down and were stuffing grass into their mouths as if it was their last hour on earth. They wouldn't be so tricky.

'Why's that big one running away?' called Digby. 'Cherry, I don't like the way it's running about like this! Shouldn't it be wearing a fucking saddle?'

'Come here and wait with this lot,' I said, waving at the Shetlands. Digby looked at me, confused.

'*Wait* with them? What the hell are we waiting for?'

'For me to catch Hester.'

'Who's Hester?'

'Just stand here and put your arms around them and keep still. They won't move.'

'Put my *arms* around them? I've heard it all now!'

'Like this,' I said, giggling helplessly, and demonstrating. Feeling someone next to them, the ponies snorted, and leaned on me heavily.

'You see – *this* is why I don't like setting foot outside the city,' said Digby, shoving me out of the way and taking up the position. As he spoke, one of the Shetlands turned and nipped him on the back of his leg.

'Fucking hell!' he shouted.

And with that, Digby shot off like a scalded cat. He grabbed his camera and within moments had vanished to the other side of the orchard, and then disappeared from view in the general direction of the house.

I looked across to where we had left Inigo, and saw him helpless with laughter. Seeing him so undone was a rare sight; gosh, he was always so *still*, so *controlled* – issuing dry asides every two seconds yet rarely appearing very relaxed himself – that to see him like this was quite shocking to me.

'If you could help me please, I need to get hold of that pony!' I shouted, pointing at Hester. *Holy Mackerel!* I thought. *I was becoming Lady W-D!*

Inigo, still snorting – held up a hand to show me that he had heard, and – taking something out of his pocket advanced towards Hester, very slowly – stopping en route to pick up a frayed black and red camera strap that Digby had left on the rug. I watched him, fascinated. Inigo and horses was not a combination I expected to have been faced with today – or any day at all. Yet two minutes later, he had Hester – quite literally – eating out of his hand, with the camera strap around her neck to prevent her from escaping again.

'What did you give her?' I asked, dragging the Shetlands towards him by their manes. I looked at Hester in alarm; she was bending up her lip and trying to lick a sticky, orange substance from her teeth.

'Reese's Peanut Butter Cups,' said Inigo smugly. When I looked blank he added: 'It's an American candy. I mean, chocolate. Utterly delicious. Leaves everything else at the starting gate, and wasted on a *horse*,' he added in disdain. 'That was my last one.'

'Well at least you caught her. I expect she's getting the biggest hit of her life,' I said. 'Makes a change from Polos.'

He walked the ponies back with me, and there was an unspoken comfort in the rhythm of their unshod hoofs reluctantly admitting defeat and following our lead, and a very English melancholy in the unselfconscious beauty of the pale pink damask roses clambering chaotically around the orchard gate as we filed through. I picked one and threaded the stem into Hester's mane.

Trellanack – from which I had done my best to distance myself since the afternoon that Lady W-D had banned me from the stables – suddenly felt more mine than it had done since I was thirteen years old.

'Matilda shouldn't sell this house,' I said suddenly.

'She wants to,' said Inigo. 'You know that, don't you? She *wants* to.'

I didn't reply.

We ambled around the back of the house, and eventually shoved Hester and her accomplices back into the park.

'This must be where they got out,' said Inigo, pointing to a broken bit of fence.

He spent a good ten minutes fashioning nearby logs and branches into appropriate shapes to try and stop up the gap. It grew hotter and hotter. I gave up helping, and sat down under the nearest lime, and smoked a cigarette, watching him. He wasn't terribly efficient with this sort of thing, I thought. Raoul, or even Imogen – would have had the job done in seconds – I daresay I could have too, but I rather liked watching Inigo.

I thought about his American girl – his secret calls to her – and wondered if he would tell her about this little escapade at

Trellanack with the loose horses. I was fed up with him forgetting everything, I thought. People shouldn't be *allowed* to forget afternoons in England like this. It ought to be against the law. After a while, he stood up.

'That should keep them in,' he said.

I doubt it, I thought.

'Yes,' I said. 'Thanks.'

We walked back to the house.

'I need to go to see Raoul,' I said. I wished, suddenly – irrationally – that Inigo was coming too.

'Good. I need to write. And before you ask, I'll check Digby's not too traumatized by the events of the past half-hour.'

'Thank you. I trust he'll survive.'

Inigo was almost back through the front door; he knew how to act in a big house. Being here wasn't the jolly jape that it was for Digby or the Alien English Experience that it was to Billy. He had come from somewhere like this, he slipped naturally back into the rhythms it dictated.

'Remember this, won't you?' I called out to him, suddenly.

'What?' he shouted back.

'Remember this afternoon! You know. The horses, and the sun, and the flowers and this house and everything.' I shrugged at him with a sort of helpless defiance – wanting him to understand me, because most of the time, I certainly didn't.

'*Gather ye rosebuds while ye may!*' I shouted, and just as soon as these words were out, I was embarrassed by them; I needed to defuse them. 'Or just go inside and have a cup of tea,' I muttered.

Just before he turned away again, I thought I saw Inigo smile.

Then again, I had thought a good many things about Inigo
Wallace that had turned out to be quite wrong. This might have
just been one more.

32

Undone

Raoul was in a different ward. I hadn't seen him for over two weeks, but to all of me, it had been ten years. Lucy and I travelled together, but she asked if she could see him alone first. She was with him for just fifteen minutes, then instead of inviting me to join them, she came back out and nodded to me.

'I'll wait for you in the car,' she said.

I didn't ask her why she had been so quick, or what was happening. I didn't want to know, and yet I knew I would have to.

When he saw me walking in, he tried to sit himself in a more upright position as though preparing for battle. I was thrown by seeing him. His face, without the sun, had paled, and his eyes were ringed with black shadows. Beside his bed stood a neat pile of books, and a big notepad and a stub of a pencil. Flowers, picked from the garden at the Rectory, were drying out in Imogen's little vase.

'You've just missed your sister,' he said.

'I know.' I leaned down and kissed him. 'She's waiting for me in the car.' I couldn't take it any more. 'What's happened, Raoul? Why was she so *quick* in here with you?'

His face seemed to fall into his hands. For a moment he said nothing, just lay in his hospital bed without talking, just closing his eyes to something that I dreaded hearing from him.

'We think it would be better if we had some more time away from each other,' he said.

He looked at me and then down at his hands.

'Why?' I whispered. 'Haven't you had enough?'

'It's all right, Tara,' said Raoul. 'Don't take on all our pain. Sweet girl, you never needed to feel it like we did.'

'It's because of the baby thing,' I said, my voice shaking. 'She thinks that it's not fair on you that she can't have babies. You have to tell her that she's *wrong*.'

'You know she's been hanging about with this boy from a group?' said Raoul softly.

I was flummoxed. 'I — I don't — Why did she tell you that?' I asked in despair.

'She is too honest not to,' said Raoul. 'It is what I expected. I am not ridiculous enough to imagine that Lucy Jupp can go to London and not make half the city fall in love with her.'

'But she hardly knows him! She's just saying this because she's trying to give you the chance to run away! She's so *stupid*!' I wailed. 'You have to tell her that you don't mind about her not having babies, Raoul.'

'It is more complicated than you imagine, Tara. Everything is.' He winced suddenly. 'I said to her that if she keeps running away then maybe it is for the best that she is on her own. I can't chase her any longer. Can't chase anything,' he added wryly, nodding at his leg still plastered up to his hip.

'Are you still in pain?' I asked, my voice shaky.

'I don't notice,' he lied. 'Sit down, won't you? Can't you tell me something that I want to hear? Please, Tara, don't talk to me about this any more. I want you to tell me about London. How was it? Who did you see? What happened?'

'Everything,' I said helplessly. 'Everything happened.'

'You made your record?' he asked.

'Yes. I did.'

'Does it sound exactly as you want?'

'It sounds exactly as Billy Laurier wants,' I said.

'Which is all that matters,' said Raoul drily.

'Which is all that matters.'

I owed him the comfort of a conversation about my life – he was too shaken to talk any further about his. Raoul, being Raoul, wanted details about everything: Napier House in particular, the recording studio, the Six O'Clock Club. I realized that Lucy had told him virtually nothing on the telephone, and my heart hardened again. Was she still outside waiting to drive me home? I didn't know and I didn't care. All I wanted to do was to sit with him, to make him feel better. An hour later, visiting hours were over.

'You should go now,' he said. 'And please, don't talk to your sister about what we have said to each other. There is no use. When I get out of here, I plan to go to Spain for a while. These things take time.'

'What things?' I asked desperately.

'I don't know yet,' he said. 'All I know is that it is no good talking now. Talking is just going to spin us into *mantequilla*, into butter. She is how she is, and you can't blame her for it. Things have happened that are quite beyond our control.'

'You *can* blame her,' I said. 'When she won't listen! When she knows that you'll always be there, no matter whether you have children or—'

Raoul cut me off mid-sentence. 'She needs you, Tara. Even

if she thinks she doesn't – she needs you. I have disappointed her. It is a lethal thing, disappointment – worse than any other emotion. Far worse. Because, you see, that first hit, that first bloom never lasts, does it?'

'I – I don't know,' I said.

'Well, let me tell you now – it *doesn't*. It can't.'

'Not ever?'

'No. But that doesn't matter. It can come back at intervals – little, slippery snapshots of what you started with – and that's enough. It's really enough.'

'But that seems very sad.'

'Not at all,' said Raoul. 'Or at least, it shouldn't be. Because it's not about the start of it all – any fool will tell you that. It's what you replace it with that's the key – something stronger, tougher – not something that you can see right through when you hold it up to the light. That's the important thing. Can you take what you've been given and end up with something even *better?*'

He actually slapped his hand down on the bed in frustration.

The young nurse appeared – she who had taken his blood pressure when Imogen and I had visited weeks ago. She was holding a little pot of what I presumed were Raoul's painkillers, though no pills were going to be able to dull the agony of losing Lucy. Seeing our faces, her own took on an expression of concern for her patient.

She gave Raoul the full benefit of her large breasts as she handed him his pills. 'He's still in a great deal of discomfort,' she said.

'When will he be able to leave?' I asked.

'It's hard to say,' she said, plainly dreading the idea of his departure herself. 'I'll come back to do your blood pressure later,' she added.

'Thank you, Rachel,' said Raoul.

Lucy would have bridled at the familiarity with which he smiled at her. As it happened, I felt nothing but relief that someone was paying him the attention that should have been coming from his wife.

'Why did you agree when Billy called you in the first place?' I asked him when she was out of earshot. 'Letting her loose in London without you – without Pa – without anyone but me to tell her what to do.'

Raoul reached for a glass of water. I wanted to throw myself into his arms and sob.

'When I was fourteen, I trapped a bird in a cage,' began Raoul.

'Oh no, please!' I said, holding up a hand to stop him. 'I don't want to hear any nonsense about if you really love something then you must give it freedom. I *hate* that!'

'The bird kept coming back,' said Raoul simply. 'Every time I set it free, it returned.'

I found Lucy sitting in the car reading an old copy of the parish magazine. For five minutes neither of us said a word.

'Did Florence tell you that Halo Jackson asked her out tomorrow night?' Lucy asked eventually.

'No,' I said, still looking straight ahead.

'I told her not to trust him. Do you remember Diane Jackson?'

'No.'

'Halo's sister. You know – she sat next to me in history. Large girl, red hair. She had a fear of being locked in, so she used to have to pee with her foot wedged under the door to stop it from opening . . .'

I didn't look at her.

'Look, I'm just trying to make some kind of conversation,'

said Lucy. 'I know you're furious with me, Tara, but you're just going to have to grow up and stop looking to Raoul and me to be your little idealized vision of married bliss. It's too difficult, all right? It's just too difficult.'

She forgot to indicate as we turned left and found ourselves stuck behind a tractor shedding straw.

'I don't understand you any more. I don't think you even understand yourself,' I said bravely.

'Gosh, Tara,' said Lucy. '*Spare* me the psychological analysis. But on the other hand, full marks for saying precisely what you're thinking for once.'

'And it's not just Raoul that you're cutting off!' I had started this now, and inside I knew that I wasn't going to stop until I had said it all. 'It's Matilda too.'

'Matilda?'

'She's damaged, Lucy, and you know it!'

'She damaged *herself*, for Christ's sake! No one forced her to throw herself into the arms of Paul Warren, or to marry Billy Laurier! Or to write notes to Raoul that broke everything into pieces. She's made every decision *herself*!'

She pulled out and tried to surge forward to overtake the tractor, but failed to pick up enough speed and pulled back in.

'And Raoul?' I said bitterly.

'I can't lie to him. Can't you get that into your head? I want to throw all of this off my back! Ugh!' She shook her whole body, to demonstrate the point. 'I could *do* that in London. At Napier House I have a purpose, *I am needed*. It doesn't matter that I won't have babies. At home, it's all that I can ever think about.'

'Raoul needs you.'

'He doesn't,' said Lucy. 'He thinks I should go my own way for a while.'

'Only because you said you'd been saucing about with the harmonica player!'

Lucy took a deep breath and seemed to gather herself back together.

'I'm doing this for him, Tara,' she said. 'Him as well as me. He'll hurt for a bit, then he'll find someone else. He has to, if he's going to be happy.'

'Is that all you can say? Raoul's going to Spain, and he may never come back, and that's all you can *say*?'

'It's *not* all I can say,' she said. 'But it's all I will say. Please.' She turned to me, her face white with exhaustion. 'Please,' she said. 'I need you to believe that this isn't easy for me either.'

'Why not tell him to stay, then?'

'Because I have no choice.' She opened her eyes wide, as though she were trying to see some explanation for everything, but couldn't. 'I don't think he wants to stay. He knows that I'm a dead end.'

'I'm glad I wasn't born beautiful, like you,' I said, unable to stop now I had started. 'All it's done is lead you into trouble. What will Pa say? You can't get *divorced*.'

The word seemed to sicken the very air around us; I don't think that I had ever spoken it out loud before. As soon as it was out there, I wanted to chase it back in, but it was too late. Lucy's hands gripped the steering wheel; she was leaning forward in her seat. It had started to rain. I loved her so much, my sister, but I knew then that part of what I loved was her certainty, her absolute confidence in everything that she had ever done. Without that, I felt my foundations shifting. Still I couldn't stop.

'I don't know,' she said quietly.

'So that's it?' I shouted. 'You're going to let it all fall apart because you've had two weeks in London and that's enough to

398

make you *leave*? Because now you've given marriage a good stab, you just can't do it any more? You can't have children? Neither can plenty of other people! Why does it have to define *everything*?'

But even as I asked the question, I suddenly knew the answer. It defined everything because it had defined Ma, and Lucy had been unable to save her. Not being able to produce babies herself had taken away that chance to redeem everything. If she had a child, it would heal the wound she had carried around with her since she was thirteen. Yet even realizing this wasn't enough to make me stop shouting. Once I had started, I felt myself out of control, throwing words into the air with force and fury – I was all over the place.

'I don't think it *is* about you and Raoul and not having children anyway. I think you're happy for him to go back to Spain because knowing you, you're *bored*. That's why you're laying your bets on the harmonica player—'

I felt the sharp sting of the slap across my face. Lucy and I stared at each other, appalled. There it was – the unhinging of that gate that had kept everything fenced in.

'Oh, Tara, Tara, *Tara*! Oh, what have I done to you!'

Lucy tried to gather me into her arms, her face aghast.

'Get away!' I wrenched myself free of her. I struggled to find the door handle, and once I had, couldn't open the damn thing.

'Let me out!' I was saying it more to myself than to her. 'Let me *out*!'

'No!' she shouted. 'No, *please*! I'm sorry. God, I'm sorry.'

I could feel every one of her fingers on my cheek, the impression they had made.

'Get me out!' I shouted. 'GET ME OUT!'

'You can't walk,' Lucy shouted. 'It's pouring.'

'We're almost back in the village,' I hissed. 'I'm hardly going to get lost.'

'You'll catch a chill . . .'

'Believe me, I've already caught one from the things you've said.'

'Tara, *please!*'

'What the hell do you care?'

Lucy stared at me for a second. At some point in this cheerful little scene she had bitten her bottom lip so hard that it was bleeding. She knew that she wasn't going to win me back right now. She ran around to my side of the car, pulling the door open for me. As I shot out of my seat and into the rain, a letter addressed to the Bishop of Oxford flew out from the door pocket and into the road. Pa's terrifying black-inked handwriting was smudged into illegibility within seconds.

'For Christ's sake!' shouted Lucy, grabbing the envelope and flinging it back into the car.

'You built your own truth on *my* marriage,' she yelled. 'That was nobody's mistake but yours, Tara!'

'If you didn't mean forever, you shouldn't have married him!'

'I shouldn't have married him when I couldn't give him what he wanted!'

'You have given him what you wanted! Yourself!' I shouted this last bit right out into the heavens themselves, louder than I had ever shouted anything before. Then I slammed the car door shut to obliterate her response.

33

How to Pass Time in a Rainstorm

It was raining harder now, but Lucy drove past me without attempting to lure me back again – and anyway, the Ten Plagues of Egypt wouldn't have got me into that car now. I was wearing Imogen's sandals, which were too small, and George's mac, which was too big. The temperature had dropped; dark grey clouds rolled around, drunk and disorderly, in a fast-blackening sky. I could taste the sea, but it could have been my tears. I felt as far from London as I had ever been; and yet I knew that without London I would never have talked to Lucy like I had. Two weeks ago, I hadn't been the person I was now.

I kept rhythm, despite the crying, which, if you've ever tried it, is harder than you think. One foot in front of the other; I knew the way through the village so well I could have walked it blindfolded. Another few minutes and I came towards the corner where the drive up to Trellanack began. Hester stood at the bottom of the drive, taking shelter under the copper beech. In my reckless days of stealing rides, I would quite often set off in miserable weather, knowing that no one else would be around. Now, despite Matilda telling me I could ride her again, I knew I couldn't. I thought of Lady W-D in India, and of Trellanack awaiting the hotel and golf club. It was all very well, everything changing. Ma had always told us that nothing ever stayed the same, that everything and everyone moves on. Yet all she had wanted to do was preserve us as newborn babies. A baby, then another baby, then another until it was too much. And then all of us left to figure out the rest of it for ourselves.

I had no intention of going up the drive. I just wanted to stand at the bottom and stare over the fence as I had done when I was little, and none of this had happened. I sang the song that was now being played on the radio, the Cherry Merrywell song that Billy hoped was going to make me a famous pop singer, and as I sang, the words were eaten up by the wind, so I sang louder and louder, tossing around my hands, trying to fight the wind and the rain with my voice.

I saw him approaching before he saw me. I knew at once that it was Inigo, for his distinctive walk, for the length of his legs. He had his head down and appeared to be walking with some sort of purpose, though what that was in weather like this, I couldn't think. Suddenly he looked up and saw me at the bottom of the drive, as though we had planned to meet. Instinctively he stopped, so that we were both still – two pawns on a chessboard, waiting for the next move.

I moved first, my feet slipping on the wet ground, pulling up the hood of George's coat. He stood still, waiting for me. When I got up close, I saw that he was carrying a magazine under his arm – just as he had been all those years ago at Milton Magna. I opened my mouth to tell him, and shut it again.

'Hello,' he said. 'Lovely weather.'

'Cornwall always gets rain in July,' I said.

He frowned. 'What are you doing out, anyway? Shouldn't you be eating cake with your sisters or something?'

'I wanted to clear my head.' I wished I hadn't stopped at the bottom of the drive. I hadn't been looking for him.

'Walking won't help to clear your head,' said Inigo. He pulled a hip flask from his back pocket. 'But this will.'

'It's not cooking sherry, is it?' I asked, thinking of Raoul.

'Who do you think I am?' said Inigo.

We stood under the limes and took glugs of whisky like we were resting in the trenches together. It was raining harder now.

'I thought I heard someone singing,' said Inigo.

'It wasn't me,' I said. 'It must have been Hester.'

'Hester has perfect pitch.'

'How do you know?'

'Because I do too.'

He tried, and failed, to spark a light for a cigarette. 'How was your brother-in-law?' he asked, trying again. I opened my mouth to reply, to say that he was on the mend and should be home soon, but what came out was quite different.

'They're getting divorced,' I said. 'At least, she hasn't told me that for certain, but it was quite clear to me. I don't think she loves him any longer.'

I don't think that he noticed at first – the rain and the fading light gave me good cover. But I felt the tears, hot down my face, and found that I couldn't stop them.

'It's just that if Lucy leaves, then that means we won't have Raoul any more! Raoul!' When I spoke his name it sounded unearthly, an inconsolable wail. 'He was the one who listened to me, and who said I could sing, and he'll go back to Spain and she'll hate me anyway for what I've said to her . . .'

I don't think that any of what I said next was comprehensible to Inigo. He put the unlit cigarette back into his pocket and stood there for a minute, while I cried; I think it was the first time that he didn't know what to do with me. There was nothing he could come back with – no smart remarks, no shadowy questions, nothing – just the awkwardness of seeing a girl he'd written a song for weeping like a ten-year-old in the rain, wearing an outsized coat and a pair of ill-fitting shoes. I must have looked about as far from Billy Laurier's vision of Cherry Merrywell as it was possible to be.

'I'm sorry,' I said. I sniffed, wiped my eyes with my wet sleeve and realized with horror who it was I was standing next to. 'I think I must be tired. The travelling and all that—'

'Don't say sorry. You don't need to.'

'I feel as though I've made an idiot of myself.'

'So what if you have?'

'You never seem to,' I said accusingly.

Inigo sighed. 'You don't know me very well.'

He took my hands and formed them into a little cave shape to provide shelter for his match.

'You'll be lucky,' I sniffed, to hide the oddness of it.

He struck, and it worked. Once the cigarette was lit, he handed it to me.

'Does this qualify for the blues?' I asked him. 'Watching someone else's marriage fall apart.'

'I don't think so,' he said.

'Why not?'

'For it to be the blues, you'd have to be in love with Raoul.'

'Which I most certainly am *not!*'

'Well, precisely.' He unfolded his magazine. It was a battered copy of *Horse & Hound* from Lady W-D's collection. I laughed, in spite of myself.

'It's force of habit,' said Inigo. 'When I was little, I carried the music magazines around with me everywhere, as though they were teddy bears. They kept me safe.'

'What was there to be afraid of in *your* world?'

I expect I sounded sarcastic; I hadn't meant to. Every word that was coming from him was sharp, hot, *real*. I had never heard him talk like this before, and I didn't want him to stop. I think both of us sensed that this strange honesty between us was a game of limited overs.

'Everything,' said Inigo simply. 'Refusing to do what anyone wanted me to do by never working hard at school, and spending all day long trying to be Elvis for a start. Knowing that we were living in a dying house, coming out of the war and fearing for the strange new world without sirens and blackouts and rationing. Most of all,' he said, 'I was afraid of my mother's sadness.'

'And I of my father's,' I said.

He didn't answer. That was it. I sensed he didn't want to say any more. He looked down at the magazine, then at me. 'You'll be on magazine covers soon,' he said.

'Not *Horse & Hound*, sadly.'

'You never know,' said Inigo.

'The truth is,' I said slowly, 'I don't want to be on the cover of anything. I never did. I only wanted to sing to please Ma. That's the truth of it. I only did it for her.'

Inigo didn't react to this, but he didn't look surprised. The rain had stuck his dark eyelashes into starfish and his shirt was soaked through. He wasn't wearing enough clothes, I thought. Imogen would have berated him for not wearing a coat.

'Billy thinks he can make me do anything he likes,' I said. 'Wear the right clothes, be seen at the right parties, talk to the right boys, answer the right questions . . .'

'So just to prove him wrong, you dress in jodhpurs and fall off piano stools and sing the blues, and suggest to me − *me*!

Bloody Father Hit-mas *himself*! –that I need to change the words in the third verse because they're too predictable. Jeez, Cherry Merrywell. You haven't exactly made his life easy.'

'I never meant to cause any trouble,' I said. 'It's just that none of this makes sense in the way that I thought it would.'

There was another silence. The wind blew my hair into my mouth.

'Your sister says that you've never been good at following everyone else in the general direction of what's expected,' said Inigo.

'Ha! When did she say that?'

'Last week. The day that we went out together. You know – the day that Digby was taking your picture for the countless multitudes who shall be buying your record.'

Oh, yes, certainly, I knew that day only too well! But Lucy and Inigo going out was news to me. I must have looked far more astonished by this news than he was expecting.

'I thought she would have told you about it,' he said in surprise.

'She's too weird for words,' I said. My voice sounded high and tight. 'Why wouldn't she tell me . . . ?'

Then something occurred to me with a terrible gong of dread. I covered my mouth with my hands, my heart jammed against my ribs. I wouldn't have been surprised if there was a crack of thunder overhead – such was the horror of what I was taking in. I had missed it. For the first time ever, it had come and gone *without me knowing it*.

'It was the anniversary,' I whispered. 'Ma's death. It was last week . . .'

'She told me,' said Inigo. 'She was sitting in the library at Napier, crying into a cup of coffee after you left with Clover.

I should have just walked out again, but I decided to ask her what was up.'

'And she *told* you?' I was amazed. 'She told *you*? She *never* talks about Ma.'

I was part horrified, part deeply impressed. Nobody asked Lucy questions like that; it wasn't how it *worked*.

'What did she say?'

'She said it was seven years since her mother had died, and that she, Lucy, had been thirteen when it happened.'

'Yes,' I said, gulping. 'Yes, she was.'

'Then she told me how much she had loved the maze at Trellanack, and how she and Matilda used to have picnics in the middle.'

'Well, yes.'

I felt thrown by Inigo's ability to have sucked information from my sister like this; I needed to regain control.

'I said that if she wanted a maze, then she should go to Hampton Court.'

'Hampton Court?'

'Yes. Substantial Tudor pile formerly inhabited by some lout called Henry VIII. I'm surprised you haven't heard of him.'

I gave him a ghost of a smile.

'Anyway, we went,' said Inigo.

'*What?*'

'I went with your sister to Hampton Court. We agreed it was as good a way as any to spend the day.'

'I don't understand. Why weren't you working?'

'I never start working until after six. It was no problem. I took the morning off, we solved the maze, we came back.'

'You solved the maze?' I stared at him in disbelief. 'I'm surprised you stopped there. Why not tackle a few other problems while you were at it? Billy says there's trouble brewing with the Russians.' I laughed out loud, such was the need to release some sort of astonishment at what he was telling me.

Inigo shook his head. 'Already dealt with that one. No need to worry. It won't happen.'

'What won't?'

'War.'

'How do you know?'

'Because there's too much music left to write, of course.'

He put his hands out and touched the bark of the lime.

'Why didn't Lucy tell me?' I asked him. 'Why didn't she *remind* me what the date was?'

'She said that you always find it hard. She didn't want you to any more.'

'Did she . . . ?' I cleared my throat. 'Did she say anything to you about Raoul? Anything at all.'

'No,' he said.

'What did you talk about, then?'

He grinned. 'Mainly the precision of the courtyard, and how many bedrooms were afforded to the servants. I have to tell you, I was glad to get back to Napier.'

'Why?'

'It's strange, being with your sister in a place like that. She lost herself completely.'

'Did she go into a trance and start quoting dates and speeches and great chunks from the letters of Anne Boleyn as though there were no one else there?'

'Yes,' said Inigo. 'Exactly that. People kept staring at this excessively good-looking girl sitting there listing off dates and times and opinions on who actually wrote "Greensleeves".'

I had never heard Inigo compliment anyone's appearance before.

'Well, who *did* write it?' I asked him.

'Well, Henry VIII gets the credit, but really, I don't think he would have had the time or the energy to compose such a song. He was too busy seducing and eating and knocking people's heads off to write a melody that was to stick around for five hundred years.'

'Don't you always say that you need experience to write?'

'Not *that* much bloody experience,' said Inigo.

The wind picked up again. I shivered.

'Come on.' Inigo rolled up *Horse & Hound*. 'Shall I walk you home?'

It wasn't that he wanted to, I realized. It was merely the force of his upbringing. You can't leave girls standing in the rain. Get them back where they belong before you think about yourself.

'Oh no,' I said too quickly. 'I'm fine. Thank you.'

Inigo glanced at his watch.

'Nearly time for you to start working,' I said.

'Yes,' he said. 'The piano dates back to the ark. But what point is there in tuning it when it will be packed away and sent to auction in a matter of weeks? I'll have to put up with it.'

'The advantage is that if it sounds good on that, it will sound good on anything.'

'Exactly.' Inigo looked at me curiously. 'You see, Miss Jupp, you even *think* like a composer.'

'Thank you,' I said to him.

'For what?'

'For what you did for her. Thank you for taking Lucy out. I think that was a good thing that you did. She won't forget it.'

'No,' he said. 'With a memory like hers, I certainly doubt she will.'

I handed him back his hip flask, now almost empty.

'Don't worry about forgetting,' said Inigo. 'I think your mother would *want* you to forget for once. It's a drag – remembering the same blackness every year. A fucking drag.'

In the same way that Raoul's accent afforded him leverage with his emotional remarks, Inigo's occasional Americanisms jolted one into believing whatever he was saying.

'Maybe you're right,' I said.

He stuck out his hand. I laughed and shook it.

'Friends?' he said.

'Yes.'

We walked off in opposite directions, each stride taking us further away from the limes and the bottom of the drive where so many of my dramas seemed to have been played out. I broke into a run, wanting to be sitting inside at the Rectory, warmed by Imogen's cakes and tea and the Littles telling me stories about school. As I ran, mud squelching over Imogen's sandals and splashing on to my bare legs, I thought about Inigo and his strange act of kindness. By the time I arrived home, I had dismissed it as something he had done because Lucy was so pretty. I wasn't sure how to take the version of Inigo that wasn't all that I had assumed him to be. When I arrived back at the Rectory, I wrote Lucy a note with one word: Sorry. Then I tore it up again. I wasn't sorry. Before, I would have said it anyway. Not any more.

It was too late, in any case. She had already left us.

'She's gone to Bristol with George,' said Imogen. 'She came in from the hospital, changed her shoes, packed her bag and she was off. She said she'd stay overnight and take the train back to London.'

'Why?' I asked, stupidly. I knew the answer far better than Imogen did. She had gone because she didn't want to be with me in the car. She was breaking away.

'She said to tell you that she was sorry,' said Imogen.

I looked at her. 'Did she *seem* sorry?'

'She seemed as though she weren't here at all.'

I turned away from Imogen.

'Sometimes things happen that are beyond our control,' she said.

'You don't say.'

'She's always been the most complicated of all of us. I don't think she even understands herself. Lucy's always been—'

'Very selfish!' I said.

'He'll be all right,' said Imogen steadily. She picked up a pair of socks and pulled a needle and thread from her work basket. 'They both will.'

'How can you be so horribly cheerful about everything all the time?'

Imogen looked at me and laughed in surprise.

'Because we have a choice, don't we? Might as well believe the best is going to happen. If that's ignorance, then I'm happy to be foolish.'

The day had been too long – it had gone *on* too long. But the one thing that I was aware of was that the terrible pain of Lucy and Raoul was dulled by just one thing. And it wasn't Digby.

It was because of *him*. It was a little bit better, because of Inigo Wallace.

34

An Effortless, Beautiful Thing

I had only one more day before I was to return to London and my new life. I had spent most of Sunday at church, watching Imogen scuttling around after Mr Bell and laughing with Florence at George's attempts to rouse the congregation to attend yet another Bring and Buy sale at Peggy Payne's house. Unfortunately for George, whose good looks were usually enough to set the choir into giggling fits without any further provocation, he read out a church notice without any awareness of the *double entendre* it provoked.

'The ladies of the congregation have cast-off clothing of every kind,' said George.

'No change there then!' shouted a wag in the front row.

'They may be seen in Mrs Payne's garden on Friday. Any money raised will go to Granite House,' continued George, oblivious.

A fit of silent hysterics with Florence temporarily dulled the pain of what had happened between Lucy and me.

On Monday morning I walked to Trellanack and watched Digby taking more pictures. I felt a terrible ache while I was there, the sort that you get when you know that someone is dying and that you may be visiting them for the last time. Even Digby – who had seemed so relentlessly unaffected by the fate of Trellanack – seemed slower now. We talked in low voices, as though not wanting the house to hear us. I heard the sound of the piano coming from the drawing room, but I didn't interrupt Inigo. I felt suddenly shy in his presence – I just didn't quite know why. I couldn't join up the pieces yet; it was too difficult.

In the afternoon, I took the bus into Truro and visited Raoul. Expecting to find him wiped out with despair over Lucy's last visit and confused about why she had returned to London ahead of me, I was surprised to see him sitting up in bed, scribbling on sheets of lined paper. He was wearing his glasses, and was so deep in thought that he didn't notice that I had arrived. I coughed, and he looked up, startled.

'Tara!' He stacked the papers together and shoved them on to the table beside him. 'I thought you were coming at two!'

'It's ten past.' I looked at him curiously. 'Working hard? You seem to have cracked your writer's block.'

'Yes. I rather think I have.'

'Capability Brown comes good at last,' I said. 'I knew he would.'

Raoul looked around the room, left and right, like a spy about to impart Key Information. I resisted an urge to laugh.

'Can I let you in on a secret, Tara?'

'Yes, please,' I said.

Raoul leaned towards me as far as he could. His eyes, although still deeply shadowed, were brighter than they had been for months. When Raoul shot his eyes at you like that, resistance was virtually impossible.

'I have abandoned Capability Brown.'

'I beg your pardon?'

'Of course not forever,' he said hurriedly. 'I *love* the man, Tara. But for now, I have left him.'

'Left him?'

'Imogen's Georgette Heyer books,' he said, holding up his hand to stop me from talking any more. 'They have given me inspiration.'

I laughed. 'What do you mean? You've written a romantic novel set in the eighteen-hundreds?'

Raoul took a deep breath. 'Well, actually, yes. Yes, I *have*. You're the first person outside of these walls to know about it. Only it's set in the *seventeen*-hundreds, and at the moment it breaks into paragraphs of Spanish when I can't find what I want to say in English. I have only a little way to go. It is nearly finished.'

I stared at him.

'Don't be ridiculous! You can't have written a *novel*! You don't even *like* fiction . . .'

'Only the most narrow-hearted of men hate fiction,' said Raoul smugly. 'You know I 'ave always felt I had it in me to write something like this.'

I walked around to the other side of his bed to where a pile of papers sat stacked on a chair. Picking up the top sheet I scanned it. 'It's typed!' I said, astonished. 'And you've misspelt "detestable",' I added, frowning at the third line down.

'You must not read that,' said Raoul, reaching over and taking the paper out of my hands. 'You have to go from the start like everybody else will, Tara. No special treatment for family members. Although I can reveal to you that Captain William Thorley is not what he seems . . .'

'All right,' I said, folding my arms and giving him the benefit of my barely concealed doubt. 'What's it about then?'

'It's about a girl from Granada coming to England and falling in love with a landscape gardener called Lancelot. Only she has *secrets*.'

'I bet she has! And who's been typing it up for you?'

'Rachel,' said Raoul simply. 'She ask what I am doing, and we started to talk. She wanted to help, so I told her that all I lacked was a typewriter. I can't use one with my leg like this, so she takes my pages home every day, and –' Raoul did a little typing motion with his long fingers to illustrate the point. 'She used to be a dentist's secretary,' he added, as though this explained it all.

'*Rachel?*'

'One of the nurses. You know, the one with the big––'

'But it must have taken her *hours!*'

'Yes,' he said lightly. 'But she has been so kind. I have been in here for nearly a month. She has work with me all this time.'

I recalled Nurse Rachel's concerned face when we had last visited and imagined that the poor girl was quite helpless under Raoul's spell. One simply didn't see men like him in Truro – he had turned her whole world upside down, and hardened her fingertips into calluses at the same time.

'You've written the whole thing in a *month!*' I said.

'Nearly,' said Raoul. 'When your heart is breaking, you'll do anything to distract yourself. Once I started, I found I could not stop. It would have been impossible for me *not* to write it.'

'Why didn't you tell us before?'

'Why should I? It was something for myself. All my life, I am giving information to people all the time. For once, this was something for me. Just for me.' He grinned at me. 'Are you impressed?'

'Of course I'm impressed.' I shook my head. 'I've been dreading coming to see you today, after – after last time. I can see that I really shouldn't ever have doubted you.'

'Oh, make no mistake, my heart's in shreds,' said Raoul calmly. 'But with Lucy – the more you scream and shout, the further she runs. So this –' he picked up his pen and twiddled it in the air – 'this has been my saviour.'

'Do you think someone will publish it?' I said.

'I don't care,' he replied. 'I don't think that far into the future. I just want to finish it.'

'Gosh, Raoul. I've never heard you speak such sense about your writing before.'

'That is because, for once, I believe in my work. All the time that I was writing about Capability Brown's *truths*, I was just standing on his shoulders to admire the scenery that *he* had created. This time I have created my own view. I have plundered every house that Lucy and I ever visited! I have made characters out of *thin air*! I can create what I want. I make a girl with eyes like Imogen's and a character like Lucy's. I make a father like my own, only with bigger feet for crushing people into the ground. I make a house that is a delicious cocktail of Trellanack and Bowood, with a little *pinch* of Castle Howard thrown in. You know I even included our little episode with *El Chico de la Catedral*!' he said triumphantly.

'You *what*?'

'I have my heroine injured in a riding accident,' he explained. 'Only more happens when she is rescued than did when I found you, I can tell you.'

I laughed, out of astonishment.

'What do you mean? It's *erotic*?' I don't think I'd ever used the word before.

Raoul nodded. 'Yes,' he said. 'There's lots of erotic. Erotic is all over the place. But good erotic, you know. Not the usual stuff.'

'What on earth is the usual stuff?'

'Once I start, I couldn't stop. The erotic imagination drives my heroine to everything that she does. She is a woman with desires.'

'Desires,' I said. 'One of Lady W–D's best hunters was called Desire.'

'Here I am, lying like a dying man . . .' went on Raoul, ignoring my remark.

'Hardly,' I said, noting the warmth back in his cheeks.

'Like a dying man,' repeated Raoul, 'unable to move, staring at the same walls and the same faces day after day, and yet I am more free than I have *ever* been. Fiction has saved me from the impossible.' He leaned forward, and there was fire in his eyes. 'It has saved me from *myself*,' he added.

I thought of Ma, and gulped.

Nurse Rachel, who I think could have been standing behind the curtain for some time, like an actress waiting for a cue, entered the scene. Seeing that Lucy was not present, her face relaxed. I'm quite sure that her uniform was at least two sizes two small.

'I have told Tara here about the book,' said Raoul as she straightened his sheets.

'It's nearly finished,' said Rachel.

'I know.' I looked at her bright, plump face – her eyes sparkling with the thrill of being in Raoul's presence. She can't have been much older than me.

'It seems that you have worked very hard,' I said. 'Raoul's lucky to have found you.'

What was I *saying*? I thought as the words left my mouth.

417

'I'm the lucky one,' said Nurse Rachel. She flushed. 'It's a wonderful book. I can never wait for the next chapter!' I smiled weakly at her. Sensing an ally, she carried on. 'I drive home as fast as I can after work, and I sit up at my typewriter for as long as it takes. His handwriting was impossible to read at first, but –' she smiled at Raoul – 'I've got the hang of it now. All those loopy y's and great long bits where he decides to write in another language! But I've grown quite attached to my Spanish dictionary. Think I'll be ready to converse with anyone soon. As long as they want to talk about intimate relations in eighteenth-century Granada,' she added, blushing becomingly. She leaned forward and plumped up Raoul's pillow. 'I've made you tomato soup for tea,' she said. 'I had some myself last night, so I brought it in with me in a Thermos this morning; it was no bother. Would you like it now? You could have some too,' she added, nodding at me without enthusiasm.

'You're too kind. In fact, I'd like to finish writing,' said Raoul.

'Oh!' She was too in love with him to hide her disappointment. 'Perhaps we'll catch up later this afternoon? When I've finished my observations?'

'I'm certainly not going anywhere,' said Raoul.

Nurse Rachel smiled at him, opened her mouth as if she wanted to say more, then thinking the better of it, left us.

'Observations?' I said to Raoul. 'The only thing *I'm* observing is the fact that she's bats about you, the poor girl.'

'Don't be silly.'

I unscrewed the lid of the Thermos. The soup smelled delicious. Nurse Rachel certainly hadn't injured herself on a tin opener, as Lucy had done cooking for Raoul six months into their marriage. Thyme! I thought, breathing in the smell that reminded me very much of Clover's window boxes at Napier

House. And a small tub of real croutons, made by hand and sprinkled with black pepper!

'For a couple of weeks I tried to fall in love with her,' said Raoul. 'It didn't work.'

'God, Raoul. Don't say things like that.'

'Tara, when you're stuck in bed for weeks on end, you'll try anything. It's quite all right,' he said. 'I would drive Rachel demented in the real world. Anyway,' he added with a shrug, 'she knows she will never get me.'

I was frantic to change the subject.

'What's it called?' I asked him. 'Your book?'

Raoul looked at me, as if considering whether he should impart such information, then obviously couldn't hold it in any longer.

'*Bernadita*,' he whispered.

'And who *is* she?' I whispered back.

Thirty minutes later, my head was scrambled with the unleashed contents of Raoul's imagination. A Spanish señorita with hair as black as her violent moods, a landowner in eighteenth-century Oxfordshire, a secret concerning a horse that had been won in a bet, an awful lot of hopping in and out of bed and Capability Brown popping up in the story like a jack-in-the-box – I couldn't really keep up. I wondered whether Raoul had been given painkilling drugs that were too powerful.

'So, you see, it is all there,' he was saying as I gulped down the last dregs of his soup. 'Everything that is worth writing about comes into this book – landscaped gardens, the English, horses, discrimination, language barriers, oranges straight from the tree and girls with big dreams, big desires and well-endowed men.'

'Oh, Raoul,' I said weakly. 'You can't say things like that if you're hoping to get published.'

'I certainly can,' he said. 'I believe I am far more likely to raise interest in people if I appeal to their honesty. Imogen said it herself. When she reads, she wants to escape, but to feel that she has learned something without even realizing it. It should be an effortless, beautiful thing.'

He picked up the Thermos and peered into it.

'Christ, it's all gone!'

'Sorry!' I said in horror. 'Shall I get you something else?'

'I work best on an empty stomach,' said Raoul. 'It's something I have discovered in here.'

For a moment, he looked at me seriously.

'How is the boy who takes pictures?'

'He's all right,' I said uneasily. I felt that just talking about Digby sent lights and sirens flashing around my body that screamed: '*She's Done It! No Longer A Virgin!*'

'You went to bed with him?' asked Raoul.

'*Raoul!* No! I mean, please don't – gosh – you can't ask me *that.*'

'So that means yes?'

'Yes.' I threw my hands in the air, admitting everything. 'Yes, all right. It does.'

'Good,' said Raoul. 'I have made my heroine something of an experimental lover. There is nothing duller in any novel than a woman who saves herself for the loins of the overcharged hero in the final chapter. *Bernadita* reverses all of that phooey.'

'You know, talking like this with you is all wrong.'

'It shouldn't be,' said Raoul.

'May I tell Lucy?' I asked him.

'No,' said Raoul. There was an urgency in this. 'No, please, Tara. You can't. Keep it to yourself for now. It is still unfinished.' He looked at me. 'Don't imagine for one moment that my heart

420

isn't splintering into a thousand pieces,' he said. 'But if she wants me to be free, she needs to know that there are no second chances.'

'There should be,' I said. 'You can't let her go, Raoul. Go after her,' I begged. 'She doesn't understand herself – you're the only one of us who does. At the moment I think that Napier House is the only thing that keeps her going. If she can save it, then I think she will feel like something she's done has been worthwhile.'

I didn't even know whether I believed what I was saying.

'You lie in bed for weeks on end, you get a perspective on everything,' said Raoul. 'If she wants me to go, then I go.'

'But *I* don't want you to go,' I said desperately.

'Love is what you make it, Tara,' said Raoul. 'You can't blame Lucy any more than you can contain her. Some people are born walking, always seeking. She is that girl looking for the end of the rainbow all the time. You can tell her that she'll never find it, but to what purpose? If you believe in the rainbow, then you believe in the pot of gold.' As I walked out, I wished, with all my might, that Raoul's accent didn't give such aching resonance to words that – spoken by anyone else – would be the last word in schmaltz.

And *Bernadita*? I confess, dear reader, that I thought Raoul had gone quietly and completely mad.

35

Black Night, No Moon

When I arrived home, George, Imogen and Florence were sitting in the kitchen eating carrot cake.

'I've been to see Raoul,' I said.

George looked up. 'I'm going in tomorrow. Was he all right?'

'Perfectly,' I said. 'He's finished his book.'

'Good for him,' said George, picking icing off Florence's knife.

'Wonders will never cease,' said Florence, batting George's hand away. 'I must say, I never thought he'd do it.'

'Well, I think it's terrific that he's finally taken Capability Brown by the scruff of the neck, and has got the thing written,' said George. He took a big gulp of tea.

'Except it's not about Capability Brown at all,' I said. 'It's a novel. He's written a *novel*. It's called *Bernadita*.'

George started to choke and spat out his tea.

'Don't be stupid,' said Florence. 'He hasn't written a *novel*?' She looked at me, uncertain. '*Has* he?'

'He has. And why not? He always had a desire to write "ficción." What else do you do if your leg's strapped up and you're lying in bed surrounded by old women with shattered hips? He thinks it will be finished by the time he's out.'

'You're not serious, Tara?' asked George, putting down his cake.

'You don't have to believe me,' I said. 'But it's true. He didn't want anyone to know about it, so you mustn't breathe a word. But I *had* to tell you all. I couldn't not.'

'It can't be true!' exclaimed Florence.

'It is true. What's more, there are lots of erotic scenes in it.'

'Erotic?' said all three of them in unified astonishment.

'Yes. It's bodice-ripping stuff.'

'But what's it about?' asked Imogen.

'All you need to know is that *Captain William Thorley is not what he seems.*'

There was a silence while they digested this. Their united amazement made me realize one thing. Raoul was on to something with this. Like me – they were already captivated, and they hadn't even read a word of the thing.

'I'm not sure it's my sort of book,' said Imogen.

'Well, he was inspired to write after an overdose of Georgette Heyer administered by *you*. He says she's a genius.'

'But she doesn't write that sort of thing!' cried Imogen in horror.

'Of course not!' I said impatiently. 'But she writes for women, doesn't she? And now so does Raoul. Only with a little more punch.'

'Punch will be the word if Pa finds out,' said George. 'How can I get my hands on a copy?' he demanded, leaning forward, eyes glinting.

The prospect of returning to London the next day was suddenly a terrible one, something that I couldn't conceive of doing. How could I leave them? How could I be anywhere else but here?

'Raoul will have to type it all out when he comes home,' said George. 'Although recalling his awful handwriting, I'd be surprised if he gets that far. Nobody but his mother could decipher it.'

I opened my mouth to tell them about Rachel, but something stopped me in my tracks. It was a knock at the front door. All of us looked at each other.

'Crumbs!' said Imogen. 'Who on earth could it be at this time of night?'

'Digby,' I said. I just *knew*.

'Can I get it?' asked Florence, standing up.

'No!' I almost raced out of the room to stop her.

Sure enough, it was him – standing on the doorstep, dressed in a black shirt and a pair of very tight tweed trousers.

'What are you wearing?' I asked him, astonished.

'Matilda's old man's strides,' said Digby. He grinned at me. 'Five bob says that if I wear them to the Marquee Club next week, I'll have half of London in them by the weekend.'

He peered into the Rectory, like a child hoping to be let loose in the Natural History Museum.

'Aren't you going to ask me in?' he demanded.

'Of course she is,' said Florence, coming out of the kitchen. Digby grinned at her delightedly. 'Florence,' he said. 'I know you from Tara's description.'

'Do you?' she asked suspiciously.

In the end, my attempts to keep Digby from my family were futile. He sat himself down at the kitchen table, and Imogen brought him a plate of bread and cheese and opened a very good bottle of red wine, as though he was a Traveller From Afar who needed all the best that Cornwall had to offer before resuming his journey.

424

'Thank you, baby,' he said, giving Imogen one of his lopsided grins. She went bright red, and for a moment I worried that Mr Bell would be forgotten. Digby was too much for someone like Imogen; she would lose the ability to speak before the night was out.

'Where's Inigo?'

'Writing, the great bore. I wanted him to play cards with me but he shoved me out of that spooky room he seems to have claimed and told me to go and annoy someone else. I told him that I was going to go and find you.'

'What did he say?'

'Not much. Actually, he was his usual delightful self,' said Digby, considering. 'He said something about you needing sleep, and didn't I realize that you were going to be working next week? I said it was high time someone showed him a good time before he wakes up one morning and realizes he's turned into a headmaster overnight. Tell me,' said Digby, looking at Florence, 'which one of you is most scared of your father?'

'All of us,' said George. 'Some pretend not to be, like Lucy, but underneath, we're all terrified.'

Tipping Inigo out of my head, I pushed my fingers towards Digby's. Without looking away from Florence, he closed his hand around mine. There was something shared between us – the unmistakable weight of the misfit's cloak – that always brought us comfort in each other's presence.

Upstairs, at two thirty in the morning, Digby sat on the window seat, looking through old photograph albums. He was entirely absorbed by pictures; it was possible for a snapshot of someone's birthday party fifteen years ago to hold him tighter than any person. I sat on my bed, smoking and looking at him, answering his questions and holding a pillow on my lap as though I were about nine years old.

'What's this?' asked Digby, flipping over a page. '"Aunt Mary's Funeral,"' he read. 'God, not even *I* take my camera to funerals. Aunt Mary must have been quite someone . . .'

Suddenly I knew that there was someone in those pictures that I didn't want him to see.

'Actually Pa doesn't like me showing those photographs to anyone,' I said, standing up and crossing the room. 'He thinks it's sinister—'

But Digby had already seen her.

'I *know* her!' he said suddenly. 'That looks like Talitha Wallace.' He frowned into the picture. I had written her name underneath in my childish hand. 'Yes, that *is* her. That's Inigo's *mother!*'

'I know that,' I said. 'I *know!*' Fear of the truth coming out made me sound agitated. I gulped, then said it.

'My Aunt Mary used to be the housekeeper and cook at Milton Magna Hall.'

Digby looked astounded. 'Does Inigo know?'

'No!' I said. 'At least – not that she was my aunt.'

'Why not?'

'I didn't want to tell him.'

'Why not?' asked Digby again.

I threw myself back on to my bed. There was a light dizziness in my head; I felt as though I were partly in a dream.

'Stop asking questions!' I hissed. 'Please just stop asking *questions* all the time! Why do you always have to *know* everything about everyone?'

Digby looked amazed; not an expression that I had ever seen him exercise before.

'All right. Steady,' he said, as though I were a tricky horse he

426

was trying to load into a trailer. But I was on the brink of something, pausing before I ran away and hid under the nearest bed, or fell forward into the unknown mists of truth that I had been avoiding all this time.

'I met Inigo when I was ten,' I said. 'He was fifteen. I was helping Aunt Mary in the Big House. He was there one afternoon. I sang to him. He played the guitar.'

'You did?' Digby laughed, in spite of everything.

'But when I met him again, just before we made the record, he didn't recognize me, so I didn't tell him who I was.'

'Why not?'

'Too ashamed,' I said. 'His father gave him a little elephant just before he was killed. I didn't know whose it was, but I didn't care. I tried to steal it, but my aunt caught me and made me give it back.' I covered my face with my hands at the memory.

'Miss Merrywell, the more I get to know you, the more I don't know you at all,' said Digby. 'I doubt it meant as much to him as you thought it did,' he said.

I had never thought like this before.

'His father *died*,' I repeated. 'And I was going to take something – for my own entertainment. I hated myself for it.'

'I think he'd forgive you if you told him—'

'It's too late,' I said quickly. 'And anyway, he doesn't ever need to know. In a week he'll be back in America and none of this will matter any more.'

'Except that it mattered then, and it matters now,' observed Digby.

He put out his cigarette and looked at me. There was a thick silence. Below us, in the hall, I could hear the clock chiming a quarter to three.

Digby rubbed his nose and looked at me.

427

'He sees through me,' he said.

'Who?'

'Inigo, of course.'

He was going to tell me, I thought. Now that I had told him something that had caught him off balance, he felt as though he needed to give me something back. That was the way that Digby worked.

'What do you mean?' I asked.

'He sees me for what I am.'

'Which is what?'

'Nothing more than . . .' He gave a short laugh. 'Nothing.'

He looked at me unmoving.

'You may as well tell me,' I said.

When he spoke again, it was like Matilda talking about Paul Warren. It was as though he wasn't really in the room at all.

'There was a girl who liked me. I liked her a bit too much for my comfort, so I did the logical thing and didn't treat her very well.'

I didn't move, barely felt like I was breathing. The one thing I was conscious of was the peculiar absence of pain. Hearing him talking about someone he had loved was almost a relief: an explanation. He actually put his hands over his eyes.

'What happened?' I asked.

He took his hands away again and stared up at the ceiling.

'I had to go to New York to work, and I asked her to come with me. She said that she didn't want to come. We had the most almighty argument – me asking her why she wouldn't come, and she trying to explain that she wasn't going to fall into my hands every time I snapped my fingers. Anyway, I got to New York and tried to call her, but she didn't want to talk to me.'

428

'What happened?'

'What do you think? I went straight out to a party where I got stupidly drunk and made a pass at the most beautiful woman in the room, of course.'

'Of course,' I said.

'Into the middle of all of this walks Father Hit-mas. Turns out that the woman I'm chatting up is his mum.'

For a moment I gulped back a shout of laughter. Digby and Talitha Wallace was not what I had expected.

'Ouch,' I said weakly.

'You could put it that way.'

'But she must have been much older than you . . .'

Digby shrugged. 'If anyone could bottle what she had, they could make zillions.'

'What happened next?'

'Inigo sent me flying across the room.'

'*What?*'

'I can see his point. His ma had just got hitched to Rocky Dakota, and here she was, almost at first base with some jumped-up little git from London's East End. It wasn't ideal.'

'What did you do?'

'Left in a hurry,' said Digby. 'We never spoke about it again, but he can't forgive me. Of course, he was screwed up beyond belief at the time. Everyone says he never got over that house burning down like it did. He was drinking that night, but he still delivered a tough left hook. Before that I was under the mistaken impression that boys who had gone to schools like his couldn't fight to save their lives. I was wrong on that count, and black and blue for three weeks afterwards. I had to tell everyone I'd fallen down the stairs.'

'I – I just can't imagine it,' I said eventually.

'Well, it's all true. More's the bloody pity.'

'Inigo just isn't like that. I don't see him *ever* losing control. How is it that you're always having to work together?'

'Billy doesn't know that we fell out,' said Digby. 'He likes to work with the best people. Inigo's the best at what he does, and I'm the best at what I do.' He rubbed his nose with his hand. 'We put up with each other.'

'What about the girl?' I asked archly. 'The one you liked too much for your own comfort?'

'Well, that was the biggest problem of all,' said Digby.

'Why?'

'She was a friend of Talitha Wallace. A friend of the whole fucking nation, in fact.'

I didn't make the connections.

'Another woman of a certain age,' he said bitterly, filling in the gaps for me. 'It was Clover.'

'Clover? You and *Clover*? But she never said anything to me about—'

'Why would she?'

He lit a cigarette. 'Bloody hell.'

I looked at him. 'God in heaven, Digby,' I said. 'I wish I'd known.'

I felt like I wanted to hold him forever; I felt like I wanted to push him out of my room. Somewhere in between these two things was the truth. I knew that Digby and I was a flimsy thing, a gulp of something pure but unsustainable. He and Clover, for all the oddness of it, immediately felt more real to me than he and I had ever been.

'You know, I never believed all that crap about telling the truth feeling good,' said Digby. 'Now I know I was right. I feel like hell.'

He glared at me as though I were personally responsible.

'Inigo told Clover about me and Talitha,' said Digby. His voice was louder now – he was right back there at the scene. 'He *poisoned* her against me.'

I wasn't used to such hyperbole from Digby. Again I almost laughed.

But I couldn't think of anything else to say to him now. I moved my hand away from his, but he pulled it back. He wanted it for comfort, to know that there was someone next to him listening. It wasn't because he wanted to tell me – at the end of it all – that he loved me, and not her. But I let him hold me still. I would have done anything for Digby, because he had *believed* in me. Now he was talking about her again.

'I only went to New York in the first place because she kept saying I was too young. She kept backing away from me all the time. She got it into her head that I was one of the bad guys, so I thought, well, what the hell – if that's what she's expecting, then that's what I'm *going* to be.'

'Wouldn't it have been better to prove her wrong, and to hang around until she believed you?'

'Of course,' said Digby. 'But I was too stupid to do that. Things start going too well, and I'm up and running.'

There was a silence between us. Used to the low throb of noise from the street outside Cheyne Walk, the stillness of the Rectory felt deafening. I closed my hand over Digby's fist again. He was more of a Lost Boy than ever now. His watch, a beaten-up thing that he wore when he was working because it had been his father's, sat stoutly on his freckled wrist, telling the wrong time. He had bitten his nails down to nothing and there was biro all up his arm where he had written the telephone number of his bank manager, who had been stalking him for days with questions about his unbelievable number of unpaid parking tickets. For the first time I was aware of Digby's youth. Certainly, he was the best at what he did, and despite his chaos and disregard for rules, his talent for being at the centre of what was happening gave an overall impression of experience and wisdom that was quite wrong. For the first time since I had first seen him, I was aware of someone else.

'If you still love her,' I said, 'find a way to show her.'

'You can't go through life sorting everything out like that,' snapped Digby. 'You know, talking like the sort of novel you pick up in an airport, where all the ends are tied up with bows and everyone ends up dancing in the arms of their one and only intended love. Fucking hell, Cherry. Life isn't sweet like that.'

'You try to tie the ribbons but you just get tangled up in them,' I said dully. 'I know.'

We didn't say anything for a long time. I don't know what he was thinking; hell, I don't know what *I* was thinking, other than that there was some sort of relief in knowing all of this. What I knew now went some distance towards completing the picture of Digby that had been so difficult to see before. I thought of him and Clover, of Lucy and Matilda and Raoul, of me and Inigo, all of us, I thought, underestimating love and making a bit of a mess of everything as a result.

Digby took my hand. 'And you,' he began accusingly. 'Don't ever think that I think y*ou're* anything less than perfect,' he said.

'Don't,' I said quietly. 'Don't say that. You don't have to say all of that stuff—'

'I know I don't have to,' said Digby. 'I know.'

He stood looking at me; I could see that none of this was any easier for him than it was for me. He hadn't planned to tell me about Clover, but now that he had, there was no use in pretending any more that he would ever love me the same way that he loved her. I was just a girl. Clover was a woman. Reading my mind, Digby looked at me.

'I've taken pictures of the most beautiful girls in the country,' said Digby. 'They don't have what you have, Miss Merrywell.'

'What is it that I have?' My voice shook in despair. 'Apart from no clue, and cold hands?'

'You've got *yourself*,' he said, as though it were the most obvious thing in the whole wide world.

I laughed bleakly. It wasn't funny.

'Black night,' he said softly, looking out of the window again. 'And no moon. I suppose I should go.'

Digby wasn't the sort who ever had to go *anywhere* except at the end of something. I knew – like even the biggest fools know – that it was the beginning of the end, and inside I thanked him for doing it, and not leaving it to me. He was experienced in all of this. He knew how to do it. One foot in front of the other until you got to the next place you were meant to be going.

'We're all right, aren't we?' he said, standing by the door.

I nodded. 'We always have been,' I said. I laughed. 'Didn't you teach me all I know?'

'I think it's the other way around.'

It wasn't until he left that I realized I had given him far more than he could ever give me. But I couldn't change that now. Might as well see it as a good thing. It could be as Imogen had said: *We have a choice don't we?* I could jump whichever way I wanted now, only I didn't know who was going to be there to catch me any longer.

433

36

He Had the Matches

I was afraid that I wouldn't find Lucy at Napier House when I returned. I wasn't looking forward to the journey back to London, but it was made easier by Digby announcing that he would be staying on an extra day and returning by train. Sitting in the passenger seat beside Inigo, I opened a copy of *Alice in Wonderland*. I didn't want him to feel that he had to talk to me. Neither of us mentioned our meeting in the rain; our conversation was confined to the lightest of subjects. I didn't know where to start with him.

'You all right?' he asked me, somewhere around Exeter. 'You haven't said much.'

'I'm perfectly OK,' I said.

'I'm sorry he's not here,' he said, reading me wrongly. 'Digby was adamant that he had more pictures to take, but I guess he was probably trying to avoid being in the car with me all day. It's been a long few days.'

He changed gear. The car was like a spaceship compared to the old crates that we drove about in at home.

'There's nothing between us any more,' I said, sounding

ridiculous. 'I mean, whatever there was – which was, which was . . . I don't know – there isn't now.'

Inigo gave me a brief glance.

'I'm going to resist the urge to tell you that, for you, that is a very good thing,' he said. 'You'll only want to hit me, and I don't fancy crashing Billy's car.'

'I never believed it was forever,' I said. 'I wasn't that stupid.'

'Still, doesn't make it any easier,' said Inigo. 'For what it's worth, I'm sorry.'

'You don't have to say that.'

'He has a remarkable ability to stay friends with everyone he . . . has *taken out*,' said Inigo tactfully.

I laughed; I couldn't help it.

'One day I might be a walk-on part in the film of his life,' I said.

'Or he in yours,' said Inigo.

We went on without saying any more about it for a while. Inigo put his foot down and we sped through the counties – Devon, Somerset, Dorset flashed past us, and people stared at Billy's car, with Inigo driving.

I thought of Digby alone at Trellanack, deep in concentration, his eye to the lens. Everything else went from him when he was working – it had been then, and was now, his escape. For the hundredth time that day I debated whether to ignore his request and tell Clover what he had told me. I pushed my cardigan behind my head and closed my eyes, aware of the movement, always the movement, and the safety of being with him. I didn't care where we were going any more.

When I opened my eyes again, we were passing a sign to Bath. Inigo was tapping his fingers against the steering wheel.

'Good, you're awake,' he said.

I sat up and shivered, pulling my cardigan around my shoulders. Outside the temperature had dropped. Spots of rain fell on the windscreen.

'Remember this tune,' he said. He lit a cigarette.

'Huh?'

'I'm going to sing you something and I don't want you to forget it.'

'Why?'

'It's a new song idea,' said Inigo. 'The best ones always seem to happen when I'm at least three hours from a piano. If I drum the melody into your head, you can remind me of it when I've forgotten it tomorrow.'

'Seems one hell of a responsibility,' I grumbled. 'What if I forget it?'

I needn't have worried. Inigo's tunes needed only to be heard once and they were inescapable. He sang it over and over, making up silly words so that we wouldn't forget it. Then he sang it as Elvis, and as Roy Orbison, and I sang it as Patsy Cline and Marilyn Monroe and he joined in with harmonies and drum solos on the steering wheel and I couldn't stop grinning for the joy of it. I pushed my feet up on to the dashboard and accepted a stick of gum.

'Does everyone in America chew this all the time?' I asked him.

'No. Only in the movies. But don't stop singing,' he said. 'We have to sing for at least another –' he checked the time – 'fifteen minutes without stopping if we want to remember it.'

I started off again, in a higher key.

'It sounds like something else,' I said, watching Inigo tearing into a packet of crisps with his teeth.

'Good.'

'Is it going to be for me?'

'Nope. I've got a new group I'm meant to have written three songs for. They're going to have it.'

'Shame. I rather like it.'

'Well, if they don't want it, I'll play it to Billy and maybe you can have it then.'

I pulled a face. 'No, thanks,' I said. 'I don't want any more rejected songs.'

'Because of course the last time you had a song someone else didn't want, it sank without trace.'

I blushed. 'You know what I mean.'

'Anyway, Billy tells me that you're to be back in the studio next week,' said Inigo.

'What?' I said. 'When? With you?'

'No,' said Inigo. 'Much to your relief, I'm sure. He wants you to record with Johnnie Wilson.'

'Who on earth is he?'

'Don't worry,' said Inigo. 'I taught him everything he knows.'

'Why won't you do it?' I asked.

'Time,' said Inigo, which seemed to explain nothing at all. 'Now you're off and running, Johnnie can take over. He knows what he's doing and he won't annoy you by talking about the *Sunday Express* and Mr O'Rourke.'

I said no more to him, but wondered how many other people were waiting in the wings to be pulled in by Billy when they were needed. I was the centre of it – the reason why all this was happening – and yet I was not part of it at all.

A couple of miles on, without warning, Inigo turned left off the main road and pulled over. He switched off the engine.

'What are you doing?' I asked.

For a wild moment I thought he was going to turn to me

and reveal an impossible secret – that he was a spy, or the il-legitimate son of the King of Greece – I don't know – nothing would have surprised me. He was still so inexplicable to me, still so unknown. Now he was rummaging around the car, looking for something with some urgency.

'I knew I'd find pencils,' he said moments later, pulling three of them out of the glove compartment. 'Billy plants them wher-ever I go. He gets terrified that I'm not going to have anything to write down my ideas.'

'Because without your ideas, there are no songs, and without your songs there are no hits, and without your hits there's no money . . .'

'What he never thinks to leave me is *paper*,' muttered Inigo.

He swivelled around and caught sight of an almost-empty packet of Grape Nuts that I had thrown into the car at the last minute.

'May I?' he asked.

'It would be an honour, Father Hit-mas.'

'Don't call me that,' said Inigo, tipping the remaining cereal into my hands and ripping the packet into three pieces.

'Why?'

'Imperfect rhyme. "Hit-mas" doesn't rhyme with "Christmas" which renders the whole name obsolete.'

I stared at him.

'And in rendering the name obsolete on those grounds, you are simply proving the point they're all making. They call you that because you notice that sort of stuff.'

He handed me his cigarettes.

'I only do this because I can't do anything else.'

'Jesus might have said the same thing,' I said archly.

He looked up and grinned.

'I hate to break this to you, Cherry, but I'm not the Messiah.'

For a minute I listened to nothing more than the uneven scratch of sharpened lead on cardboard. I fought the desire to look at what he was writing, instead, I stared out of the window; we had caught Wiltshire unawares. When he had finished, he shoved the bits of card under his seat and looked at me. When he yawned, he looked fifteen again and I bit my lip for wanting to tell him.

'What time did you go to sleep last night?' I asked instead.

'Too late.'

'Do you want me to drive?'

'Ha!' said Inigo. 'Don't make me laugh. What would Billy say if he knew *you'd* been at the wheel?'

'I don't think he'd expect anything less,' I said. 'You should get some sleep. I've been driving since I was twelve.'

'Not legally,' pointed out Inigo.

'Well, I . . .'

Inigo handed me the keys.

'Go on, then.'

'You mean it?' I laughed in amazement.

He opened the door and walked around to my side of the car. Grinning like a mad thing, I slipped into the driver's seat.

'Find us somewhere to stop for lunch,' he said. 'And for God's sake, take it slow.'

He pulled my discarded jumper up behind his head for a pillow, closed his eyes, and left me and the Mercedes to our own devices. Pressing the car into first gear, I can only compare the experience to riding the mint-fresh Cathedral Boy after one of the Shetlands. George would be mad with envy, and Billy with agitation, I thought. I had better go slowly. I need not tell you, O reader, that hadn't actually passed my test.

When I glanced at Inigo, ten minutes later – he was still fast asleep. *I could go anywhere,* I thought. *I could turn around now and go back to Cornwall. I could drive us to Southampton and board a ferry to France. I could, I could, I could* . . . But I think I *knew* where I was going. Even if I told myself that I didn't know – that I'd lost my sense of direction – I can't believe that there wasn't some part of me that realized where I was taking us. Where I was taking *him*.

I stopped the car just short of Westbury station, and Inigo opened his eyes. I picked up the map from the back seat and studied it intently.

'We're lost, aren't we? he said, yawning. 'I knew it.'

'No, no.' I frowned and looked down at the map again to hide my nerves. 'We're *not* lost. I think I should have come off here –' I pointed at the map – 'but we're *here*.'

He said nothing for a moment – just lay back on the seat and rubbed his eyes as if the action might transport him away from me and back to New York where he didn't have to deal with the discomfort of the English countryside. Then he sat up and looked out of the window and I waited for him to realize where we were.

'Shit!' he said. He sounded astonished.

'What? What is it?'

'God, Cherry, this is where I used to live. We're right by Magna.'

He was speaking to himself more than to me.

'Where?' I asked, my voice thick with feigned innocence.

'This is the station! We used to – this is where I grew up. How the hell did we end up *here*? Did you *know*?'

The directness of the question took me by surprise.

'Of course not!' I sat on my hands and squeezed my fingers together into knots. 'I just lost track of where we were. I had no idea we were anywhere near your old house. I thought we might find somewhere to have lunch here. I'm sorry,' I said. 'I didn't know.'

'We can't have lunch here. Nowhere *here*.'

He believed me, at least. He had no reason to suspect that ending up where we were had been intentional on my part; that was the thing about Inigo. He always had me marked as a loose cannon with no clue what direction I was going in.

'Let's go then,' I said, playing my ace earlier than I had expected to. 'We should get back on the right road again. You don't want to hang around here. Do you?'

I looked at him, then quickly away again. Lord above, I was no actress. And what was I doing? Driving here on a whim, and thinking that it was going to spark something. And I didn't even know what I *wanted* it to spark.

Pa! I thought. Why were we here at all, for crying out loud!

'I thought you said that the house had burned down, in any case.'

'It had. It *has*. It's not there any more. At least . . .' he tailed off, looking out of the window. 'Let me drive,' he mumbled.

I climbed back out of the car and around to the other side again. It was up to him now.

I had placed him too close to the village where he had grown up to drive away without looking. It was just as I thought; the pull, once close enough, was too strong. To anyone who had

441

never been there before, we could have been anywhere – but *I* knew, even if he didn't realize that I knew.

He stopped the car by the village green, close to the shop where Aunt Mary had sent me for supplies and Lucy had flirted with the boy behind the counter. The house was just a little further up the road, up that drive that had so impressed me the first time I had clattered up it on the old bicycle that Aunt Mary kept in her back garden. I let Inigo walk ahead of me – if only to give him time to think of what to say to me about what he had decided to do.

A woman and her young son passed us; the little boy was slicing nettles on the verges with a stick as he walked. Two girls on fat grey ponies ambled past talking about pressing flowers for a school project. They barely registered us, and it didn't occur to me that they should. It didn't feel as though we were entirely there at all.

Inigo – rake skinny, wearing a black shirt, carrying the car-keys tight in his right hand, looked wrong here – as though he were an actor on the set of a film that was set some years into the future. He had become too modern for this place. I spat my chewing gum into a tissue and hurried to catch him up.

'It looks the same,' he said. 'The village looks exactly the same.'

'How long has it been since you were last here?'

'Six years. Feels like sixty.'

Still we walked on. The rain started to fall in a thin mist; swallows were diving for insects above the village pond.

'What is it about us?' he said. 'Every time we're in the same place, it rains.'

'I know,' I said. There was no romance in what he was saying – if anything, the words coming from his lips were simply a bleak statement of misfortune, but I liked how he put it. *What is it about us?*

He stopped in front of a row of tiny cottages. Four of the five were thatched. All were tiny; I recall walking past them with Lucy and considering them houses for gnomes.

'Mrs Daunton's place,' he said, waving at one with a green door.

'Who was she?'

Inigo shrugged. 'Just an old lady I used to know. She let me watch *The Grove Family* with her on Fridays. She never said much to me, just sat there, sewing and eating licorice from a paper bag.' He laughed. 'She was almost deaf and half blind so I don't know how she came to be the first person in the village with a television set.'

'I never watched *The Grove Family*,' I said, not without bitterness. 'Pa doesn't approve of soaps.'

'I bloody *loved* it. And I loved this house too – so stuffed full of things and so wonderfully *small*. I remember Mrs D never stopped banging on about how there wasn't enough room in there to swing a cat, so one afternoon, I did just that.'

'What do you mean?'

'I picked up Albert, and swung him around the room a bit.'

'Albert?'

'Her Persian tabby. We knocked over several teacups and I hit my elbow on a table covered in ration books and broke an unwashed cup of last night's cocoa. It turned out she was right.'

I laughed. 'Sometimes I think you're a very strange person.'

'Not strange at all,' said Inigo. 'I just wanted to prove her point. People like that.'

The rain was heavier now. I tilted my head up into the sky and felt it on my face.

'Lucy always liked the idea of being an only child,' I said, thinking out loud. 'Yet Matilda longed for brothers and sisters. I suppose being somewhere this tiny made you feel quite different to how you felt in the Great Hall down the road.'

Once again, I feared I was saying too much. Inigo didn't seem to have noticed.

He hesitated, as though part of him wanted to march up to the front door, knock briskly and insist on joining Mrs Daunton and Albert for another half-hour's viewing, as though no time had passed at all – but he stepped back instead.

'I don't want her to see me,' he said. 'I'm not sure what I would say. Back then she had one line that she used to say to me every time I saw her. "*You up there, in that big house, with no father. It's a shame, so it is.*" She had two boys and three girls, but she lost both her sons in the first war.' He looked at me as though registering this fact for the first time. '*Both* of them,' he repeated. 'But I never felt sorry for her, because she was the one with the television.' He snorted. 'I thought if I had my own television then I would always be happy.'

I didn't trust myself to speak any longer, but I walked on beside him. Down through the village we went; past the houses that I had seen as a little girl, the houses that had seemed so very far from home to me back then when I had slaved away at my aunt's beck and call. Inigo slowed down as we approached the bottom of the drive to Milton Magna Hall. Then he stopped and looked at me.

'You took us the wrong way,' he said. 'And now we're here.'

'You drove us here,' I pointed out gently. 'We could have turned around.'

'Why didn't we?' he asked, suddenly angry. 'Why didn't we? I don't know *why* I'm here. I don't know at all.'

'My father says that most of the time our reasons for doing things are very obscure, even to us,' I said. I reached out, and hardly knowing what I was doing, only recognizing that it's what Pa would have done for me – I took his hand and squeezed it tightly. He looked at my hand in his.

'What's *this?*' He half laughed in surprise.

'I just thought you might want to know that there's someone walking next to you.'

What was I doing! I dropped my hand away again.

'That's nice,' he said slowly. He looked at me with the same expression that Digby wore when struggling with a difficult clue in *The Times* crossword.

'Nice,' I said. '*Very useful word, nice.*'

He hadn't remembered his remarks to me in the studio that day, I thought – he registered no recognition of being quoted. Once again, I had to stop thinking that he remembered everything like I did, it was too painful when I found that he didn't.

'If you don't mind,' he said. 'I'd like to walk on alone. Just round the corner, that's where the house was. I just think I'll stand at the bottom of the drive for a minute. That's all.'

'Of course.'

'I'm glad you're here,' he said, then he added, as some sort of caveat: 'It makes it easier having someone here.'

Someone, I thought. *Anyone, as long as it's someone.*

'Can I take a smoke?' I asked him, merely for something to fill the gap. He handed me the packet of Lucky Strike.

'You should go and sit in the car,' he said. 'In case you hadn't noticed, it's pissing down now.'

'I'm all right,' I said.

He walked on, but I didn't go back to the car, although the wind had picked up, and I was cold. I went back to the old recre-

445

ation ground, where Lucy and I had sat on the swings and talked into the early evenings, and when I sat down I realized that I couldn't smoke because he had the matches. He had the matches, I thought, pushing myself back. He had *always* had the matches.

Not knowing why I was doing it, I laughed out loud at myself. I hated myself for taking his hand, at the same time as feeling that it was all I could have done. Since I was ten years old, Inigo Wallace had been my imaginary plaything – a vision of guitar-playing loveliness something to fill my head when I lay awake at night – but none of that was real.

How could I have been anything other than shattered by meeting him again all those years later? I wanted a fantasy – someone who could make everything all right just by looking at me – but I had encountered someone quite different. Damaged? Yes, he was, I thought, shoving the cigarette back into my pocket – but so much the more precious for it.

He had never pitied himself, I thought. He never felt as though he had the slightest right to. Despite losing his father, and the house he had grown up in, he had never been sorry for anything. He had taken what he had and used it, and worked it and had actually done what he had set out to do.

Soon he was out of sight. I resisted the urge to run after him, and believe me – the urge was there all right. I thought of him as a little boy – with this village the centre of his world, his only truth. How strange it was, that people in the same family could live in the same house, sharing the same space, and yet breathe the air around them so differently.

I would hum our new – sorry – *his* new song, I thought, I would keep singing so that we wouldn't forget it. I had only got halfway through the chorus when I saw him again. I jumped off the swing and walked towards him.

446

'How – was it all right?' I asked.

'Nothing there,' he said. He had his hands in his pockets – *Oh God! In his pockets! As though he feared I would start reaching out for them again!*

'It's hard to see anything at all in this weather,' I said.

'I walked a little way up the drive,' he said. 'One of the gates had gone. Then, where the house was – there was – nothing.'

He looked at me, as though I was about to provide an explanation beyond the obvious.

'Nothing at all?' I asked. In some way I think I felt as surprised as he.

He shook his head; seemed to haul himself up back on to dry land. 'God, Cherry. You're soaked. Come on.'

We ran back to the car as the rain started to fall harder, and thudded down on the seats inside. The clock on the dashboard said two o'clock. I opened the flask of sweet tea from Imogen and unwrapped the rolls she had made for my lunch.

'They're a bit squashed,' I said. 'Tomato and parsley. My sister thinks parsley cures all ills.'

'Thank you.'

He shivered. We sat and ate in silence, while the rain hammered down on the car so hard I thought it might break us. The blood-red leather seats turned black from the rain on our clothes – I didn't think Billy would be best pleased – but this was not the moment to comment on such trifles.

I poured him tea and we shared the cup. When we had finished, he sighed and turned the key again.

'Now please tell me you haven't forgotten that song,' he said.

'Of course not.'

★

447

As we drove away from the village, the windscreen wipers became our metronome, and we sang, and I knew that this day was going to stay with him, forever – and perhaps he'd always recall that there had been a girl with him, on that rain-soaked afternoon when he had gone back to find the house that wasn't there.

I felt shadows lifting from him, and I closed my eyes and said a prayer for him – and believe me, I didn't go around praying for any old person, like the Church would have us do. But I prayed for Inigo Wallace. That's how much it meant to me, you see. *That's how much it meant.*

37

The Marquee

Once back in London, Inigo seemed to distance himself again, but he had every excuse to. He was writing all day and most of the night, and was about to return to New York. I felt as though there were another part of him that was a little ashamed of what he had done on our journey back to London together – it seemed as though he had given too much away. I stepped back and pretended I hadn't noticed. It wasn't as if I wasn't busy too – Billy had thrown me into the deep end with an endless string of interviews and record signings. No one knew who I was as I walked down the street, but I had a feeling that Billy was capable of changing that. I had the impression he was merely deciding which button to push to make it happen. He was free to be the person he most wanted to be. Billy Laurier, the only man worth knowing if you wanted to get yourself known.

I had other things on my mind too – namely my sister. On my first night back in London I had closed my eyes and prayed that she would be there when I awoke. Once more, my hotline to God was proving to be distinctly faulty.

'She hasn't come in,' I said to Clover the next day.

'Thank you, Sherlock Holmes,' said Clover briskly.

I looked at her. 'We both know who she's with.'

'She can't stay with the harmonica player,' I said. 'She *can't*. Digby says he doesn't even have a proper home—'

'If I were you I'd sit tight and not even *ask* where she is,' said Clover. 'It will only make things worse. Let her come back in her own time.'

'But what about her work here?'

'She came over to collect three boxes that need to be sorted out this week. She can go through those papers anywhere – she doesn't need to be under my thumb for that.'

'It sounds to me as though you don't mind her going.'

'What possible use is there in me making a big fuss over where she is, Cherry? She's a grown woman. I feel she's had an awful lot of opinions shoved in her direction. Give her peace. She hasn't run away to be with Brian. She's run away to try and work something out.'

'How do you know?'

'I don't know. But if you went to see his group, it might make her feel a little less like you disapprove of everything she does. You're her sister, for God's sake.'

'Where are they playing?' I asked sulkily.

'The Marquee,' said Clover. 'It could be dreadful, but there's a small chance that it could be earth-shatteringly wonderful – I find that English boys playing American music is rarely mediocre. Digby will take you if you like. He's convinced that Brian's on to something.'

'My sister, probably,' I said in despair.

The place smelled of jazz and cigarettes. Our feet walked stickily down the steps to the basement where the band would be playing. Already the crowds were in; self-conscious girls with hairstyles that would have taken them the whole day to perfect, boys counting their cash and handing money to the girl behind the bar. It was two seconds before Digby had found people he knew, and, as always, the presence of others seemed to fuel his fire. He sparked up, became the person that they expected him to be. He was here for a reason now. Very quickly I gulped down several mouthfuls of gin from Digby's hip flask; he recognized that I needed it. Then he bought me a beer and found us a little table to the left of the stage and for a while we sat and watched the musicians setting up. I was high on something – not happiness, but *something*. Gin, cigarettes, beer and the darkness of the room all conspired to contribute to the sensation of being there but watching myself from the outside.

'Hey! Brian!' shouted Digby.

I watched as the skinny, short boy with blue-green eyes fiddled around with a guitar just in front of us. He looked over and grinned at Digby, a cigarette between his lips. His very manner made everyone else look conservative. It wasn't so much what he was wearing, rather the way that he walked, his ownership of everyone around him. Just as when Lucy had clapped eyes on him at Digby's party, he stood out with the force of his confidence. Whether it was real or not didn't seem to matter. If it was a mask, then he wore it well.

'I can't see Lucy,' I said.

'Do you want me to go and ask him if he knows where she is?'

'No,' I said. 'She'll be here. She has to be.'

Digby signalled to a waiter and asked for wine and cigarettes. There was a nervousness in the air, a sense of an uprising. I expect the Marquee was more used to hosting stoned jazz-heads, none of whom were about to burn the place down with energy.

451

But the crowd who had come to see Brian and his band looked pent-up, expectant.

Clover came in, sat down next to us, ordered a drink and didn't take off her sunglasses. A soon as Digby saw her, I was aware of his body language changing, of some invisible defence going up. How I hadn't seen it before, I don't know. It explained everything: his restlessness, his constant jibes at her, his outrageous suggestions, dismissed as just being part of his act. It was an odd thing – being in the presence of two people who couldn't tell each other how they felt. I saw Digby through Clover's eyes: restless, immature, flighty. I saw Clover through Digby's eyes: impossible, distant, spiky. They were as apart as two people could be; what bound them together was nothing more than a little word, unspoken, unattended to. But it was there all right. He loved her and she loved him. Obvious.

When I next looked up, Inigo was loping towards our table. It took him a while to reach us, because everybody wanted to say hello to him: Father Hit-mas, coming to talk to his subjects. We were not worthy! Seeing him walking in on his own, having made no effort to look right and yet somehow making a mockery of everyone else in the crowd, I was hit by the second great reveal of the night: Inigo Wallace was even more powerful than Billy, because he was *living* it all too. Where Billy stood back and issued orders, Inigo was actually part of the scene, creating the scene – and unlike Digby, who crashed around London like a puppy – he did it with such lack of show, so little fanfare, that it was difficult to know where he stopped and everything else started. He pulled up a chair and sat down between Clover and Digby.

'Brian's looking good,' he observed.

The place was rammed to the rafters, and escape was impossible.

'You might as well enjoy it,' said Inigo, reading my mind.

There was a deafening screech from one of the speakers near the stage, and the group started to play. I hesitate to say that they had me from their first chord, but it was true. Escape? How the hell could I? They were too powerful, too strong. I leaned forward in some kind of trance. Where was Lucy? How was Raoul? Why did Inigo have to leave for America? It all dissolved for the time that they stood on that stage. It vanished, replaced only by music.

The singer was stick thin, beautiful, with a deadpan pale face and an amazing American accent when he sang, considering he was from Dagenham – I recognized him as the boy with the big mouth who had been playing records at Digby's party. He threw himself into spasms, and as he did so, twisting bodies surged forward into the nearest space, ricocheting off tables, hair drenched with sweat, drinks cast away in one gulp. *My God!* I thought. Something took hold of me, something that I couldn't control, and wouldn't have wanted to anyway.

I looked at Digby. He was amused, a spectator, staying dry while everyone else jumped off the edge of the cliff into unknown waters below. 'You go ahead.'

Clover didn't dance either. Taking off her sunglasses, she looked at us and pointed at the group.

'Go worship,' she said.

For the first time, I was aware that she was not just older than us but from another generation. Clover had been born just a year after the First World War. She was *twenty years* our senior, old enough to be our mother, and that was what had kept us close to her. Where I never had before, I could see those twenty years of experience in her eyes. She had lived through more than all of us.

Suddenly Inigo was up on the table.

'What are you doing?' I shouted up at him, laughing.

'Get up here!'

I clambered on to a chair first, and he reached down for my hand and pulled me up there with him.

'You get to see how they play from up here.' Inigo was talking to me but looking, eyes intense, at the band. But he hadn't let go of my hand. *He hadn't let go of my hand.*

'Quick! Down again!' he shouted, seeing the woman behind the bar indicating in our direction. Two men – jazz-heads in suits – looked ready to come and evict us from the place.

'Let's go!' shouted Inigo.

Still holding hands, we ran into the crowd. We laughed out loud, the breath knocked out of us – we laughed because we couldn't *not* laugh. As we spun round, throwing ourselves into unfamiliar shapes, crashing feet with those next to us, I was intensely aware only of the safety in all this movement, the pushing forward all the time – there seemed to be some kind of strange comfort in it – the heat and pressure and power, a united abandoning of all of us to some greater force, some primitive urge to surge.

'I didn't think you were the kind who danced,' I shouted at Inigo, in between songs.

'Tara Jupp, of *course* you've got to dance. If you don't dance, you don't *get* it.'

'Get what?'

He raised his eyebrows at me and grinned. 'Anything you can think of.'

There was nothing sweet about that night – nothing you'd associate with the Swinging Sixties of books and movies, no neat skirts and beehive hairdos and twisting nicely with the boy

454

you had a crush on in the class above you at school. It was sheer chaos, it was everything on the brink. I felt the heat and the urgency of the boys on that stage and I realized that more than anything else, all of this was about sex. Sex and magic, and something new and urgent that made it impossible to imagine being anywhere more important that night than in the Marquee Club listening to that group play. The drummer was pounding his sticks like a primitive being, the piano player was hitting those keys so hard I wondered how they didn't fly off altogether. It was wild. That was the only word for it. *Wild.*

I could have stayed like that forever, suspending everything in that music, shouting out as each song finished, jumping into the next one like I knew what it was all about when none of us did, really. We were England's post-war babies, grown up and gone crazy, born to the wailing of air-raid sirens, but possessed by sounds stolen from black Americans with very different blues to our own. Something about it must have worked, because whatever train they were all on, I wanted to be on it too. I could go back to worrying about the harmonica player when it was over, because it was impossible to resist his call when he was on stage.

Through the sweating shirts and faces, I looked back at our table. Digby and Clover were still there. Digby looked amused but unaffected. This was mere fodder for his camera, and he wasn't touched by it as we had been. For us, it was different. When the band finished playing, something had changed, for all of us who had danced in that crowd. I don't exaggerate when I say it. It had changed something *forever.*

Clover looked at me.

'I never knew you were a dancer. I thought you just stuck to the singing.'

'Can't have one without the other.'

Digby was watching the group packing away their instruments.

'I should go and say hello,' he said, more to himself than anyone else. 'If I get them in the studio next week, I can have them in *Vogue* next month.'

'Tell him he's got the greatest group you've ever seen and I hope they're still together in fifty years' time,' I said, still reeling.

'I wouldn't go that far,' said Clover, alarmed.

Digby waltzed across to Brian, ruffling the hair of a red-headed boy on the way past, and taking a cigarette from the fingers of a sweaty blonde.

I watched him, feeling conscious of Inigo's eyes on me.

'Well? What did you think?' I asked him. 'Did they live up to it all?'

'I knew they'd blow the place apart.'

'How? How come you seem to know everything before it happens?'

'I know the guy on the piano, Nicky,' said Inigo. 'He didn't want to do this gig, but I bet he's pleased he did it now.' He lit a cigarette. 'What did *you* think?'

'Incredible,' I said. 'I have a rare feeling that I'm going to able to tell my grandchildren that once upon a time, I was in the right place at the right time.'

'The right place at the right time,' mused Inigo. 'Don't think I've been there since I accidentally walked in on Charlotte Ferris in her underwear in the Blue Room at Milton Magna, Christmas 1954.'

All around, the place was getting louder and louder, more and more unhinged. I saw the men who had threatened us when we had been standing on the chairs looking disturbed by it all;

it was their club, and they had lost control of something.

'Do you wish it was you onstage?' I asked him.

'Not any more.' He looked at me. 'Do you?'

I watched Brian, smoking with the singer.

'When I hear a boy from Kent singing the blues like he grew up in Mississippi, yes, I do.'

Inigo lit another cigarette. I kicked my heels under the table with frustration at how he was capable of putting me so on edge. I wanted to feel my shoes hit the floor, I needed to ground myself, to realize that this wasn't a dream – because there was something about being with Inigo Wallace that still left me feeling as though I was a little girl watching my older self.

Digby showed no signs of moving back to where we were sitting; he was still throwing his hands around and finishing glass after glass of wine. Occasionally he'd glance over to us, see I was still sitting with Inigo and look like he was going to come back to sit with us again. Then some other member of the group would come up, or a girl wearing good shoes, and he would get distracted again.

'Digby's happiest when surrounded by people who hardly know him,' I said.

'Not like us,' said Inigo.

When he stood up, I saw a packet of guitar strings sticking out of his back pocket. All I could think at that moment was how *hard* I felt I was trying, sitting there so stiffly unrepentant and uncomfortable in my dress, smoking away as though my life depended on it, yet how completely himself he appeared to be.

'I've had that song going round and round in my head,' he said. He didn't need to tell me which one. Since we had arrived back in London, nothing had stolen more of my mind than that melody, written by Inigo on the way back from Cornwall.

'It's a hit song,' I said simply. The truth wasn't hard to admit.

'"May to September" is a much *better* song of course,' said Inigo, grinning. 'Much more meaningful.'

I laughed and sang up at him, putting on the American voice that I had used for the recording.

> *'I met him when the cherry was red*
> *Took hold of my heart, forgetting my head.'*

Inigo joined in, clicking his fingers.

> *'He loved me through the summer and more*
> *Now we're getting married on Malibu shore.'*

'You're right.' I said. 'Who needs the blues when you're getting hitched in America?'

He glanced at his watch.

'My flight's at ten o'clock tomorrow morning,' he said. 'I haven't packed. I should get going.'

The room, and everything in it, seemed to deflate in front of my eyes.

'All right,' I said.

Inigo stood up.

'When will – when will you be back?'

'I don't know,' he said. 'Depends on what happens next.'

'What happens next? What do you mean?' I asked quickly.

'Your music,' said Inigo.

Of course, I thought. What the hell else would he mean?

'Billy wants to start work with Johnnie Wilson,' said Inigo. 'You'll be recording again soon.'

'What – what about you?' I asked, childlike.

'He needs me to work with a couple of his groups in America,' he said. 'I might be back here at Christmas.'

He leaned down and kissed me on the cheek.

'Don't let anyone tell you what to do,' he said. 'Unless they've consulted me first.'

That was it. I let him walk out of the room. *I let him go.*

Digby was beckoning me over to him. I walked over to where he was standing with the hippest crowd in the room. He had pulled some Polaroid pictures out of his wallet and was showing them to a couple of girls by the bar.

'We're going to go to the Pheasantry after this,' he said. 'Joanna's going to share a cab with us.'

I looked at Joanna, who was at least three years older and wiser then me, and infinitely more beautiful.

'I'm going to go back to Napier House,' I said firmly. 'Will you tell Clover?'

'If you want,' he shrugged. 'Got enough bread?'

'Yes.'

He pressed a pound note into my hand. I tried to give it back to him.

'Don't be crazy,' he said.

I shot out of the club as fast as I could. Two men were arguing loudly on the stairs.

'We can't have that sort of group here,' one was saying. 'They come in like they own the place, and they bring the bloody riff-raff in with them. You mark my words, that lot will be nothing but trouble.'

'But the kids love them! And the kids bring their friends—'

'Who will tear this place *down*. Get with the picture, Ray.'

Outside, Oxford Street felt like walking into a poster – the whole place lit up like a funfair. I was afraid Inigo would have already jumped into a cab, but there he was, standing at the bus stop, smoking. I tapped him on the shoulder.

'Inigo,' I said.

He turned around. 'Tara!' He looked surprised. 'What's happened to Digby?'

'Spontaneously combusted with the effort of telling Brian how great his group is,' I said.

'Ah. Well, that makes sense.'

There was a pause. I felt little and awkward, afraid that it was perfectly plain that I had run after him because I didn't want him to leave for America again. He looked at me. 'Where are we going, then?' he asked.

'What do you mean?'

'Well, since you've ditched the Marquee Club, we might as well do something else.'

From anyone else, it would have sounded like the last word in stylish chat-up. From Inigo, incapable of flirtation, it sounded like an invitation to watch him change the tyre on his bicycle.

'Whatever we do, it mustn't involve vodka,' I said.

'Of course not. It's crème de menthe frappé all the way from now on,' said Inigo.

I looked at him and then said in a great rush, 'Shall we go back to Napier, and will you please show me your writing room?' He hadn't ever promised me that I could see the room, but it was worth taking a gamble on it.

'You promised me I could see it before you go.'

'Did I?' asked Inigo, frowning.

'Yes.'

'When?'

'I don't remember exactly. Somewhere near the beginning.'

'Beginning of what?'

'The beginning of me being here.'

'Yes, when *was* that exactly?'

'It feels like it was a million years ago,' I said. 'But it was last month.'

Inigo stuck his hands into his pockets.

'Show me where you write,' I said. 'Please. This is the Last Chance Saloon. I want to know where all the magic happens.'

Inigo grinned and hailed a cab. 'And afterwards, I may well have to kill you, Miss Merrywell,' he added in a German accent, jumping in after me.

Ten minutes later, and we were rocketing alongside Hyde Park, and Inigo pushed down the window in the cab and the night air smelled sweet and warm, of mown grass and motorcycle fumes. When we pulled up outside Napier, I felt a kind of odd happiness that the cab driver might think we were more than we were. There was someone, somewhere on the planet, who didn't know us at all, but who thought that we were one and the same. Inigo paid and we stood outside the house together. I dithered a bit.

'Come on, then,' said Inigo. He placed a hand lightly on my back and the match was lit.

38

Lord Napier's Study

Stepping inside the familiar hall at Napier House, I caught sight of myself in the mirror.

'I look a scruff,' I muttered.

'Doesn't matter,' said Inigo. 'You're seventeen and you're pretty, so you're excused everything.'

It was that one sentence that did it. He had said I was pretty. As I kicked off my shoes and followed him upstairs, I felt as though I wasn't entirely present; a part of me was watching us from another room, willing him to take my hand. Walking beside him at midnight, the very space between us was like straw beside that lit match; any moment now and it would burst into flames. He seemed unconcerned, unaware as ever. He yawned, pushed his hand through his hair, picked at a loose button on his jacket.

'My sister says I should stop wearing black,' he said.

'You'd look good in a hessian sack,' I said.

He looked surprised.

'Thanks,' he said.

When he pushed open the door of his writing room, I tried, and failed, not to draw in my breath.

He had obviously left the room mid-work; his notepad stood

on the piano, and there was a half-drunk cup of tea on the window seat. All over the walls, crammed into every conceivable space, were photographs of people in fancy dress; black and white pictures of men and women in turbans and feathers, hooped skirts, fur rugs, silk dressing gowns and – in some cases – nothing at all.

'Photography was Lord Napier's great hobby,' said Inigo.

'Oh!' I cried, leaning down to look at a photograph of a man wearing black tie, carrying a duck and standing next to a horse. 'Digby has this exact same picture in his . . .' I paused and gulped. 'Bedroom,' I muttered.

'It will be a copy,' said Inigo, ignoring my discomfort. 'Digby's obsessed by Lord N's work; I expect he told you.'

'No,' I said. 'Actually, he didn't. I think there's quite a lot he hasn't told me.'

'As long as there's quite a lot you haven't told *him*, it doesn't matter.'

'That girl he was with tonight,' I said. 'Joanna. I think I've seen her before. She's very pretty.'

'Dull as paint,' said Inigo. 'I sat next to her at some dinner party a while back. She thought the *Cutty Sark* was a shoe shop in South Kensington.'

'*Isn't* it?'

'Very funny.' He looked at me. 'Well, did you mind?'

'Mind what?'

'Him and Joanna. His ability to be – er – distracted.'

'He'll always be distracted until he tells Clover that he loves her.'

Inigo stared at me. 'Who told you that?'

'He did.'

I looked at him. 'I know about what happened in New York. He told me about that too.'

There was a moment of silence while Inigo took in what I had said.

'He's never got over Clover,' I added.

'He has a strange way of showing it.'

I sat down at the piano, feeling the cool comfort of ivory under my hot little hands. I played a D-minor chord and I sang:

> '*I don't think he'll get over*
> *That girl he lost called Clover.*'

Inigo grinned, stepped up to the piano and played a G-major chord.

'*The guy's an idiot,*' he sang.

'Doesn't rhyme,' I said, taking my hands away and looking at him.

'Still an idiot. You know the first time I met him, he was shooting Marina Hamilton in Los Angeles.'

'The actress?'

Marina Hamilton was greatly loved by Pa and George because she had rejected her wild past and had discovered God.

'Do you know her?'

Just like it had been on the morning that I had faced him about the elephant, I didn't want the conversation to stop.

'Yes,' said Inigo. 'Marina was a drunk,' said Inigo. 'She drank for years without anyone really knowing quite how much was going down. I met her when I was fifteen – had the biggest crush you could imagine.'

So perhaps when he had sung to me that day in the kitchen, his thoughts had been entirely with Marina Hamilton and her ample breasts, as well as Charlotte in her underwear.

'Who *wouldn't* be obsessed?' I said.

'Then I bumped into her at the Governor's Ball after the Oscars a few years back and she looked completely different. She was sober, I suppose, that was why. I asked her how she was and she said, "Isn't it wonderful? I've found Jesus." I was with my brother-in-law Harry at the time, who said, "Where the hell was he? I've been looking everywhere for him!" She didn't laugh. Then she looked at me and said "Oh, Inigo, will you ever love again?" and I said, "What do you mean?" and she said, "That wonderful house! Burned to the ground!"' Inigo stopped suddenly, as though checking himself. 'I said to her that it was years ago, and that I had been in New York ever since and she said, "Darling, of *course* you have."'

'What did you say after that?'

'Nothing.'

'What do you think she meant?' I asked him, full of curiosity.

'How should I know?'

'I suppose she meant that losing a house like that is something that you don't ever really get over,' I said cautiously.

'Maybe,' said Inigo.

'What did she say next?'

'Nothing. Marlon Brando came up to talk to her, and that was the end of that.'

'Oh. I *hate* it when that happens.'

'Me too. The man's a menace.'

He laughed, and I beamed back at him.

'Can I tell you something?' I asked him.

Inigo nodded.

'I feel like a fraud,' I said.

'That's the whole point of being a pop singer,' said Inigo.

'But Billy has such hopes for me,' I said. 'He thinks I'm going to sell thousands and tour around the country shaking everyone's hands and making little girls weep with joy when they touch me, but I don't think I can do it. I never *wanted* to be famous,' I said. 'I just wanted to make my family think I'd done something good.'

'Jesus might have said the same thing,' said Inigo with a ghost of a smile. Had he actually *remembered* me saying the same words to him in the car? I didn't know.

'Billy'll never understand,' I said. 'Here am I, some pipsqueak from Cornwall, some girl who used to go around stealing other people's horses to ride because she couldn't afford lessons of her own, running around London pretending to be the next big thing. I'm as fake as Clover's fingernails.'

Inigo laughed. 'You can always get off at the next station.'

'There is no next station. I'm stuck. Didn't you hear?'

'There's *always* a next station.'

'But I can't let him down.'

Inigo took a bottle of whisky from the lid of the piano and poured himself a stiff shot.

'Christ, I've spent my whole life letting people down. My mother, my stepfather . . . I gave up beating myself up about it when I realized it was unutterably pointless.' The more he spoke, the more he lost the American-ness in his voice. 'The only person you shouldn't let down is yourself,' said Inigo. 'Sorry to be so terribly clichéd, but I'm very much afraid that it's true. Ask your mother. Shit. I'm sorry, I forgot.' He cursed.

'It's all right,' I said.

'My father's dead too,' said Inigo. 'He died in the middle of the South Pacific, fighting a war so that I could prance off to New York doing Elvis impersonations. Get over it.' He seemed to be talking more to himself than to me. 'There's nothing more pointless than being cut up about it,' he said. 'Your mother, my

466

father – they wouldn't want us hurting for too long.'

'How on earth did you get round to that way of thinking?'

'I don't remember him. Makes it easier. I can believe what I want to believe about him. I can create my own fairy tale, you know?'

'Ma would have wanted me to come to London,' I said. 'She would have wanted me to have the chance to get out of Cornwall. She used to play the piano to us every night. She wanted to be a singer herself.'

'Then she went and had eight hundred children and couldn't do it any more?'

'Something like that.' I played a scale to hide the fact that I was shaking. 'I just wish she was here.'

Inigo lit a cigarette and passed it to me.

'So, do you think you're doing it for her?' he asked.

I nodded. 'I think so. Because I know she would have been disappointed if I said no to this chance. I can't let her down.'

I suddenly felt wiped out.

'You know what I do when I'm worrying about something?' said Inigo.

'What?'

'Write a song.' He pushed back his hair. 'Why don't we?'

'What?'

'Write a song. Now. Here.'

'*Together?*'

I sat up straight.

'Give me a line,' he said. 'Go on.'

'All right.' I looked at him. '*I don't like you, I love you.*'

Inigo looked at me, and I felt the adrenalin in my fingertips.

I laughed, but when he started to play – singing the line over and over – he was so good I shivered.

467

'You don't like the happy stuff,' he muttered. 'But the happy stuff is harder to write.'

'It's hard to write about being crazily in love when you haven't been.'

'I don't think so,' said Inigo.

'What do you mean?'

But he had moved on.

'If you get it right, you're made for life,' said Inigo. 'If you get it wrong, it'll haunt you forever. Come on,' he went on. 'And stick to what we're saying here. No going off on any unnecessary tangents.'

I scribbled something else, my hand arching over the page as though I were taking an exam and feared that the pupil next to me might copy my work. Ten minutes later, I handed it to Inigo.

'Not at all bad,' he said. He read the words again. 'Room for improvement, but not bad at all.'

He started to play, reading my words off the page. I was almost afraid of his capabilities; for the first time I was seeing him at work and realizing how unbelievably good he was. It made me feel jealous and frantic and glad all at the same time.

I don't know how long we were there together, working on that song. The only signal that time was passing came from the dull chime of the carriage clock on the mantelpiece telling me that another hour had passed, but I was afraid of talking about anything that might draw Inigo's attention away from what we were doing.

By the time we had finished the song, morning had broken.

'It's good,' said Inigo.

'I can't tell,' I lied.

'It's also very late,' he said. 'Or early,' he added, walking over to the window and creaking open the shutter. Light spilled into the room. The sky, pale blue, cloudless, had obliterated our night together. The sun had returned from the other side of the earth. It was over.

'I should go,' he said. 'I've got to be at the airport soon. I didn't expect to be writing into the early morning with you like this.'

'Me neither.'

Without thinking about it, without even having any awareness of myself at all, I rested my head on his shoulder. We stood together, two little upright figures in Lord Napier's study, and suddenly his hand was in mine. My fingers were blotted with black ink from all that writing and rewriting; they knotted around his, but it didn't seem real at all. When we had talked to each other before, there had been oceans between us. Now I may as well have been naked.

On cue, the clock struck six.

'Good morning, Tara Jupp,' he said.

I had no knowledge of the fact that there was a telephone in Lord Napier's study, until it rang, and its shrill interruption made me jump. Then I remembered the notes in the telephone book. For a moment, I had forgotten them. *New York called Inigo Wallace.* Just two entries in Clover's book of five simple words that let me know it could never be anything more than *nothing*. Eyes wide, I looked at him.

'Don't – don't answer it,' I heard myself saying in a whisper.

'I have to,' he said.

The spell had been shattered; he sounded jumpy – as well he might – standing with his fingers in mine, not hers. Poor girl, I thought. Oh she who little knows what he is doing.

'Wait,' he said to me as the bell rang on. '*Please.*'

Wait.

He crossed the room and picked up the receiver, turning his back to me.

'Hello?' he said quietly. 'Yes, thank you.'

I knew that was the operator putting him through to that land over the sea.

How could I wait? It was wrong, dangerous. I didn't want to stand there any more, listening to him talking to her.

'Yes. I'm coming in tomorrow night,' I heard him saying as I closed the door gently behind me. Heart thumping, I found myself back upstairs, though how, I don't know.

Over, I thought. It had to be over. Take those few hours and compress them into every song you'll ever sing. Take them, and do with them what you will.

Just for those brief hours, he had been mine.

39

Me versus the Standard

Three hours later, I was awake again. Automatically, I glanced at Lucy's bed. Still empty. She was never coming back, I thought. She would never forgive me. Clover, immaculate in a black and white jersey and tight black trousers was standing in the bedroom doorway, actually ringing a bell. I sat up.

'Has he gone?' I asked unthinkingly.

'Who?'

'Inigo. He had to catch his plane.'

'Yes. He's gone. I had toast and marmalade with him at seven. He said he hadn't slept.'

'No,' I said. 'We were writing a song.'

'Well, hurry up and get yourself presentable. Billy's downstairs. He's got some news for you. There's scrambled egg and tomato if Mr Laurier hasn't scoffed the lot.'

Billy was sitting waiting for me. When I came into the room there was a good deal of chat about the group at the Marquee, and how he had heard that they had left the place in tatters, and half of London was talking about them. I didn't mention the high probability of Lucy still being with one of these tearaways; it was too terrifying to think about.

'I had a call this morning from the producer of *Sunday Night at the London Palladium*,' said Billy. 'Harry Delancey's dropped out. He can't perform this weekend.'

'Why?'

'He's broken both arms,' said Billy gleefully.

'*How?*'

'Some say he fell out of a stationary hot-air balloon on Brighton beach. Others say he fell down the stairs tripping over his wife's new dog.'

'Poor man,' I said. Then, because I couldn't resist, I added, 'Couldn't he magic himself better again? And do Raoul while he's at it?'

'Evidently not,' said Billy. He paused for dramatic effect – something that he did rather a lot, but I was never easy with. 'The producer says they'd like to fill the slot with a female singer. I suggested to him that you should do it. What do you think?'

I laughed, because it seemed like such a joke, and because it was so sudden, such a thing to throw out to me, after no sleep, and feeling Inigo's hand in mine. I stared at him, realizing suddenly that he was serious.

'Me? Sing at the Palladium? On Sunday night?'

'It's the most *astonishing* opportunity,' said Billy. 'You'll go straight into the home of every television-owning family in the country. We couldn't ask for anything more.'

I'd like to say that I was 'in shock' at the idea, or that I couldn't gather my thoughts due to the astonishing prospect of standing on that most famous of stages and singing for the world to hear, but everything that Billy had just said entered my head with the absolute clarity that in my view *always* accompanies earth-shuddering news. Within seconds of him announcing it, I was on that stage, up there in lights, and terrified. That meant that

472

if I didn't want to do it, everything would fall apart.

'What if I forget the words?'

'You won't,' said Billy.

'What if they don't want me?'

'They do.'

'It's too much,' I said. 'I don't know if I can do it.'

'Cherry, you can do this standing on your head.'

'Can I?' I stared at him, not nearly so sure.

Billy took a different approach. 'You don't have to do anything other than perform to the people in the theatre. Don't even think about the television.'

'But there will be cameras!'

'Of course.'

'So how can I *not* think about the television?'

'It won't be half as intimidating as singing at our wedding. You don't know anyone you'll be singing to. That makes it much less frightening.'

'What will I wear?'

Billy grinned. 'That's what Clover's here for.'

I think he heard me ask that question and took it to mean that I was excited about selecting an outfit; I was now behaving precisely how he expected a girl in my position to behave. Get told you're going to sing at the Palladium: seize the chance to buy more clothes! It was how every other girl he had ever worked with would have behaved. He didn't hear the anxiety in my voice, an anxiety built on the knowledge that whatever I wore, however I dressed, there was no turning back. I knew, from how I had felt when I watched Alma, that this was serious.

'It will be the most wonderful night,' predicted Billy.

'How do you know?'

473

'Only wonderful things happen at the Palladium. It's unlike anywhere else. Digby will tell you that. He's been there several times.'

'Digby?'

'Remember him? Nice guy, takes pictures for *Vogue*.'

'Very funny.'

But it was true; I hadn't thought about him since I had walked out of the Marquee Club.

'You should ask him to come with you,' said Billy archly.

'So that everyone can see us together and think what sensational lives we lead?'

Billy took my hand in his. He was so big, so powerful, that I felt dwarfed by him. Compared to Inigo, he was a mammoth of a man.

'You know you can do this,' he said. 'You can do this, Tara Jupp. It's what you were born to do.'

Overwhelmed by the lack of sleep and the sure knowledge that Inigo was on his way back to America, I wobbled. Biting my bottom lip, I choked down the tears.

'That's just the thing,' I said. 'I don't know any more. I used to think that the only thing that mattered was escaping. You'd get on the first horse you could see and ride for the open gate. Now I'm not so sure about the open gate. Now the open gate makes me . . . makes me nervous.'

'I hate to break this to you, but this is nothing to do with open gates or horses,' said Billy. He shook his head. 'You've been spending too much time with Clover. She's forever coming out with that sort of nonsensical rubbish. Just try not to overcook all this in your head, all right?' He didn't add the word 'little' before 'head' but I knew it was there anyway. Looking thoughtful, he poured me two inches of brandy.

474

'It's not even nine o'clock in the morning!' I said weakly, taking it anyway.

'Precisely. It's still last night.'

He loaded these words with something that felt like empathy. Did he know how much last night had changed everything? Was he able to read it in my face? Was it that obvious? I didn't want to say any more; I willed him to understand. Where I had thought I had loved, I had not. Where I had thought I had *not* loved, I was now aching with bittersweet agony. The new world was made up of nothing but Inigo.

'The group at the Marquee were very good,' I said.

'So I gather,' said Billy.

I looked out of the window. 'I feel . . .' I paused. 'I feel odd.'

'Don't you always feel odd when you've been dancing with people you're usually just walking with?'

I smiled at him. The idea of Billy ever experiencing aching feet from dancing seemed absurd, and yet he seemed to twig all right; there was no question that he realized I was a different person that morning. He hadn't been there, but he knew I had been dancing with Inigo. He had eyes all over London.

'You won't have much time to rehearse,' he said, gently swinging us back to the subject in hand. 'But that's all right. You don't need it. I said to the producer: "Harold," I said, "Cherry Merrywell is a professional. You could put her onstage with no orchestra, no fanfare, no make-up, and she'd have the audience in the palm of her hand. That's just the way she works."'

'But it's terrifying,' I said. I was too tired to think about it; nothing of what Billy was saying seemed remotely part of my life at all. Perhaps that was why I found myself agreeing to do it.

'And in the meantime,' said Billy, 'you're going to perform at the Palladium.'

'And in the meantime,' I said, 'I think I may need some new shoes.'

'That's my girl,' said Billy.

The following afternoon, Billy and I had lunch with a woman who wrote for the *Evening Standard*.

'What if she asks me questions about Digby?' I asked Clover at breakfast that morning. I didn't want to say the wrong thing to the papers. For all that I pretended to be cooler-than-cool about the popular press, it was hard not to be affected by seeing your name and photograph in black and white, surrounded by adjectives of dubious authenticity. The reports on my record appeared to be gathering pace. Whenever a fresh piece appeared, I would stare at it, without a shred of recognition. Whoever was writing about me had me pinned as something I really wasn't:

"*Beguiling little Cherry Merrywell from Somerset cuts her first disc*" [sic] (*The Times*). "*Seventeen-year-old Miss Merrywell sounds as sweet as a Cherry*" (*The Daily Herald*). "*Sensitive, charming Bishop's daughter Cherry Merrywell joins Billy Laurier's stable*" (*The Daily Mail*).

'Well at least they have you in with the horses,' Clover said drily on reading this particular gem. Now she looked at me in the manner of a parent patiently explaining Road Safety to a wayward member of the Tufty Club.

'Listen to me. If she asks about Digby, you must look her right in the eye and say that he's taken you under his wing,' she instructed.

'But she could take that any way she wants to.'

'Exactly,' said Clover, turning back to her magazine.

'But I don't want people to think that we're – that we're – you know – when we're *not* any longer. When it was never really

anything other than – well – *you* know – and when – when . . .'
I wanted to add 'when he really only loves *you*' but stopped
myself.

'A girl only has to ask Digby for change at the bus stop and
the world thinks they're in love with him,' said Clover. 'It's how
it works with someone like him. But if I were you, I'd keep
your mouth shut. The last thing you want to do is rock the
boat.'

I thought of that night at his party and nodded.

In any event, Billy had obviously told Evening Standard too
much before we sat down. She looked terribly old to me, but
I suppose she can't have been more than thirty-five. It was quite
plain that the stardust and glitter that I was seeing in London
had been replaced by nothing more than dirt and dust for her.
She reminded me of the girls from the village who had had too
many babies, then tried to look young again, but only ended
up looking even more care-worn.

She was wearing a hooped skirt, like a gypsy, and red earrings
in large lobes. She ordered an omelette and a cup of tea, which
alarmed Billy, I could see. He believed that hot drinks should
only be consumed at the beginning and end of the day, never
in the middle. For him, it exhibited a worrying lack of urgency;
if one had time to sit and wait for a hot drink to cool, then
one had too much time on one's hands.

'I expect you want a Coca-Cola,' Evening Standard said,
barking with laughter and pouring too much milk into her cup.

'Just water, please.'

'What makes you special, then?' she asked me. I looked at
Billy, and shrugged helplessly. What sort of question was that!

'No thank you, no tartare sauce today, Margaret.' Billy smiled

477

at the waitress, then, shaking white pepper liberally over his fried potatoes, he turned his attention back to us.

'Cherry's young and fresh, and she sings like a dream,' he said firmly.

Evening Standard, clocking my knotted hair and seedy appearance, looked as though she strongly doubted all but the first of these statements.

'Who wrote the song?' she asked, taking a black biro from her handbag, and scribbling on the back of a paper napkin to get the ink running.

'Inigo Wallace,' said Billy and I together. I felt that curious mixture of pain and elation at saying his name; it was so powerful, this feeling, that I felt certain that Billy had noticed it too.

'Father Hit-mas,' she sighed. 'Of course.' She looked at me. 'Did you like him?'

'He's very clever,' I said.

'But did you *like* him?' she spoke slowly, as if addressing a particularly backward child.

'Of course she likes him,' said Billy. 'And Inigo knew, as soon as he first met her, that he'd heard something remarkable.'

If only you knew, I thought.

'I've heard he's difficult.' She took a cigarette from Billy.

'He can be whatever he likes, he's the most successful songwriter in the country,' I heard myself saying. I felt keyed up and defensive. *Say what you want about me*, I thought. *Just don't say anything bad about Inigo Wallace.* You don't *know* him.

Billy looked at me and frowned.

She asked all the questions that Billy had prepared me for: what did I most like about London? Which singer did I most admire? But even though I answered her carefully and politely, there was a dagger between us, hanging invisible in the air. For

478

every reason I could imagine, she didn't like me, and for every reason left, I didn't like *her*.

After twenty minutes of discomfort, Billy had bolted down his fish, and stood up to leave. I wanted to bleat at him to take me with him, but I could sense that he had no intention of me moving just yet. In his mind, I had come here to ingratiate myself to this woman, and that was what I was going to do.

The moment Billy' had left us, Evening Standard opened her compact and started dabbing her nose with powder.

'Digby O'Rourke,' she said, squinting into her mirror. 'How long have you known him?'

'A couple of weeks,' I said, my voice taut.

'Nice to come to London and start walking out with the most celebrated photographer in the city. How did you manage that?'

'I fell off a piano stool,' I said.

'He doesn't strike me as the type who's drawn to girls who fall off piano stools.'

'Well, a change is as good as a rest.' I was giving too much away. In any case, she was out of date, this woman. I was no longer *walking out* with Digby, as she had put it.

'When I first got here, he took me under his wing,' I said dutifully.

'To be quite frank, I'm surprised there's room for anyone else under there,' she said.

I gulped at her frankness.

'I don't know what you mean,' I said, feigning confusion.

'No, naturally, you don't.' She laughed, without mirth. 'If I can give you one piece of advice, darling,' she said, leaning forward, and looking me in the eye, 'it's this. For God's sake, watch out. He won't stick around forever, you know. Let me put this in the plainest possible terms,' she said when I remained silent. 'He's not the sort of man your mother would like you to end up with.'

Something heating up inside of me hissed and fizzed.

'My mother's dead,' I said.

She didn't miss a beat. 'Well, my girl, I can tell you this much. *Were* she here, she would be telling you not to get your heart broken by a man like him.'

'Were she still here, she would be shocked by your manners,' I said. 'And even more so by your horrible taste in skirts. Good afternoon.'

I got up and walked out. Part of me wanted to shout with hysterical laughter and run for the hills. The other part wanted to shout it all out to Inigo. *You see! I didn't let her tell me what to do!* Was I destroying everything, ruining my chances of people writing nice things about little Cherry Merrywell because I didn't really want to be her, anyway? But I had to be her. Sunday night was waiting for me.

40

Into the Heat

The Palladium was so far into the realms of fantasy, that it was impossible to believe it would actually happen at all. In the next two days – between rehearsals, and hair appointments, and endless sessions with Clover and huge piles of clothes – I realized that I wasn't merely nervous as hell, I was shockingly ill-prepared. When Billy had told me, all that time ago, that he wanted to take me to London to make a record, I don't think that I had ever got further than that in my head. The idea of showing myself to millions of people on television was a slippery notion, impossible to grasp.

'It doesn't really matter what happens,' Clover lied. 'Have a drink before you get up there, and try to enjoy it.'

'I don't think that's likely,' I said. 'Although the drink bit I can manage. Inigo always says you shouldn't before you perform,' I added. Just mentioning his name was irresistible.

'He *would*,' said Digby. He paused. 'I've got a new record to play you,' he said.

'Oh yes?'

'Bob Dylan. It will blow your mind.'

'I don't think I need my mind blown,' I said. 'I should get back to Napier House.'

We had to get to the Palladium some hours before the show started. I felt that if I had simply walked in ten minutes before, it wouldn't have been so hard. As it happened – rather like sitting in the dentist's waiting room for too long before your appointment – arriving early merely served to increase the tension.

Billy had organized a car to take us there. Outside the theatre stood a gaggle of teenagers, no doubt waiting for someone of far greater significance than I. Billy swept us in through the stage door.

'When you leave the building tonight, you won't be able to move for people wanting your autograph,' he said to me.

If he was attempting to encourage me, he was only making it all much, much worse.

'When will Clover be here?' I asked Billy, as we were led to my dressing room by a man called Harold, who was harassed and smiling, and wearing a crumpled black suit and red socks. We walked through corridors that smelled like the contents of Lucy's make-up bag. We had been engulfed by the place; I couldn't imagine us ever getting out.

'Wonderful that you could come and sing for us tonight, really wonderful, Miss Merrywell,' said Harold. 'This is such a big, big show. I'm sure I don't need to tell you that. Billy promises me that you're the one to fill in *terrifically* for Harry Delancey.' He gave me an encouraging smile, which I interpreted as sincere doubt on his part.

'I'll certainly try,' I said.

Poor man; I could see how worried he was. This was the biggest show on television, and he was taking Billy's word for it that I was going to be all right. Despite the make-up I had attempted to apply before I left Napier House, I knew I still looked like the undernourished schoolgirl I really was. My hair, washed, dried, curled and sprayed to within an inch of its disobedient life, had already flopped. I glanced at myself in the dressing-room mirror, and quickly looked away again, but everywhere I stood or sat, there was my reflection. I was inescapable.

'Would you like a glass of water?' asked Harold.

'Would it be rude of me to ask for something stronger?' I asked. Inigo need never know, I thought savagely. He wasn't here anyway.

'I'll get you a gin and tonic.'

'Go easy on the gin,' advised Billy.

Harold looked at me and I shook my head and mouthed, *No! Don't!*

'We'll call you for her run-through in an hour. Norman Wisdom's just on at the moment. He's a perfectionist – we won't get him offstage for a good forty minutes.'

'My father loves him,' I said.

'Everybody's father loves him,' said Harold, with perfect truth. 'He's a professional. Miss Merrywell, I shall see you later. Break a leg, my dear. Break a leg.'

'Wrong choice of phrase,' I muttered through chattering teeth as he left the room.

Broken legs only reminded me of Raoul and Lucy, and of my own bloody limp.

Billy laughed at my expression, motivated, I suppose, by relief that we were here and there was no escape until I had performed. I joined in, because if I hadn't laughed I would most certainly have cried.

'Welcome to the theatre, my dear,' said Billy, taking off Harold's voice with spot-on accuracy.

'A whole hour to kill,' I said. 'I don't think I can sit in here looking at myself. I shall go stark, staring mad.'

'Of course you shouldn't stay here,' he said briskly. 'We shall go and have a look around. Stare at Mr Wisdom and pick up a few tips.'

A theatre without its audience is a strange place. I was hoping that the Palladium would be smaller in reality than it looked on the television, but unfortunately, this was not to be. It felt huge, all-encompassing, powerful, not just because it was upholstered in red velvet and gold, but also because it held in its grasp the ghosts of everyone who had ever walked on that stage. It was alive with both the magnitude and brilliance of what had been before, and the glorious hope of what was to come. In the meantime, it waited, quietly biding its time. I could have leapt into the air with relief when Clover walked in, her shoes silent on the thick carpet.

'How are you?' she asked me.

'Terrified,' I said.

'You'll be fine. I've brought you some shepherd's pie. I've left it in your dressing room. You should eat something.'

'I couldn't,' I said. 'I feel sick.'

'Of course,' said Clover. 'Naturally you do. You're about to perform in front of an audience of more than two thousand people, not to mention four million television viewers. But still, you should eat. An army can't march on an empty stomach, or whatever that expression is.'

'I'm one person, not an army.'

'You know what I mean, for goodness sake. And I've got you the most beautiful little dress,' went on Clover. 'Green and red sequins, and made by Mary Quant. I had to beg her for it. It's the only one like it.'

I said nothing. My teeth chattered together, but I was far from cold.

'It's all a little fantasy, darling,' soothed Clover. 'It's dresses and smiles and make-up for the little girls.'

'But I don't know if *believe* in all that any more. At least, not for me. Not for *me*.'

'But *they* do. They believe you! The girls in the crowd, or more to the point, the girls sitting at home watching their parents' television sets, wishing that they were anywhere but where they are. You're living the dream *for* them, darling. It's a tough job, but someone's got to do it.'

I looked at Clover's face. She was terribly intense; for once she had shed her customary languor. I thought about all those afternoons in Napier House – the Six O'Clock Club and all the times we had talked long into the evening. She had listened to me – and I mean *really* listened. She was the first grown-up to have treated *me* like a grown-up. I felt a wave of gratitude towards her, not just for looking after me, but for everything that she stood for.

'I'll leave you,' said Clover. 'Look out for me later. I'll be shouting out that I'm your landlady to anyone who'll listen. Charlotte's coming tonight. She used to come here to watch Johnnie Ray so she's probably sitting in the stalls already, fantasizing about being seventeen and free of all responsibility.' Clover looked thunderstruck for a moment. 'What *all* of us would give to be seventeen again,' she said.

'Amen to that,' said Billy from the side of the stage.

Clover picked up her bag. 'She's nervous,' she said to Billy. 'Treat her with care.'

After my run-through, which I struggle to recall with any accuracy at all, Clover was gone, and we walked back to the dressing room, Billy and I – and it was just us shut into that little space, and it felt as though the whole world waited outside

485

the door to see what was going to happen next.

'I'm nervous,' I said.

'You'd be a fool if you weren't,' said Billy. 'But you're going to be all right.' Coming from Billy, it was an order. Normally his confidence was exactly what I needed. Now it felt threatening, terrifying.

I stretched out for water, but my hands were shaking so much that I had difficulty even bringing the glass to my lips. I looked at Billy's face, the perfect symmetry of his features, and wondered how well he actually knew me at all.

'Inigo's song,' I said. '"May to September."'

'*Your* song,' he corrected me. 'Sure, he wrote it, but it would be nothing without your voice. He needs you as much as you need him.'

Not true, I thought.

I was spared saying anything else by a knock at the door. A face peered into the room.

'Darling,' said Billy, standing up. 'Are you sure you're feeling well enough to be here?'

'Of course.' Matilda stepped inside and kissed him on the cheek. 'Dr Wilson says everything's fine. In any case, I'm not here to talk about me. Tonight's for Tara.'

Every word was making it worse!

'I don't know that I can do it,' I said slowly.

Billy looked at Matilda.

'Harold needs me to sign a couple of forms,' he said. 'Can I leave you with her?'

He spoke as though I wasn't in the room, although, poor man, I don't know what else he could have done. Removing himself from the situation was sensible; he must have been able to sense that nothing he was saying was working. He left us. I looked at Matilda, steeling myself for the usual discomfort of her embrace, where I would feel the bones in her spine as I held her, and the odd swell of the baby in front of her, and smell the lily of the valley she always wore, that reminded me of Trellanack and leaning over her shoulder while she excelled at backgammon, mixed with the inevitable undertones of alcohol. But she didn't move towards me.

'I thought you'd be worried,' she said. 'That's why I came.'

She looked tired, but famous. Her blue eyes were made up as they had been for the photographs she had posed for earlier that day. She was wearing heels, but kicked them off and into the corner of the room as she used to at Trellanack.

'I was worried that you'd feel as if you've been pushed into this,' she said.

'I don't know if I have,' I said. 'Anyway, most girls would do anything to be pushed here. It's what I always wanted to do, and yet now it's happening.'

'You should be careful what you wish for,' said Matilda. 'Everyone knows that, don't they?' She gave a laugh, and sat down next to me. We looked at our reflections in the mirror. I would tell her, I thought suddenly. Why not? Lucy had vanished with the harmonica player, everything was different now. I felt rather as though we were two passengers aboard a sinking ship. I had nothing left to lose.

'Inigo's gone back to New York,' I said.

And she knew. She looked at me, and she *knew*.

'He'll hear about tonight,' she said. 'Even if he can't watch it.'

She had taken me the wrong way.

'No,' I said. 'I don't care about *that*. I just wish he was here, that's all. Not to hear me sing. Just to be here. I've only just realized how – how . . .' I shook my head.

487

'What are you singing?' Matilda asked me. She picked up my lipstick and coloured her mouth in red.

'Two songs,' I said. '"May to September" . . .'

'Of course,' said Matilda.

'And "Over the Rainbow".'

'Why *that?*'

'Billy thinks it's important that I show what else I can do,' I said. 'He says it shows off my voice. It's the B-side,' I added helplessly.

'Too sentimental.' Matilda smacked her lips together, pouted and pulled my hair back from my shoulders and tied it back from my face. 'You were *never* sentimental,' she said. 'Sad sometimes, but not sentimental. Who are you singing for, in any case? Not the grown-ups,' said Matilda dismissively. 'You have to sing something for the little ones – you know – the ones at home. All we ever wanted to do was shake everything off and look at the pretty boys. The dreamboats, honey!' She attempted an American accent and didn't quite pull it off. 'Whether they were right under our noses in the pub on a Friday night, or arriving from Spain carrying books about landscape gardening in the eighteenth century, they were all that we ever wanted. I don't think I knew how to escape until I discovered how to look at boys in the same way that your sister did.'

She laughed. I just sat there, realizing that she was right. Of *course* she was right. "Over the Rainbow", for all its beauty and purity, was a wistful, little-girl thing, sung at the start of the film, when Dorothy didn't know any better than to wish herself away from everything she knew. It wasn't about me any more. I had been to the end of the blessed rainbow, and had found that the pot of gold wasn't worth nearly as much in London as it was in Cornwall.

'There's nothing I can do now,' I said. 'I have to just sing it, and get off. That's what Billy's said to me. And I *must not* talk to the audience,' I added, quoting Billy's instructions. 'Just "Good evening", and "Thank you". I'm not Judy Garland yet.'

'Nor will you ever be,' said Matilda, taking this literally. 'Can I do your make-up?'

I laughed. 'If you want.'

'What are you wearing?' Matilda asked me.

I pointed at the Mary Quant dress that Clover had hung up for me.

The door swung open suddenly and two dancing girls dressed in red and green sequin leotards burst into the room, all legs and arms, sparkling like a couple of damsel-flies dipped in glitter. I recognized them from a dance routine that had been in rehearsal as we had arrived.

'I missed the third kick in the opening sequence!' giggled one of them. 'My mother'll kill me. She's been glued to the telly since Wednesday, waitin' for tonight!'

They stopped, suddenly, registering the two of us.

'Oh my Gawd!' muttered the first.

'Bloody 'ell, you're Matilda Bright!' cried the second.

'And you're in the wrong fucking dressing room,' snapped Matilda. 'Get out, will you? Can't you see we're having a crisis?'

The girls shot out, alarmed.

'And I recommend that you phone your mother and apologize!' she yelled after them.

When she looked at me again, she was grinning from ear to ear.

'Well!' said Matilda, not without a certain amount of satisfaction. 'They say girls get more and more like their mothers as they get older. I'm certainly proving that to be the case. Now sit down and let me do your face.'

I closed my eyes and hoped that she hadn't been drinking.

For five minutes, neither of us said a thing. I could hear the ticking of Matilda's watch as she painted me; once or twice I actually saw the imprint of the baby kicking through the thin blue material of her skirt. I jumped – she didn't react at all. I reached out and touched her stomach gently, and she looked at me in surprise.

'Sometimes I have these moments when I actually believe it's going to happen,' she said.

'I feel the same about tonight, I whispered. Matilda smiled at me and placed her hands on my shoulders. How could someone so frail, so unhinged, feel so strong, so comforting?

When she next spoke, it was as though we had been conducting a conversation without actually talking. She came in at precisely the point where I was.

'If you could sing anything as your second song,' she said, 'what would that be?' She picked up an eyebrow pencil.

I took a breath.

'You remember that Alma Cogan song called "Dreamboat"? That's what I'd sing if I could.'

As I said it, I knew that it was exactly what I should be singing: the song that had started it all for me – the song that I had sung to him that morning before either of us knew the first thing about what lay ahead – that scruffy, fluffy, true-to-me song that I had sung to Inigo before I had taken the wretched elephant and shamed myself forever. And even if Inigo weren't here, and even if he never knew that we'd met before, it wouldn't matter. I would sing it for him anyway.

Matilda stopped. I opened my eyes.

'Then you shall sing it,' she whispered.

'I can't,' I said. 'The orchestra haven't practised it. No one's prepared it—'

'Good Lord, how difficult can it be? *Everyone* knows that song!'

She was the Matilda of old – wide-eyed and refusing to believe that things were the way they were – whether it was Raoul loving Lucy or carrot cake for tea rather than her favourite drop scones.

The door opened, and Billy came back in.

'Oh, just in time,' said Matilda blithely. 'Tara and I have been talking about what she's singing and we don't think "Over the Rainbow" is quite right.'

'Really?' asked Billy sharply. 'Why's that?'

'It's just not a Tara sort of song,' said Matilda patiently.

'Cherry,' corrected Billy automatically.

Matilda ignored him and picked up a pot of rouge and peered inside. 'Tara wants to sing "Dreamboat". I think you should let her.'

'"Dreamboat"?' asked Billy. 'The old Alma Cogan song?'

'Not as old as "Over the Rainbow",' pointed out Matilda, perfectly accurately.

'You can't,' said Billy. 'This decision was made days ago. You need to give the crowd the B-side, Cherry, sweetheart. The band are ready to play . . .'

'Where can we get the sheet music from?' asked Matilda calmly, looking at Billy expectantly, as though he were about to produce it from his inside pocket.

Billy looked at her with something verging on bewilderment. '*What?*'

'Where can we get the music from? For the Alma Cogan number. For the band.'

'She can't sing a different song. Not *now*,' said Billy. 'We've rehearsed what she's doing—'

'She doesn't need to rehearse,' said Matilda. 'You can just go on and do it, can't you, Tara?'

I nodded at her, not daring to look at Billy.

'I know the song backwards,' I said. 'If they can play it, I can sing it.'

Billy slammed both hands down on the table. Several eye pencils flew to the floor. Stepping forward without seeing, Billy crushed one of them into the carpet.

'This is fucking crazy,' he said. 'You don't do this. You don't behave like this! I assured the producer that you're *a professional*. It's all set and ready to go, there's an audience in the theatre waiting to be entertained, and there are millions of kids sitting at home—'

'Then give them something they want to hear,' said Matilda simply.

'It's all right,' I said. I was afraid of all this – I didn't like Billy angry. 'I'll sing "Over the Rainbow". I realize it's impossible to change now.'

Billy looked at me, his jaw set.

'Wait here,' he said. 'Either of you two moves an inch from this room, and I'll have you jailed for the next three months.'

'I'm going to be jailed anyway, darling. I'm having a baby, remember?' said Matilda with little irony.

He slammed the door behind him. Matilda turned to me, her face lit up like a Christmas tree.

'You touched the Achilles heel,' she said. 'Bravo, Tara.'

'What do you mean?'

'Telling him it was impossible to sing something different this late in the day. He can't stand being told that anything is beyond his cosmic powers. Now he'll do all he can to make it happen.'

'Not even Billy can swing this one,' I said. I looked at her. 'But thank you,' I said, realizing I meant it.

'Sit still, like he told us. I want to finish your face,' said Matilda. 'Oh, hang on. Do you think we can order a glass of something? It's terribly warm in here.'

'No.'

Ten minutes later, and the orchestra were flexing their fingers over "Dreamboat".

'I've squared it with Harold,' said Billy, taking out a hand-kerchief and mopping his brow. 'You know something, Cherry Merrywell? Inigo said you'd be trouble. He was quite right.'

Didn't I know he'd said it!

Matilda glanced at me.

'Five minutes, Miss Merrywell,' said a voice through the door.

'Goodness. I must get somewhere to watch you,' said Matilda.

She floated out of the room, not letting go of the glass of white wine she had appropriated from some minion in a uniform. Billy looked at me.

'You all right now?' he asked uncertainly. I think he was a little afraid that I was about to demand something else – the whole theatre to be moved a little to the right, perhaps.

'Yes,' I said. I clamped my teeth together to stop them from chattering.

'I know what it is to be scared,' he said suddenly.

'Do you?'

'Tara,' said Billy slowly, 'you *know* I do.'

I looked at him. It was the first time he had used my name since he had rechristened me for public consumption. His eyes met mine, and they didn't look away. What had he felt when Paul Warren had died? *What had he felt when he had kissed another man?*

'I want to sing,' I said. 'It's all right. I'll be all right.'

I was singing for Inigo now – even if he didn't know it.

Something came over me in that moment. I stepped up to Billy, and – taking both his hands in mine – kissed him quickly on the cheek.

'In case I don't get through this, I want to thank you,' I said.

Billy laughed; he was terribly embarrassed but not unpleased.

'For what?' he asked me.

'For making me do this. For bringing me to London. For forcing me on to the world's biggest stage in front of millions. Thank you for all of it.'

My teeth clattered together like teeth in cartoons. How on earth I was meant to sing now, I couldn't think.

'Stop it,' said Billy, laughing. 'I'm no good at this sort of thing.' He pushed me gently forward. 'Do it for him,' he said.

'Wh-who?' I asked.

'You know who.'

He took my hands in his again, and held them until I was called to the stage. As I walked that long plank, I thought about why the hell I was doing it. I was doing it for Ma, and for Pa and for my brothers and sisters, for all those little girls who wanted someone to believe in. Most of all, I was doing it for *him*.

The one person who I didn't think about when I walked on to that stage was Tara Jupp. I was Cherry Merrywell now. I had to go out and prove she was worth all the effort.

41

Soho and What Happened First

Standing onstage, I was aware of two things: the heat and the expectation. I wasn't the great magician Harry Delancey, and for much of the crowd this was not a good thing – even though they were too nice to show disappointment. They clapped me politely as I walked on – but it was damning with faint praise. I would have rather taken silence. *I know what it is to be scared*, Billy had said. But what had he done when he had been afraid? He had risked everything, and loved anyway. I sat down at the piano. What had Billy told me to say? 'Good evening'? *Was* it evening? It felt nothing like any evening I had ever known. Was it evening in Cornwall? Was Pa watching me?

'Hello,' I said. 'I'm Cherry Merrywell.' I paused. 'At least, that's what they call me.' Someone laughed. Mostly there was nothing; they were still waiting. Just get out there, smile and sing the song, Billy had said. Well, I'd blown that one already!

'This is a song some of you might know,' I said. 'It was recorded by Alma Cogan a few years ago, and I used to do impressions of Alma when I was growing up.' I could vaguely make out the shapes in the orchestra pit – the poor musicians who were having to play a different tune for me at the last minute. 'I suppose you could say I still haven't grown up,' I added. 'Anyway, if Alma's watching somewhere, I've got a message. Please invite me to one of your parties. I hear *good* things happen at your parties.'

Laughter, punctuated by shuffling, a little bit of surprise. I saw the conductor stand up.

'A long time ago, I sang this song for someone I wanted to impress,' I said quickly. 'I suppose I *still* want to impress him.' I laughed – astounded at myself holding court in the middle of the stage at the Palladium. 'But I should just stop talking and get on with the song,' I said. 'And when I finish, I'm going to sing you another song that you might have heard on the radio in the last couple of weeks. Here we go.'

So there was nothing more to do but sing – every other choice had eliminated itself. *As it was in the beginning, and evermore shall be*, I thought. *Amen.*

The orchestra started, and suddenly I was Alma again – as I had been when I had first met Inigo at Milton Magna Hall. He would know afterwards – and if he didn't, then he never would. I sang exactly how I had sung back then, and with my eyes half closed I could see us in the kitchen, I could feel Aunt Mary's presence beside me, and suddenly the air under those hot lights felt sharp with life, with the activity of something important, something real. *It was as it had been.*

Halfway through the first chorus I think I sensed Billy, standing in the wings. Halfway through the second, I saw Clover sitting next to Matilda in the front row. I sang, or at least I must have done, because people say I did. I'm not saying that lightly, but it *happened* lightly. I knew that I had learned from the best performers in London – every one of the people I had grown so close to was performing in their own way: Matilda, Billy, Lucy, Clover, Digby and Inigo. All dancing as hard and as fast as they could away from something that threatened to hold them back – that threatened the *truth*.

By the time I sang 'May to September' I was in my stride. Several of the girls near the front must have heard it several times on the radio; they were singing along, itching to stand up and dance. I felt a wave of gratitude towards them, for believing in me when I wasn't at *all* sure that I did. I felt a light sweat breaking out on my brow, and I imagined Imogen and Florence watching at home, astounded and laughing, and Roy and Luke making fun of me, because it was all they knew how to do.

'May to September we were fine
May to September – oh how I wish he was mine
Why can't he come back home to stay?
No other girl could love him more in Malibu, C.A!'

In the back of my head, as I sang, one thought remained constant: *God, Inigo was good.* This song – that I had objected to, and scorned for its simplicity – was exactly what everyone in that theatre wanted. "The happy stuff is harder to write," he had said to me. Yet he did it, and every time, it worked.

When I finished, the applause sounded too big for me, too important for what I had done. It should have been for him, I thought, grinning madly and curtsying and waving into the black space. The applause was really for him, and Alma. I looked out into the crowd, searching, searching for him, yet knowing perfectly well that he was nowhere to be found. Two girls sitting with their mothers, wearing their best dresses and clutching on to each other's arms, stood up and waved at me. I waved back. *Do it for the little ones*, I thought.

'Now, Alma Cogan – if you're out there – you heard what

the lady said!' cried Norman Vaughan, weaving back on to the stage and winking at me. 'You know, I think my own invitation to her last party must've got lost in the post,' he added. 'I'm sure that's what happened.' (More laughter from the crowd.) 'You know what? Tell Alma Cogan to get herself here, to *Sunday Night at the London Palladium* – she can join our party, ladies and gentlemen! How about that? *Swingin'!*'

I nodded, smiling as though he was the funniest man to have walked into my life, and ten seconds later I had left the stage, and everything that had just happened was confined to the same memory bank as my most unlikely Wimbledon dreams.

Harold walked me back to my dressing room.

'What a *swell* performance, Miss Merrywell. You know, if Norman Vaughan says your swingin', then you're swingin'.' He laughed, and I saw that all the doubt I had seen in his eyes before I had stepped onstage had vanished.

'Thank you,' I said, grinning at him like a fool.

'And that dress,' he added. 'What a look! You'll have every girl in the country wanting to dress like you come Monday morning.'

'It's Mary Quant,' I said.

Billy was waiting for me.

'God in heaven, Cherry, what the hell were you doing spouting off like that?' he demanded. But he was glittering. Matilda was crying again. Pulling out a handkerchief, she looked up at me.

'It was perfect,' she said.

'I don't know,' I said, taking a glass of champagne from Harold and gulping down an enormous mouthful. It fizzed into my nose.

'Come here,' said Billy, taking me gently by the arm. 'The papers want to see you.'

'Not before *I* see her,' said a voice.

I turned around and nearly fell over myself. It was Lucy. All

498

dressed up like she was going out to the pub with the village boys, black kohl around her eyes, her short, dark hair softer now that it had grown back a little. Harold's glasses fell off. Suddenly, there was no one else in the place, just her.

'You saw?' I asked her.

She nodded. 'You didn't think I'd miss you, did you?'

'Yes,' I said. 'I rather thought you would.'

'You do realize,' she said, 'that there's no getting away from any of this now? If you wanted not to be famous, then you've gone utterly the wrong way about it. There isn't a single person out there who isn't in love with you, or who doesn't want to be you, or isn't desperate to talk to you.'

'Oh, Lucy.'

She held my hand tight in hers. My eyes fell on the sign at the end of the corridor. *Exit.* She glanced around and understood, through the miracle of our wordless communication, honed through hours of sitting next to each other in church.

Together we slipped away from the crowd, out through the back door of the theatre and into the night.

We went to a little bar somewhere in Soho. It was Sunday night, but the streets were alive with people – young people – girls with big hair and too much slap, boys with cheap jackets and bad shoes, but all of them dusted with the magical essence of youth, everyone hanging about and waiting for everything and nothing to happen. It was London, I thought. That was all it was really about. Wandering around hoping that you're somewhere in the general direction of the right place, but never really being sure. Lucy and I ordered black coffee with sugar, even though neither of us was very keen on it, and Lucy sat opposite me and pretended not to notice the boys giving her looks from the other side of the room.

'I suppose you're not going to tell me where you've been staying,' I said.

'I didn't want to be in the room with you,' said Lucy. 'I wouldn't have slept next to you last week.'

'I know. I suppose I felt the same.'

I rubbed my eyes, almost expecting to wake up and find myself back at the Rectory before this whole fandango had even begun. The night had become dream-like. First the Palladium, then running away from everyone and seeing Lucy again – it was too much for one evening. The sequins on my dress were rubbing my legs. I itched to step out of it, and into my jodhpurs. Lucy reached out and touched my cheek.

'Your face looks so pretty,' she said.

'Matilda did my make-up.'

'It's not the make-up,' said Lucy. 'It's something different about you. Like you've grown up.'

'It's only been a week,' I said. But I knew she was right. You don't have a week like I had and not feel older.

'I've been wanting to say sorry,' I said. 'For saying all that terrible stuff. Everything you think about me is right. You and Raoul is your thing, not mine.'

The relief at saying this to her was almost too much. Only in saying it to her did I know it was true.

'It's never as clear as all that,' said Lucy. 'I realize that now.'

'After that journey back from the hospital, I wanted to throw myself off the planet,' I admitted.

'Good thing you didn't,' said Lucy. 'Or who the hell would have replaced Harry Delancey at the Palladium tonight?'

'They would have found someone,' I said. 'Billy would have concocted someone else out of thin air. It's what he does.'

'How did it feel?' asked Lucy.

'Strange, and over very quickly.'

'Funny, I think I said the same thing after that night in Plymouth with Martin Adams.' She gave me the ghost of a smile. 'Dear Tara,' she said. 'I couldn't have done that. Not in a million years.'

'You could have done,' I said. 'If there's one thing all of this has taught me, it's that we're all capable of much more than we give ourselves credit for.'

'You sound like Pa.'

'I can't tell you how much I've missed him this week.'

'And that's the second lesson,' sighed Lucy. 'Sometimes you have to step away from everyone to see who actually matters the most. Up close, it's hard to tell.'

There was a pause while a waitress with bored eyes came over and asked us if we wanted anything to eat, then Lucy leaned forward.

'I don't want to lose him,' she said urgently. 'Raoul, I mean.'

I looked down at the table, then up into her eyes again.

'So why did you run off with the harmonica player?'

I didn't want to say his name.

'Because he paid me attention, and I thought it might help me to forget Raoul,' said Lucy. I jolted at the speed of her response, and at her frankness.

'You've been gone a whole week,' I said.

'I know.'

'Did you . . . ?'

'I thought I might,' she said. 'But then when I had the chance, after the night at the Marquee, it didn't happen.'

'Why not?'

'I didn't want to. I needed to think, and he's a thinker too. I told him about Raoul, and he listened.'

'You could have told me about Raoul, and I would have listened.'

'No, you wouldn't,' said Lucy truthfully. 'You would have stamped your own opinions over everything that you said.' She held up her hand. 'And I don't blame you for that. Brian doesn't know Raoul. He barely knew me.'

'Are you telling me that you sat around just *talking* to him?' What I wanted to add was that, having watched him on that stage, I was not sure that any girl would have been immune to Brian's charms. Even from an entirely objective viewpoint, it was fair to say that he was certifiably irresistible. That was what had scared me about him from the start.

'He's very young,' said Lucy. 'During the day he mucks about with his guitar and his friends, and smokes non-stop – when he can afford to buy tobacco. For seven nights in a row, all we did was lie about talking. He couldn't afford to go out. Poor boy, he must have been bored senseless by the sound of my voice, but he can't afford to go out much, so he was stuck with me.'

'Why did you need to be away for a whole week?'

'It took me that long to sort through all of this,' said Lucy. She tapped the side of her head. 'I sat in his room, going through Clover's boxes, reading Colette Napier's diaries, and the simplest things kept leading me back to Raoul.'

'And all this time, the harmonica player didn't lay a finger on you?' I asked her.

'He tried,' said Lucy. 'Then I think he rather liked the novelty of having a girl around who he didn't have to try to pull all the time.'

Her lip was trembling. She took several short breaths – her hands stiff around the coffee cup.

'I've realized that my husband is the only one I've ever wanted to hang about with.' She laughed without mirth. 'A bit inconvenient, now, isn't it? Now that he's backed away from me.'

She pushed away her coffee, infuriated, as if it were distracting her from saying what she needed to say. 'Back when I was friends with Matilda, it was all about the game. You know. Getting people to fall in love with me, and then giving up on them once they said it. Then I met Raoul and all of that changed, but I knew nothing about him! Nothing except that he liked the Victorians, and appreciated the work of Nikolaus Pevsner. The rest – his family, where he was from, what it meant to be Spanish, what he wanted from the rest of his life – none of that even entered my head. It was always just about me, and my happiness, or my desire to be desired and *my* inability to have children. To think!' she said in amazement. 'I may have never even *told* him! Matilda did me a favour by writing that note. If she hadn't, then it would have been years before he found out.'

'She did you a favour?' I looked at her from under peeling false eyelashes. 'Do you mean that?'

'I didn't think of it that way till now,' said Lucy. 'All I could see was that she had done something to me that I couldn't forgive.'

'Matilda did it because she was angry, and because she believed herself to be in love with Raoul. I don't think she was capable of thinking beyond that,' I said. I had thought this many times before, but this was the first time that I had told Lucy. Matilda had never been entirely to blame.

Lucy took a deeper breath and looked at me. Rubbing her eyes, she streaked mascara down her left cheek. And there was me, in my Mary Quant sequins, fresh from the London Palladium, but about as far from Alma Cogan as I could ever have been. The pair of us must have looked like a real couple of dolls.

503

Lucy fished up her sleeve for a handkerchief, and found none. I handed her a paper napkin.

'What she did was to let him know about the baby thing, and from the moment that he knew, I started looking away again and blaming Matilda. But really, it was never her fault at all. It was mine. I've just spent the last three years predicting that he's going to leave me, then making tracks myself so that it wouldn't hurt as much. I'm very good at that, don't you think?' She blew her nose again. 'Now I've driven him away forever. I practically told him that I was shacked up with another boy, and that it was over—'

'You shouldn't be telling me all of this. It's for him to know. You need to go back to him—'

'But that's just it,' said Lucy. There was anguish in her eyes. 'He's not in hospital any longer.'

'What do you mean?'

'He got out a few days ago. He's gone.' Her voice was flat, dull.

'Well, surely he's gone home.'

'He's certainly done that. Only not back to our home. He's gone back to Spain, Tara. Like I told him to.'

My heart thumped into my shoes.

'But he'll come back.'

'I don't know,' she said. 'He said that he would be back some time to collect some things from the cottage. That doesn't sound promising, does it?'

'But surely if you tell him how you feel – tell him what you've told me?'

'How could I?' she said. 'This is his chance to start again. God, it's hardly too late for him, is it? He'll find another girl in seconds. He can have his family, after all. Perhaps even that slut of a nurse who wouldn't leave him alone . . .'

'Rachel,' I said.

'Whatever her bloody name is,' said Lucy.

'She was only helping him.' I looked at her. 'She's been typing out his work for him.'

'She *has*?' Lucy looked disgusted. 'What on earth gave *her* the right to . . .'

What the hell? I thought. *I would tell her.* Why not? It would hardly make any difference now, if he really had gone back to Spain forever.

'He's been writing fiction,' I said, all in a rush. 'A book called *Bernadita*.'

'Ber-na-*di*-ta?' Lucy gave the name the full whack of its four syllables. 'What do you mean, writing fiction?' She gave a bark of laughter. 'I don't believe you.'

'I didn't until I saw part of the manuscript and heard him describing the plot to me in graphic detail.'

As it had with me, it took more than a moment for this to sink in. Then Lucy said: 'Why didn't he tell me? And what about Capability Brown?'

I shook my head. 'Oh, he's in the book,' I said. 'He's writing one of those novels where real historical people pop up and get involved with the characters he's invented.'

'Dangerous,' said Lucy.

'I don't think that he had much faith that you'd think it was any good.'

It was a hard thing to tell her, but it was the truth, and I felt that the truth was the only currency worth trading in now. Lucy said nothing, just twisted the coffee spoon around and around in her empty cup. The waitress was eyeing the door – she wanted to go home. It was late now – nearly midnight, and a Sunday to boot. We ignored her. I think we were both afraid that if we moved, we wouldn't be able to talk like this any longer. It was a precious thing, this space between us, and if we stood up, or changed the scene, something might just switch back and make it impossible to communicate again.

'He didn't want to tell me because he didn't think that I had faith in him. When all along . . .' She paused, speaking slowly and shaking her head, as she articulated something that she had only just worked out. 'When all along, it was me not having any faith in *me* that was the problem. It was me I never believed in, not him.'

I wanted to snap my fingers and tell her that she had got it in one. I wanted to laugh and pat her on the back for saying it. I wanted to cry, because I never thought that either of us would get to this point at all.

'Now it's too late,' she said. 'Too fucking late.'

Hearing Digby swear so often had numbed me to Lucy's use of that word, but I knew that she didn't use it lightly. She looked into her cup again as though expecting some magical solution to emerge from the grains in the bottom.

'Go back to Cornwall, and find him,' I said again. 'He has to come back.'

'You know, that's exactly what Brian said,' said Lucy.

'I feel I should thank him,' I muttered.

'No,' said Lucy. 'I'd steer clear of him if I were you. The only way I was able to put up with his mess for a week was because I couldn't face the idea of being in the same bedroom as you after I'd slapped you in the face.'

'I never stopped going on,' I said. 'I think I deserved it.'

Lucy shook her head. As we stood up, I thought of something else.

'You know, right after that I bumped into Inigo Wallace, and he told me about your little outing to Hampton Court.'

Lucy picked up her cardigan.

'Gosh,' she said.

'I never knew you'd gone.'

'Seems he's good at keeping stuff to himself,' said Lucy.

'Was he – all right?' I asked her.

'Very all right,' she said. Something in my face must have given it away. 'You still haven't got over him, have you?'

'Not really,' I admitted. 'Fuck it, there's nothing to say.'

Lucy looked shocked. 'You better not take that language home to Pa,' she said.

By the time we got back to Napier House the birds were starting to sing. Lucy, exhausted, pale and halfway through her second packet of cigarettes, fell into bed. I lay and thought about every-thing and nothing. How I could stand onstage in that famous old theatre and sing a song for a boy who didn't love me, in front of a load of people I didn't know, and how I could feel so lonely when I had my sister back, but how miserable she was without Raoul, and how, through all of this, the only place that I really wanted to be was with my father, and for him to put his arm around me and tell me that it was all all right. I wondered what Matilda was feeling – with her bump and her fame and her loneliness without Lucy, and without Paul Warren, a lone-liness shared by Billy – and I thought how it was all a very big muddle, but that it would change, because the one thing that I seemed to have learned was that things always changed.

And the change started the very next morning, when the telephone didn't stop ringing. Everyone had seen my perform-ance. There were telegrams and flowers and invitations and notes through the door of Napier House and at Billy's offices, but none of these salutations were from him. And I realized that the plain and simple truth is that none of it made any sense – none of it added up – without the right people next to you. Then, in the evening, he called.

'Inigo for you,' said Clover, chucking the telephone at me and running to shoo away more girls from the door.

'Hello?' I could hear my voice shaking, even if he couldn't.

'Cherry?' said Inigo.

The delay across the Atlantic was disarming. I felt he was even further away than America – he might as well have been calling from Mars.

'I heard what you did,' he said. 'You know, you should have listened to Billy. You can't go around changing everything the whole time. He had a plan for you, and you need to believe that he knows what he's talking about.'

I was shocked – although I don't know what I'd expected him to say. I suppose I thought he might know me by now, but he didn't.

'Everyone said it was good. The audience loved it—'

'That's not the bloody point.' I could feel his irritation, hear him sighing with annoyance.

'I couldn't sing "Over the Rainbow",' I said, finding my voice again. 'It wasn't true to me.'

'Why do you have to be so difficult? Billy busted a gut to get you on that show. You may have gone down well, but you took a massive risk.'

'But the risk worked! It paid off! Everyone liked it – the audience went wild for it!'

'Making them laugh by impersonating Alma Cogan is not what you were meant to do.'

'You weren't here! You didn't see it. You can't judge me on what you've been told!'

'I can,' he said.

There was a terrible silence. I felt the hiss through those wires that were letting us talk like this, and I felt that they were listening.

'All I'm saying is that you need to pay *attention* to Billy. He knows what he's doing. You're only seventeen and you don't know the business like he does. If you want to stick around in this business then you need to *listen* to him.'

I did it for you! I wanted to shout.

'Listen, I don't want to call you up like some annoying big brother, telling you what you can and can't do, but you've signed up for something that you can't always control. You need to be careful, Cherry.'

'How is it out there?' I asked him, my voice trembling.

'Huh?'

'How is it? In America – the weather?'

'I don't know. I haven't opened the curtains yet.'

Silence again.

'This must be an expensive call,' I said.

'Take it from me, Cherry,' said Inigo. 'You're good. But I don't want to see you blowing your chances – you know what I mean?'

There was the sound of another telephone ringing in that far-off place, wherever he was.

'I should go,' he said.

'Will you be back at Christmas?' I asked him.

'Perhaps. Why? Are you worried about working with Johnnie Wilson? He's a great guy . . .'

'N-no. I just was wondering when I might see you again, that's all.'

'The only thing you need to wonder about is how to make

the most of what you can do. Don't cock everything up with Billy, and you'll make a lot of money. Take too many risks, and you'll be out on your own.'

With that, the call was over. Wearily, I picked up the pen and scribbled into the telephone record book.

Inigo Wallace to Cherry Merrywell from New York. Purpose of call: severe telling off.

How was it possible for him to be so different again? Was he the same boy who had stood with me, bewildered, by a village green in Wiltshire just a few weeks ago? The same boy whose hand I had held in mine after we had sat up all night writing a song that I couldn't get out of my head? He had made his decision, I thought. I was just another singer to him. Not even Alma Cogan had made him realize that he had known me for longer than he thought. I would forget him, I decided savagely. And push away the ache forever. There was only one problem with this, of course: it was impossible.

Part Three

The Misinterpretation of Tara Jupp

42

The Storm

On Saturday evening two weeks later, Lucy and I spent the evening watching my little brothers playing tennis. Billy had driven Matilda and me back to Cornwall for just three nights – anticipating the lack of time that we would have at home later on. The big push on Cherry Merrywell had accelerated. I had spent the fortnight following the Palladium in the recording studio, and in a constant round of interviews and live perform-ances of 'May to September'. After the Palladium, nothing scared me. Perhaps it was because nothing else felt as big. Perhaps it was because without *him*, it didn't seem to matter anyway.

My time in the recording studio with Johnnie Wilson did nothing but remind me even more of Inigo. Johnnie talked about him a great deal, forever referencing what he had taught him and speaking constantly of his musical genius. Tall, amiable and softly spoken, with a pale round face, soft brown eyes and a liking for girls who could sing and make him laugh, Johnnie gave the impression that he was a little bit in love with me, but on the one occasion that he asked me to dinner with him after an afternoon in the studio, I refused.

Back at the Rectory, I wanted everything to be just the same, yet of course it wasn't. Raoul was still in Spain, so Lucy was back with us. I didn't blame her. Why would she want to be in Rose Cottage on her own – surrounded by his clothes and his books and the certainty that it was never going to be the same again? On the evening that we arrived home, she and I took pieces of cold apple pie and a bottle of lemonade to the bank of daisies beside the court.

'Ta, Lucy – are you watching?' yelled Roy, and I was jolted out of myself for a moment, because he served a sensational serve. But Luke returned it, and the ball flew back across the net at his brother.

'Out!' cried Roy. 'Wasn't it, Ta?'

'You're both so good that I can't even see any more. You hit too fast. Can't you slow down a bit?' shouted Lucy.

Pa appeared. 'Don't get complacent, boys,' he shouted. 'Roy, that was in. Luke's point.'

Pa sat down next to me on the grass bank beside the court.

'*You* may think they've improved,' he said. 'Actually, they both came to me last night to say that they only want to play for fun in the future, For fun! I ask you!'

'Oh, Pa . . .'

'No. There's nothing you can say. I shouldn't have placed so much hope in two players who were always going to be more interested in what was on the other side of the court fence than within the service box. It was my mistake.'

I was shocked, first by the boys' courage, secondly by Pa's confessing his error to me.

He looked at the boys, who were laughing together under the grey sky. A storm was forecast later in the evening. For now, the air was clingy and humid, unwilling to succumb to the rain just yet.

'I should never have pushed them so hard,' said Pa.

'You pushed them hard because you believed in them,' I said.

'Like you pushed me to read Pevsner and expand my mind beyond boys and the pub,' said Lucy wryly.

Without looking at her, Pa took her hand in his. Lucy couldn't hide her smile – she was thirteen years old again, and probably living out her fantasy that she was Pa's only child.

'If he doesn't come back, then know this,' he said. 'Know that you can come back here and stay for as long as you like. You belong here, Lucy Janet Persephone Jupp.'

'Goodness,' I said. 'That really *is* her name. Well done, Pa.'

'Thank you,' said Lucy.

She looked down, but I saw her brushing away a tear. Whether it was for Raoul or Pa, I didn't know. But I knew it was for love.

Pa stared out at the court. His grey hair was blown about, and he was wearing a blue jumper that Imogen had knitted him years ago, that was ripped at the sleeve. For the first time, I looked at him and saw him as he had been as a boy, and as he had been when Ma met him. For the first time, I looked at him and saw Lucy in him too. Roy served to Luke, a ball that was plainly out. Pa bit his lip, trying to resist the urge to bellow, but it was just too much for him.

'OUT!' he yelled. He staggered to his feet.

'Pa . . .' I tried telling him. 'You said that they wanted to play for fun now—'

'Luke, you're playing like a big baby!' Pa shouted. 'Pull yourself together and remember what we talked about yesterday. And why were you so late out this afternoon?'

'Science project,' said Roy automatically, and Luke said, 'Helping make the beds.'

'Time wasting!' shouted Pa.

He looked down at Lucy and me and sighed.

'Force of habit,' he said, with an unapologetic shrug. 'As Jesus realized at the Last Supper, once you've invested time and energy in something, it's *powerful* hard to let it go.'

The sun had gone in. As I walked inside there was a rumble of thunder, and the distant sound of horse hoofs breaking into a trot along the village road as their riders realized that they would need to get back soon to escape the downpour.

After supper, the rest of the family had melted away, as they tended to when there were plates to be washed up. For me, fresh from Napier House and Clover's ability to create stylish interiors simply by virtue of her presence in the room, I felt wearied by the sight of the stacked plates, the cracked glasses, the grotty, twice-used napkins in the kitchen – but I wanted to be with Imogen. I wanted to talk about Matthew Bell and about the village, not about anything else. Lucy had taken the car to Rose Cottage to collect a bag of fresh clothes and books. Relief that she was welcome at the Rectory would have propelled her all the way there and back without petrol. The telephone rang, filling me with hope doubled now – that it would be either Raoul or Inigo.

'It's for you,' said Imogen, coming back from the hall. 'It's Mr Laurier.' Nothing could make her refer to him as Billy. 'He said it was urgent.'

I didn't want Billy and his urgency, I had come here to escape such things. Padding into the hall, I picked up the receiver. Billy would be calling to make plans for our return. He wouldn't want to leave anything to chance – not after the Palladium and everything that had been written in the papers about me.

'Hello?' I said cautiously.

'Oh, thank Christ. Cherry, is that you?'

'Yes.'

'I think Matilda's having the baby.'

'Huh?'

'She's going into the – you know – she's in labour. Or rather, she's already some way into it. At least, I *think* she is. I don't know what the hell's going on. I had the nurse booked to start in London next week—'

I couldn't hear what he said next because his voice was drowned out by an ear-splitting wail. She was in labour all right.

'Have you rung the hospital? Called for an ambulance?'

'Of course.' I could hear the rising panic in his voice – a strange thing. I had never known Billy to be anything other than completely together.

'I'll come over,' I said.

I slammed down the phone and raced into the kitchen.

'I'm off,' I shouted to Imogen.

'Goodness, I thought you were here till Tuesday,' began Imogen.

'Emergency at Trellanack,' I said. 'Matilda's having the baby.'

'*Now?*'

'Apparently so,' I shouted. 'Billy needs someone to wait with them until the ambulance arrives.'

'Ambulance? They've diverted all the traffic through town because of the tree felling.' Imogen looked thunderstruck. 'They won't be able to get through unless someone stands at the junction and diverts them up through the back route to Trellanack. I'll go.'

'Would you?' I gasped. 'It may be a long wait . . .'

Imogen ran to the hall, and pulled on her wellies, Pa's raincoat and Roy's sou'wester. Racing back into the kitchen she rammed a packet of Rich Tea biscuits and a torch into her pocket.

517

It started to rain when I was halfway down Mrs Otley's path. I don't mean the usual way in which rain begins – a few suggestive little spots followed by a light shower, possibly easing into something more substantial in time for you to put up a brolly. No, this was a downpour of biblical proportions. The dusty earth, shocked by the drama, had nowhere to contain the water – the rain bounced off the path as though falling on to hot concrete. I was wearing my sandals and within seconds they were drenched. I pushed my hair out of my eyes and carried on running, as above me the wind picked up sinister pace, scudding dark clouds across the blackening sky, sending wild rumours through the limes at the bottom of the drive, forcing the Shetlands to scurry for shelter. Hester stood apart from the others, her head high. It was as if she knew I was coming.

Throwing myself through the fence, I grabbed an old halter abandoned on the side of the gate-post. Stretching out a hand, I walked quickly towards the pony with nothing to offer her but the hope of her help. She came towards me, ears pointed. She wanted rescuing as much as Matilda. Quickly, I vaulted on to her back, and bent down and kissed her mane, at the precise moment that a deafening clap of thunder sent her squealing into an uncontrolled trot, throwing her head back and banging me on the nose. Pushing her into a canter, half blinded by the rain, I aimed her at the top of the park and hoped for the best.

If I fall off and break my leg, who the hell's going to come after me? I thought, in sudden panic.

'Please!' I shouted into the spaces in front of me as I rode. '*Please* can everything be all right!'

Dismounting at speed, and leaving Hester at the top of the park with the merciless abandon of John Wayne, I climbed over the fence and up to the front door of the house. The little gap that Inigo had stopped up with logs was still closed. Where was he? I thought. I needed him now more than ever. It wasn't until I ran through the open front door that I realized that my nose had been bleeding all over my T-shirt.

'Billy?' I called. 'Matilda?'

'Upstairs!' shouted Billy. 'Her mother's bedroom! How d'you get here so *quick*, Cherry, you little angel?'

I had never seen inside Lady W-D's bedroom, and not possessing Lucy's Photographic Memory for Houses (Trademark), it took me several wrong doors before I found them. I had expected noise; when I arrived there was none. Matilda was lying on the bed, her head drenched in sweat. Irrationally, all I could think in that moment was what a feminine room it was for such a woman as Lady W-D, who one imagined would have slept well on bare boards. There was a rose-patterned bedspread, and heavy pink and white silk curtains. Even in the midst of the mayhem, I noticed the faded velvet top hat she had worn at Hickstead, on the dressing table, beside an ancient copy of *Of Mice and Men*.

Clutching Matilda's hand, Billy looked up as I walked in, and noticing the blood on my T-shirt, he stood up in alarm.

'It's nothing,' I said quickly. 'Just a nose-bleed.'

'Thank God you're here,' he said.

He thinks I'm going to make it all right, I thought in sudden panic. He thinks that because I'm a girl, I'll know what to do; that some sort of primal instinct will come over me and, if I have to, I'll get that baby out of her somehow.

'Matilda?' I moved over towards the bed, kneeling down as though worshipping.

She looked at me. Her face was white; any trace of make-up had transferred itself on to the pillows.

'Tara!' she said. 'Please, darling thing. Make this pain stop. I can't do it. I just can't do it.'

'You can. You absolutely can.'

But, Lord above – *could* she do it? Who was I to know?

I picked up a glass beside her bed.

'Water?'

'I keep wanting to be sick,' she said. 'I think it's the fear. It can't come now, can it? Why's it coming now? I thought first babies were always meant to be late.'

'Not with Billy at the helm,' I said.

Trying to joke was the wrong thing to do. Matilda started to cry, great sobs that wrenched through her entire body. I looked at Billy, who was looking at me in horror.

'I can't watch her suffering like this, for Christ's sake. I just can't.'

'Don't, then,' I snapped. 'You shouldn't be up here anyway. What man is in the room when his wife has a baby, for God's sake? Go downstairs and make some tea. Bring up some clean sheets.'

I was aghast at my own outspokenness. Matilda looked at me as he left the room.

'Good,' she said through gritted teeth. 'At times like this, people need to be told what to do. He'll thank you for it tomorrow.'

Was there going to be a tomorrow? I wondered. It felt like the last night on earth.

'Clean sheets,' said Matilda with a weak smile. 'Don't people usually ask for towels and hot water?'

Oh Christ, *did* they? I didn't know.

'Stay with me, Tara,' said Matilda. 'You won't leave me, will you?'

She started to cry again.

'When did you last have a contraction?' I asked her – more for the sake of having something to say than anything else.

'Is that the agonizing bit?'

'Jesus, Matilda, did you read nothing about all of this?'

'Of course not,' she said. 'Denial's served me jolly well all throughout this pregnancy.'

I didn't laugh. She looked up at me, her big eyes full of fear.

'I had an awful moment about twenty minutes ago, when Billy called you. I think that was the last contraction thing.'

'We'll just have to breathe through them,' I said shakily.

'Will you hold my hand?'

She switched positions suddenly; she was crouching on all fours, animal-like.

'It feels easier like this!' she gasped. 'Don't know why. I feel like a *horse!*'

It was so unlike any image of Matilda that I had ever known, I was almost ready to laugh. And there *was* something bleakly comedic about Matilda and I upstairs in Lady W-D's old bedroom, just a few months before Trellanack was supposed to be out of her hands for good, going through labour together. And it *was* together; every time Matilda had a contraction I felt such horror I wanted to rush for the door. Something stopped me. Something made me sit still, and hold her hand, and listen to her crying, waiting for it to end. They had to be here soon, they had to be, I thought, calculating how long it would take for the ambulance to get to Trellanack from Truro. Forty minutes? An hour at the most? But the rain, still hammering down outside the window made everything uncertain. Cornish nights like these could stop anyone in their tracks, except – perhaps – this baby. For one reason or other, it was coming sooner than any of us could cope with. In the odd moments of calm in between, Matilda climbed back on to the bed, and rested her head on the faded rose-patterned pillow-case and talked about the past.

'The last time I came into this room,' she said, 'it was the morning after Lucy told me that she was going to marry Raoul. I was crazy with it all; I exploded at my mother like some awful creature of the night. I couldn't stop, on and on about how I had lost the one person I had ever really loved.'

'Raoul would have driven you crazy, you know,' I said.

'Oh no,' said Matilda. 'It's not him I'm talking about. It's Lucy.'

I looked at her.

'You make it sound as though you were married to her!'

Matilda reached for a glass of water, wincing.

'But we were, in a way. That intense friendship between two girls of school age is something built in rock. You don't know anything else when you're seventeen and you find someone you can talk to about anything at all. The funny thing is,' she went on, 'all the time that I was ever with Raoul on my own, I think I was just trying to impress Lucy. I wanted to have something sensational to talk to her about. I wanted her to be . . . to be proud of me.'

I looked at Matilda's face, those world-famous blue eyes, the big rosebud mouth full of white teeth now stained with red wine.

'The thing about that sort of love,' she said, as though she knew what I was thinking, 'is that it doesn't anticipate hurt, or failure. That was my downfall. I couldn't believe that she was prepared to hurt me like she did, so I went after her with the only thing I knew I could use to hurt her.'

'She was broken,' I said. 'You had the power to break her, more than she broke you.'

'I know,' whispered Matilda. 'I've hated myself for it ever since.'

'Is that the reason why – why you drink so much?'

Matilda shook her head violently.

'Even if it is, it doesn't make it all right.' She clasped her hands together and fixed me with the sort of intense look that her mother used to give me when she wanted to underline the importance of the eggbutt snaffle for ponies with soft mouths. 'The only thing that can make it all right is what I do now. Now that she's forgiven me. You see?' Then the cloud came over her again. 'Oh my God, it's happening again. Oh God, Tara, Oh God in *heaven!*' She gripped my hand. 'Tara,' she said. 'This is not funny.'

'Believe me, I'm not laughing.'

'Tell me,' she said through gritted teeth. 'Tell me why the hell anyone goes through this, darling?'

The door opened. *They were here!* I thought, nearly fainting with relief. It was going to be all right.

'Right,' said a voice. 'Have you been timing the contractions?'

I looked up and nearly blacked out for the second time in as many seconds. It was Lucy.

43

Debut

'What are you doing here?' Matilda and I asked the same question together. I moved forward, stumbling up from my position on the floor towards my sister.

'How did you know we were here?' I gasped.

'I was coming back from the cottage when I saw a ghostly vision in the middle of the crossroads.'

'Imogen,' I said.

'She told me what happened.'

Matilda sank into her pillow and closed her eyes.

'You shouldn't be here,' she whispered. 'It's too difficult.'

I looked at Lucy. She was wearing her shorts and the same little top that she had worn the day that we had first met Raoul, those three years ago, only now she had an old tweed coat over the top. She had pulled her hair up, which somehow seemed to have lifted the clouds that had been there since Raoul had left away from her eyes. I sensed the urgency in her, I could smell the heat from her body; she had raced here as quickly as I had. Lucy, who feared nothing but the blame she had placed on herself for our mother's death, was facing the very same situation again.

'If the baby comes tonight,' she said, trying to keep her voice steady, 'it will be *how* early?'

'Six weeks,' said Matilda without opening her eyes.

'I thought so,' said Lucy. 'All right. It's going to come, and it's all going to be fine. Do you understand me, Miss Wells-Devoran?'

Matilda opened her eyes and gave Lucy the ghost of a smile.

'No one's called me that since I left this place.'

'Perhaps they should have done,' observed Lucy. She looked at me. 'Good, you're here,' she said confusingly. I think that she started seeing the room properly all of a sudden, weighing up how on earth we should go on from here. I pulled her by the sleeve of the tweed coat into the corner of the room, out of Matilda's earshot.

'Listen, the ambulance should be here soon. You didn't need to come. This is too hard for you. We can't pretend we know what we're doing, but I'm all right with her. I really am. You could go and see how Billy is—'

'He's perfectly fine, sitting downstairs gulping down Scotch and distracting himself by trying to mend the wireless. The ambulance *won't* be here soon,' she said. 'The road is entirely blocked by felled limes. And if you think you know of any one person who's read more than me about how to stage-manage an un-attended birth, then I'd like to know who they are.' Lucy pulled her arm away from me and spoke with absolute calm. 'Get a grip, Tara. I know exactly what I'm doing. What do you think I was reading all those times you used to come into my bedroom and catch me with the torch on under the covers?'

'I'd always assumed it was something about either great country houses or sex.'

Lucy looked mildly startled. 'Well, *no*, actually.'

'Well, what, then?'

'I was reading books on childbirth in the vain hope that if it ever happened to me, then I would survive it.'

'I don't believe you.'

'Don't beat yourself up over your mistakes,' said Lucy. 'Learn from them.'

Learn from them! It was the advice that Raoul had given her when I had overheard them talking in the dining room before they were married.

Matilda reached for her water again, and knocked it over the bed.

'I think I'm going to be sick,' she croaked.

'Don't worry,' said Lucy. 'That's perfectly normal. Around thirty-nine per cent of women experience sickness in labour.'

I looked at her.

'Great country houses and sex! Ha! I didn't need to read about either of those things,' she said tartly. 'I was getting *quite* enough of both in real life.'

She looked at Matilda.

'We need more water, towels, and something for her to be sick into.'

'All the bed linen, towels and everything have been stored in the Red Bathroom,' said Matilda. She wanted to say more, but quite plainly could not. Wailing into the next contraction, she screamed as though she were being murdered.

'Oh God! Oh *God*!' I shouted, too alarmed not to.

'Red Bathroom, Red Bathroom . . .' mused Lucy, ignoring me, and allowing Matilda to squeeze her engagement ring into her hand so far that it drew blood. Lucy winced. I could see her Photographic Memory For Houses (Trademark) setting to work.

'Red Bathroom, Red Bathroom,' she muttered again. Suddenly

she snapped her fingers. 'Ah. Got it. Byron's valet's bathroom, wasn't it? Tara, cross to the East Wing, third floor, fourth door on the left, walk through and turn left again. Bring as much as you can, and for God's sake, hurry up.'

I shot out of the room.

For the next two hours we operated on an entirely new level. Lucy, in absolute control, belted out orders as I scuttled around the house for her.

'Open the window! No, close it again, it's too draughty. Actually, throw it slightly open – just *slightly*, Tara, we're not re-enacting *Peter Pan* here. Go to the Poppy Room on the second floor, West Wing, and get me the little lamp beside the bed – the one with the lambs painted around the edge – it's too dark in here.'

Matilda was panicking now.

'And she needs something to drink. Get her a whisky.'

'Is that the right thing for her to have?'

'YES!' yelled Lucy and Matilda at the same time.

Occasionally, Billy poked his head around the door.

'For Christ's sake, how long does it take to get an ambulance out here?'

'Forget the ambulance,' snapped Lucy. 'And she's doing very well without it, thank you very much.'

Her confidence calmed Matilda, who, just as in days of old, was susceptible to Lucy's reality being the only one that held any truth.

'Thank you,' she kept saying to Lucy. Over and over again. '*Thank you for being here. Thank you for being here.*'

'Stop talking,' said Lucy. 'Come on, deep breaths. It won't be long now.'

She looked at me, hovering for her next instruction.

'Get a couple of rugs,' she said. 'She'll be cold after the baby's born if we don't keep the heat in. And more towels. You can never have enough towels.'

I bolted downstairs to the kitchen. I found the kettle, coated with limescale, and with shaking hands found matches to light the gas. Tearing open cupboard doors, I found teabags, a nearly empty pot of sandy-looking honey, a couple of ancient tea towels and a bottle of Scotch. By chance, I found a hot-water bottle without a cover in the cupboard under the stairs, so I wrapped one of the towels and my sweater around it and poured in the first lot of boiled water. I ran a chipped, dusty teacup under the tap, chucked in three inches of whisky, gulped it down, rinsed the cup again, filled it with water and brought it back upstairs to Matilda, who spilt most of it in her agony.

Back upstairs, I distracted myself by rummaging through Lady W-D's cupboards, searching for bedding, and found nothing but two old horse blankets. The two New Zealand rugs had 'Desire' woven into the corner of one and 'Prudence' into the other, evidently belonging to the legendary mares she had ridden at Windsor. I held them up in despair.

'Better go for Prudence,' said Lucy crisply. 'I think Desire's somewhat inappropriate at this stage, don't you?'

Matilda yelled out in agony again; it was the worst cry yet. I looked at Lucy, and for a moment I saw her falter. There it was, that little flicker of fear, that fleeting second when Lucy was the thirteen-year-old girl in her mother's room. I felt my heart clench with terror, a hot sweat forming on my brow. It was Ma all over again.

'I've found more pillows,' I announced, with all the triumph of Columbus discovering the Americas.

'They're disgusting,' said Lucy, switching into action again.

'You can't put those anywhere near her, for crying out loud. We need pillowcases.'

'Wrap them in something else. I don't know where there are any bloody pillowcases.'

Lucy wrenched open Matilda's suitcase, and wrapped the two greying pillows in one of her dresses.

'That's Mary Quant,' gasped Matilda. 'Be careful!'

The next time Matilda cried was just a few moments later. It felt as though she were trapped inside this pain – how on earth it was ever going to end, I didn't know.

'It's nearly time to push,' said Lucy. She wiped Matilda's brow with an old vest of Lady W-D's.

'It smells of Mother,' wailed Matilda.

'Is it upsetting you?'

'No,' said Matilda, wrenching it back into her hands. 'It makes me feel like she's here. I wish she was here. *Why* isn't she here?'

'Were she here, she would be telling you to shove every emotion you're feeling and every little bit of pain into a tiny ball and to pretend that everything's fine.'

'And she'd be right!' sobbed Matilda. 'It's the only way to get through this!'

If it hadn't been so terrifying, the whole thing would have been almost hilarious. She turned to me.

'*You* would have been a better daughter for her. I always used to think that. She *loved* you. After all, you could ride.'

'Don't be silly,' I said. Gosh, Matilda could really pick her moments.

'Keep breathing,' said Lucy. 'It won't be long now. Breathe.'

As the end drew closer, Lucy was by her side. It was as though someone had pressed a button – freed her from something she had been struggling with all her life. 'You're going to be OK,' she said, and this time her voice was firm, steady. 'This is going to be the most unbelievable experience of your entire life.'

'Even more so than fish and chips from the back of the van outside the Bull on a Saturday in 1958?' asked Matilda.

'Well, that's pushing it.' They looked at each other, their eyes locked. 'And speaking of pushing it . . .' she said. 'It. Is. Time.'

I framed that moment somehow, and clicked down the shutter in my head.

There was Matilda – red-cheeked, swollen-hipped, kicked, hijacked, tilted moon-wards and forced into submission by the death-like inevitability of her baby's imminent birth – and beside her stood Lucy – tight with sadness but all-powerful with the certain knowledge that any hope, any possibility of feeling the swell of new life in her own being, was over. Without having it herself, she was going to be there for the girl she had lost. *She was going to be there.* Then Matilda started to push, and *my* bravery ran out.

Escaping the noise of her screams was impossible. My whole body shaking, I raced downstairs to where Billy was standing in the kitchen, his brow soaked with sweat, tears running down his face.

'Christ in heaven!' he kept saying. 'I had no idea it would be like this!'

'No one does,' I said. 'Or they would never do it.'

We said nothing to each other for the next ten minutes. Occasionally he took my hand in his and squeezed it until I winced with pain. He finished another glass of whisky and opened another bottle. Then, suddenly, the screaming stopped.

'What's happened?' he demanded, as if I had psychic powers.

'*I* don't know.'

'Go up,' he urged me. 'Go up and see if she's all right. Please, Cherry. Quick.'

Back upstairs I went, and pushed open the bedroom door.

'Has it happened?' I heard my voice loud in the room, anxious, clanging.

The baby had arrived. Unmoving, grey and blood-splattered – he was lifeless in Lucy's hands. He looked dead.

My instinct was to turn away. 'What's happened?' I whispered. 'Is he all right?'

'Talk to her,' gasped Lucy. 'Turn her head away. Distract her.' She closed her eyes and clenched her hands into a praying position. 'Pray, for God's sake, Tara. *Jesus, please God, help me. Please God, help me.*'

I repeated her words in a whisper, holding Matilda's hands.

'Jesus, please God, help me. Jesus, please God, help me.'

Matilda was whispering the words with me, her eyes tight shut. I watched Lucy, my hand clasping Matilda's.

'Jesus, please God, help me. Jesus, please God, help me.'

Lucy cleared his nose and his mouth, then very gently, pressed her hands on to his chest.

'Come on,' she muttered. Then a little louder. 'Come on! Come *on*!'

It felt like three years, but it was probably just twenty seconds. Suddenly there was a crackly cry, and a gasp for air, and as I watched, that tiny little body changed from grey to dark red.

'He's all right,' said Lucy in a low voice. 'He's going to be all right.'

She carried on working, and with each passing moment the cries grew louder. She cleaned him, she wrapped him in a towel, and then she held him close for what was probably no longer than ten seconds, but to Lucy I think they were the most important ten seconds of her life. Matilda stared at her – her old friend holding her baby. *Her baby.*

'You saved him,' she whispered to Lucy. 'You saved him.'

Tears were streaming down Lucy's face.

'Enough,' she said, her voice shaking. 'What's his name?'

'Joseph,' said Matilda. 'His name is Joseph Paul Laurier.'

Lucy's lip trembled. She looked at the baby, and placed him on to Matilda's chest.

'Go on,' she whispered. 'You may as well put her boobs to good use. She's never got them out for any other man in this village before.'

'Billy,' whispered Matilda. 'Where's Billy?'

I found him sitting on the bottom of the stairs, his head in his hands. He looked up at me.

'It's all right,' I said. Then I shouted it out. 'It's all right! It's a boy. It's a *boy.*'

'A boy?' Billy stared at me. 'A *boy?*' he repeated.

'He's Joseph,' I said. 'Joseph Paul Laurier.'

The ambulance, and a sodden Imogen arrived ten minutes later. There was a lot of fuss about how small the baby was, and who had delivered him, and whether they should risk taking mother and child back to the hospital through the storm.

'If he can get through a birth like that, he can get through anything,' said Lucy.

Imogen looked at me and squeezed my hand.

It was nearly light. An hour later, news came through that the road had been cleared.

Billy insisted that they should go to the hospital.

'I don't care where you take me as long as you don't take him away from me,' said Matilda.

'Do you want me to come too?' asked Lucy.

Matilda nodded, wrapping Joseph tighter to her chest.

I watched them help her into the ambulance. I should have felt anxious, but I knew – despite his size, and being early, and Matilda's problems – everything was all right now. I felt a powerful urge to say thank you.

'I'm going to Pa's service,' I told Lucy.

Billy looked up at us.

'Thank you,' he said. 'Thank you.'

Matilda gave a faint smile.

As she left Trellanack, as if to illustrate that the wound between her and Matilda was healed forever, Lucy – who had never fallen anywhere unless it was into the outstretched arms of a boy – tripped over the rug by the front door.

'You're tired,' said Billy. 'You should go home too.'

Lucy looked at Matilda.

'No,' she said. 'She needs me.'

'I'll save you some soup for lunch,' I said.

I went home, watching my feet walking, one step in front of another, spacey with tiredness, overheated with spent adrenalin. It had been only seven weeks since the wedding and that meant seven weeks since we had seen Matilda again for the first time. The summer was still here; seasons had barely changed, the leaves were still on the limes. And yet everything else had: Inigo, Digby, me and the Palladium, Lucy and Raoul, Matilda and Billy, and now there was Joseph. The world around me had changed again. I laughed out loud with the strangeness of it, with the beauty of the whole thing. With that first cry, that baby had wiped everyone's slate clean again, and as I walked I realized that there was something different happening to me too, an evenness to my stride, a certainty. I walked home without my limp. Let me say that again. *I walked home without my limp.* Madam was right. I could cast it off. I didn't need it any longer.

44

The Three of Them, the Two of Us

Later that day, Billy telephoned the Rectory to thank Lucy again, and to say that Matilda and Joseph were both well but were to stay in hospital for two more nights as Joseph had arrived so early. When they came out again, they would stay at Trellanack until Christmas, under the wing of a maternity nurse from York-shire, called Miss Johnston. After that, they would leave the house for the last time and return to London for good. Lucy and I walked to Trellanack to clear up Lady W-D's room.

'Thank God they've got a few months' reprieve,' said Lucy, as we walked up the stairs to the bedrooms after ten minutes in the park with Hester, the Shetlands and a bag of carrots. 'Perhaps they'll change their mind about selling.'

'I don't think so,' I said. 'And apparently Lady W-D called from India in floods of tears.'

'I beg your pardon?' demanded Lucy. '*Crying* for her daughter? Wonders will never cease!'

'Billy says that she couldn't get over the fact that she wasn't there. She'd been planning on arriving a week before the baby was due, but obviously that's all up the spout now. Then he told her that it was you who had saved Joseph's life.'

'I expect that shut her up.' Lucy grinned at me. 'You know, it's a good thing I can't have children. I don't think I could ever produce anything as sweet as he is.'

'Does it make it harder?' I asked her. 'Knowing that you'll never do it yourself?'

'I've got seven brothers and sisters. Do you suppose I'm going to go into a decline every time one of you lot produces a child? I shall be certifiable by the time I'm fifty. Anyway,' she added, 'I shall be the terrible old aunt who leads them into romance and adventure.' She gave me a sidelong glance. 'After all, it was Aunt Mary who introduced *you* to Inigo Wallace. Not that I ever had her down as Cupid, I must say.' Just hearing his name spoken aloud made me draw in my breath.

'Cupid misfired badly if he was trying to hit Inigo.'

'When do you think you'll see him again?' Lucy persisted.

'I don't know. He said he might come over here again before the end of the year. Even if he does, who cares?' I added unconvincingly.

Lucy threw four blood-stained towels into a pile with Prudence's rug.

'We shall return to London triumphant,' she said. 'You to your adoring public, and I to conquer those who wish to destroy Napier House.'

'You love Napier, don't you?'

'When you've spent weeks on end reading Colette Napier's diaries, you can't help falling for it,' said Lucy.

I was achingly aware of the fact that we were saying all this at Trellanack. It felt like a betrayal; admitting love for another house in front of the original heartbreaker within whose walls we stood.

'Nowhere will ever have me like this house,' admitted Lucy,

feeling it too. 'It's Raoul and me. The House of Dreams,' she added, ironically. 'But Napier makes for a good distraction, doesn't it?'

As soon as they returned from hospital, it was impossible to imagine them as anything other than a trio. Matilda, Billy and Joseph were a force of nature now – a threesome of impenetrable strength. Once back at Trellanack, Miss Johnston – who had a sharp sense of humour, calm, cool hands and fierce loyalty to her charge – soon had Joseph sleeping well, and Matilda recovering faster than any of us had thought possible. Matilda moved into an existence that had its roots in a word I had never thought would be associated with her: *happiness*. From that stormy evening when her son had been born, she had stopped drinking entirely and found an entire new vocabulary, populated by such items as muslin squares, nappy pins and bibs. It was as though birth had released her from all that had haunted her.

But in the same way that Napier House could never fully take Lucy's mind away from Trellanack, nobody could take Lucy's mind from Raoul. We were to return to London, but I sensed anxiety from my sister, the sure knowledge that when we went back this time, we were leaving Cornwall for more than a few weeks. Pa took me aside before we set off.

'Keep Lucy close,' he said. 'She's like a puppy without a master without Raoul.'

'Oh, Pa!'

I wanted to dismiss the absurdity of what he had said, the silliness of implying that a woman couldn't be complete without the right man guiding her in the right direction, but in Lucy's case it was so very true that I couldn't say anything else. I nodded.

'The thing about the Spanish is that they don't wait around. Look at the Armada.'

'What do you mean, Pa?'

He ignored me. 'And *you*,' he went on. 'I think you should stop fussing around over this American boy.'

'What?' I looked at him, confused. 'Oh, Pa. He's not American . . .'

'If he'd rather be with someone else – then he's not worth the ink on the paper.'

I blushed to my roots with horror. The night before I had been composing a letter to Inigo that I had no intention of sending. Having screwed it up and shoved it in the waste-paper basket, I hadn't accounted for my family's absolute refusal to keep their noses out of anyone else's business.

'I read nothing more than to whom you were writing,' said Pa. 'But I can well imagine what you were saying to him.'

'It was nothing important.'

Pa picked up a pile of papers from his desk.

'Mind you're back for Christmas,' he said. 'Matthew Bell and the choir could certainly do with your presence. That Jones girl has a voice like a strangled heron.'

'Of course, Pa,' I said.

He turned and nodded at me.

'And mind you know this, my girl . . .'

'What is it, Pa?'

'I'm proud of you both for what you did for Matilda and that baby. Lucy showed bravery. I'm ashamed to say that I never thought she had it in her.'

He walked away before I could say anything else.

I arrived back in London on Friday afternoon. Having slept on the train and then bundled myself into a taxi, I was a weary, hungry traveller. I made bets with myself on what Clover would be preparing for the Six O'Clock Club, without really caring either way. Lucy was staying another week at Trellanack to be with Matilda and Joseph. Last night she had telephoned Clover to tell her, and had been shocked by Clover's despair over the house.

'No, darling, you stay down there,' she had said, her voice weary. 'Not much use coming back up here at the moment. I had the man who's arranged to pull the place down here this morning. He was very jolly and efficient and told me that I should take the money and run, and count myself lucky. *Lucky!*' she repeated. 'When the only thing that I give a damn about is being ripped apart.'

'What's more,' Lucy had said, her face creasing with worry, 'she says that they want to bring the demolition of the houses in the terrace forward by two weeks. This means that Pevsner will turn up to nothing more than a pile of rubble. She can't get hold of him to ask if he can make it there any earlier.'

'But they can't do that!'

'Have you noticed how that's all we have ever said about these people, and yet they still carry on doing it?' said Lucy. 'They can, and they will.'

As I rang the front doorbell, I saw the Happy Couple descending from a taxi carrying shopping bags from Cee-Cee's. On the street in front of me, the world played out as usual, as though the earth hadn't been tilting on a different axis at all. There were people coming back from work, men in suits, typists in heels, carrying on their lives whether we were there or not. As soon as I was inside, I kicked off my shoes and stood in the hallway, breathing in the now familiar smell of Clover's Penhaligon's and the polished wood of the telephone table. I turned to the book, flipping to the latest entry: *1st August: Clover Napier made call to Victorian Soc. No answer.*

It was then that I noticed something on the hall chair – something that at first was so familiar to me that it didn't immediately strike me as being out of place. I walked slowly towards it, as though it were some rare species of bird that I might frighten off with too sudden a movement. I picked it up, and from the pocket fell a pocket guide to Hampton Court. I dropped it, as though it were on fire.

It was Raoul's coat.

45

The Harmonica Player and the Refugee

I think I must have said something – though I'm not sure what it was – because within moments the hall was occupied by Clover and Raoul himself. Both of them came out of the drawing room together, like something out of Noël Coward. The William Morris pomegranates on the wall in the hall – olive green, peeling and fading in the corners, seemed to ripen once more as he stood there; everything had to step up its game to accommodate Raoul's dark vitality, the rich luxury of his skin.

'Where have you *been*?' demanded Clover. There was great relief in her voice. 'You were due back here two hours ago!'

'*Raoul!*' I rushed into his arms, which I'm not sure he was entirely prepared for.

'Tara,' he said gently.

'Why didn't you tell me you were? How did you get . . . ? *When* did you . . . ?' I didn't know where to begin. 'I thought you were still in Spain! Lucy doesn't know you're back, does she?'

'No,' said Raoul. 'And nor need she. I just wanted to do something for her, to help her before it finishes.'

'Before it finishes?'

'I remember what you told me about this house. "Napier

541

House is the only thing that keeps her going. If she can save it, then she will feel like something she's done has been worthwhile." So I've done what I can. I flew back from Spain yesterday and I went straight to find help. Even if I've lost your sister to some boy who plays the harmonica, at least I can help her to keep this house standing.'

'Raoul – I need to talk to you,' I began.

'Cherry,' said Clover, gently interrupting me, 'can it wait? Please, come this way. We have company.'

I followed them into the morning room, wordless. But there was no Rachel. Instead, standing with his back to us, staring intently at the fireplace, was a man in a grey suit. Scribbling something into a notebook, it took him a moment to notice we had walked back into the room. Then, turning to face us, round glasses forerunning John Lennon's by several years, he smiled.

'Good afternoon,' he said, nodding at me. Then, turning back to Clover, he said: 'May I see zee rest of the house now? I'm afraid I don't have as much time as I would like.'

'Tara,' said Raoul. 'This is Professor Pevsner.'

'Professor Pevsner?' I turned to Clover, my eyes wide. 'Professor *Pevsner*?' I repeated idiotically.

'Yes indeed,' said Clover, and she started talking to him about the room, in a low voice as though she were afraid that Colette Napier herself might walk in and start contradicting her. For a minute I did what Ma had always told us not to do, and stood and stared.

Professor Pevsner resembled an intelligent mole. The thinning, whiskery grey hair combed off his face made him look every one of his sixty years, yet in his shrewd eyes there was a curious innocence that stood at odds with his formidable intelligence, making him seem much younger.

'This Morris paper,' he said to Clover, indicating the walls, and giving me a sympathetic look as he spoke, 'does it run all the way through into the dining room?'

'Why don't you come and see for yourself?' said Clover.

She led him into the next room. I stared at Raoul.

'How did you get him here?' I whispered.

'I have my ways,' he said.

'What kind of ways?'

'I showed up at his offices this afternoon and offered him a lift here,' said Raoul. 'He said I was extremely lucky to find him, as he was going to be in Cambridge all week lecturing. Then I mention Trellanack, and the Rectory, and your father's name. He recalled everything of course, but more than the houses – he remembered your mother's iced lollies. Then he said to me, "You know I don't drive?" and I said that I had a car waiting. He couldn't very well refuse me after that.'

Raoul delivered all of this information in a loud stage-whisper that would have been very funny, were it not for the despair in his eyes. Here was a broken man, I thought. He had lost his wife, and loved her so much that he had tracked down Professor Pevsner to save Napier House for her.

'She wants you back,' I said. 'But she doesn't believe you should come back. She thinks it's too late—'

Raoul held up his hand to me. 'No,' he said. 'Don't tell me this, Tara. You've always believed in us too passionately. You have to accept it, as I will. It is *over*. We must not speak about it,' he said. 'Please.'

Clover stepped in.

'I have fish pie,' she said. 'Perhaps we can eat while the professor continues to look at the house?'

Raoul looked at Clover. 'Such a wonderful house,' he said.

'Were it not for my despair, I would be beside myself with joy at finding myself in such a place as this. If anything can keep me from breaking down like a lunatic for a second time, it is your superb aesthetic principles, my dear.'

'Your wife's been a great help to me,' said Clover. I knew her well enough by then to tell how moved she had been by what he had said.

Food had always been a great comfort to Raoul, but he scarcely ate a thing. For me, seeing him at Napier was completely unreal; it didn't feel as though he was entirely there at all. I told Raoul about the Palladium and how nervous I had been, and how I had changed the song, but how everyone had liked it.

Raoul raised his eyebrows.

'How nice,' he said. 'To know someone who actually did what she said she was going to do.' He looked at me. 'Are you happy?' he asked.

The directness of the question shocked me. I gulped.

'I don't know,' I said.

'Ah well. In that case, you probably are. I never knew I was as happy as I was when I was sitting in Truro with your sister. Now I'd do anything to . . .' He put down his fork, and to my absolute horror hung his head and covered his face with his hands. Despite having his roots in a country defined by passion and heat, I had never seen Raoul cry before. Without thinking about it, I went around to his side of the table and put my arms around him. There was such heat coming from him, he was on fire for her. *Que te miro y tu hermosura me quema.* I see you, and your beauty burns me up. It had come true for him again.

It took him a while to stop. He made little noise, but his whole body shook, as though rocked by the weight of Lucy's absence. Eventually he sat up again, blew his nose and spoke.

'I'm sorry,' he said. 'What a terrible bit of drama. I dislike running true to my origins.' He turned his head slightly to address Clover.

'If it's any comfort,' she said, her voice unsteady. 'I lost the only man I ever loved because I gave up trying to get him back.' She didn't look at me as she said it, but I think she knew that *I* knew.

Raoul stood up and moved towards the mantelpiece, upon which stood a box containing the collection of Christmas cards from 1881. Taking off the lid, he dropped the box on the floor. Bending down to pick the cards up, he winced with pain. His leg was obviously still not fully recovered. I bent down to help him, rescuing a frail piece of paper depicting a robin delivering presents to a family of blue and grey rabbits.

Clover took our plates away, and Raoul propped his leg up on a stool.

'I feel a hundred and three,' he said.

'A hundred and *free*,' I corrected him. 'You're out of the hospital now, aren't you?'

'Funny,' he said. 'I rather miss it. Rachel was very good to me.'

I opened my mouth to ask precisely what he meant by this, but was distracted by the unexpected sound of the doorbell. Clover came back into the room carrying a trifle and a jug of cream. Setting it down on the sideboard, she looked at me and frowned.

'More little girls after your signature?'

I must have gone pretty red at this remark, and Raoul looked at me in amazement.

'Are you serious?' he asked.

'Last night, there were a couple of them hanging around for

at least half an hour,' said Clover. 'In the end I gave them a piece of chocolate cake and told them to buzz off. They were very persistent. "*We want Cherry! Do you know where she got her dress from?*"' she wailed in over-the-top impersonation.

'I don't see how they knew where I was staying,' I said. I wanted to sound as though it was the last word in peculiar, but really, I knew that these girls were just like me. They wanted to be me in the same way that I had wanted to be Alma.

'Are you going to have to go out in disguise if you want to do anything from now on?' asked Raoul.

'I'm already in disguise,' I said. 'Who *is* Cherry Merrywell anyway? She's not me.'

I shrugged and grinned at him and he laughed an amazed, delighted laugh.

'She knows how to deal with everything that's coming her way,' said Clover, nodding at me. 'She knows about putting on the mask and pretending.'

And not just with reference to the music, I thought, taking more trifle than I needed because Clover had put in an extra tin of raspberries in honour of my return. I was pretending to myself too – some sort of idiotic game where I tried to fool myself into believing that I didn't miss him as much as I did. That I didn't . . .

My thoughts were interrupted by the doorbell again.

Clover sighed. 'Keep quiet and I'll go and tell them you're out of town,' she said.

We heard her opening the door.

'Raoul, you . . .' I leaned forward to tell him that he had to find Lucy, that she had run away from herself more than from him, but I stopped talking the instant that Clover returned to the room. Following her into the drawing room at Napier House was Lucy's harmonica player. It was Brian.

'Hello,' I said, shocked.

He nodded at me.

'I would stand up . . .' began Raoul, who had no clue who he was.

Brian nodded at him and reached into his pocket for a single skinny roll-up.

'Light,' he said, without looking up. Whether this was a command to God, or to us, I never knew, but in the event he spotted the lit candle through the doors that led to the abandoned dining-room table. He crossed the room towards it, briefly distracted by a painting of a Victorian feast by candlelight, painted by Colette Napier's godfather, Horatio Thomas.

'I like this,' he said, not taking his eyes from the picture. 'How much can I give you for it?'

'Don't make me laugh,' said Clover.

He was dressed in a pair of black trousers and a brown roll-necked jumper and must have been terribly hot – but if he was, it didn't show. His skin wasn't great, his pale blond hair had been badly cut and looked as though it hadn't been washed since the band played the Marquee Club, and there was a large hole in the toe of his right shoe, but he had That Thing going on and no mistake. I glanced at Clover, who was rolling her eyes heavenwards behind his back, but I noticed she had hitched up her skirt a little and had checked her hair in the mirror in the hall. He was one of those boys who did that to you and that was all there was to it. Aside from his arresting looks and confidence, his attractiveness was in his Englishness, in much the same way that Raoul's was in the utter opposite of this.

'Get me a drink, would you?' Brian said to Clover. His speaking voice was soft and wispy, not how I expected at all. 'Whatever Miss Merrywell's just had,' he added sardonically, indicating my empty glass.

'Look, Brian, I told you before, I'm not a bloody public house,' snapped Clover.

'The Wetherby Arms is closed,' said Brian. 'Anyway, I've come here to talk to him.'

He waved his cigarette at Raoul, who looked astonished.

'*Me?*'

Oh, help, I thought. *He's going to tell Raoul that he and Lucy are running away together!* I stared at him, feeling slightly sick. I wanted to leave the room, but where could I go? I was too nervous of bumping into Professor Pevsner to go upstairs, and outside it had started to chuck it down with rain.

'Yes, *you*.' Brian was talking to Raoul, while staring at the portrait of Great-Uncle Hanley.

'I don't think I know you, do I?' asked Raoul. He must have had his suspicions by now, but he wasn't going to be the first to show his hand. Clover practically flung a glass of wine at Brian and folded her arms in front of her.

'I don't want any scenes in this place,' she hissed. 'You may not give a monkey's that Professor Pevsner's upstairs trying to work out if I can save this house from being torn to shreds, but *I* do.'

Brian looked up at her.

'Who?' he asked politely.

'Can't you just bugger off back to the dump you call home and practise your mouth organ,' said Clover icily.

Brian snorted. 'Stop feeding me lines, baby.'

'Don't "baby" me!'

'Hey – if they get rid of this place, you can come and stay

with us down the road if you want,' said Brian. He stifled a yawn. 'Help us with the washing-up.'

'I didn't think you bothered with that? Last time I saw you boys, you were throwing dirty plates out of the window,' said Clover.

'That was Keith,' yawned Brian. 'He fucking hates Spode.'

I saw Clover's mouth twitching.

'Actually, there's a place come up on Edith Grove,' he said. 'It's going to be beautiful.'

'I sincerely doubt it,' said Clover.

Brian ignored her, focusing his green eyes on Raoul again.

'She doesn't know I'm here,' he said.

'Will you stop talking like Hercule Poirot,' said Clover irritatedly. 'By "she", I imagine you're referring to his wife?'

'Can't you stop being the bloody headmistress for five seconds?' said Brian, appropriating an ashtray from behind the sofa. 'You're only pissed off with me because one of your guests chose to spend a week sharing all her problems with *me*, instead of paying your bloody smart-arse doctor boyfriend ten quid an hour for an inferior service.'

'She's not with Henry any more,' I said quickly. 'That finished ages ago.'

'Cherry, for God's sake!' Clover looked exasperated, but Brian had moved back to Raoul.

'Lucy told me everything,' he went on. 'I've heard it all – should've charged her a fucking fortune – but when you look like she does, you get away with shit, you know? Anyway, she's the reason I'm here.' He dragged on his cigarette. 'I've come over to knock some sense into you.'

Come on! I thought. *Please, Raoul. Step up to the mark!* Brian was too assured for me, way too cool for Raoul, who didn't trade in this sort of languid chat. I need not have worried.

Suddenly, and without making a sound, Raoul jumped, cat-like, across the room, took Brian by the scruff of the neck and held him up against the Morris wallpaper as though he were trying to work out whether to hang him up next to the Waterhouse or the Francis Owen Salisbury portrait of Colette's Aunt Sybil.

'Give me a reason why I shouldn't rip you to shreds,' he shouted.

'Oh my God!' shouted Clover. 'If either of you touches a single thing in this house, I will kill you both, and that is a *promise!*'

'Raoul!' I cried. 'What are you doing?'

'Put me down, for Christ's sake!' hissed Brian. He half laughed, then coughed. He was still holding his cigarette, I noticed. 'She still loves you, for crying out loud!'

'Don't mock me!' yelled Raoul.

'It's true, Raoul!' I shouted. 'Give him a chance to speak!'

'What have you been doing with my wife?' demanded Raoul, hoisting him even further up the wall.

'Professor Pevsner! Professor Pevsner!' Clover kept hissing, over and over again, rocking backwards and forwards like a possessed woman in a horror film.

'Put him down, Raoul, good *God!*' I whimpered.

I was more afraid of Clover than of Raoul or Brian.

'Jesus, man! I never touched her. We're fucking friends, man! That's all!' protested Brian.

'I don't believe you!'

But Raoul flung him down. Brian nearly fell over, but stopped himself, straightened his sweater and took a long drag on his cigarette. His pale face was flushed with colour; this was certainly not something he had expected to happen.

'I love the Spanish,' he muttered, glaring at Raoul, then laughing and shaking himself off. 'Good with their hands.'

Raoul went for him – really went for him – but Brian was fast. As he ducked out of the way, Raoul sent the mid-Victorian side table, with the pair of yellow and blue china lamps purchased by Clover's grandmother on a holiday to Paris in the Spring of 1884, flying on to the floor. The crash was dulled by the Japanese silk rug underneath them, and by some miracle, nothing broke. Rushing forward, I retrieved the lamps and stood holding them up to my chest like a couple of shields.

'*Stop it!*' yelled Clover. 'This is *my* house! *My HOUSE!*'

Raoul turned towards her, and his hair was all over the place, his eyes as wild as Cathedral Boy's had been on that morning he had sent me flying.

'I'm sorry,' he said steadily. 'But please – get him *out!*'

Brian was standing behind an armchair, poised to run for the door. He looked nervous, but as though he were having a thoroughly good time. Protected not just by the chair, but also by two red and green velvet footstools and a glass-topped table from nineteenth-century Berlin – he felt safe to talk again.

'I just walked past to see if she was back,' he said, breathing faster, but keeping his voice calm. 'I looked through the window and I saw you all standing around in Clover's front room, looking like you're having a meeting or something. I thought, Christ, who the hell's the tall guy with the tan? Then I thought, It's him. It's the one she won't stop going on about. So I walked right up the steps and now here I am. You can hear all of this straight from the horse's mouth.' There was a pause. He laughed under his breath. 'I'm the horse,' he added, bowing his head.

'I know several women who would disagree with that comparison,' muttered Clover.

'Watch it,' warned Brian.

He turned back to Raoul, this time speaking slowly, as if Raoul wouldn't understand anything but the most basic of statements. 'You know, she still loves you. Lucy. Your wife is still in love with you. She misses you, she wants you back, all of that. You know, she's *into* you. She *wants* you.'

Raoul, trembling but very still, looked at him through narrowed eyes, his fists still clenched into balls. He looked as though he had stepped right off the set of *West Side Story*. I thought of what Pa would say when the Littles fought at home. Ignore it when you can – all fighters like an audience. Brian paused and flicked his cigarette ash into the empty fireplace. Clover looked at *me* expectantly, I know not why.

Raoul spoke without blinking, without looking away from Brian's face.

'Is this some kind of a joke?'

'I'm not interested in joking,' said Brian. 'But I just thought you should know, that's all. She's quite a girl, you know.'

'Of course he knows,' I said.

'Tara, stop it,' said Raoul.

'*Tara*.' Brian turned his attention to me now. 'Yeah. Lucy told me. Old Billy Big-Shot changed your name, didn't he?' He looked at me intently, taking his attention from Raoul for a moment. 'How does that *work*? I'm trying to get people to call me Elmo—'

'I wouldn't bother,' interrupted Clover. They won't be calling you anything but a number in prison, which is where you're going if you destroy so much as the *tiniest* piece in this room.'

'I want another drink. Are you going to attack me again, Raymondo, or can I get myself a Scotch?'

Raoul relaxed his hands. Brian walked to Clover's drinks cabinet and poured himself a whisky.

'I should come here more often, I really should.' He looked at Raoul again. 'Great night out, this is. You come to help a man out, he goes for you like he's Sonny fucking Liston.'

'I don't trust you,' snarled Raoul.

'Neither would I,' said Brian. 'But you might as well believe me on this one. She's a wreck. A fucking pretty wreck, but a wreck all the same. It's not because she can't have kids or any of that crap,' he said dismissively. 'It's because of *you*, and how she thinks you won't want to stick around any more.'

'Who told you all of this?' asked Raoul. Now he sounded more amazed than angry.

'Who do you think? *She* did,' said Brian. 'I've heard nothing but your stories since I met her. Never let a girl rabbit on so much as she did. She wants you to be free, but I just thought I'd come and check whether that's what you really want. Because if you do, then – believe me – there's a fucking queue forming. You know what I mean? Mick hasn't even clapped eyes on her yet. You don't want to wait around for *that.*'

'Can you try and complete a sentence without swearing?' asked Clover.

'I'll give it a fucking try,' said Brian seriously.

'It's true,' I said. 'You have to listen to him, Raoul. She told me too. She's undone without you.'

'She's not,' said Raoul. 'She told me to go. She said it was over. She practically paid for my flight back to Spain—'

'Because she was scared!' I said, at the same time as Brian said, 'Because she loves you, you great Ernie!'

Raoul threw his hands in the air and swore – in Spanish.

'I came back from Spain to tell her that I cannot live without her. She was not at home. All her clothes are gone. I got straight on to the train to London. I thought that perhaps if I could find the professor and bring him here, then even if she didn't want me back, some good would come of me appearing here.'

'The professor?' asked Brian. 'Oh, you mean the bloke who's casing the joint now?'

There was a soft knock on the door. All four of us swung around; Clover pulled down her skirt again, dusted down her blouse and assumed an expression of unconvincing serenity.

'Good evening,' said Professor Pevsner, acknowledging the fact that there were now four of us where there had been only three. He looked confused. 'Is everything quite all right? I thought I heard noises . . .'

'Yes,' said Clover brightly. 'Everything is *quite* all right. Mr Jones, er – tripped over the rug.'

'Yeah, that's right,' said Brian. 'A Spanish carpet, fraying a bit round the edges.' He snorted with laughter. 'Professor,' he said, bowing his head. 'Good to make your acquaintance.'

Clover frowned at him.

'This is Brian,' she said.

'Elmo,' corrected Brian. 'Elmo Lewis.'

Pevsner shook his hand.

'Would you like a drink? Something to eat?' Clover asked him faintly. The Great Man shook his head.

'No, no. I must be on my way. No need to see me out. I will telephone you tomorrow morning when I have had a think about the best way to proceed.'

'Would you like me to order you a taxi to the station?' asked Clover, pulling herself together.

'If you would,' he said. 'It's only Paddington.' He looked around at us and smiled thinly. 'Thank heavens it's not Euston. I have not been there since they sent the diggers in.'

'It's murder,' said Raoul, wrenching his mind back from Lucy.

I'm quite sure that the professor made his remark merely to get himself out of the room and on his way – but Brian's eyes flashed.

'Wankers,' he said.

Clover widened her eyes and glared at him, I ducked my head into my wine glass, horrified and delighted in equal measure. Clover's grandfather's carriage clock ticked watchfully on the mantelpiece. Raoul swivelled from the professor to Brian.

'Wankers!' repeated Brian defiantly.

'Wh–who do you mean?' asked Clover faintly. Brian was un-deterred.

'The morons who took down the arch. And the fucking idiots in the government went and let it happen.' He dragged on his cigarette. 'You can't let shit like that go on, you know! Before you know it we'll all be living on top of each other and not speaking, just – you know – *mind-reading* and then we'll go back to all the books, and take them down off the shelves and open them up and say, "What the hell happened to that bloody great arch at Euston? Can we have it back, please?"' He looked at us, his audience, not without satisfaction, and paused. Flinging an elegant hand in the air, cigarette ash spilling from his fingers and floating lightly on to the carpet, he closed his eyes.

'*Each generation can load a load of old stones with its own poetry!*' he proclaimed in little more than a whisper.

We became very still, waiting for his next move – he was the king of cats with that angelic face and that odd voice. He opened his eyes again, and knew that he had us.

I could say that Brian was on drugs that night, but he wasn't. Drugs weren't really freely available at the time. He was drunk, but he believed what he was saying.

'Hear, hear,' said Raoul quietly. Brian looked at him, and grinned, and Raoul – suddenly deciding to believe him – crossed the room and shook his hand.

Professor Pevsner watched all this, unable to hide his fascination.

'Your views are sadly not shared by many, Mr Elmo-Lewis,' he said. 'We are in a minority – a very passionate minority, but a minority, nonetheless.' He walked to the window and looked out into the gathering dusk. 'It will be the Coal Exchange next,' he said. 'They have it marked, and believe me, it will be down before the end of the year.'

'Why can't they just leave it alone?' asked Brian. 'The Victorians knew what they were doing,' He was warming to his subject now. 'The clothes were good. The lace and the hats and all that. They had a bit of *style*, you know?'

The professor looked amused. I don't think I imagined that he would ever look amused, but after Brian Jones had spoken to him, he did.

'I must call for your cab,' said Clover. She seemed shell-shocked.

'Taxi? I'll find you a taxi,' said Brian expansively. 'If you promise to drop me off at Earls Court.'

'Would you? That *would* be kind,' said the professor, not reading Clover's nervous expression. 'I shall speak to people about these wonderful interiors,' he added to Clover. 'But I have to tell you that Victorian interiors such as these are held in even more contempt than the exteriors. I am afraid you shall have to prepare for the worst.'

He spoke with the calm, sympathetic yet detached tones of

a doctor issuing a warning to family members before he performed a life-threatening operation on one of their number.

Clover pursed her red lips together.

'It's not over yet,' she said defiantly.

'Mr Jones?' said Raoul suddenly.

Brian looked up at him.

'Yeah?'

'Thank you. Thank you for coming in. Sorry I tried to kill you.'

Professor Pevsner looked startled; his glasses slipped off his nose.

'I think I really must be going,' he said.

They left together – the German refugee and the harmonica player – into the wet night. I'm sure that the last remark I over-heard as they stepped into the street was Brian telling his new companion that he had played the organ in church as a young boy.

'And where was this church?' asked Professor Pevsner politely.

'Oh, you won't know it, man,' said Brian.

'Humour me, Mr Elmo-Lewis,' said the professor.

'Brian,' sighed the harmonica player. 'Just call me Brian.'

46

Some Kind of Freedom

Back inside Napier House, Raoul turned to Clover.

'I am so sorry,' he said. 'My God, I don't know what came over me.'

'Nothing was harmed,' said Clover. 'And don't think that there haven't been times when I've wanted to boot my guests across the room. Not that he *is* a guest,' she added vehemently.

Raoul sank on to the side of the armchair that Brian had used as refuge.

'Where is she?' he asked. 'Tara, where is your sister?'

'Oh, Raoul,' I said. 'I've been trying to tell you. She's at Trellanack.'

'*Trellanack?*'

'With Matilda. She had her baby early. Lucy's with them for the week. Matilda begged her to stay.'

'She's with *Matilda?*' He stood up. 'Then back I go,' he said simply.

Clover looked at him. 'Don't be ridiculous. You can't go back at this time of night. You might as well stay here.'

But he wouldn't do it. Not even Napier House and all its Victorian wonders could pull Raoul in for another moment.

'I shall take the night train back to Penzance,' said Raoul.

'Sounds uncomfortable. What about your leg?' asked Clover.

Raoul sloshed another two fingers of whisky into Brian's glass, gulped it down and shook his head.

'My leg is fine,' he said. 'Nothing compared to the pain of my breaking heart.'

With that, he kissed both of us on both cheeks, and was gone.

'If she doesn't want him back, then I'll have him,' said Clover, closing the front door behind him. 'I've always wanted a man who'd fight for me. Not in my drawing room, however,' she added, shuddering. 'Now, who else are we expecting tonight? I hear Elvis may be passing this way later this evening.'

Elvis. Inigo. Milton Magna Hall. Why did everything have to come back to him?

That night I fell to my knees in a way that I don't think I ever had before. I prayed for Raoul on his journey back to Cornwall, and I prayed for Lucy with Matilda and her baby. Please may it all work out, God. Please may it all be all right.

He has many prayers to listen to, Pa said. Make sure yours get his attention. *Please God, if you restore Raoul and Lucy, then I shall sing in the choir every day when I go home for Christmas. I shall never ask You again about Inigo Wallace, but shall wish him nothing but happiness with the girl he loves in America.* It was one hell of a deal, I thought. He would *surely* have to listen to that one.

I woke up the next morning to the sound of Clover running up the stairs.

'Telephone,' she said. 'It's your sister.'

As soon as I heard her voice, I knew that I would be seeing a great deal of Matthew Bell and Antonia Jones over Christmas.

'He came back, Tara,' she said. 'He came back, and he wants to stay.'

'And you believe him?' I asked her anxiously. 'You believe him when he said that he didn't care about the children thing?'

'Yes,' she said. 'I believe him. I actually *believe* him, Tara!'

'Please,' I said, 'don't put me through anything like this again. I just want you and Raoul to settle down in Rose Cottage and never question anything ever again.'

'That may be impossible,' said Lucy.

'Why's that?'

'*Bernadita*,' said Lucy. 'I've read four chapters, and I think it's going to be bigger than Anaïs Nin.'

'Gosh,' I said. 'He really *does* go to town with all the erotic stuff?'

'Wait until you've read it,' she said happily.

I put down the telephone and picked up the pen.

Lucy Fernandez to Tara Jupp, I wrote. *Reason for call.*

I hovered over the page.

Reconnected, I wrote, with a shaking hand.

Then, grinning, I added an exclamation mark, and danced all the way up the stairs.

Professor Pevsner, against all the odds, managed to wangle a temporary reprieve for Napier House, by insisting that it was viewed by the National Monuments Record, but I think we all knew that it was only prolonging the agony. However, it gave Lucy and Raoul the chance to be in London together – Clover had asked them both to stay and finish the cataloguing of items destined to leave their surroundings forever. So for three months I had the company of my brother-in-law and my sister, when I wasn't all over the place promoting a part of me that I wasn't convinced by any longer. Had I ever been? I didn't know. By November, the second Cherry Merrywell record had been released, with plans for the third in the new year. Seeing myself on the cover of magazines, hearing my voice on the wireless, still did little to establish any truth as to what I was becoming, but I knew, as Matilda had known before me, that I was well-known. It wasn't just the invitations, the parties, the opinions sought, the letters from thirteen-year-old girls that stacked up in Billy's office alongside those destined for his other acts, but it was the odd feeling that I was being watched all the time – that when I went to the cinema, or to a bookshop, people noticed me. Or rather they noticed Cherry. Every night I put her back in her box, and every morning took her out again, made her up, walked out of the door with her. Lucy and Raoul remained at Napier until December, when the demolition of the road was to begin. Their newfound love was everywhere in the house, affecting everything, yet Clover felt as unapproachable has ever where Digby was concerned.

'The man that you loved and lost,' Lucy asked Clover one night. 'Who was he?'

'No one,' Clover would sigh.

'Where will you go when this place is no longer standing?' Raoul asked her, sensing her agitation and changing the subject.

'Rome, probably,' said Clover briskly. 'Doesn't everyone go to Rome in a crisis?'

The rooms were being packed up now. Boxes appeared, empty one minute, and closed up with tape the next, labelled and stacked to be taken off to Clover's Aunt Nettie's pile in Somerset.

'What she'll do with it all, I do not know,' Clover said as we sat in the drawing room, knee deep in tissue paper. 'The only words I've ever heard her speak are: "If it's of no use, throw it away."'

I looked up at the walls where many of the paintings had been taken down, revealing darker wallpaper, or in some cases, no paper at all and choked back tears.

'They were more economical than I realized,' said Clover. 'They wanted to splash out on William Morris, but only as much as they had to. If they knew a painting was going to be there for years – why hide expensive paper behind it?'

'Where's Horatio Thomas's picture?' I asked. 'The one of the feast that Brian liked?'

'Oh, you mean *The Beggar's Banquet*?' Clover sighed. 'I gave it to Lucy to give to Brian.'

'You *didn't*!'

'I know,' said Clover grimly. 'I think I'm losing my mind. Lucy wanted to get him a present to thank him for having her to stay, and she caught me at the right moment. I said she may as well take it to that dump in Edith Grove and hope to God that Brian stares at it for long enough to get some sort of inspiration from it.'

'Well done,' I said. 'I think you did the right thing.'

Clover laughed. 'I never really liked it myself.'

I had to stop myself from stealing the box marked 'Lord N's Study. Photographs.' Inigo's piano had been collected weeks ago, leaving no evidence of his presence in the room. Further and further away from that night I drifted, and yet every day it was the same. He filled my thoughts from the moment I woke up until the second I closed my eyes. Christmas, I kept thinking. He may be back at Christmas. Even if it meant just talking to him for five minutes, it had to be better than nothing.

Then, three weeks before the bulldozers were due, someone turned up on the front door.

'Digby!' I said. I was always pleased to see him; nothing had changed that.

'Move aside, Famous Girl,' he said. 'I need to speak to the owner of the house.'

'She's not here,' I said. I looked at him curiously. 'What do you need to say to her?'

'Oh, nothing much,' he said.

'Shall I give her a message?' I asked politely.

'No,' he said. 'I want to say it myself.'

He turned to go, but then seemed to think better of it. Racing back up the steps of Napier House, he stood in front of me and placed his hands on my shoulders.

'I did what you suggested,' he said. 'I thought I might as well show the grumpy cow that I mean business.'

'You *what*?'

He wasn't really listening to me. I had never seen Digby so sure of himself before, and that was saying something.

'I've sold Cheyne Walk,' he said simply. 'So Clover and I are both homeless. I thought she might want to come and live in Paris with me for a while. I was thinking of buying a suitable house off the Champs Elysées and forgetting all about London.'

I stepped back inside the front door of the house and nearly fell over.

'You've sold your house? But how is that going to help her? She's losing this place too!'

'Well, there's nothing like two people, both in the same boat, realizing that they have more in common than they knew.'

I laughed; Digby with a plan was almost unnerving.

'And what about your dad?'

'Gave him half of what I made from the sale,' he said simply.

'But I thought you said that he didn't want money, he just wanted his house?'

'Yeah, well, turns out I was wrong about that. He's buggered off to Brighton with Susie Farriner's mum.'

'He *has*?'

'Anyway,' went on Digby, 'I have an awful feeling that the rest of the world is about to descend upon Chelsea. It's all Brian Jones's fault. When everyone else catches on to whatever he's up to, it's time to get out.'

'And you really think Clover will come with you?'

'She might.' He looked at me. 'What have I got to lose?'

'I don't know,' I said. 'Perhaps you're right.'

Digby looked up at the house.

'She's done all she can do,' he said. 'Sometimes you have to realize that the bastards are going to win in the end.'

He walked down the steps again.

'Tell her I'll come and take some snaps of Napier tomorrow,' he said.

'And you may as well tell her to stop fighting. I'm not going to give up. I've sold my bloody house for her.' He grinned up at me. 'I'm *free*!'

He actually jumped down the steps and skipped down the road – Puck in a leather jacket, ready to start stirring up magic and chaos all over again.

I hadn't accounted for the coldness of that December. The village had been dusted in icing sugar, all memories of Billy and Matilda's wedding temporarily covered up under frost-hard mornings. When I arrived home for the ten-day break, Imogen was balancing on tiptoe to stick holly above the portrait of Aunt Mary.

'Has Christmas come early to those whose hearts belong to Matthew Bell?' I asked her slyly.

Imogen descended from the stepladder and grinned at me.

'We've been out twice this week,' she said.

'And he's not been catching any more crabs?'

'Not as far as I know. Oh! And one other thing, Tara.'

'Yes?'

'Well, he was thinking that you might like to sing in the carol concert. You know – famous singer isn't too famous to sing in the church she grew up in, and all that.'

'Oh, please, no, Imogen. I don't think I could bear it . . .' I remembered my deal with the Almighty, and shoved it out of my mind. I needed to *rest*.

'Don't be so imperious,' said Imogen airily. 'Although it doesn't *really* matter. He said that if you didn't want to do it, then that was fine because Antonia Jones can always step in.'

'I think I can find time for it, after all,' I said.

That afternoon, Lucy, Raoul and I were to walk over to Trellanack. Matilda and Billy had invited us to visit Lady W-D, who wanted to thank us for our part in Joseph's arrival, and see the house for the last time. In the new year Trellanack would belong to the hotel owners, and everything would be forever changed. Lucy was nervous about seeing Matilda's mother, with whom she had parted on such terrible terms.

'We'll just stay for a quick cup of tea, and then off,' she said. 'I don't think I could bear to have to watch her having to be nice to me.'

'The poor woman,' I said. 'She's come all the way from India to see her grandson and make amends with the woman who delivered him. Anyway, Matilda says she's returning to India in two days' time. You won't have to put up with her for long.'

'And so we leave one sinking ship for another,' sighed Lucy, pulling on boots.

Raoul squeezed her hand. 'As long as you're here . . .' he began.

'You could live in a cardboard box and not be bothered,' I concluded for him. He grinned at me.

'And it's absolutely *not* true, anyway,' I said. 'Unless the cardboard box was designed by Vanbrugh.'

'And listed by Pevsner,' added Lucy.

Matilda, Billy and Lady W-D were in the morning room when we arrived. Matilda looked edgy, nervous, as though something was wrong. Seeing the open whisky bottle on the drinks tray made my heart sink. Immediately I wondered whether the arrival of her mother had set her off again. She hadn't changed, I thought. Three months in, and she was back to business as usual. As soon as we had kissed Joseph hello, and he had been swept off in the capable arms of Miss Johnston, Lady W-D entered the room. She looked fatter, darker, the picture of health. Any nerves that I had had vanished in her presence. I was twelve years old again, and she was about to give me a lecture on how to assemble the curb chain on a Kimblewick bit.

'Dear girls,' she said. 'What a thing! Here again.'

She turned and saw Lucy. Reaching out, she took her hand and shook it ferociously.

'Hear you came up trumps,' she said. 'Well done.'

Lucy laughed out loud. 'I just did what anyone would have done.'

'You did not,' objected Raoul. 'No one else I know could have done it. She did what only *she* could have done,' he said.

Lady W-D nodded.

566

'I know,' she said. 'I know.'

The house was cold; outside the sun was breaking through layers of thick white cloud, shining watery light on the dust on the table where Lady W-D had sat all those years ago, writing letters to her cronies about such subjects as the state of the Rising Trot in the Youth of Today.

'Mother's going in two days,' said Matilda.

'Yes, we'd heard,' I said.

'Had to see you. Had to see you to talk to you both about an idea Matilda's had. Well – *more* than an idea—'

'Don't say any more, Mother.'

Suddenly standing up, Matilda crossed the room to where Lucy and Raoul stood and handed them a letter. Then she looked at them both, at their puzzled expressions, as though she were considering snatching it back again right away.

'Read it,' she said. 'Just read it aloud.'

'Aloud?'

'I want Tara to hear too,' said Matilda.

Lucy cleared her throat.

'"Dear Raoul and Lucy . . ."'

Lucy paused, half laughed as though what she was doing was absurd, then, meeting nothing but silence, continued:

'Trellanack House is to be sold, and is currently under offer from a firm who promise to turn the area into a successful business venture. They plan to demolish the house and build a new hotel, modern, efficient, and yet, as they put it, maintaining the old views from new windows.'

Lucy grimaced as she read, Raoul stared straight ahead.

'*We were, at first, eager to accept this plan. As you know, my mother has no desire to keep the house, and felt that it was best to get what we could and move on. However, the birth of our son has changed that forever.*'

Lucy put down the letter. Her hands were shaking.

'You're going to keep it,' she said. 'For Joseph.' Her eyes filled with tears. 'We'll do all that we can to help, Matilda. We'll work here while you're in London, we'll do anything. Oh, thank you for keeping it for him, thank you!'

Matilda looked alarmed.

'Oh God, no,' she said. 'We're not keeping it. No, not at all. Read on, read on.'

'*We know how much Trellanack means to you. We also know that without Lucy, there would be no Joseph. This is a fact that my mother has had to face, and now that she knows the truth, she wants to put right the wrongs that were done all those years ago.*'

Lucy looked up as she read this, and her eyes met Matilda's.

'*We would like to give you the chance to take on the house and to run it as a hotel. We believe that you are the only people who will do it right. You need pay us nothing – just a peppercorn rent, so that it's official. But it's yours. Trellanack is . . .*'

But Lucy couldn't read any more. Sitting down, eyes blinded, she handed the letter to Raoul.

'*Trellanack is yours more than it is ours, and always has been. These places belong to those who love them best, and in the case*'

of this place, that is certainly you. We have told the people who
wanted to buy it that it is not for sale. We have said that we are
keeping it for ourselves, but it is all yours to take on and make
live again. It was never not.'

Lucy looked up at Matilda, her hands shaking.

'You can't just *give* us the house,' she said, half laughing, half sobbing.

'Oh, I can,' said Matilda. 'And believe it or not – I just did. I couldn't say it out loud, that's why I wrote it down. I'd only cry and ruin it all.'

'But you might change your mind! What about when Joseph grows up and wants to know why it's not his?'

'He shall be told that the only way he is able to ask that question in the first place is because you saved his life,' said Billy simply. 'Anyway,' he added. 'I can't see Joseph wanting to live in Cornwall, can you? His roots are in the Mississippi Delta.'

It was Billy's way of telling us that he knew that *we* knew.

Matilda looked at us steadily; there was no shadow of drink and fame hanging over her, no fear of her father, no weight from the disappointment she had been to her mother. She was, at last, a woman, not a little girl crashing from one room to the next with a beautiful face but no confidence.

'I really don't want the house hanging over me any more,' she said. 'I can only really be free without it. So you see, you'd be doing me a favour if you took it. I want to feel that it's going to the right people, and that was you. As I wrote in the letter, that was *always* you.'

'But the money!' I wailed. 'What about the money?'

'Cherry,' said Billy, 'there comes a point in life when money doesn't matter.'

'That point is when you marry a very rich American,' said Matilda. She laughed and looked at Billy.

'It's what she wants,' said Billy. 'So you'd better take it.'

I looked at Raoul, and he looked at Lucy, then back to Matilda.

'Well. I very much hope that you'll let Joseph come to stay in the school holidays,' said Lucy.

47

Christmas Eve, 1962

The concert was on Christmas Eve. The air was as still as it had been the day of Billy and Matilda's wedding, but sharp with cold. Cornwall was at its most staggering. The holly trees with their berries the colour of Clover's lipstick, the stream, frozen over and cracking in places like Imogen's best crème brûlées and coated with a thin powder of frost, and in the distance the sea, grey as the sky, white horses breaking over its iron cold surface. If I had to be without him, it might as well be somewhere as knockout as this, I thought.

When I got to the church, Mr Bell was giving out sheet music. Imogen was helping with the choir robes, and she spotted me before he did.

'Tara!' she said. 'Oh my goodness! You're going to do it?' She went pink with delight, and pressed her hand down on Mr Bell's arm. He turned to look at me.

One by one, the girls in the choir looked over. Sarah shot out of the stalls and rushed up to me.

'You came back!' she said. 'Antonia owes me two shillings.'

Mr Bell gave me a barely perceptible nod.

'Sarah, will you get back here, please?' he said.

'Raoul's sent his Nurse Rachel here,' said Imogen. 'He kept on and on about how much she appreciates choral music and loves old churches. She bumped into George on the way in, sent his papers flying. I stopped to help him pick them up and heard him suggesting that she comes back to the Rectory for sherry afterwards.'

'I think she ticks all his boxes,' I said, grinning.

'I've read *Bernadita*,' said Imogen. 'Finished it this morning.'

'And?' I demanded.

'It's wonderful,' said Imogen. 'I was up all night reading about Captain William Thorley and his secrets. Although I was a little bit shocked by some of the more . . . *intimate* moments,' she added, blushing again. 'Whoever would have thought that Raoul had it in him?'

'Raoul did,' I said.

'Lucy says she got talking to a woman about not just the book, but the film too.'

'Who on earth is this woman?' I asked, feeling disloyal to Raoul in my amazement.

'Well, you may know better than I. She's been living opposite Napier House, but she and her husband are getting divorced.'

'Divorced!'

The Happy Couple, I thought. That would make Clover's day.

'*Bernadita* is all about a strong woman,' said Imogen. 'Apparently people are looking to publish books where girls actually go out and get what they want, in every sense. The fact that Raoul's a man writing about such females makes it all the more appealing.'

'Lessons to be learned then,' I said. 'Be strong, and don't let men get the better of you. But if you want to, jump into bed with them.'

'Oh, Tara,' said Imogen, horrified. 'Not before I'm married. Not even Raoul could persuade me to do such a thing.' She looked over to Mr Bell, waved and sighed. 'Worst luck,' she added quietly.

Thank goodness one of us girls was still behaving like the daughter of the vicar, I thought, recalling the way that I had fallen into Digby's arms without even knowing him.

By six o'clock the church was full.

'Good, Tara,' was all Mr Bell said. 'You don't need to run through anything, do you? No time, anyway,' he added. 'Just do it, as you always would. Everyone else knows what to do.'

I nodded, hardly trusting myself.

The church was full of candles. The smell of wax and pine needles and myrrh overwhelmed me. I was a water-boatman skimming above the surface, without dipping down to feel anything, because as long as you kept on moving, kept singing, kept recording the next song, and running, always running, then why should there be the need to look at anything for longer than a moment? Growing up, church had forced us to sit still, even if we were playing marbles under the pews or fiddling with boiled sweets in the darkest depths of our winter coats. Church forced us into listening, even when we claimed that we hadn't heard a word. It took us away from things, while giving us the chance to contemplate for as long as we wanted.

I wasn't sure that I wanted to contemplate anything right now. Contemplation felt like a threat. I had run off the cliff, and as long as I was in London, I could carry on running. Now I was back at home, there was always the chance that I was going to look down. But if I did, I feared I would fall.

My brothers and sisters crowded into one row, Roy and Luke

dressed in ties and new jackets. They were growing up, I realized, no longer the babies any more.

Just before I stood up to sing, Mr Bell spoke up.

'Now, many of you in the church with us tonight know that the rest of the country think that this girl here goes by the name of Cherry Merrywell. But tonight, she's just our little Tara Jupp, and she's going to sing the solo in the next piece.'

Halfway through the second verse I saw him, and when I did, the whole song fell apart. My voice wobbled and crumpled out of tune, I forgot the words and had to close my eyes because I thought I was dreaming and didn't want to wake up and find he was a figment of my imagination. But when I opened my eyes again, he was still there, sitting at the back of the church as real as he had been on that first morning I had met him. When my solo finished, I felt paralysed, rooted to the spot, my eyes frozen on his; I was terrified of moving and him vanishing again. Then the rest of the choir took their places around me and we somehow muddled through the descant of 'Hark the Herald', and as we proclaimed with the angelic hosts that Christ was born in Bethlehem, he stood there, singing too, and he could have been anyone really, anyone who had come to our little church on Christmas Eve, 1962, except he wasn't anyone, he was Inigo Wallace. And I loved him.

Afterwards, everyone waltzed out, the choir holding candles, and as I walked past the pew where he was sitting, I dared not even look his way for fear that he might have already left. Once outside, I shot back into the vestry before any of the other girls could catch me, tore off my robes, flung my denims and jersey on, and pulled my hair up off my face.

He was waiting for me, just a little further up the road, away from everyone else. When he saw me, he shook his head.

'You were terrible,' he said.

'I know,' I said. 'You're cold.'

'I'm in love with the cold.'

It was odd hearing him use such an expression, so I laughed. He looked up at the stars. It was too unreal to me, too impossible, that he was here, in the village, on Christmas Eve, when all I had done since he had left London was miss him. His black hair nearly covered his eyes now, as it had when I had first seen him. He looked watchful and pale.

'I can't believe you're here,' I muttered.

He looked at me. 'Couldn't stop thinking about everything.'

'Everything?'

'England,' he said. 'I couldn't stop thinking about England.'

'So you came over to check it was still here?' I was only half joking.

'Sort of.'

And as we walked, our hands touched. I didn't look at him, and we didn't slow down. He pulled a cigarette out of his pocket.

'Didn't she mind about you coming over here?'

'Who?'

'You know. The girl in New York. The one you had to go back to. Clover told me about her right from the start. She heard you calling her . . .' I stopped, aware of how this was sounding.

'Calling her *what*?'

'Calling her *baby*,' I muttered, embarrassed. 'She said you spoke to her three nights in a row when you first arrived. She said that no one makes long-distance calls like that unless they mean business. She did an impression of you, sounding all serious. "*I hope everything's still all right with you, baby*".'

'Clover,' he said. 'Someone should give her a special award for her disgraceful assumptions. I don't sit on the telephone calling *anyone* baby. I'm not some jerk from –' he laughed, realizing something. 'Oh I know what she heard.' He put his hand up to his forehead in a gesture of amused frustration. 'She heard me saying I hope everything's all right with *the* baby. I was talking to Julia.'

'Who's she?'

'The poor woman who runs my mother and stepfather's lives in New York. She was talking about my mother. My mother's having another baby. She's pregnant.'

'She's *what?*'

He laughed at my expression.

'But she *can't!* Can she?'

'Apparently she can. She's forty-four. My stepfather always wanted children, so I suppose this is her last shot. I needed to get back out there to tell him that he should employ a staff of eighty to manage my mother's mood swings alone.'

'Why couldn't you *tell* me?' I asked. 'I thought you were going back to some beautiful American heiress with black hair and green eyes.'

'Rocky told me that no one was to know about the baby until she was past sixth months. I was sworn to secrecy.' He looked at me. 'And just for the record, I'd rather have a girl with green hair and black eyes than the other way around. You *know* I don't rate conventional beauty.' I felt myself back to that moment when I had heard him speak those words at Trellanack, and how much I had hated him for what he had said. How much had changed. I couldn't see when, or how, or put my finger on the moment. All I knew was how different it all was now.

'Anyway,' said Inigo, 'I thought you were still mourning for Digby.'

Making a joke of it didn't work.

'That was never real,' I said. 'Nothing was ever real except you. Right from the start – it was only ever you.' I stopped and looked at him. I didn't need to read what he was thinking, I just wanted him to know. I wanted to tell him so that – whatever happened afterwards – he would always know that I had loved him. I shivered again. He reached out and put a hand to my cheek.

'*You're* cold,' he said. 'You're shivering.'

'It's not the cold,' I said. 'I'm in shock that you came, that's all.'

We walked together back to Trellanack, crunching through the snow. I had told him that I loved him – I felt everything else falling away, disregarded. That was the only truth. What he did next wasn't up to me. I couldn't do any more than what I had done. I had done it as Digby had taught me. *Think less. Act more.* Inigo looked at me. Then, frowning slightly, he stopped walking and pulled something out of his pocket. It was wrapped in brown paper.

'For you,' he said. 'Go on. Open it.'

'Wh–what is it?'

He said nothing, just watched my hands shaking as I tucked my gloves under one arm and undid the parcel.

It was the elephant. Perfect, and just as it had been. I stared at it, unable to focus properly. Then I was crying, but for what? I didn't know. A past remembered? A past forgotten? We were grown-ups, where we had been but children.

'Seems like yesterday, doesn't it?' said Inigo.

I couldn't look at him.

'Why didn't you tell me that you knew?'

I don't even know if I managed to ask the question in its entirety, but he understood me all right.

577

'I *didn't* know,' he confessed. 'Not to start with anyway. But then you sang Alma Cogan at the Palladium and I shouted at you for it.'

'Oh, that,' I said in wonder, still looking at the ornament that had haunted me for so long. 'I deserved it. You were right.'

'I was out of my mind,' said Inigo decisively. 'Because I realized it was you, and I didn't know how to tell you. All I could think when Billy told me what you had sung was that your rendition couldn't possibly be better than that of a ten-year-old girl I once met in my kitchen in 1955. Then I did the sums, and once I realized . . .' He shoved his hands into his pockets. 'Why didn't you just *tell* me?'

'Because of this,' I said, turning the elephant over in my hand. 'I thought you'd think less of me if I reminded you what I'd done, and I didn't *want* you to think less of me.'

'Crazy,' he said.

'I can't believe you brought it with you,' I said.

'It should be yours,' he said.

'Why?'

He shrugged. 'It's a thank-you,' he said.

'For what?'

'Singing my song.'

I looked at him and spoke out loud the thought that had been crouching in the back of my mind since the moment I first arrived in London.

'I'm not sure I want to do it any more,' I said.

'What do you mean?'

'I'm always pretending to be someone I'm not. In the new year, I'm not going to go back.'

As I said these words I felt light-headed.

'I want to write songs,' I said. 'I suppose it's what I've always wanted to do. I just thought that I owed it to my mother and father and everyone else to be Cherry Merrywell too.'

'You never *were* Cherry Merrywell,' said Inigo. 'You were always Tara Jupp. You were misinterpreted, that's all. Not just by Billy, but by me, and Clover, and even yourself. Here. I want to show you something else.'

He pulled a picture from the inside of his jacket and handed it to me. It was one of the photographs that Digby had taken of me in Cheyne Walk, sitting at the piano, wearing my riding clothes.

'That's me,' I said stupidly. 'How did you get this?'

'Digby gave it to me. I suppose he was the only one of us who could see from the start who you actually were.'

'*Digby?*'

'He actually sent it over to New York with a note.'

'What did the note say?'

'"Go and find her because wherever she is, she's missing you."'

'*Jesus!*' I cried. 'Why did he do that? He's got the wrong idea, I was just – I said to him that—'

'Don't worry!' Inigo laughed at my reaction. 'He just added it at the end of a note saying that he liked this photograph more than any of the others that he took of you.'

'He never liked me in anything Clover put me in,' I said. 'He only ever believed me when I wasn't dressed up.'

'He was right,' said Inigo. 'Although, I was rather hoping that you might have been,' said Inigo softly.

'Been what?'

'Missing me.'

I said nothing, just looked down at my feet and smiled.

He took off his coat and wrapped it around my shoulders

and together we walked up the drive, saying nothing. I felt the warmth from his body, the heaviness of the coat dwarfing me, and there was Trellanack in front of us. I started to sing – Alma Cogan, as I had done all those years before. He said nothing, but walked beside me, so close, so *very* close. When I came to the end of the second chorus, we were nearly at the front door. I could see Lucy and Raoul walking across the hall towards us.

'You know, you really should do something with that voice, kid,' said Inigo.

Afterword

Two months after Inigo came back down to Cornwall to find me, I returned with him to New York, where we started to write songs together. Within a year, we moved to the Brill Building, and the rest is apparently history. We're always being asked how it works: who writes what, and how we manage to stay happy and together when we work side by side every day. Sometimes I say that we feel like a couple of aliens – two cut-out-and-keep characters from England who, unlike everyone else around us, have the same pronunciation for a word that means journey and a word that means beginning: root and route. We came together, from the same soil, to another land. Inigo usually dismisses all of this and says that we still fight over middle eights and chord changes, and what song would suit what singer, and where to go for the best cocktails on a Friday night. There's one thing we agree on every time. We're *better* than we used to be. And we know that one day we'll come back for good, to that pretty little island that we started from. England holds no fear for Inigo now. And me? Well, the truth is – I miss Imogen's cooking. When I come back, I shall sit in the kitchen of the Rectory and eat her shortbread for hours on end. That's all I feel like doing, sometimes.

Billy, Matilda and Joseph come to stay often. Joseph grew up with Matilda's beauty – and like Paul Warren, he sang before he could talk. He too has problems with his coordination when doing the simplest of things – like walking across a room or tying his shoelaces. Matilda is convinced that one day there will be a proper name for what she has always felt was a disability – a condition that needs understanding and treatment, rather than mockery and punishment.

In their first year at Trellanack, Lucy and Raoul restored the tennis courts. At the end of the year, they adopted a South American baby, whom they called Carlos. As soon as he could walk, he picked up a racket and began smashing aces around the court. Roy, Luke and Pa have all vowed to get him to Wimbledon.

The demolition of Napier House was not unusual. Between 1950 and 1965, hundreds of Victorian houses and buildings in London and beyond suffered the same fate. Clover was never going to let it go quietly. On the morning of Napier's demolition, she and Digby chained themselves to the fireplace in the drawing room, and got themselves arrested and jailed for two nights. By the time they came out, Clover had decided Digby meant what he said about loving her. Whether he understood it at the time or not, Digby's photographs of Trellanack and Napier House catalogued something quite extraordinary. The house that lived, and the one that died.

I can't think of London without recalling Napier House in 1962. I've never forgotten those evenings at the Six O'Clock Club. We didn't know anything – we were just blundering about being young. And really, that's about the most magical state that anyone can be in.

Brian Jones and his band went on to become way more famous than any of us.

He drowned seven years after he stood in the drawing room at Napier House and talked to Nikolaus Pevsner about the Victorians. He was just twenty-seven.

Acknowledgements

Bouquets to . . .

Claire Paterson and all at Janklow and Nesbit UK, Susan Watt, Caroline Proud, Bethan Ferguson and all at Quercus Books, and Talya Baker and Nick de Somogyi; Donald 'Capability' Rice, Cynthia Liebow, Kate Weinberg, Lucinda Vaughan, Petrus, Roo, Bilco, Kicko and Dad. Thanks to Mum, Auntie Jan, Clarewyn Rice and Antonia Bell for reading early drafts. Susie Harries and Simon Bradley helped me hugely with Professor Pevsner and I hope find him as they would like him within these pages. Diana Pullein-Thompson inspired the bits about horses and is a legend.

Thanks to all who put up with me 'finishing the book' for so long. I owe you a Blue Riband.